For everyone who believes in second chances—may this be your reminder to never give up, there is always someone or something waiting to feel like home.

Copyright © 2025 by M. Hartley

All rights reserved.

No part of this book may be reproduced in any form or by any electronic or mechanical means, including information storage and retrieval systems, without written permission from the author, except for the use of brief quotations in a book review.

Cover design by Caravelle_Creates

❀ Created with Vellum

Where we Call Home

M. HARTLEY

Content Warning

If you or someone you know is struggling with substance abuse and is looking for help, you can contact the SAMHSA's National Helpline to find resources available to you.

If you or someone you know is struggling with their mental health, you can utilize the 988 Suicide & Crisis Lifeline. You can also call or text 988, or chat with a crisis counselor at 988lifeline.org.

If you are outside the United States, please check your national/local resources.

Remember, you all are worthy of love and affection. Give yourself grace.

Trigger warnings:
Parental death (discussed)
Alcohol dependency (discussed)
Pregnancy (through book)
One page explicit sexual content

CONTENTS

Prologue	1
Chapter 1	7
Chapter 2	20
Chapter 3	28
Chapter 4	34
Chapter 5	42
Chapter 6	50
Chapter 7	58
Chapter 8	69
Chapter 9	76
Chapter 10	82
Chapter 11	89
Chapter 12	96
Chapter 13	103
Chapter 14	109
Chapter 15	115
Chapter 16	123
Chapter 17	129
Chapter 18	134
Chapter 19	146
Chapter 20	153
Chapter 21	163
Chapter 22	168
Chapter 23	180
Chapter 24	190
Chapter 25	211
Chapter 26	219
Chapter 27	228
Chapter 28	231
Chapter 29	239
Chapter 30	247
Chapter 31	254
Chapter 32	260
Chapter 33	269

Chapter 34	280
Chapter 35	294
Chapter 36	307
Chapter 37	318
Chapter 38	327
Chapter 39	339
Chapter 40	344
Chapter 41	353
Chapter 42	359
Chapter 43	366
Epilogue	373
Acknowledgments	379
About the Author	381

Prologue

Rhodes (Three Months Earlier)

EVERY THURSDAY NIGHT was the same.

I'd leave work, hit the grocery store late enough to avoid the crowds, grab some takeout, and head home to eat in front of the TV—alone.

It was the part of my routine I liked best.

First, because I didn't have to spend half my time helping little old ladies reach the top shelf—not that I minded, but after a long day, I craved peace and quiet. Second, because it minimized the chance of running into particular people, which did wonders for my sanity.

This Thursday was no different. I moved through the aisles on autopilot, mentally checking off my list. I used to write things down, but nine times out of ten, I'd leave the list at home anyway. Eventually, I just stopped bothering.

At the register, the same teenage girl rang me up. *Indie*, her name tag read. We'd never introduced ourselves, but over time, we'd settled into an unspoken rhythm—her faint, practiced smile, mirrored by mine, and only the necessary words exchanged.

She took my money, counted out my change, and I did what I always did: tilted my head back, pretending to admire the fluorescent lights while the soft hum of country music drifted through the empty store.

It was late. Quiet. Just the way I liked it.

Indie held out my change, waiting for me to notice. A simple *here you go* might've been nice, but that wasn't how we did things.

This was our thing, it was silent, steady, predictable.

And I wasn't one to mess with routine.

Bag in hand, I gave her my usual closed-lip smile and stepped outside into the sticky May heat.

Summer was coming fast, and before long, I'd be sweating through my days on the ranch. Not that I minded. The hard work was good for burning off excess energy and emotions. My therapist swore by physical exertion as a tool for mental clarity. Lucky for me, I had a built-in outlet.

Pausing beside my truck, I drew in a deep breath and glanced up at the sky. The sunset stretched in soft golds and pinks, the last light of the day clinging to the horizon.

Main Street lay in front of me, a familiar stretch of small-town life—the hardware store, coffee shop, a handful of restaurants, the grocery store, and The Tequila Cowboy. Everything within walking distance.

One of the many perks of Faircloud.

One of the many reasons I stayed.

Before climbing into my truck, movement down the cobblestone sidewalk caught my eye.

I turned, squinting to get a better look.

A woman in the distance wrestled with a large cardboard box, trying and failing to shove it into the passenger seat of a classic Camaro.

Curiosity piqued, I tilted my head like a puzzled puppy.

Whoever she was, I didn't recognize her, and in a town as small as Faircloud, that was rare.

She had split-dyed hair—jet black on one side, golden blonde on the other, with a few highlights weaving between. Overalls and cowboy boots completed the look, her tattooed arms flexing as she struggled with the box. I couldn't make out the designs from here, but her entire presence was *striking*. Different.

And I couldn't seem to look away.

She clearly needed help, so being the gentleman my mama raised me to be, I set my groceries in the truck and approached her cautiously. The last thing I wanted was to startle her and send her running.

"Excuse me, do you need a hand?" I asked, my voice calm, easy.

She turned sharply, blowing a stray strand of hair from her face with an exasperated sigh.

And *holy shit*.

Theo Matthews.

It had been years, but damn.

Hazel eyes, full lips, and those damn pigtails framing her round face. She was *stunning*. My heart thudded against my ribs, my pulse kicking up faster than I cared to admit.

"No, thank you. I'm okay," she said, polite but distant. There wasn't even a flicker of recognition in her eyes.

Heat crept up my neck.

"I, uh, didn't realize it was you," I fumbled, feeling like an idiot. "Nice to see you again."

Smooth, Rhodes. *Real* smooth.

Theo and I had gone to school together, but we ran in

completely different circles. She and her two best friends had always kept to themselves, never bothering much with the rest of us. From what I remembered, she wasn't a Faircloud native. Theo moved here later and never fully assimilated into the small-town culture. She gave off a *don't fuck with me* energy that kept most people at a distance.

She had one of those faces you didn't forget, though: naturally gorgeous, fair skin dusted with freckles, a button nose, and those hazel eyes flecked with specks of brown and blue.

Theo stared at me, expression blank.

I braced myself for the sting of embarrassment—until her gaze softened.

"You too," she said, her eyes scanning me from boots to ball cap. "It's been a while."

So... she did recognize me.

"Yeah, it has."

I hoped she liked what she saw, because I sure as hell did.

"I'm sorry to hear about you and Jess."

The shock must've shown on my face because she smirked, clearly amused.

Everyone in high school had known about Jess Cunningham and me. We'd been *the* couple—inseparable, the kind of love people bet on lasting forever. *Most Likely to Get Married* in the yearbook. Homecoming King and Queen.

And when we broke up? Yeah, that had been the talk of the town, too.

"It is what it is," I said, pulling out the same rehearsed line I'd used a hundred times before.

Theo scoffed, like she saw straight through the bullshit.

"You didn't recognize me until you got closer, huh?" she teased, popping her hip out with an infuriating little smirk. "Do I really look that different?"

"It's the hair," I admitted, motioning toward it. "How'd you get it like that?"

The second the words left my mouth, I cringed. *Seriously?*

"I mean—it looks great. *You* look great. *Really* great."

And there it was. Full-blown crash and burn.

Heat crawled up my neck, my cheeks going red-hot. If I weren't standing in front of the most beautiful woman I'd seen in years, I probably would've face-palmed. Instead, I debated fainting. Just right here. Right now.

But Theo only laughed, throwing her head back, her throat glowing in the fading sunlight.

God, I was *so* screwed.

"Rhodes Dunn," she said, grinning, "are you trying to flirt with me?"

"Is it working?" I asked, half-joking, fully mortified.

"Actually, yes," she teased. "The awkward country boy thing kinda suits you."

Awkward country boy. *Awesome.*

Desperate for a distraction, I pointed to the box. "Let me help. My mom would *kill* me if she knew I left you struggling."

Theo hesitated, clearly torn. She looked at the box, then at her car, then back at me before finally sighing.

"Fine," she said. "I'm sweating, and I hate sweating."

I bent down, easily maneuvering the box into the passenger seat. Mission accomplished.

And now?

Now, I stood there like an absolute fool, wanting to say something—*anything*—but coming up completely blank.

"Well... I'll see you around?" Theo offered, taking a small step back.

I nodded, forcing a smile as I watched her slide into her car. Then because my brain *hated* me, I gave her a pathetic little wave as she drove off.

The second she was out of sight, I groaned and dragged a hand down my face.

What the *hell* was wrong with me?

One look into those hazel eyes and I'd turned into a bumbling idiot. I'd had an opening. I could've asked for her number. Asked if she was free to catch up. Something.

Instead, my brain had short-circuited, leaving me standing there like some love-struck moron.

Shaking my head, I pivoted on my heels and walked back toward my truck.

Maybe I wasn't as ready to get back out there as I thought.

Because tonight?

Tonight, I'd completely crumbled.

1
Theo

September: 21 weeks pregnant
Baby is the size of a carrot

MY MOM always told me never to hook up with hot foreign men who spoke pretty languages and had legs for days.

"They're always hotter overseas," she'd say. *"Don't fall for the charm."*

Right now? I *really* wished I had listened.

I sat on my bed, crammed into what my mom generously called the guest room. Realistically? It was more of a *guest closet*. Soon enough, my belly would be bigger than this entire damn space.

"For the love of God!" I groaned, struggling to reach my feet and attempting to tie my boots. This, along with the inability to get my pants on without a fight, was a new development of pregnancy. I'd been showing for a while, but now the real struggles were setting in.

I wasn't even in my third trimester yet, but my body

clearly had other plans. Since the moment I saw those two pink lines, I'd been deep-diving into Reddit threads, gathering every piece of information possible to prepare myself. Because if there was one thing I hated, it was the unknown. If I couldn't control it, I could at least anticipate it.

But nothing had prepared me for *this*.

With an exhausted breath, I flopped onto my back and stared at the ceiling. And then because apparently pregnancy had *completely* rewritten my emotional wiring, I started crying.

Shoving down emotions had always been easy. Hell, when my father passed away, I didn't shed a single tear. I kept myself in check through every *I'm so sorry* and every unwanted hug because that's what "big girls do."

Another one of my mother's brilliant life lessons.

Maybe that was the moment I started changing. Instead of processing emotions, I learned to bottle them up, lock them away. It was easier to push through than to sit in the uncomfortable.

But now? Now I couldn't stop feeling. Every tiny inconvenience set me off like a ticking bomb. My body felt foreign. My emotions felt out of control. I had a sinking feeling that the bottle I'd spent my whole life carefully filling was about to burst.

I sucked in a deep breath, trying to rein it all in. One more attempt at the damn boots, and then I'd accept my fate of slip-ons and flip-flops for the foreseeable future.

But Texas summers only lasted so long, and fall was creeping in fast.

"Is everything okay, Sweetie?" My mom's voice floated in as she stepped into my *closet*—I mean, room.

"Yup. Everything is *just peachy*," I snapped, my voice laced with sarcasm. "Why can't the baby grow the other way so I can still tie my damn shoes?"

With a defeated groan, I collapsed back onto my twin-size bed.

My mom chuckled softly, walking over and bending down to finish the task I couldn't.

She had been unbelievably helpful through my pregnancy, more than I ever could've asked for. I didn't know what I'd do without her.

She was also one of the most *selfless* people I knew. But when it came to emotions, she buried hers as deep as I did. My dad had been the opposite, always talking things through, confronting feelings head-on.

"If you don't deal with your emotions, they'll rot inside you and make you all stinky."

His words. Not mine.

Whenever I struggled, he was the one I'd turn to. But losing your father at ten years old does something to you. It changes the way you cope. Or, in my case, the way you don't.

Now, I was emotionally stunted, a lifetime of feelings bottled up with nowhere to go. And this pregnancy? It was shaking up everything.

"You know, all you have to do is ask," my mom said after tying my laces, giving the top of my boot a gentle pat.

"I know," I muttered. "I just don't want to give up all my independence yet. It's only going to get worse."

She sighed and sat beside me, lying back against the bed, her fingers finding mine, intertwining them.

We lay there in silence.

And for the first time in what felt like forever, I welcomed it.

"You're going to be an amazing mom," she whispered, still staring at the ceiling.

Just like that, the tears were back.

She knew how much I doubted myself. How much I worried I wouldn't be enough—not that I'd ever told her. Call it mother's intuition.

Most of the time, I was barely getting by. I'd worn the same carefree, unbothered face for so long, but underneath it? I was in a constant fight.

Now, my mind was a full-blown battlefield.

I needed this baby out of me.

I needed to stop crying over everything.

The hormones were as impossible to manage as the cravings. And *Lord, have mercy*, the *cravings*.

This baby wanted everything spicy. Hot sauce, red pepper flakes—if it didn't make my mouth burn, it wasn't good enough. Which was ironic, considering I'd spent my whole life *hating* spicy food.

"Thanks," I sniffed, swiping at my nose with the back of my hand.

"Where are you off to, anyway?" my mom asked, sitting up and holding out a hand to help me up.

"Boone's throwing a party for Aspen. She finished her first novel, and he wanted everyone to celebrate."

I groaned as I pushed myself up, and my mom yanked

me the rest of the way, nearly toppling backward into the wall.

Told you—lack of space.

Seeing Aspen happy with Boone warmed my cold, dead heart.

Boone Cassidy had quite the reputation. He was Faircloud's own cowboy Casanova, notorious for one-night stands and zero commitment. But the moment he met Aspen, that all changed.

Now, they were that couple. The kind that made you sick with how in love they were. So much so that Aspen had literally written a romance novel about their love story.

Barf.

When the fiasco of getting ready was over, I slung my purse over my shoulder, hugged my mom goodbye, and stepped out the door.

Another struggle in my life? Getting in and out of my 1969 Chevy Camaro.

This car wasn't just any car. It was my dad's pride and joy. The day I got my driver's license, I claimed it as mine.

Driving this car meant I got to relive all those nights I spent as a kid helping him restore her. By "helping," I mostly meant handing him the screwdriver or holding the flashlight just right.

Turning the key in the ignition, the engine rumbled to life, smooth and strong, just like it always had.

There wasn't a damn thing I wouldn't do for this car.

And no one else drove her. *Ever.*

Well, except for Gus.

Gus owned a mechanic shop in Faircloud and had

made a name for himself by being grumpy as hell and a little too blunt. I liked him for it. He was middle-aged, had a mop of unruly red hair, a beard that would make a Viking jealous, and tattoos from his neck to his knuckles.

If I were a few years older… *bow wow*.

One day, Betsy—my Camaro—started making a weird noise, and I needed a mechanic I could trust. Word around town was that Gus was the best when it came to classics, but he had a mouth on him that could offend even those with the thickest skin.

I walked in that day ready to throw down. We went toe-to-toe from the moment we met and its been a beautiful relationship ever since.

While I was away traveling, he'd stop by to check on my car. Though, I had a sneaking suspicion he was more interested in checking on my mom. I'd told her *so* many times she should ask him out, but she always got shy and shut down the conversation.

The trees blurred past as I drove toward Cassidy Ranch, the sun sinking lower on the horizon. Boone was throwing the party at his parents' place—because nothing said rugged cowboy like a romance-themed celebration. Love made people do crazy shit, I supposed.

One thing I gained by moving back to Faircloud was spending more time with my friends. Seeing them again made me realize how much I was truly missing out on.

Don't get me wrong, I loved what I did. Adventure and photography were my passions. But lately, being back in this town meant something in a way it never had before.

I'd always been a lone wolf.

As much as I adored my friends and my mom, I knew

it would be me and the baby until the end because I came to terms with the fact that no one was guaranteed to stay.

Finding out I was pregnant had rattled me to my core, forcing me to confront feelings I'd buried for years. I've noticed that even my internal thoughts are a bit more... emotional.

I wasn't sure if I ever wanted kids. Honestly, I'd always leaned toward not. But the moment I saw those two pink lines, something in me shifted. I looked in the mirror and saw someone else—someone I could be. And just like that, my entire life changed.

Giving up a piece of myself to anyone had always scared the shit out of me.

I'd spent years avoiding attachment, burying myself in work, in adventure, in meaningless one-night stands. I was in my late twenties with zero real relationships to show for it. My priorities had been simple—figure out what city to get drunk in and what guy would keep my bed warm that night.

And now?

Now, I was forced to grow up. To settle down. To reevaluate everything.

I had been content with the way things were. But how much longer could I really sustain it?

Finally, I pulled into the driveway and parked, letting out a deep breath as I stared at the main house.

Nerves twisted in my stomach at the thought of seeing Aspen and Penny again. A strange, uncomfortable flutter, like butterflies fighting to escape.

Since the gender reveal a few weeks ago, I'd been pulling back. Retreating into myself. I couldn't shake the feeling that I was becoming an outsider—watching life happen from the sidelines.

I was growing up, and Aspen and Penny... well, they were still diving headfirst into reclaiming their youth.

There was nothing wrong with that.

But I wanted them with me on this journey. They were the only two people I had outside of my mom, and I needed them now more than ever. Meeting them was the greatest blessing a girl could've wished for.

Moving away after my dad died had been necessary. Oklahoma stopped feeling like home after he was gone. Every street, every memory—constant reminders of what I'd lost.

My mom packed up our SUV and drove us to Faircloud, Texas, and this town gave me something I hadn't had in years.

A fresh *start*.

Here, I wasn't that girl—the grieving kid everyone whispered about. No teachers pulling me aside, no pity-filled glances in the hallways. I was just Theo.

Reaching for the "oh shit" handle, I tried my best to get out of the car.

I failed miserably.

With one hefty pull, I almost straightened.

Then my knee locked up.

And just like that, I collapsed back into the driver's seat.

I groaned, staring up at the ceiling of my car. "I am fucking going home."

Muttering a string of expletives, I leaned back, taking a breather before attempting one more time.

It was impossible to describe how demoralizing it felt to be unable to do something as simple as getting out of my own car.

Especially for someone who had always done everything for herself.

"Need help?" A deep voice carried across the driveway.

That word *help* still made me cringe. It used to be foreign to me, something I prided myself on never needing. Now? It was quickly becoming a permanent part of my vocabulary.

"No thanks," I replied, shifting in my seat, still fighting my body's limitations. "I was just leaving."

The sun was in my eyes, casting a golden halo around the figure near my car.

Then he stepped closer.

Rhodes Dunn.

One of Boone's closest friends.

He leaned down, resting his forearms on the frame of my open door, flashing a grin that sent a bolt of heat through my stomach.

"You sure?" he asked, arching a thick brow. "I don't think Aspen would be too happy knowing you came all this way just to leave because you couldn't get out of your car."

I scowled. *I could do it myself.*

Determined, I extended my knee, only to feel a sharp jolt of pain shoot up the back of my thigh.

Fuck.

He was right.

I'd made it this far—it wasn't worth turning around now.

With a groan, I swallowed my pride and held out my hand. His fingers wrapped around mine, engulfing them entirely. Damn, he was big.

This was the second time he'd come to my rescue.

And the second time I'd *let him*. That? That was the alarming part.

The first time I saw Rhodes after coming home, my stomach dropped *like a* ten-pound weight in quicksand. I'd always known he was attractive, but *wow*, he'd aged like fine wine.

I'd been home periodically over the years, but somehow, I'd never run into him.

Rhodes and Jess had always been a pair—practically attached at the hip. The golden couple. When Aspen and Penny told me Jess had left him, shocked didn't even begin to cover it.

They had been the small-town Hallmark romance—the kind of couple you'd bet your money on.

And when I saw him for the first time after hearing the news?

I cringed just thinking about it.

I'd awkwardly blurted out some poorly worded condolences, stumbling over myself like a total idiot. Not exactly my finest moment. And ever since, I couldn't help but feel off around him.

Every interaction since Boone and Aspen started dating had been a struggle to keep my cool.

On the outside, I managed to look calm and collected.

On the inside?

I was burning up.

His flirty comment from a few months ago still played on repeat in my mind.

I'd wished—more than once—that I'd just handed him my number that night.

But even if I had... what then?

By the way, I'm pregnant with a random guy's baby! I hooked up with him once while traveling in Greece! Want to grab some decaf coffee sometime?

Yeah. No.

I didn't have the emotional bandwidth for that conversation then, and I sure as hell didn't have it now.

I'd have to live with wondering what could have been.

Looking at him now, Rhodes was all man—tall and broad, with muscles that had muscles. A bear of a man. Messy jet-black hair tucked under a backward trucker hat. Grass-green eyes that could wreck a girl if she stared too long.

And I was definitely staring too long.

"Thanks," I muttered, smoothing my hands down the front of my black overalls.

Rhodes' gaze dragged from my boots to my braids, his lips quirking slightly.

When I stepped away from the car, he reached in, grabbing my cowhide tassel purse from the passenger seat. As he did, his black t-shirt rode up slightly, revealing a sliver of toned, tanned skin.

I nearly swallowed my own tongue.

There was nothing sexier than a man's muscular back, and I'd bet *everything* I owned that Rhodes was perfectly sculpted beneath that shirt.

"Thanks again," I muttered, taking my purse from his massive hands and tossing it over my shoulder.

"No problem." He shoved his hands in his pockets, dragging his eyes down my body *again* before glancing at the ground.

For a beat, we stood there. Neither of us moved. The tension between us thickened, stretching tight like an invisible cord pulling us closer.

I cleared my throat, desperate to break the moment.

"Should we head in?"

Normally, when Rhodes and I were around each other, our friends acted as buffers. But now? Now it was just us and I didn't know what to do with that.

We walked in silence, the pressure to speak hanging between us like a heavy weight.

I chose to ignore it.

"Were we supposed to bring a gift?" Rhodes murmured, leaning in close enough that his warm breath tickled the shell of my ear.

A full-body shiver ran through me, goosebumps prickling my arms.

Inside the backyard, balloons arched over long folding tables, and a massive banner reading *"Way to Kick Romance Ass!"* hung from the gazebo entrance.

Boone's family had a pool, but my pregnant ass was *not* about to get in. I'd happily watch from a safe, dry distance.

"I'm her gift," I teased, flashing him a smirk. "Guess you're shit out of luck."

Rhodes let out a short laugh. "I helped her gift out of the car. *Technically*, that makes you *my* gift, too."

I snorted.

Rhodes was funny.

There was something alluring about a big, broad, brawny man with quick wit and a little shyness beneath the surface.

"Theo! Rhodes!" Aspen's voice rang out as she jogged toward us, practically vibrating with excitement. She pulled me into a hug before stepping back, her hands still on my shoulders.

"Did you two come together?" she asked, eyes bouncing between us.

"No!" Rhodes and I blurted in unison.

I glanced at him.

He was already looking at me.

"He just helped me out of the car," I explained, smiling lopsidedly. "The belly gets in the way."

"My gift to you," Rhodes said smoothly, bowing like a butler, hand over his stomach.

Aspen cooed, nudging me. "Aww. You didn't need to bring me a gift, but I'm glad it was this one."

She looped her arm through mine, dragging me toward Penny and the rest of our friends.

I didn't need to look back to know Rhodes was watching me go.

I felt it.

But I forced my legs to keep moving.

Because no matter how much I wished things were different…

There was no room in my life for Rhodes Dunn. No matter how devastatingly good he looked in a backward hat.

2
Theo

MY FRIENDS SPLASHED around in the pool like carefree teenagers, savoring the last rays of summer before the season slipped away.

Boone had Aspen perched on his shoulders, locked in a fierce game of chicken with Mac and Penny. Laughter rang through the air, carefree and unfiltered.

Meanwhile, I stayed exactly where I belonged—planted on a lounge chair under an umbrella, perfectly positioned to observe without getting involved.

Just how I liked it.

At least, that's what I told myself.

All of these men looked ridiculously good shirtless and dripping wet.

Honestly? Even *I* was wet. Thankfully, no one could tell.

I had never looked at my friends and entertained such raunchy, absolutely filthy thoughts before, but today? My judgment was clearly MIA.

Luckily, my sunglasses hid the direction of my gaze. Sure, they all looked great, but Rhodes?

Rhodes had my *full* attention.

He lounged at the edge of the pool, arms braced behind him, and his hands gripped the neck of a beer bottle.

I'd like to feel those hands wrapped around *my* neck.

The thought struck like a lightning bolt. I shook my head, trying to dislodge it.

This was ridiculous. Rhodes was a friend. With Boone and Aspen dating, we'd be spending a lot more time together, which meant I needed to get my hormones in check—for the sake of the group, if nothing else.

Then, as if the universe wanted to test me, Rhodes took a slow sip of his beer.

The muscles in his neck tensed as he swallowed, his lips parting just enough to make my head spin.

Was it getting *hotter*?

I fanned myself with the napkin on my lap, hoping it would do something to counteract the heat creeping over me. Then, for good measure, I dabbed my chest.

Desperate for a distraction, I decided to cool off the only way I could, sticking my feet in the water.

Swinging my legs over the side of the chair, I reached down to untie my boots. Getting them off was infinitely easier than putting them on. Once the boots and socks were discarded, I made my way to the pool's edge, choosing a quieter spot, out of the splash zone.

Sliding my feet into the water, I sighed in relief as the coolness rushed over me, though my pants weren't so lucky—soaking at the edges. Not that I could bend far enough to roll them up anyway.

The water swirled around my ankles as I kicked my feet back and forth, tilting my head up to the sun.

This was my happy place.

Being outside, surrounded by nature—it was why I'd chosen wildlife photography. Out there, it was just me, my camera, and the quiet, steady rhythm of the world around me.

Then, something brushed against my ankle.

I jolted, my head snapping toward the water, heart pounding, only to find Rhodes smiling up at me.

His hat was gone, wet black curls clinging to his neck, curling behind his ears.

"Your pants were in the water," he said, voice low, lips tilting into a smirk as he reached for the cuffs of my overalls, rolling them up until they were safe.

What the hell was he doing?

Better question—*why* the hell was he doing that?

My face twisted into some bizarre expression of confusion, mild embarrassment, and a bad case of heartburn all mixed together.

"Um… thanks?" I mumbled, shifting my gaze toward the others in the pool.

Rhodes didn't move far.

He stayed close, floating lazily, his broad shoulders just above the waterline, his back resting against the pool's edge.

The silence between us dragged on until, finally, I blurted out the first thing that came to mind.

"Why aren't you over there with the rest of them?"

Rhodes took another slow sip of his beer, then cleared his throat. "Games aren't my thing," he muttered, still not looking at me.

I studied the back of his head, the unruly curls brushing just above the bump of his spine.

Scoffing, I dragged my gaze away from him and back to the chaos in the pool. "Same. People who like games are… weird. Most of them are pointless anyway."

"Right?" Rhodes laughed, turning his head slightly toward me. "Plus, who actually enjoys losing?"

I adjusted, leaning back on my hands for support, when suddenly, a familiar sensation fluttered in my belly.

My breath hitched, my muscles tensing.

Instinctively, my hand flew to my stomach, pressing against the strange movement beneath my skin.

Every time she moved like that, it startled me a little.

Still, I liked it.

It was a reminder that she was *thriving*, growing, and becoming more real with every passing day.

Rhodes noticed immediately. His head snapped in my direction, and he adjusted his position in the water, turning to face me fully.

"You okay?" he asked, green eyes wide with concern. His hands hovered just in front of him, ready to catch me if I toppled over.

I let out a soft laugh, the discomfort passing as quickly as it came. "Yeah, I'm fine. She's just practicing her gymnastics routine in there."

Rhodes' tense expression softened, relief washing over his face as he nodded. His gaze drifted to my belly, lingering there for a beat longer than expected.

Seeing him *relax* like that was... kind of cute.

"How's it going?" he asked, tipping his bottle toward my bump.

I exhaled, tilting my head slightly. "If I'm being honest? It's getting harder every day. I cried this morning because I couldn't tie my boots."

His lips twitched into a slight grin. "How far along are you?"

"Just over halfway. Twenty-one weeks." My hand found my belly instinctively, a habit now and one I barely noticed anymore. It was my way of staying connected to the little life growing inside me.

I liked when people asked about her.

She was already my proudest accomplishment, even though she wasn't here yet. What I'd once thought was a mistake had turned into something bigger, something more. She gave me a purpose beyond my career, something I hadn't even realized I was searching for.

Rhodes let out a thoughtful grunt, his gaze flicking back to my stomach, like he could see her through my skin. "If you need anything, let me know," he said, voice steady, serious.

Then, his eyes lifted to mine, and something in them stuck, made my heart stumble over itself.

"I mean it," he added, low and firm.

The warmth of his words curled through me, slow and all-consuming, like sitting too close to a fire on a cold night.

"Okay," I whispered, offering a small smile before looking away. His gaze was too much, masculine in a way that made my stomach flutter. I could only take so much attention before I retreated.

AS THE SUN DIPPED LOWER, the air cooled, signaling that it was time to head out.

Driving at night wasn't my favorite, especially in this car. My old Camaro wasn't built for dodging deer, and somehow, the chances of running into wildlife always seemed higher after dark.

We'd spent the rest of the evening just existing together, but I kept my distance from Rhodes.

Too much exposure, too many eyes on us. The fact that we walked into the party together was more than enough to get Aspen and Penny following a lead that wasn't even there.

Instead, I sat next to Logan, keeping things surface-level—city restaurants, his parents' careers, baby talk.

"I'm gonna head home," I said eventually, tapping Aspen's shoulder to get her attention.

She was curled up in a plastic chair, her signature glass of wine in hand.

"You can stay over with me and Penny!" she offered, standing to hug me. "We're having a sleepover. Staying up late, drinking wine, probably passing out on the couch."

I hated saying no to their invitations.

But lately? I just *couldn't*.

Long nights and makeshift sleeping arrangements weren't in my wheelhouse anymore. I needed my own bed, my coziest pajamas, and an uninterrupted night of sleep.

"I wish I could," I murmured, hugging her a little longer than necessary. "But my back needs a real bed."

Aspen laughed, letting me go. "Fair enough," she said, though I knew she didn't quite understand.

One day, she would.

"I'll see you around."

I lifted a hand in a half-wave to the rest of the group, who sang their goodbyes.

At the start of my pregnancy, I could still keep up with them.

Now? My energy was spent.

Life was changing. I couldn't just drop everything for spontaneous plans like I used to.

It was easier to entertain myself than to inconvenience everyone else.

As I turned to leave, my gaze lingered on Rhodes.

I gave him an extra smile, and he caught it—nodding, returning one of his own.

I regretted not pushing past the weird tension and talking to him a little longer.

But my mind and body had other plans.

The fact that I wanted to stay—wanted to engage with him, despite my exhaustion—spoke volumes. I heard it loud and clear.

Despite that, I walked out the gate and chose to go home.

When I plopped into the driver's seat, I let my head

rest against the steering wheel, allowing the quiet to wrap around me.

Nights like this were hard.

I missed my friends.

I missed the *ease* of saying yes to plans without a second thought. Pregnancy was isolating in a way I hadn't expected. It was hard for people to understand how much my body and mind were changing.

Sometimes, when I looked in the mirror, I barely recognized the woman staring back at me.

Slow and steady wasn't who I'd been, but things had to change at some point. I reminded myself—these feelings were temporary.

They would pass. I just had to push through. Because this baby—my little girl—would be worth it all.

3
Rhodes

THE PARTY SHIFTED to Boone's cabin after his parents finally had enough of us "rowdy kids" keeping them awake.

If only they knew what we'd really been like as teenagers—*this* was nothing in comparison.

Boone, Mac, Logan, Penny, Aspen, and I gathered around the bonfire, the warm glow flickering across our faces as we drank, laughed, and swapped stories from our younger days. The fire crackled in the quiet moments between, embers spiraling into the night sky like tiny fireworks.

Back then, most of us hadn't known each other well. Sharing childhood memories as adults felt like peeling back layers, learning each other one story at a time.

"Aspen, I don't even think *you* know this," Penny said, sucking in a breath. Her voice dropped into something sly. "Please don't look at me differently."

All eyes turned to Aspen, whose expression tightened with curiosity and a hint of apprehension.

Penny hesitated for dramatic effect, then dove in. "One time, I spent all night driving around with Jasper Martin. We ended up at the overlook, and... I let him get to second base." She stifled a laugh behind her hand. "When he dropped me off, my dad was waiting on the porch with a shotgun across his lap."

Aspen's jaw dropped. The disbelief on her face was *priceless*.

Looking around the fire, we were all equally shocked. Apparently, Penny had a side to her none of us had ever seen.

"Your *dad*? A shotgun?" Mac asked, tugging at his collar like he was imagining himself in Jasper's shoes. "Did the poor guy piss his pants?"

Laughter echoed into the night, but I wasn't fully present.

My mind was elsewhere.

On someone who wasn't here.

Theo.

Her bold style, her don't-give-a-shit attitude—she'd drawn me in the second I saw her again after her return to Faircloud.

And I'd *blown it*.

I'd had a chance to ask her out, but instead, I fumbled through some half-assed attempt at flirting, let the moment slip through my fingers.

Now, she was stuck in my head.

I wanted to punch the air, frustrated at myself. at the years I'd wasted being blinded by Jess, not seeing things clearly until it was too late.

Loyalty had never been something I joked about.

When Jess left, it shattered something in me. I shut down. Bottled everything up so tight I refused to feel it.

That's what therapy uncovered—the way I'd buried my emotions, pretending they didn't exist.

In the year and a half since she walked away, I'd done the work.

Therapy. Medication. Letting myself be vulnerable again.

It wasn't easy. But it made me better.

Seeing Theo felt like a jolt of electricity. Like a spark reigniting something I thought had died long ago. For the first time in ages, I felt *alive*. Like I was ready to step back into the world, to open myself up to something new.

But her?

She was slipping away.

I saw it in the way she pulled back from the group, the way she sat off to the side when she did show up. I recognized that kind of loneliness. Hell, because I lived it. I knew what it was like to *drown* in your own solitude.

If I could use my own experiences to help someone else out of it, I would.

I was feeling reflective tonight, thinking about all I'd worked on and past in the time since Jess left.

I put *my* dreams on hold to make her happy. I was young. In love. Stupidly hopeful. I gave up a chance to play college football—maybe even go pro—because she didn't want me moving across the country without her.

And then she left anyway.

Standing on her porch that night, watching her walk away, was one of the lowest moments of my life.

The doubts had crept in and taken root.

Was I the problem? Was I not enough?

The spiral came fast and hard.

If someone who'd been with me for *years* didn't love me enough to stay, why the hell would anyone else?

The weight of it all dragged me under, drowning me in a bottle at twenty-four, hiding my struggles behind easy smiles and long hours at the ranch.

I still showed up. Still worked my ass off.

But I barely saw my friends.

The joy I used to feel? *Gone*.

I'd retreated so deep into my own mind that crawling out seemed impossible.

Then came my version of rock bottom. A run-in with a friend. Too much Jack. A night that could've gone way worse than it did.

And in the raw, ugly aftermath, I sat awake for hours, scouring the internet for help.

I couldn't keep going like that.

I missed the man I used to be—the one who felt *alive*.

That's how I found Jenny, my therapist.

She saw through the bullshit. Through the walls. She made me confront the fear and rejection I'd carried for too damn long.

It took over a year of hard work, but I was finally coming out the other side.

I wasn't just surviving anymore.

I was living again.

My job at the ranch was solid. My friends—though they didn't fully understand—had *stuck by me* anyway.

And for the first time in years, I felt ready.

Ready to open myself up. To try again.

"Do you agree, Rhodes?"

Logan's voice yanked me out of my thoughts.

I blinked, caught off guard. "Uh—yeah."

Logan narrowed his eyes, skepticism written all over his face. "You have no idea what we were talking about, do you?"

Mac chuckled, shaking his head. "Since you were off in la-la land, I'll catch you up," he said. "We were talking about Ellie leaving a couple months ago. Think Buck deserves forgiveness if she comes back?"

Ah. *Buck*. That asshole.

"Hell *no*," I said, my voice firm now that I actually knew what we were discussing. "That guy doesn't deserve *shit*."

Mac grinned. "Good. I plan to deviled-egg his car every day until I die."

Penny *lost it*—head thrown back, laughter ringing through the night. "Not the *Gilmore Girls* reference! I'm picturing old Mac with a walker, chucking deviled eggs at Buck's car and shuffling away as fast as he can."

The whole group cracked up, even Mac, who shrugged like, *What can I say?* He shot Penny a smirk, like they were sharing some kind of secret.

"How's Ellie doing?" I asked Boone once the laughter settled.

Boone tilted his head side to side. "She's been better, but she's making an effort. She calls once a week now, and I think she finally talked to my mom and dad. Last I heard, she was in Pennsylvania."

Mac scoffed. "*Pennsylvania*? Who the hell *chooses* to go there?"

Boone shrugged. "Something about Hershey Park and an all-you-can-eat Pennsylvania Dutch buffet."

Aspen smiled, resting her head on Boone's shoulder. "Whatever makes her happy."

The moment *hit me* harder than I expected.

Watching them together, seeing the ease between them, made the ache in my chest flare up, sharp and sudden.

And before I could stop myself, my mind wandered.

I wanted *that*.

I'd spent eight years with someone else, but was it too soon to try again?

Doubt tried to creep in.

Tried to pull me under.

But I shoved it aside, choosing instead to focus on the electric current that shot through me every time I thought of her.

Her boldness. Her fire.

Her *pigtails*.

She made me feel something I hadn't in a long, long time.

Hope.

4
Theo

22 weeks pregnant
Baby is the size of a red bell pepper

> Penny: Girls night?
>
> Aspen: Yes please!
>
> Penny: Tequila and margs?
>
> Aspen: You know the way to my heart
>
> Aspen: I'm free after I close up for the day!
>
> Penny: Boone better watch out! I'm coming for ya 😈
>
> Penny: I'm ready to FEAST and DRINK
>
> Aspen: Theo? What do you think?
>
> Penny: Earth to Theoooo

IT WAS MID-AFTERNOON, and that meant one thing: time for a snack run. Since nothing at home could satisfy this craving, I headed to the pharmacy for something different.

Buying food here was always a gamble, you ran the risk of snagging something expired. I'd learned that the hard way. For me, convenience often won out over quality.

I stood in front of the snack aisle, tapping my finger against my chin as I surveyed my options. The bags on the top shelf were slightly faded from the harsh fluorescent lights, a clear sign to steer clear of those, a trick I learned from being a regular.

When I'd left the house, I was craving something sweet—maybe a chocolate bar or kettle corn. Standing here now, surrounded by brightly colored bags, my baby and I decided salty and spicy was the way to go.

I grabbed the last bags of Flaming Hot Cheetos, along with some Hot Fries and Takis, clutching them tightly against my chest like someone might try to steal them from me. Over my dead body. I'd protect these with every fiber of my being.

"Why are you white-knuckling six bags of chips?"

The voice startled me, and I spun around, ready to fight, chest-to-chest with a man, a very tall and sturdy man.

My eyes trailed up from his broad chest, which was right at my eye level, to a pair of green eyes staring back at me. I'd recognize those anywhere. I stepped back, suddenly too close for comfort.

"Seriously," I quipped, smirking. "We need to stop meeting like this. I'm starting to think you're following me. Or are you here to stock up on your weekly value pack of condoms?"

I hoped the joke sounded casual because, suddenly, I felt embarrassingly self-conscious about my snack hoard. Rhodes's eyes lingered on the absurd pile of bags in my arms.

Was it insecurity or nerves? Rhodes looked good today—too good. His hair was tucked under a backward cap, and he wore a long-sleeve sun shirt that clung in all the right places. His dark-wash jeans were worn, and his boots caked with dirt. Not my usual type but, it was working on me.

He held up a small white pharmacy bag.

"I'm just here to pick up my meds," he said with a smirk, shaking the bag lightly so the pills rattled inside. "Thanks for the reminder about the condoms, though. I'll grab them on my way out."

My face instantly heated, and my palms grew clammy. Good job, Theo. Way to be an *ass*.

"I'm so insensitive," I muttered, unable to meet his eyes. I needed a T-shirt that read *World's Biggest Asshole* with two arrows pointing at me.

"Don't worry about it," Rhodes said, dipping his head to catch my gaze. "It's not something I'm embarrassed by, mental health needs to be talked about."

When I finally looked back at him, his perfectly pink lips curved into a lopsided smile. His reassurance did little to calm the frantic thudding of my heart.

"I shouldn't have assumed," I stammered. "That was an asshole move."

Rhodes shrugged. "Now you know." He nodded toward the snacks I was still clutching. "What's going on there? I'm sensing a theme."

I let out a scoff, followed by a self-deprecating laugh. "I came here craving something sweet, but when I saw the bright yellow and red Cheetos bag, my mouth started watering. Lately, spicy always wins the craving war."

Rhodes hummed thoughtfully. "I make a pretty good spicy pasta."

"Are you a good cook?" I asked, curiosity getting the best of me.

Rhodes tilted his head. "Good is subjective. I like to think I have a few signature dishes. Spicy pasta happens to be one of them."

A pause stretched between us. Was he offering to cook for me? Or just making conversation? Either way, pasta sounded amazing.

"You could come over one night, and I'll make some for you," he offered, his smile widening.

"Oh, please!" The words slipped out before I could stop them, sounding way too eager. Internally, I cringed, my subconscious seemed to be rooting for this.

Rhodes reached into his back pocket and handed me his phone. I took it gingerly. I felt like I had too much power. His lock screen was a picture of him and his friends, arms slung around one another and grinning wide. How sweet.

Swiping up, his phone immediately unlocked. Who didn't lock their phone these days? That was borderline psycho behavior in my book.

I typed in my contact info and sent myself a quick text so I'd have his number, too, and then handed it back.

"You even put your last name in here?" he teased,

shaking his head. "We're already friends. No need for formalities."

"Noted," I said, smiling down at my feet.

There was something about Rhodes. His presence felt effortless yet magnetic, like low stakes with a high reward. He was practically a stranger, someone I'd been around a handful of times and knew very little about. I should feel timid, scared to be so open but that seemed impossible around him.

"Do you need anything else, or are you all set?" Rhodes asked, his tone light, easy—completely free of judgment.

I nodded, then immediately second-guessed myself.

Actually...

I spun on my heel, heading toward the next aisle. "Wait. I should grab something sweet. Just in case."

Rhodes followed, stuffing his hands in his pockets as he watched me scan the shelves.

Finally, I grabbed a big bag of kettle popcorn and turned back to him, victorious.

"Now I'm ready."

His lips twitched like he was fighting back a grin. "Good to know you take snack decisions *very* seriously."

"Only the important ones." I clutched the bag to my chest like it was a prized possession. "Besides, you never know when a craving for something salty and sweet is gonna hit."

"I'll take your word for it," he teased, waving a hand for me to go first.

He stuck with me through checkout, then followed me

out to my car, the comfortable silence between us making my chest feel... *weirdly warm.*

At my driver's side door, Rhodes reached out, pulling it open for me.

I hesitated—just for a second—because for someone who prided herself on independence, I had an undeniable soft spot for chivalry.

"I'll, uh, see you soon?" Rhodes asked, almost hesitantly.

I nodded, biting back a smile as I tucked a pigtail behind my back and climbed into my car.

When I glanced up again, he was leaning against his truck bed, arms crossed, watching to make sure I pulled away safely.

And, okay... *that* made my chest ache a little.

By the time I got home, I was a puddle of emotions thinking about my interaction at the store. Rhodes was kind. Gentle. Thoughtful. Typically traits I stayed far away from. And those green eyes? A whole other level of trouble.

I sprawled out on my bed with snacks spread around me, and queued up a true crime documentary. No matter how much I tried to focus, my thoughts kept circling back to him.

He seemed interested in me which made me nervous. Men didn't have that effect on me, in fact, they were typically the ones quaking in my presence. I was to the point and often clear on my expectations. A woman who set things straight tended to send men running.

I'd been confident in who I was but lately, I was starting to question a lot about who I really *wanted* to be.

At some point, with my thoughts distracted, I grabbed my phone, hovering over Rhodes' contact. Should I text him? Call? Wait for *him* to text first? I was overthinking this and I wasn't an overthinker.

Before I could decide, my screen lit up with his name flashing in big, black letters. Was he reading my mind?

I squealed, tossing the phone onto my bed like it shocked me and covered my face. When the buzzing stopped, I cautiously picked it up, only for it to buzz again. A voicemail.

Not only did he leave his phone unlocked, called instead of texted–he left voicemails too? That should've been a red flag but it was oddly refreshing.

I hesitated, then hit play.

"Hey, Theo. It's, uh, me, Rhodes. You already know that, so I don't know why I said it. I was calling to follow up about dinner sometime. I guess… give me a call back. See ya."

The message ended with a soft click, and I instantly wanted to replay it. Rhodes was adorable.

Contradicting every ounce of badass energy I'd tried to channel earlier, I sent him a text instead of calling back.

> Theo: Sorry for missing your call! I had my phone on silent. I listened to your message. I'd love to come over for dinner!

Why was I so affected by this? I didn't like the feelings of anticipation and anxiety that short-circuited my system.

> Rhodes: Cool! What times and days work best for you?

I was free all the time. I had so much free time. Maybe I shouldn't answer right away, or maybe I should tell him I'll have to check my schedule. Exactly, add some mystery.

> Theo: Let me check and get back to you!

> Rhodes: 👍

Why didn't I say yes and be done with it? Nerves took over and controlled my actions. Tilting my head back and letting out a deep groan, I locked my screen and tossed my phone as far away on the bed as I could.

5
Theo

TODAY WAS PACKED with doctor appointments and bloodwork. The visits were more frequent than usual because of my mom's history while pregnant. Those issues have put me at higher risk.

My mom struggled to conceive, so when I came along, it was nothing short of a blessing. During her pregnancy, she was diagnosed with gestational diabetes and faced a slew of other challenges.

I was at a high risk of having the same. A diagnosis like that came with a lot—medications, injections, strict dietary changes. Because I was measuring larger than expected, my doctor added "keep a close eye" to the checklist. I was patiently waiting for the milestone to have that testing done to officially have my answer. The worry lingered, not because I doubted my ability to manage a new routine, but because of what it could mean for the baby's health or the delivery itself.

Pregnancy could be terrifying.

At first, the idea of a tiny human growing inside me was unnerving. Now, I'd bonded with her so deeply I couldn't imagine not carrying her. The connection was overwhelming and I could only wonder how much stronger it would feel when she was actually here. I couldn't wait to hold her, kiss her tiny cheeks, and watch her grow.

Sometimes, when I think too hard about the future, guilt creeps in for not finding her father. But just as quick as the thought comes, I always manage to pull myself out.

The truth is, I don't want the stress. Having someone drift in and out of her life wouldn't be fair to her. Even if I wanted to, I wouldn't know where to begin searching for him. Greece is a place I'll never see the same way again.

I laid back on the examination table, staring at the stark white ceiling. The walls were covered in outdated blue wallpaper and framed pictures that seemed older than I was.

This was the only doctor's office in Faircloud, serving as a one-stop shop: primary care, OB-GYN, dentist, and optometrist. The practice had been running since "B.T."—Before Theo. That explained the decor and the faint musty smell clinging to the wallpapered walls.

"There's her hand," the technician said, pointing at the screen. My chest swelled with pride and warmth as I gazed at her—my little girl.

I wanted to reach out and touch the screen but held back, watching intently as the technician adjusted the angles.

Every time I saw her, I dreamed of dressing her in cute

outfits, imagining her as my mini-me. I thought about what her voice might sound like, what color her hair would be. Would she be tall or short? Athletic or artistic?

Being a mom was going to change me, hell it already has. I'm realizing I can't handle everything alone. I'll need to accept help, open my mind, and set my stubbornness aside.

Focusing on the ultrasound, I reminded myself of what mattered most. All the anxiety and fear melted away whenever I saw her. She's my biggest accomplishment, and she isn't even here yet.

AS I SLIPPED BACK into my clothes after the appointment wrapped up, my phone buzzed repeatedly. A series of text messages came flooding in, one after another.

> Penny: Tequila Cowboy tonight? 😊
>
> Aspen: Yes! Boone and I will be there!
>
> Penny: Do we know if Mac is bartending?
>
> Aspen: I'll ask Boone!
>
> Aspen: Boone said, "How the hell would I know?"
>
> Aspen: But I'm making him ask...
> Men. Smh.

> Penny: 💅
>
> Penny: If he isn't, I'm not going.
>
> Aspen: Confirmed, Mac will be working!
>
> Penny: I'm doing a happy dance.
>
> Penny: Where's Theo?
>
> Aspen: DON'T IGNORE US!

Theo: I was at a doctor's appointment. I don't think I'll join.

> Aspen: Why nooootttt!
>
> Penny: Yeah, come on! We miss you going out with us.
>
> Aspen: I feel like we never see you anymore. Do you not like us?

My face flushed with frustration. My thumbs hovered over the keyboard.

They didn't see me anymore because everything they wanted to do involved drinking or late nights—things I couldn't do.

I loved them with everything I could but sometimes I felt like I was the third wheel. I didn't enjoy reading, I wore dark colors and was as far from bubbly as one could be. Being the odd one out at their hangouts was my personal hell.

They seemed oblivious, continuing as though nothing had changed. It left me feeling alienated, like I was being left behind. Over the past month, I've noticed a shift. Did they not feel it?

When I told them I was pregnant, they were thrilled. I assumed they'd want to include me in activities I could enjoy, be overbearing and involved every step of the way. Maybe I was naive to think that.

Right now, I felt like I was shouting into a void only I could hear, my expectations too high.

"Forget this," I muttered, locking my phone while walking out of the doctor's office. My pulse pounded in my ears, my thoughts a chaotic tangle. If I replied now, I'd say something I'd regret—something I couldn't take back.

Outside, I leaned against my car, the cool metal grounding me. My phone was already in my hand. Without thinking too much, I tapped Rhodes's name.

Why him? I didn't know.

The line rang, each trill tightening the knot in my chest.

"Hello?" His deep voice answered, slightly out of breath.

"Am I bothering you?" I asked, the words tumbling out too fast. Under my breath, I muttered, "This is why I text."

Rhodes chuckled, a warm, rumbling sound that somehow made my heart ache and ease all at once. "Nah. Just tossing a hay bale into the truck. What's up?"

I hesitated, kicking a pebble on the pavement. "Nothing. Just... finished a doctor's appointment."

"Everything okay with the baby?" he asked, his tone dipping into genuine concern.

"Oh, yeah," I said quickly, trying to keep it light. "She's measuring almost eight inches already."

There was a beat of silence before he asked, laughter in his voice, "Is that big?"

"Kind of, but nothing I can't handle," I said, then immediately slapped a hand to my forehead. Did that sound as suggestive as I thought it did?

Rhodes let the pause hang, just long enough to make me squirm. "Are you free Friday?" I blurted, desperate to change the subject.

"For you? Always. What time?"

"How's five?" I asked, cringing at how casual I tried to sound while my stomach flipped like a damn pancake.

"Works for me. Any requests? Besides the pasta, of course."

I thought for a moment, closing my eyes and letting myself tap into the craving. "What about a dark chocolate cake and ice cream?"

He scoffed, the sound airy, teasing, and entirely too attractive. "Deal. What kind of ice cream? Let me guess, I'll make all your chocolate dreams come true."

I laughed, nodding like an idiot at my phone, as if he could see me.

Something about the way he said it, low and easy, made my chest tighten in a way that wasn't unpleasant. His soft promise seeped through my jagged thoughts, smoothing the edges. I exhaled, the weight I'd been carrying lifted just a little.

"Yes." I exhaled, the word coming out like a release of pent up tension.

Somehow, Rhodes had reached into my chaotic mind and plucked out exactly what I was thinking, as if he understood me on a level no one else did. It was a familiar connection I couldn't quite grasp but didn't want to let go of.

"Perfect. I'll see you Friday."

"Wait, can I bring anything?" The words rushed out, a little too eager. I winced at myself. Truthfully, I just wanted to keep him on the line a moment longer.

"Just yourself."

His response was simple, but it hit me harder than it should have. My throat went dry, and I swallowed audibly.

"Well, I'll, uh, see you Friday?" The sentence hung awkwardly in the air, more like a question than a statement. Why did I say it like that? We'd literally just agreed on this.

I groaned quietly, slumping into the driver's seat. My head thunked against the headrest, my frustration bubbling over.

"I'll see you Friday," Rhodes said, his voice steady, confident—everything I wasn't in that moment.

Trying to channel the calm, mysterious woman I always aspired to be, I ended the call without a proper goodbye, my thumb tapping the screen just a little too quickly. Tossing my phone onto the passenger seat, I let out a groan, covering my face with my hands. The last thirty minutes of my life replayed in my head like a cringeworthy montage.

After a moment, I reached for my phone again, determined to distract myself. The group chat was still sitting there, waiting. With a resigned sigh, I typed out a generic response that was polite yet detached.

> Theo: Maybe next time.

Satisfied with my emotionally evasive response, I set the phone down again and leaned back, letting the quiet of the car settle around me. Alone with my thoughts, I let the emotions I'd been holding back swirl unchecked.

6
Rhodes

BOONE LET me leave work early today. I wasn't entirely honest about why, but a little white lie didn't hurt anyone. I needed time to grab the groceries for dinner with Theo. If Boone knew, he'd run straight to Aspen and spill. I wasn't ready for that.

For the first time in a while, my heart fluttered in a way that wasn't tinged with dread. The sensation was warm, like butterflies shifting inside my chest. Usually, the only woman occupying my thoughts was Jess, and the spike in my heart rate then wasn't pleasant, it was hammering anxiety. Tonight felt different, and I clung to the feeling.

As I wandered through the grocery aisles, I was laser-focused on making tonight special. Boxed pasta wouldn't cut it. I was making everything from scratch.

The store's fluorescent lights buzzed faintly overhead, and the only sound was the hum of old-school country music. My basket was filled with flour, eggs, red pepper flakes, and tomatoes. Most of the other seasonings were already at home.

When I talked to Theo earlier, I was smiling like an idiot. Thank God she couldn't see me. She might've hung up and never called again, and I wouldn't have blamed her. Still, hearing her agree to dinner felt like a win.

Turning into the freezer aisle, I froze. A puff of teased black hair, unmistakable and too familiar, caught my eye. My chest tightened, the air around me suddenly feeling too thin.

Jess's mom.

She wore her usual uniform: capris, a short-sleeved shirt, and that gravity-defying hairstyle. My palms dampened as old, unwelcome memories surged like a wave breaking over me, each one sharper than the last.

I clenched my jaw and squeezed my eyes shut. *Ten, nine, eight...* I counted backward, willing myself to stay calm, to stay grounded. The knot in my stomach only twisted tighter.

You don't have to stay. You can leave. The thought was a lifeline, something solid to hold onto. I opened my eyes, scanning for an escape route.

Every nerve in my body screamed the same command: *Get out. Now.*

Spinning on my heels, I decided ice cream could wait. Instead, I veered into the baking aisle to grab double chocolate chunk cake mix. No ordinary store cake for Theo. Sure, it was box mix, but I knew my limits. I wasn't much of a baker, and asking Aspen for help would only give her more ammunition to tease.

For me, this wasn't just dinner, it was a shot at something new. Theo wasn't just stunning; she was effortlessly cool in a way that made you want to lean in and stay a while.

Maybe I was chasing something familiar. Or maybe it was the timing—she'd come back to town just as I was beginning to feel whole again, like some kind of nudge I couldn't ignore. Either way, this was a step I had to take, even if it scared me.

Eventually, I circled back to the freezer aisle, relieved to see Jess's mom had vanished. My chest loosened, and I let out a breath I hadn't realized I was holding. Grabbing the ice cream, I ran through my mental checklist.

At the last second, as I was heading to checkout, I spotted something. Without overthinking, I reached for it and tossed it into my basket. A small, impulsive gesture but one that felt just right.

To my surprise, Indie was working the register. This wasn't my usual day to shop, but it was comforting to know at least she was my one constant. Her reaction to seeing me was as flat as usual, minimal talking, quick exchange of cash, a fake smile.

Bags in hand, I jogged to my truck to quickly drive home.

My little bungalow sat on several wooded acres. The dark gray paint and metal roof gave it charm, while the wraparound porch pulled it all together. Inside, it was too big for one guy—three bedrooms, two bathrooms, and a decent kitchen, however, the rent was a steal thanks to the sweet couple who owned it. I'm pretty sure they just felt bad for me.

This place was just a house. Every night, I came back

to the same thing: lights off, darkness swallowing the space, and an eerie silence no one could explain. Being just a few years shy of thirty, I never thought I'd be here—starting over. Alone. Spending my nights tossing frozen pizzas in the oven, living like a bachelor.

Over the past year, I've had to be okay with being on my own. Therapy taught me that I needed to find peace within myself before I could truly be with someone else, and I did. I became content. I'd realize though, being content wasn't enough anymore.

I wanted more. I wanted a family.

I could see it so clearly: little versions of me running around, their laughter filling this empty house. A partner who wasn't just someone I loved but someone I could call my best friend.

Was that too much to ask?

Balancing all the grocery bags in one trip, I barreled through the door and dumped everything on the counter.

I'd start with the pasta first, leaving out the eggs and flour. Mid-washing my hands, my phone started to ring and a picture of my mom popped up on the screen. Quickly, using the towel to dry my hands, I swiped and accepted the video call.

"Hi, Sweetie!" she greeted, her face filling the screen, way too close for comfort. She and I were spitting images; people said I looked like the male version of her. She had black hair, which she kept cut to above her shoulders, and vibrant green eyes.

"Ma, pull the phone back." I laughed, leaning on the counter.

She huffed and adjusted the angle. "Better?" Behind her, I caught glimpses of a hotel room.

"Where are you?" I asked.

"Rob surprised me with a trip to the city! He knows how much I love to shop." She grinned like a teenager, clearly thrilled.

My mom and Rob still lived in Faircloud. Even though she was still close, I didn't get to see her as often as I should have. She worked the night shift as a nurse in the city, which meant she would work when I was getting off. Rob was a saint in that he always supported her and had nothing negative to say about her job. Instead, he gloated about how amazing and committed she was.

We chatted as I worked, but the moment she noticed me making pasta from scratch, her mom instincts kicked in.

"Homemade pasta? Who's the lucky lady?"

I hesitated. Lying to my mom wasn't an option. Lying in general wasn't something I did. "Theo Matthews," I admitted, keeping my tone casual.

"And you're making her a meal? From scratch?" Her voice carried a hint of worry. "Isn't she... pregnant? Oh my God, is it—?"

"No, Ma. Definitely not. If it were, you'd have known months ago."

She softened, but doubt still lingered in her eyes. "I'm just looking out for you. I saw what Jess put you through. I don't want you to get hurt again."

"I know," I said, focusing on the dough beneath my hands, kneading it like it could absorb the tension. "It's just a date. She's a nice girl, and she needs a friend right now."

"Are you sure it's worth it? That's a lot to take on if this becomes more than just a date."

I paused, pressing the heel of my palm into the dough a little harder. "I'm not thinking that far ahead. I'm taking baby steps, Ma, trying to get back out there. And she's a friend. It's okay, seriously."

Her expression softened on the screen, worry etched in the lines around her eyes. "I trust you. Just be careful, okay?"

Her words hit deeper than she probably realized. She'd been there, picking up the pieces. My mom had spent countless sleepless nights sitting with me, pushing through her own exhaustion to make sure I didn't drown in mine. Back then, the bottle had been my crutch, my escape, and she'd been the one forcing me to face the reality I kept trying to avoid.

"I will. Always," I promised, meeting her gaze.

Still, I needed to steer the conversation away. Even though she said she trusted me, I could hear the judgment in her voice, subtle but unmistakable.

Just because Theo was pregnant didn't mean she deserved less care or attention. The weight she carried didn't make her less worthy of kindness or companionship.

Would my mom feel the same skepticism if the baby were already here? If I invited Theo and her child over for dinner, would she still see it as a risk?

The questions churned in my mind as I shaped the

dough, but I didn't voice them. Some battles didn't need to be fought out loud.

We'd continued our conversation about work and other little stuff before it was time for them to leave for their dinner reservations.

After we hung up, I put the final touches on my meal. Luckily, I had my mom on the phone because it had been a while since I had made this dish. The recipe was hers, which came from her mom, and so on. It was a generational thing.

Cake baking, sauce simmering, everything felt right. When I glanced at the clock, the nerves hit me like a truck.

Was the house clean enough? Would Theo feel comfortable?

Walking around, I made a few last-minute adjustments. I made sure my bed was made and my bathroom cleaned up, and I even wore a little cologne. A lot depended on the first impression.

Should I light a candle for the table? Was that too forward?

Forget the candle.

I ran my hands down the front of my jeans, looking down to check out my outfit. Suddenly, I hated this shirt. The fabric was too tight. I needed to change.

Taking off in a jog towards my bedroom, I mentally flipped through all four shirts I owned and I landed on a standard Black Carhartt tee.

While I was mid change, there was a knock on the door, barely enough for me to hear. Panic took over, and I ran down the hall while *also* trying to put my shirt on.

Pro tip: don't do that.

As my head came through the hole, I barely stopped myself in time from running into the wall. I needed to calm down, take a deep breath, and put on my game face. I repeated those steps in real time, shutting my eyes and counting back from ten. When I steadied myself, I approached the door as calm and collected as I could be.

There she stood, her overalls unbuttoned on one side, her tube top hinting at fair and smooth skin beneath. Her pigtails—damn those pigtails—made my heart stutter. She wasn't even trying, and I was already completely under her spell.

"Hey there, Honey," I said, plastering on a confident grin while desperately hoping she couldn't tell I was one step away from falling to my knees.

7
Theo

> Aspen: Do we want to hike Hawke Peak tomorrow? I could die for some fresh air and sunshine
>
> Penny: I have to go to work in the morning. Our weekend kid's reader called out, so now I'm in panic mode to find a replacement
>
> Aspen: Maybe I can convince Boone to do it
>
> Penny: Boone Cassidy, reading to children? My ovaries wouldn't be able to take that.
>
> Penny: I can go after
>
> Aspen: DEAAALLL

MY KNUCKLES BRUSHED the door lightly, so lightly that if no one answered, I could pretend I'd tried and leave. A perfect excuse to retreat. However, retreating would do nothing except make me angry with myself.

Was I really ready for this?

This wasn't just any visit. This was the first time Rhodes and I would be alone—no friends to buffer awkward silences, no distractions to hide behind. The thought sent my pulse skittering, my breath hitching in my throat. I had to stop overthinking, but it was too late. My stomach twisted harder, the imaginary indigestion turning into full-blown contemplation for even showing up.

The seconds dragged, stretching out like an eternity. I stood there, frozen, my heart pounding in my ears. Then I heard it, a shuffle of muffled footsteps, the faint clatter of something. He was home. And he was coming to the door.

There was no turning back now.

A waft of air blew the strand of hair falling from my braids and Rhodes appeared in front of me with an easy grin that screamed confidence. His deep voice, smooth as butter, greeted me.

"Hey there, Honey."

Honey. The nickname rolled off his tongue, sending a tingle straight through me. Butterflies collided with the knots already twisting in my stomach, and even the baby shifted, as if reacting to the deep timbre of Rhodes' voice.

I couldn't read him. One moment, he seemed nervous and uncertain around me, and the next, he exuded confidence. It was maddening, trying to figure out if he was just as unsure as I was, or if I was the only one overthinking every little thing.

Biting my lip, I reached up to push my pigtails behind my shoulders, a nervous habit that made me feel both childish and exposed. My fingers brushed the strap of my purse, fiddling with it as I tried to ground myself. "Hi," I whispered, the word barely audible, my voice trembling.

"Come in," he said, stepping aside and holding the door open for me.

The scent of pasta hit me immediately, rich and tangy, curling around me like a warm invitation. My stomach growled, loud enough to be embarrassing, but I couldn't even bring myself to care.

I stepped into the living room, glancing around. The space was simple, functional. Dark forest-green walls framed a cozy L-shaped couch and a modern coffee table in front of a TV. A long table sat near the entrance, the room lacked personal touches—no photos, no art.

Following him further inside, I found myself in the kitchen. The dark wood cabinets and matching floors gave the space warmth, while the marble countertops, streaked with gold veins, added a touch of luxury. It wasn't what I expected for a ranch hand's home, still, it suited him.

"I hope you're hungry," Rhodes said, stirring something on the stove. Then, with a simple, commanding tone, he added, "Here."

Like a moth to a flame, I moved toward him, drawn by the man and the intoxicating aroma wafting through the room.

Without a word, he dipped a spoon into the simmering red sauce, wiped off the excess, and offered it to me. Instinctively, I leaned forward, my lips parting as he gently placed the spoon against them.

The flavors burst across my tongue. A perfect harmony of garlic, rosemary, and the kick of red pepper flakes. The spice was bold and satisfying, scratching every itch. My eyes fluttered shut as I savored it, my tongue darting out to catch a stray drop that had escaped.

When I opened my eyes, Rhodes was staring. His Adam's apple bobbed as he swallowed hard, gaze following the slow, deliberate path of my tongue.

Heat crept up my cheeks. Was it from the spice—or from the way he was looking at me?

"That's delicious," I muttered, not breaking eye contact.

We stared at each other, a thick silence hanging between us. I could feel an invisible force holding me in place. Tilting my head slightly, I took in his wide eyes and slack expression. Something flickered across his face, something I couldn't quite identify.

Rhodes was looking at me like he thought *I* was delicious.

An urge swelled inside me to reach out, to close the space between us, but he broke the moment with a simple clearing of his throat, shattering my thoughts.

"Mhm." His groan was soft. Turning back to the stove, he wiped his hands on a towel. "I, uh, have something for you."

Before I could ask, he disappeared into another room, leaving me standing there with my curiosity building. When he returned, he was holding a bouquet of vibrant flowers, their colors so bright they almost seemed to glow.

The sight of them caught me completely off guard. My chest tightened, and before I even understood why, tears pricked the corners of my eyes.

"I'm sorry. I didn't mean to upset you," he said quickly, his grip on the bouquet tightening as I reached for it. "I just... I saw these on my way out of the store and thought they were pretty."

"Thank you." My voice cracked as I grabbed the flowers, my gaze fixated on the arrangement of Gerbera daisies in every shade of the rainbow with delicate baby's breath and lush greenery. "They're beautiful."

Our hands brushed as I accepted the bouquet, and I glanced up at him, a small smile tugging at my lips. "You can let go now. They're mine," I teased, my voice barely above a whisper.

Rhodes chuckled, the sound warm and rich, and the tension in the air dissolved. I couldn't help but laugh with him, wiping away a stray tear that escaped down my cheek.

I'd never had a favorite flower, I loved them all equally, but these? These I loved just a little more.

Rhodes took a step back, leaning casually against the kitchen island. I appreciated the distance. His proximity was intoxicating, his cologne—a blend of cedar and coffee—assaulting my senses in the best way.

In the short time I'd known him, Rhodes had exceeded every expectation. He helped me out of my car, held doors open, and now, he'd brought me flowers. No man had ever given me flowers before. I didn't know what to do with them. Should I put them down? Thank him again? Ask for water?

Why was I panicking over *flowers*?

I tried to calm my spiraling thoughts, reminding myself that Rhodes wasn't judging me. He didn't care if I said something awkward or stumbled over my words. If he hadn't already been scared off by my blunders, he wasn't going anywhere now.

I placed the bouquet gently on the island next to my bag and turned to face him. "Can I help?" I asked, desperate for a distraction from the chaos in my head.

Rhodes shook his head, stepping back toward the oven. When he opened the door, a wave of rich chocolatey aroma filled the air.

He'd baked a chocolate cake.

Rhodes *baked* me a fucking chocolate cake. My ovaries were officially done for.

My gaze fixed on his broad back as he moved effortlessly around the kitchen. Watching a man cook was undeniably sexy, and Rhodes was making it impossible to say no to...well, anything. If his goal was to get me into his bed tonight, he was certainly on the right track.

"Are you sure? Please, let me help," I begged, teetering on the edge of dropping to my knees, though it wouldn't just be to beg.

"Fine," he relented with a smirk. "You can grab the pitcher from the fridge and bring it to the table."

Grateful for the task, I opened the refrigerator and blinked in surprise. It was nearly empty.

If Rhodes liked to cook, why was there nothing in his fridge?

I grabbed the pitcher, careful as I removed it from the shelf. The pale liquid inside sloshed as I carried it to the table, my curiosity piqued.

"What the hell is this?" I asked, eyeing the contents skeptically.

"Peppermint tea," he answered, his voice casual as he plated the last bit of food. "It's supposed to help with heartburn. I read online that it's safe during the third trimester."

I nearly dropped the pitcher.

Rhodes had researched pregnancy-safe foods, then bought ingredients—ingredients that clearly weren't staples in his nearly barren fridge.

Swoon.

Rhodes was thoughtful, gentle, and undeniably caring. How could anyone choose city life over someone like this?

That made me wonder, were there skeletons in Rhodes' closet?

"Wow, that's amazing," I whispered, pouring tea into my glass until it was nearly full. I repeated the process with his glass, leaving the pitcher on the table between us.

My legs began to ache, so I sat, easing the pressure off my ankles.

"Can I get you anything else?" Rhodes asked, his tone sincere.

I glanced at the table in front of me: pasta coated in rich red sauce, warm bread, and a pitcher of peppermint tea.

I smiled. "No, this looks *fucking fantastic*," I said, laughing in partial disbelief. He'd truly outdone himself.

Rhodes sat across from me, his eyes meeting mine, and I couldn't help but grin. "I'm so excited to eat this right now. My mouth is literally watering."

He chuckled, gesturing toward my plate with the silverware in his hand. "You try it first. Be gentle with me —it's been a while since I made this."

Twisting my fork into the noodles, I gathered as much as I could before taking a bite. The spice hit me immediately, but oh my God, it was *good*. An explosion of flavor burst on my tongue, a mix of heat and richness that was downright addictive.

"Oh yeah," I moaned, my eyes rolling back. "That's it."

Rhodes cleared his throat. "I'm taking that as a compliment."

"I'd make love to this pasta," I confessed, covering my mouth as I laughed. "I'm going to need you to make this for me every day."

The sauce was perfect—creamy, smooth, and balanced. If I hadn't seen him stirring the pot when I arrived, I might've thought he bought it pre-made and passed it off as his own.

"Your wish is my command," Rhodes replied, his eyes crinkling as he tried to hide a smile.

"Where did you learn to make this?" I asked, eager to learn more about him, to peel back the layers one by one.

"My mom," he said. "It's a recipe that's been in my family for generations."

"That's so cool. So, you're close with your mom?"

"Oh yeah," he said with a nod, taking another bite.

"Me too," I said. "How about your dad?"

Rhodes shook his head, washing down his food with a sip of tea. "I never met him. He left my mom before I was even born."

For fuck's sake, it was only my second question, and I'd already made things weird. Why couldn't I have just asked his favorite color or something? I managed to say the wrong thing around him... again.

"I'm sorry. That must've been hard on your mom," I said carefully.

"Yeah, she worked hard to give me the best life possible. I owe her everything."

I felt that to my core. My mom had taken on both roles after my dad passed away. At least I had ten solid years with mine, Rhodes never even had a chance.

"I get that. My dad passed away when I was ten," I said. "My mom handled everything with so much grace, even though her whole world was turned upside down."

The conversation had taken a serious turn, but with Rhodes, it didn't feel uncomfortable. He listened, really listened, giving me his full attention.

"That's why we moved here. After he passed, we needed a change," I continued. "I'm glad we did because who knows where I'd have ended up if we'd stayed in Oklahoma."

"I can't imagine what that must've been like," he said, his voice soft. "That kind of pain doesn't really go away, does it? Was it sudden?"

His words cut deep, but not in a bad way. Not many people knew the details of my dad's death. It was sudden and devastating, and I never got the chance to say goodbye. Thinking about it still tore me apart.

I nodded, deciding to share a little more. "He died in a car accident. Not having closure keeps the wound open."

I spared Rhodes the haunting details: my dad driving late from a job to surprise me at a soccer game I'd begged him to attend, the accident that robbed me of him forever. After that, I stopped asking for things from anyone.

"Jesus, Theo. I'm sorry," Rhodes said. Then, to my

surprise, he added with a crooked smile, "Now we're both assholes."

A laugh escaped me, a snort, really, and once I started, I couldn't stop. Rhodes joined in, and for the first time in forever, I didn't feel weighed down by my grief.

"We can call it even now," I said, wiping my eyes as I took another bite of pasta.

The rest of dinner flowed easily. Conversation came naturally, and when the plates were clean and dessert devoured, I didn't want the night to end. Usually, by this time, I'd be curled up in pajamas, watching TV. However, I craved more time with Rhodes.

"I'd suggest playing a game, but neither of us likes losing," I teased, leaning back in my chair.

"I've got a game we can play solo. No losing to someone else," he said with a smirk.

Rhodes disappeared down the hall and returned holding two decks of cards. "Solitaire."

"Ugh, I've heard of it but I've never actually played it."

He feigned shock. "Theo. You've never played? It's the ultimate game for an only child."

"That's definitely not true. I'm an only child, and I've never heard of it."

Rhodes handed me a deck, then cleared the table to demonstrate. "We have more in common than I thought," he said.

"What? No dad and an only child?" I quipped.

"Exactly," he replied, smirking as he winked.

I fumbled with the cards, trying to follow his lead as he patiently showed me how to shuffle and set up the game. Despite my clumsiness, he was encouraging, guiding me through each step.

At first, I was slow, asking a million questions and second-guessing every move. With Rhodes' help, I got the hang of it, and soon we were playing in companionable silence.

Every so often, I'd catch him stealing glances at me, and I'd sneak looks at him too. Without his usual hat, his tousled black hair curled behind his ears. Freckles dotted his sun-kissed nose, softening his rugged, masculine features. He was...beautiful.

"You know what game I love?" I asked, breaking the quiet.

"Hmm?" he hummed, giving me his full attention.

"Scrabble. Specifically, the digital version. I play it every morning and night before bed."

"You play against strangers?" he asked.

"Yeah, I've got at least five games going right now," I said.

The tradition had started with my family. Tuesday nights were game nights with Mom and Dad, and Scrabble was always the highlight. After Dad passed, Mom and I kept it alive as long as we could. Playing online now gave me a way to hold onto those memories.

Rhodes nodded thoughtfully, waiting for me to return to my game before resuming his own.

When I couldn't stop yawning and my eyelids grew heavy, I knew it was time to go. Rhodes offered to drive me home, but I refused. There was no way I'd admit I couldn't keep up—even if it was true.

8
Rhodes

"DO YOU EVER LEAVE THIS PLACE?"

Mac glanced at me, a snarl on his lips, as he squatted to grab glasses from the bottom shelf of the bar.

"No, smartass. I live here. Literally," he said, setting the glasses on his workstation.

Mac lived and breathed this bar. Even on the rare occasion he had a night off, he was still here. Considering he lived upstairs, it wasn't much of a leap. Tonight, Dudley and the other bartender had both called in "sick." Ironically, they were sleeping together. Being the workaholic he was, Mac stepped in to cover the bar himself.

It was Tuesday, which meant Tequila Night. Since the day started with a "T," tequila shots were half off, and all tequila-based drinks were $4. The special usually drew a decent crowd for a weeknight.

How did I know this? Because if I ever wanted to see Mac, this was where I had to come. At this point, I'd watched him behind that bar so many times, I could probably do the job myself.

After a long day at work, I figured I'd swing by tonight and check in on my friend. Mac always loved it when we showed up just to watch him work.

Sike.

"Why don't you call someone else in? Just because they both called out doesn't mean you have to take the hit," I said.

Mac didn't allow himself much beyond bartending. The only thing that could pull him away was his dog, Angus.

And speak of the devil—there was a loud thud, followed by the sound of paws skidding across hardwood. Angus, Mac's massive 120-pound black Lab, came barreling down the stairs.

Nearly knocking me off my stool, Angus pounced, planting his front paws on my lap.

"Hey there, buddy," I cooed, scratching behind his ears. His head tilted left and right, his pink tongue lolling from his mouth as he panted eagerly. Angus was a beast of a dog. Standing on his hind legs, he was as tall as an average man.

"Oh, shit," Mac muttered, rushing around the bar.

Rule number one: no animals in the bar while it was in service.

"You know better, boy," Mac scolded, shooing Angus toward the stairs. He disappeared, presumably locking him back upstairs. Depending on how the night went, I might head up later and keep him company.

Left to myself for a moment, my thoughts drifted to

dinner with Theo. She'd been on my mind ever since. She was so nervous, which I found sweet. Then again, I'd been nervous, too, though I tried not to show it. Especially when she licked her lips and gave me those big, beautiful eyes. It took everything in me not to say "fuck it" and finish cleaning her up myself.

But my anxiety had other ideas. I called her *Honey*. She didn't seem to mind, but was she just being polite? Showing her how to play Solitaire—was that too much? Did I come off as cocky?

The questions came one after another, relentless.

I took a deep breath and brought my beer to my lips. The cold liquid slid down my throat, a welcome distraction. *It was okay.* I reminded myself of that. No matter how loud the anxiety got, I had to pull my mind back.

Mac returned from upstairs, mumbling something under his breath. When he got closer, he shook his head and smiled.

"That damn dog. I swear, he knows exactly what he's doing."

"Oh, yeah, he's no dummy," I laughed. Angus was just like his owner, always up to something.

A faint breeze swept through the room as the bar door swung open and shut. Mac turned his back to light a cigarette.

"Oh, for fuck's sake," he grumbled, exhaling smoke and planting both hands on the bar. "I got a full audience tonight. Don't you guys have anything better to do?"

That's when I noticed the beginnings of a mustache on Mac's face. Ironic.

Two hands clapped down on my shoulders, and I craned my neck to see Boone, wearing his signature khaki hat, with Logan close behind.

I hadn't told anyone I was coming here tonight, so our unplanned reunion was pure coincidence.

I'd come because I needed to think. Mac wasn't the type to push for conversation, which made this bar the perfect place to work through my thoughts.

Boone, though, he was different. I loved him like a brother. He was a born lover, through and through, and our bond was strong and unspoken. He'd seen me at my lowest and hadn't turned away.

There was a night, a year ago, when things had gone south for me, bad enough that I didn't think I'd climb out. I'd been a real asshole to Boone back then, but instead of letting it ruin our friendship, he stayed. He sat with me through the storm and promised we'd never speak of it again.

Even now, his cheeky grin and khaki hat brought me back to that night, a memory that was both painful and defining.

Everything was blurry. Was I spinning? The space around me moved on its own, but my thoughts remained steady, consumed by one thing: failure.

I sat in my truck, parked outside my house. Why I chose to be here was beyond me—I didn't even have my keys. The house was empty; my mom was working an overnight shift, leaving me vulnerable. Nights like these were the worst, when the silence crept in and the thoughts hit hardest.

Loneliness felt heavier in the dark, suffocating in the absence of sound. My dad was nonexistent, Jess was gone, and my fragile ego had been shattered into pieces.

People said Jess leaving wasn't my fault, but how could I believe that? I'd given up everything for her. I threw my dreams in the trash and stayed in Faircloud because she begged me not to leave her behind. I'd done my best to love her, but it wasn't enough.

"You can't leave me here alone, Rhodes. Everyone will talk. What about the girls who'll throw themselves at you? I can't take being here without you."

It was funny now, she didn't care about me. She left without a proper goodbye, dropping the news on her front porch just moments before crossing the county line.

Where did all her pleading get me? A one-way ticket to Pity City.

Reclining slightly in my seat, I tipped the bottle of Jack to my lips. One gulp. Two. Three. The burn didn't make it better. The thoughts of inadequacy kept looping, and the liquor wasn't dulling the ache anymore.

It was a physical pain now. My chest felt heavy, my mind a chaotic swirl. Exhaustion loomed, but relief stayed just out of reach. I drank because being drunk was better than feeling broken.

Her leaving cracked something inside me, exposing the festering darkness I'd kept hidden. I was unraveling, bit by bit, like a yoyo spinning out of control.

Why wasn't I enough? Jess left. My dad left. What was so unlovable about me that people walked away? My mom had to step into roles he abandoned, teaching me to shave, talking me through puberty, throwing a football with me in the yard. It wasn't fair to her.

Would I ever be good enough for anyone?

I leaned back in my seat, staring at the gray liner of my truck.

Tears rolled down my face, splashing onto the leather. One after another, steady and silent.

I was a grown-ass man, spiraling because my girlfriend left me and my father didn't love me. How fucking pathetic.

If I were sober, I probably would've flinched when the truck door flew open. I wasn't, and the fresh Texas air filling the cab did nothing to shake me. I didn't care who it was.

"Rhodes, what the hell is going on?" *Boone's voice was cautious but firm.*

The seat snapped upright and despite it, I kept my eyes forward, refusing to acknowledge him. Boone reached into the cab, his hand closing around the bottle. The warmth of the glass disappeared from my grasp, leaving me feeling emptier than before.

The bottle had become my safety net. The burn of the whiskey was a hug, comforting in its own cruel way.

Boone helped me out of the truck in silence, his arm steadying me as he led me inside. He didn't say a word as he laid me down on my bed. His concern was heavy in the room. It was suffocating.

"Talk to me," *he said, sitting on the edge of the mattress. The bed dipped under his weight.*

I shook my head. I couldn't speak. Where would I even start?

"I was worried," *Boone said, his voice gentler now.* "You weren't answering our calls or texts. I know you've needed space, but this isn't you. Whatever you're going through—"

"You don't fucking know what I'm going through," *I snapped, venom lacing every word.* "You don't know me."

Boone flinched, not backing down. "Stop. I'm worried about you. Logan and Mac are worried about you. You've been distant. Showing up to work, sure, but you're not hanging out with us anymore. I've sat back and let you deal with your shit your way, seeing you like this? That was a mistake."

I clenched my jaw, swallowing against the lump in my throat. Let him lecture me. I probably wouldn't remember it by morning anyway.

"If you don't want to talk to me about it, fine," Boone said, exhaling sharply. "But you need help, real help. Drinking yourself stupid isn't the answer. You're lucky none of the guys know I came here tonight. I won't tell them, and I'll never bring this up again, however, you need to hear me, Rhodes."

I didn't move. I didn't look at him.

"Words," he pressed. "I need words."

"I hear you," I muttered finally, my voice barely audible.

He nodded and stood. "I'm not leaving until you're sound asleep, and I'm taking your keys."

Boone gave me a sad smile before walking out of the room, leaving me alone with my thoughts.

That night, he slept on my couch. The next morning, I woke up with my head pounding and found him passed out, his feet propped on the coffee table.

Despite my best efforts, I remembered everything. Boone kept his word, and we never spoke about it again.

9
Theo

IF I STAYED in this house any longer, I'd lose my ever-loving mind, not to mention run out of true crime documentaries to watch. It was unsettling how much crime happened without us even realizing it. The human psyche was a strange, dark place.

I needed to get out of bed and shower, if only to feel a little more human. Without much to do, I could easily spend all day here, eating my body weight in snacks.

Exhaustion was my constant companion, dragging me down even when I *wanted* to move. It wasn't like I was working anymore. My days of traveling the world, camera in hand were behind me, for now, at least.

Could you imagine me, heavily pregnant, running to capture the perfect shot or lying in a field waiting for the right moment? Sure, I'd never been on a safari or in any real danger, but agility was a requirement. These days, I was about as nimble as an elephant.

Life looked so different than it had just a few months ago. I'd never been one to stay in one place for long, always on the go. Being confined felt like a shock to the system. My mind still wanted to move, but my body? It screamed, *Who are you kidding?*

I couldn't argue with the backaches and swollen ankles. Even putting on shoes had become a huge task. Slip-on Birkenstocks were my saving grace, unless my mom was around to help me wrestle into a pair of boots. With her schedule as a vet tech at a 24-hour emergency clinic, I couldn't rely on her every time I needed something. And then there was the looming question: how would a baby fit into her already hectic life?

With effort, I rolled out of bed, planting my feet firmly on the floor before hoisting myself upright. Waddling to my dresser, I pulled out a fresh pair of pajamas, a cute set with cartoon tigers, because I wasn't about to let pregnancy rob me of that small joy. I'd be a matching set girl until the day I die.

Clutching the clothes to my chest, I made my way to the bathroom and shut the door. I paused there, hands braced on the vanity, head hanging low between my shoulders. I needed a moment to gather myself.

My thoughts were relentless, racing endlessly through my mind—negative, intrusive, exhausting. Loneliness was a constant presence, and since the texts during my last doctor's appointment, I hadn't answered Aspen or Penny. Saying no or explaining myself had become too tiring. How could I expect them to understand when they hadn't lived this?

That realization only made me feel more like an animal on display, navigating this unfamiliar territory while everyone else stood on the outside, watching.

I glanced up, catching my reflection in the mirror. The face staring back at me was barely recognizable—puffy, but at least my skin was glowing, right? Stepping back, I surveyed the rest of me. My belly peeked out beneath my shirt, a sliver of skin catching the light. I lifted the shirt over my head, exposing stretch marks and the strange new shape of my belly button.

This body wasn't mine. At least, it didn't feel like it. The changes were undeniable, physical and otherwise. I'd been warned that pregnancy would be hard, but no one could've prepared me for how disorienting it would be. My sense of self felt like it was unraveling, slipping through my fingers. I wasn't just Theo, the photographer, or Theo, the friend anymore. Soon, I'd be Theo, the mom.

The weight of it brought tears to my eyes. One slipped free, and I wiped it away with my thumb. Being the first in my friend group to have a baby meant I didn't have many people to confide in. No one truly understood what it was like to stand at the edge of a life-altering change.

Sniffling, I turned to the shower and twisted the faucet. Baths had once been my sanctuary, but my mom's house didn't have a tub, and even if it did, getting in and out would've been a whole ordeal. I'd never stoop to asking for help with that.

The warm water hit my back, soothing the aches and tension. I closed my eyes, letting the steam envelop me, and tried to redirect my thoughts to something lighter.

To Rhodes.

The storm in my head quieted, replaced by a gentle warmth that spread through me. Rhodes had been a constant in my mind lately, his calming presence and shy demeanor something I wasn't used to but craved all the same.

I thought about the way he'd approached me on Main Street, his awkward attempts at flirting making my heart flutter. Despite everything, he'd come back into my life, and that meant something. He saw something in me worth coming back for.

The way he'd looked at me during dinner, his gaze darkening when I'd licked the sauce from my thumb. That spark of desire had been unmistakable. It was thrilling, seeing him so affected by something as simple as that.

The memory made my breath hitch. My thoughts wandered to what he might look like shirtless, his broad shoulders and strong hands. A heat pooled low in my belly, spreading through me like wildfire.

I tilted my head back, letting the water hit my chest as the tension inside me built. My hands moved instinctively, one sliding up to cup my breast, the other trailing lower, teasing over sensitive skin.

I imagined Rhodes' hands instead, rough and calloused, leaving trails of fire wherever they touched. His voice echoed in my mind, low and commanding.

"Do you like that, Honey?"

A gasp escaped my lips. My knees trembled, and my head fell back against the tiled wall–breathing quickly as I imagined him behind me, his body pressed against mine, his touch guiding me.

The fantasy was so vivid it consumed me, every nerve on fire.

Groaning in frustration, I pinched my nipple and let

out a yelp. Toying with the peak again before bringing my free hand to the other breast.

No one was home, so I had this space all to myself. I could let loose as much as I wanted.

"Rhodes," I moaned, his name a plea.

If I had my way, I'd be in Rhodes's shower while he took advantage of my body. They were his hands roaming my body, sinking lower and lower and teasing my throbbing core. It was him panting in my ear and grunting with satisfaction.

The thrill consumed me. Unable to stop now, I reached up and grabbed the shower head, knowing exactly what I had to do to dull the ache.

"Yes," I panted again, the constant pressure beating against my clit. My legs shook, vibrating with desire. "Rhodes, yes." I huffed again, holding the showerhead still until I felt my climax build stronger, my body convulsing at the steady pressure.

Rhodes was behind me, holding the water against my clit. He was in control, and I was putty being mended by his touch.

"Just like that?" He'd ask, not letting up no matter how hard I begged.

"Please. Please. Oh, yes."

I bet Rhodes was a dirty talker.

"I love hearing you beg. Do you want to come?" he'd growl.

The water streamed against me, relentless and steady, amplifying every sensation until I shattered. Stars exploded behind my eyelids, and my body convulsed with the release. My grip on the showerhead slackened, and I braced myself against the wall, trying to catch my breath.

My mouth fell open, and my head flew back. I was panting like a damn dog.

As I came back to reality, one thing was certain: thoughts of Rhodes weren't enough. I wanted the real thing. And somehow, I'd have to figure out how to make that happen.

10
Theo

24 weeks pregnant
Baby is the size of an ear of corn

> ** Rhodes2324 Has Won**

> ** Rhodes2324 Wants To Start A New Game With You**

> ** Rhodes2324 Played 'Jeux' For 18 Points **

> ** Rhodes2324: Better luck next time, Honey. ;) **

> ** Rhodes2324 Has Won **

> **Rhodes2324 Wants To Start A New Game With You **

TELLING RHODES I enjoyed Scrabble was a mistake—but also the best thing I could have done. It was a mistake because he beat me every single time.

Sure, I technically won a few games over the past few

weeks however, it was only because he let me win. He'd play absurdly low-scoring words on purpose. This man was insanely smart; there was no way he'd start a game with "tin" and expect to win.

I wanted a fair and square victory, not a pity win. Sometimes, the nagging feeling of losing control would take over, leaving me irrationally angry and tempted to cheat with Google. This was why I didn't like games. Yet, I couldn't stop playing because I liked spending time with Rhodes. It wasn't just the game—it was the conversations afterward. Honestly, I liked his attention, especially since it came from someone other than my mom.

Meanwhile, Aspen and Penny had gone radio silent after I decided not to join them at The Tequila Cowboy. Aside from a few texts in our group chat, they hadn't reached out. I knew they were spending time together without me, and it hurt.

When I dwelled on it too much, I spiraled into negativity—first angry, then sad, then laughing it off, reminding myself I didn't need anyone but me. After all, I was the only constant in my own life.

Still, the bad thoughts sometimes overshadowed the good. Right now, I needed to focus on the positive: my pregnancy, my future, and the moments I could spend with Rhodes.

When my dad died, a cloud of gloom settled over me and stayed for years. I worked hard to overcome it, but it never disappeared entirely. Lately, it was harder to push away. My friends seemed distant, my body was changing, and my thoughts were a chaotic mess, magnified by these wild hormones.

My phone rang, breaking through the haze. Rhodes' name lit up the screen.

Over the past few weeks, I'd grown comfortable talking on the phone, a big shift for me. Rhodes was a talker, not a texter. He believed it was "better to communicate and understand someone when you could hear their voice." How adult of him.

"What's up, Honey?" Rhodes' deep voice was music to my ears. Another reason I caved to his phone calls was just to hear it. His slight Southern drawl had a soft lull that calmed me.

"What did you just call me?" I laughed, flopping back onto the bed. I felt like a high schooler again, the cute boy was calling, and I had to keep quiet so my mom wouldn't overhear. Next thing you know, I'd be twirling my hair like in the movies.

"Uh, it slipped out," he replied, sounding uncertain.

I felt a twinge of guilt for calling him out on it because, truthfully, I liked it. That simple word warmed my cold heart.

To save us both from embarrassment, I steered the conversation away. "That last word you played was total bullshit. It's not even real!"

"Shvitz? It means sweat," he replied, smugness dripping from his voice. I could hear the grin, the bastard.

"How do you even know that?" I laughed, staring at the cream-colored ceiling.

"Let's just say I spent a lot of time alone last year and turned it into a learning experience."

"Ha, same," I admitted. "Except, I've been stuck in my head, not learning obscure Scrabble words."

Rhodes' next question caught me off guard. "What are you wearing right now?"

"Geez, Rhodes, I didn't peg you for the 'fuck boy' type. I thought we'd at least make it to date two before the dirty talk," I teased, adding a sultry edge to my tone.

Rhodes let out a laugh, full of vigor and amusement. "I was asking because I'm parked outside and need your help with something. But I do like being called a good boy."

Why did that simple admission make my skin prickle and my mouth water? I was hot and bothered over something so small, but lately, everything turned me on.

I fanned myself, trying to refocus. "You need my help?" I glanced at my ratty cow-print pajamas. "If it involves leaving the house, I'll need to change."

"Yep. Grab your camera, and I'll explain on the way. Want me to come to the door to help you?"

"No!" I shouted, louder than intended. The last thing I needed was for my mom to see Rhodes and bombard me with questions. "I'll come down. Just give me a minute to get ready."

I got out of bed and shuffled to my dresser in the corner. Trying my best to open the drawer that held my undershirts, I yanked and yanked until finally, I could reach my hand in to grab the first shirt I could find.

"Can you tell me what you need my help with? Or, is it a super secret mission?" I asked, placing him on speakerphone as I got dressed. Pulling off my shirt, I slipped into a padded sports bra, the only thing big enough to get over my boobs. They had doubled in size; I kind of liked it.

"Mac's sister hired a photographer for marketing stuff,

but they flaked. I may have mentioned I know a cool photographer."

"I hate to tell you this...I have little experience doing marketing photos. I deal more with slow-pace, landscapes, and cute animals." My craft hones in on the beauty of wildlife and broad detail. In marketing, it's all about timing and ambiance, which are two things that differ heavily from my skill set. Hell, I don't even know how to properly edit indoor photos. "I can still see what I can do."

Being with nature was calming. I didn't feel boxed in or restrained when capturing wildlife and exploring the landscapes. Capturing images that elicit emotions from the viewer is both an art and a science. Traveling around the world, I learned from many great artists how to use natural lighting to my advantage and make the photos speak for themselves with little editing or changes.

Rhodes cleared his throat before responding in a hushed tone. "I didn't think about that. I heard 'photographer' and thought of you."

I stepped into my overalls, clipping one side and leaving the other open. Grabbing the phone, I waddled over to my full-length mirror to make sure my outfit looked presentable. In the reflection, I saw a pair of dark-washed ripped overalls paired with a tight white T-shirt. My belly was on full display, and I looked *good*.

"Thank you for thinking of me. I needed an excuse to get out of this house." I confessed, even though it wasn't necessarily what I expected. Running the comb through my hair, I made the part as even as I could to showcase both colors.

"You know, you can always give me a call when you're

bored. I can beat you in Scrabble in person if that will make you feel better about losing," Rhodes bragged, practically dangling the win in my face.

"Oh, please!" I scoffed and shook my head. "I'm just going easy on you. I don't want to come on too strong."

I grabbed the best camera I had for this type of job and filled my carrying bag with everything I thought I might need. The worry from before washed away, and excitement flooded in. I was thrilled to get behind the camera again; I missed it. It'd been four months since I even uncapped the lens.

Who knows—maybe I'd like to do gigs like this. Learning was never-ending, and the more tools I added to my tool belt, the better my craft became.

Minutes later, I was outside, heading to Rhodes' truck —a towering, lifted Chevy that screamed rugged masculinity. Rhodes stepped around to greet me, wearing a backward hat that made my ovaries scream.

"You're gonna need some help getting in," he teased, opening the passenger door. He held out his hand, and I gave him my stuff so he could put it in the back. "Do you care if I pick you up? It'd be easier."

Before I could argue, he scooped me up like I weighed nothing. His earthy scent enveloped me, and my arm instinctively looped around his neck.

Rhodes placed me in the front seat and reached for the seatbelt. His arm brushed against my breasts, and I let out a raggedy breath. The air came out choppy as I tried to keep my composure. His touch set my nerves on fire, and the clothes on my skin felt like too much. I was brought back to my fun in the shower. It was no longer my imagination creating the sensations but the real thing.

"Precious cargo," he said softly, buckling me in.

Our eyes locked, lingering a moment longer than usual. My stomach fluttered, and I couldn't fight the growing tension between us. For once, I didn't want to back away.

11
Rhodes

WATCHING Theo in her element was fucking exhilarating. The moment we stepped into The Tequila Cowboy, she got straight to work. Without hesitation, she pulled out her camera, adjusting settings with practiced ease as she confidently directed people into position.

No one so much as blinked at the sight of a pregnant woman calling the shots, telling everyone where to stand and how to pose. At one point, she even quipped at Mac, "Would it kill you to at least pretend you're having fun?"

For someone who had no background in events or marketing, Theo had adapted effortlessly.

She moved through the bar with purpose, testing angles and adjusting for the perfect lighting, her sharp gaze scanning for the ideal shot. The bar was shut down for a few hours to prep for tonight's event. Lizzie had a videographer lined up to capture the action once the crowd rolled in.

Personally, I thought turning the bar into a production was overkill. Lizzie was determined to expand the bar's reach, hoping to attract tourists and folks from nearby cities. The citizens of Faircloud wouldn't be thrilled about that, though. I could already imagine the town hall meetings filled with bitching about how their quaint little town was being overrun by "city folk." Honestly, I kind of agreed with them.

The Tequila Cowboy had been a low-profile staple in Faircloud for generations. That started to change when Mac's sister, Lizzie, inherited it after their dad passed. The whole situation was a sore spot for Mac. Their dad had secretly updated his will, giving the business to Lizzie. Sure, Mac could be a bit reckless, but that didn't mean he wasn't capable of running the place.

"Jesus, fuck," Mac muttered, leaning his forearms on the bar, a cigarette dangling from his lips, holding on by hope and a prayer. "This shit is stupid. The bar's doing fine. I know because I've been managing it for years. Lizzie doesn't know a damn thing."

I adjusted on my stool and took a sip of my drink. "I don't get why your old man thought she'd run the place better than you."

"Right?" Mac exclaimed, standing up to his full height. He jabbed the cigarette in the air for emphasis. "I busted my ass in this place while he sat around drinking and betting on red three landing in the corner pocket. Lizzie's got a degree in communications. How's that supposed to help her run a bar in Faircloud?"

Mac was tall and wiry, his arms inked with tattoos. His perpetually messy brown hair added to his signature grungy bartender vibe. He'd always been the family's black sheep, while Lizzie could seemingly do no wrong.

Sometimes, I counted my blessings that I didn't have siblings to rival with like that.

"Your guess is as good as mine," I replied.

Across the room, Theo's voice rang out. "Mac! Get your ass back over here, will you? I'm not done yet!" She stood with her hands on her hips, the camera dangling from her neck, exuding authority.

Mac shot me a look, cigarette now hanging from his fingers as he pointed it in my direction. "She means business," he muttered, stubbing out the smoke in an ashtray before heading back to Theo.

I smirked and raised my drink in a mock toast. "Told you I knew someone who'd get the job done."

When Mac mentioned his sister's photographer had dropped out, Theo had been the first person I thought of. I'd made it my secret mission to keep her engaged. That day at Boone's, I'd seen her retreating, and I couldn't let her spiral. From the way Aspen talked about Theo, photography was her safe space—something she'd never say no to.

I understood what it was like to feel like an outsider, to watch everyone else move forward while you stood still. Knowing what I did about mental health, I knew she'd need support, whether she admitted it or not.

That's why I'd downloaded Scrabble on my phone for *her*. It gave me a way to connect through something she enjoyed. Besides that, I liked toying with her. I'd taunt her over messages and edged her to keep going. After a close round, she would call and accuse me of letting her win. I'd turn an accusation into a conversation to spend a little more time getting to know her. That'd been my game over the last few weeks.

Sneaking a glance at Theo now, I smiled. She'd wrangled Mac and Dudley into posing with their backs to each other, each holding a bottle of tequila and pouring it into their mouths. The neon lights behind them cast sharp silhouettes. Wildlife photography might have been her specialty, but Theo had a natural, creative eye for everything she touched. She was an artist, through and through.

Theo pulled the camera away from her face and glanced at the screen, a smile spreading from ear to ear. If staying perched on this barstool meant I could see her smile like that, I'd gladly stay here all day.

She turned her head and caught me staring. The apples of her cheeks lifted as her joy was on full display. Something stirred in my stomach, and my heart thudded against my chest. A simple smile shouldn't have this much power over me, but it did. I couldn't look away.

Even the sound of the door opening wasn't enough to pull my attention from Theo—until her smile faltered, replaced by an expression of pain. My focus snapped to the entrance, desperate to identify the source.

Paint me as fucking shocked when I saw Aspen and Penny come through the door. Were her two best friends really the reason for her change in mood?

My gaze returned to Theo. She pretended not to notice them, redirecting her focus to the guys she was photographing, moving them into different poses. I'd thought she'd be happy to see Aspen and Penny. After all,

I'd asked them to come to the bar to support her. Clearly, that had been a mistake.

Taking a swig of my drink, I tried to swallow the lump forming in my throat.

"Hey, Rhodes!" Aspen called, sliding onto the barstool to my left. On my right, Penny mirrored her.

"What's up, ladies?" I smiled, nodding and tipping my hat in acknowledgment.

"We decided to take you up on your offer," Aspen said. "I wanted to see Theo in action."

"I've never watched her work before," Penny added.

I glanced at Theo, still engrossed in her task. She seemed determined to keep herself busy, her body language screamed avoidance. Mac and Dudley wandered back to the bar, leaving Theo alone with her thoughts.

The room closed in on me. The voices around me dulled, and my attention narrowed on Theo. Her face looked like she was about to cry.

"Excuse me," I muttered, sliding off the barstool.

With one foot in front of the other, I approached Theo cautiously, just like I had that night a few months ago. This time, she sensed me. She sniffled but didn't turn around. A soft sob escaped her lips as she tried to regain control.

Her features struck me: the tip of her nose red, her hazel eyes glassy, her pouty lips pressed into a tight line.

"There's no way the wall is that interesting," I teased, nodding toward the wooden paneling she was pretending to photograph. It held a few faded photos of patrons and old metal signs.

Theo scoffed, wiping her nose with the back of her hand. She looked up at the ceiling, drawing a deep breath.

I placed a gentle hand on her arm and guided her to a bench near the bathrooms. I didn't say a word, waiting for her to speak first.

"It's the hormones," she mumbled, still refusing to meet my gaze.

"Okay. What are the *'hormones'* saying?" I asked, adding air quotes for emphasis.

Her head snapped toward me. "It's a pathetic story. It's hard to explain." Tears spilled down her cheeks, and her bottom lip quivered.

"Try me," I said softly, bumping her shoulder with mine.

She exhaled, her words shaky. "I've been feeling lonely. When I told people I was pregnant, I thought I'd be fine on my own. But everyone got so excited, and I started to believe it too. I painted these pictures in my head, got my hopes up... instead, I feel like a burden. People don't want me around because I can't do the things they want to do."

"By people, you mean..." I nodded toward Aspen and Penny, who were deep in conversation with Mac and Dudley.

Theo hummed in agreement. "I feel stupid even saying it, but... I can't go out dancing or drinking. I can't hike or stay up late. My body just can't handle it. I feel like they don't get that. I don't want to hold them back."

She'd been withdrawing, isolating herself because she felt misunderstood. Welcome to the club.

"Have you talked to them about it?" I asked, unsure if I should reach out to comfort her or keep my distance.

Theo let out a dry laugh. "No way. I'd sound crazy."

"No, you wouldn't. They love you. The people who care about you will never see you as a burden. They'll help you through your lows—you just have to let them." I didn't know if I was overstepping but, it had to be said.

She didn't respond, sitting in contemplative silence. I leaned back against the wall, mirroring her posture.

I knew the feeling all too well. When you go through something no one in your circle understands, it's isolating. I'd been there. Trying to explain heartbreak to people who'd never experienced it felt impossible.

"I get it," I said finally, breaking the silence. "I'll spare you the details, but if you ever need to talk, I'm here."

Theo nodded, a small grin forming. I smiled back and placed a hand on her thigh. Her expression shifted, her gaze dropping to where my hand rested.

"Why don't we get out of here?" I asked softly. "Say our goodbyes and leave. I'll play sick."

Theo sniffled, giggling. "I'd like that. Let's blame you this time."

We stood in unison, and she led the way back to the group. I put on my best performance to sell the story.

Theo took charge, offering a quick hello to Aspen and Penny before an even quicker goodbye to the whole crew. I nodded along, agreeing with the tale she spun about me being sick.

Apparently, I'd been so ill I was throwing up in the bathroom, and she had to rescue me. I then told her how amazing she was and that she was the queen coming to *my* rescue. Even though the story was extreme, I didn't protest. For tonight, she could have the win.

12 Theo

MY HANDS GRIPPED the fabric of my camera strap as I sat ramrod straight in the passenger seat of Rhodes's truck, refusing to speak.

Embarrassment simmered beneath my skin. I couldn't believe how I'd reacted to seeing Penny and Aspen. My emotions spiraled the moment they walked in considering it was the first time I'd seen them in weeks.

The more I thought about it, the angrier I became. Was I wrong for pulling back? Maybe it was petty, but why should I be the one to reach out? My feelings were hurt, and I hadn't done anything wrong.

At the bar, Rhodes told me I should talk to them. But in my head, that would only lead to awkward conversations I wasn't ready for. It felt easier to let the distance grow, to avoid the pain altogether.

I stared out the passenger window, the passing scenery doing little to distract me. Rhodes cleared his throat, breaking the silence. I glanced at him, catching his gaze as it flickered in my direction.

"Yes?" I asked, turning slowly to face him.

One hand rested on the steering wheel, the other on the center console. His profile caught my attention—the soft curve of his jaw, stubble dusting his tanned skin. The slight bump in his nose hinted at an old break, and his messy black hair curled at the nape of his neck. I found myself wondering what it would feel like to run my fingers through it.

"You don't have to act like everything's fine," he said, his voice gentle but firm. "Especially not around me."

His words hit a nerve. I raised my eyebrows slightly, his tone stirring something familiar. *Holding it in does no good.* A pang of déjà vu tightened my chest.

I locked my emotions away long ago. I hadn't let anyone in—not fully. Not even the therapists who tried to help. But Rhodes? He felt different. Safe. Familiar.

"I know," I confessed the words coming out in a hush. I squirmed in my seat, unable to bear the weight of my emotions. Uncomfortable that I'd not been able to keep myself in check.

But Rhodes noticed so that meant something.

There was a beat of silence before Rhodes spoke. "Did you want to talk about it?"

I did. I wanted so badly to let it out.

With a shaky exhale, I took a leap. I stood on a cliff, ready to take the emotional plunge. My mind screamed at me to let him in. I didn't understand why, but the thought of sharing my feelings, of being vulnerable with the man sitting next to me didn't scare me.

"It all just... sucks. I don't know who I am anymore," I

admitted, my voice trembling. "I look in the mirror and don't recognize myself. Inside or out."

The tears came fast, hot streaks laying paths down my cheeks. Once I started, I couldn't stop.

"I feel like a burden. Nobody wants to be around me. I'm not the same person I was a few months ago, and it's terrifying. I used to be strong, independent. Now I'm... I don't even know. Everything lingers. I'm angry constantly. Emotionally unstable. I'm tired all the time. My ankles are swollen. I've gained so much weight. And the stretch marks—"

"Enough." Rhodes' voice cut through my rambling, sharp but not unkind.

I blinked at him, startled by the change in his tone. He flicked on his blinker, changing lanes abruptly to pull onto the shoulder. The truck jolted to a halt, the engine idling as he threw it into park.

"What the hell, Rhodes?" I snapped, glaring at him.

He turned to face me, his expression a mix of frustration and determination. My anger flared, contorting my face into a scowl.

We were just outside of town, the traffic still steady as it whirled past us. I silently prayed no one would stop to check on us because my anger was pooling and sizzling just beneath the surface, ready to boil over. No one else needed to see me go toe to toe with a man nearly double my size. Right now, I'm pretty sure I'd win too.

"I'm not going to sit here and let you talk about yourself like that," he said, his tone firm. "Anyone who can't see how incredible you are is an idiot. You're being hard on yourself, setting these expectations that you need to be what, *perfect*? Everything I'm hearing you describe is normal. You're growing a human being, Theo. There will be changes, you will feel out of control."

I'd never seen Rhodes so rigid and stern before. It was a shock to my system, short-circuiting the emotions swirling inside me and replacing them with something quieter. Calmer.

"Rhodes…" I replied.

"You're beautiful," he continued, his voice softening. "You're kind, funny, and so damn strong. I need you to realize that you're doing enough. You *are* enough. You need to give yourself grace."

My throat tightened. What was there to say? I nodded, unable to form words.

"Say it," he pressed. "I need to hear you say it, Honey."

"I know," I whispered, though I wasn't sure I believed it.

Rhodes sighed, the tension in his shoulders easing. "Those thoughts you're having? They're trying to protect you, in a twisted way. But they're not helping. I know what it's like to look in the mirror and not see yourself. To feel like you're disappearing." The expression on his face fell softer. The red tone on his skin began to dissolve.

His voice cracked slightly, and I saw something shift in his eyes—a flicker of vulnerability. My hand moved on its own, reaching out to touch his face. The stubble on his cheek was rough against my palm, grounding us both.

"Rhodes," I said softly, searching his gaze.

For a moment, we stayed like that, connected in a way words couldn't explain. Then he cleared his throat and leaned back, breaking the spell.

"I get it, Theo," he said, his eyes on the road again. "I know how it feels. But you're stronger than you think. And you're not alone."

His words settled in my chest, a comforting weight. Maybe he was right. Maybe I didn't have to carry all of this by myself.

"Tell me," I demanded. "Tell me what it's like. Does it ever get better?"

I didn't know what I was looking for in my question. Did what get better? The feeling of loneliness. The uncertainty. The feeling of not wanting to be a failure. The feeling that life as you knew it was slipping away.

I didn't know what it was like to be a mother, what if I fucked it all up? What if I failed my daughter? I was adding another identity, another role I'd be stepping into. Friend. Daughter. Worker. *Mother*.

Rhodes nodded. "I have my moments where the thoughts come back, but I'm able to shove it into a box and tuck it deep into the corner of my mind."

"I'm sorry you went through that," I spoke softly. I assumed he was referring to what happened between him and Jess.

"I used to feel sorry for myself but I'm glad it happened when it did. If she was willing to leave me after all those years together, what's to say she wouldn't have done the same after marriage and a family."

"You planned a family and future with her too," I don't know why that's what I chose to respond with. It was more so in sadness thinking about what he'd lost.

"I haven't thought much about what my future looks like now. When Jess left, she took a big part of me with her." Rhodes looked at me, *really* looked at me. The rumbling of the idling engine filled the silence before he spoke again. "That created a lot of self-doubt, and I didn't handle it well. I felt like I couldn't turn to my friends because they didn't get it. Instead, I turned to some not-so-healthy ways to numb the pain."

Sitting here with him, listening to his side of the story, I couldn't shake the feeling that we were meant to find each other at this exact moment. Like some unseen force had nudged Rhodes Dunn into my life right when I needed him most—when I needed to be seen, to be understood.

"How did you change?"

"Therapy. Opening up and allowing myself to feel things. Shoving it away made it worse."

I used to open up, but my person was no longer here. Nearly sixteen years later, I was still living with the impact of their sudden departure.

"You should also talk to Aspen and Penny. I wish I had opened up more to Boone or Logan when I needed someone." Rhodes added. "But know, you don't need to hide from me."

"Thank you, Rhodes," I said, looking down and playing with my hands. "I'll try not to hide, on purpose."

I looked up at him, and he met me with a knowing smirk. His hand found my knee, a gentle squeeze that sent warmth through me. It wasn't just from his touch, but from the unspoken understanding between us.

"Let's get you home," he said, putting the truck in drive.

"I do have a question."

"What's up, Honey?" Rhodes cooed back.

Each time he called me that, the little butterflies living in my belly did a twirl and created a flutter. I often wondered if the baby felt it too.

"Why not Mac?"

Rhodes turned to me, cocking his head to the side in a question.

"You said before you wished you'd turn to Boone or Logan. Why not Mac too?"

Rhodes let out a deep belly laugh, one that rumbled against my heart. "Mac wouldn't know what to say or do. He'd probably laugh uncomfortably or offer me a cigarette. I wouldn't want to put him in that awkward position."

I laughed, too; I guess I didn't see Mac as the comforting type.

As the truck rolled back onto the road, I let out a breath I didn't realize I'd been holding. For the first time in weeks, I felt like I could breathe.

13 Rhodes

TheoTheGreat09 Wants To Start A New Game With You

TheoTheGreat09 played QUEEN for 14 points

**TheoTheGreat09: suck it **

Rhodes2324 played VICTORY for 15 points

**Rhodes2324 has won **

**Rhodes2324: you were saying? **

"LET ME IN!" A loud *thud* echoed through the door, definitely more of a kick than a knock. I didn't have to think too hard about who it was. I was expecting Theo any second.

I twisted the handle, and there she was: five-foot-two and gorgeous, her face twisted in a mix of exhaustion and determination. She flashed me a tight, pained smile, the kind you give when you're in over your head but too stubborn to admit you needed help. A large pizza box balanced steadily on her belly, and a two-liter bottle of soda dangled from her hand.

I'd told her I could pick up the pizza on my way home, but Theo insisted. She'd practically begged over the phone, saying she needed something to do that gave her "purpose." Apparently, pizza delivery was just enough responsibility to make her feel useful.

I grabbed the box and soda from her, hoping to ease her discomfort, and stepped aside to let her in.

Theo waddled into the kitchen, dropping her purse onto a chair at the island before collapsing half over the counter. She sighed dramatically, resting her forehead against the cool surface.

"Why is picking up pizza and walking like fifteen steps to your door *so* exhausting?"

"Maybe because you're carrying an entire human inside you?" I teased, placing the box on the counter and leaning on the edge.

She groaned but pushed herself upright, heading toward my cabinets. "The exhaustion is strong, but the hunger is stronger." She opened a cabinet and reached for the plates I kept on the top shelf. "You're lucky a slice or two isn't already missing. The smell in the car nearly broke me."

I leaned back, crossing one leg over the other as I watched her struggle which was mildly entertaining. Theo was determined to handle it on her own, even if she had to stretch onto her tiptoes and exert the energy knowing she'd never be able to reach the plates anyway.

As she reached higher, her sweatshirt rode up, exposing a sliver of soft, smooth skin. My grip on the counter tightened, my fingers curling as I fought the urge to reach out and touch her.

"You know, I wouldn't have cared if you ate some on the way," I said, trying to keep my voice light.

She huffed, dropping back onto her heels in defeat, blowing a stray hair from her face.

I sighed, stepping forward. That was enough struggle for her. "Let me get it."

Stretching past her, the movement closed the space between us. For a moment, she stayed perfectly still, caught between me and the counter. I could feel the warmth radiating from her, and the proximity made my heart race.

I grabbed the plates and stepped back quickly, putting distance so I could regain my composure.

When Theo turned to face me, our eyes met. The dim light of the kitchen made hers glow, and her freckles stood out against her flushed cheeks. For a moment, I couldn't move. The air felt heavy, like a rubber band stretched too tight.

"Um, thanks," she said, breaking the tension. She glanced down, her voice quieter than usual.

"No problem." I turned away, inwardly cursing myself. I'd been so close to crossing a line I wasn't sure either of us was ready for.

I focused on opening the pizza box and setting out plates like nothing had happened. Baby steps. I had to take baby steps.

Would I love to kiss Theo right here in my kitchen?

Absolutely. Would I love to take things further, to explore every inch of her body? No question. But I couldn't risk pushing her or myself too far too fast.

"Make it two slices for me," Theo said, standing way too close.

I smiled, grabbing an extra slice for both of us. "Want red pepper flakes?"

Her faint smile returned. "Oh, yeah."

I'd already set out the shaker, knowing she'd say yes. Generously, I sprinkled her pizza until every inch was covered.

"Take a seat," I said, nudging her gently. "I'll bring it over. Just need to grab the tea first."

She must've been tired because she didn't argue, which was rare for Theo.

I poured the tea and brought everything to the table. Theo perked up immediately, clapping her hands like an excited kid.

"Dinner is served." I bowed dramatically as I handed her a plate.

"Oh, why thank you, kind sir," she said with mock formality.

"So," I asked, taking a bite of my slice, "how much longer until the baby's here?"

"Fourteen weeks," she replied. "She'll be here before I know it."

"You nervous?"

"A little," she admitted. "More about my next doctor's appointment, though."

"Why's that?"

She explained the gestational diabetes test and how her mom had it during her pregnancy. She tried to brush it off, but I could see the worry lingering in her eyes.

"You know, it's okay to feel nervous," I said softly. "You don't have to handle everything on your own."

Theo gave me a small smile, though she didn't respond.

After a few moments of silence, she set her pizza down and wiped her hands on her pants. "I could actually use your help with something else, though."

I froze.

"Sure," I said, keeping my tone casual even though my heart was pounding.

Theo took a sip of her drink, clearly delaying the answer. The gears in her head were turning; a look in her eyes screamed contemplation.

"I need to find a new place," she said. "My mom's house is too small, and her work schedule makes it hard. I was hoping you'd come apartment hunting with me?"

"Of course," I replied without hesitation. "When were you thinking? I'm free Saturday afternoon."

She nodded, looking relieved. "Saturday works."

I smiled, feeling a warmth spread through me. Theo trusted me, piece by piece letting down the walls she'd built over the years.

"What's that goofy grin for?" she teased, her own smile lighting up her face.

"Nothing," I said, grabbing another slice of pizza. "Just thinking of all the ways I'm going to beat you at Scrabble later."

Theo snorted, nearly choking on her tea. She started laughing—a raw, unfiltered laugh that made my chest ache in the best way.

I missed this feeling.

14
Rhodes

AUTUMN IN TEXAS was my favorite season. You didn't have to deal with the unbearable summer heat, and at least you could keep your shirt on—though Boone didn't seem to get the memo. He always found an excuse to go shirtless, probably hoping Aspen would drop by unannounced. Honestly, you'd think he's still trying to win her over, but we all know she was hooked the moment she saw the mustache.

Today, the vet was coming to check on the ranch's cattle, so Boone needed Logan and me there early to get things ready. One of the heifers was close to calving, and having the vet on-site was standard procedure to make sure everything went smoothly.

I tried focusing on the task at hand, but my mind kept wandering to Theo and the apartment hunt. Lately, I felt this overwhelming sense of protectiveness over her and the baby. I'd been mentally ticking off a list of requirements for her new place: ground floor for easy access, two bedrooms so she had her own space, and close enough to town for quick errands. Faircloud had options, though none seemed to check every box.

I tilted my head back, letting the sun warm my face as I shook off the thoughts. I knew it wasn't my place to dictate where Theo should live, but I still couldn't help but want the best for her and the baby. With each passing day, Theo was becoming more of a permanent fixture in my life, not that I was complaining.

She'd call me after work to chat about some random documentary she'd watched, asking me the most bizarre questions.

"Are you a serial killer?"

"You sure you're not just putting on a nice-guy act to lure me in before chopping me up?"

She even joked about not having life insurance, just in case of her "accidental" demise I'd know there wouldn't be a profit.

Boone, Logan, and I rode on horseback trying to herd cattle into the holding pen. Horses made the cattle less skittish, which made our job easier. At Cassidy Ranch, we believed in working smarter, not harder.

We were still a ways from the barn when Boone, wearing his usual khaki hat and shirt slung over his shoulder, turned to us. "You two free Halloween weekend?"

"Thinking about throwing a party?" Logan asked, riding between us.

Boone smirked. "Well, it was Aspen's idea to get everyone together. The one rule is that you have to wear a costume."

"I'm in," I replied, shifting in my saddle. The crisp air

carried the faint scent of earth and livestock, and the mountains loomed in the distance under a clear blue sky as the cattle walked lazily in front of us.

Logan chimed in. "How're you and Aspen doing?"

"Better than ever," Boone said with a grin. "Her book's coming out in a few months, and she's knee-deep in 'beta edits,' whatever that means."

"Does it feel weird knowing the book's about you two?" I asked, genuinely curious. I don't know how I'd feel if someone wrote a book about my life, putting it out there for people to read like that.

Boone shrugged. "Not really."

"From the jump, Boone was helping her with 'inspiration.'" Logan laughed, putting air quotes around the last word. "He knew what he was getting himself into."

I grinned, nodding. "In the name of science, right?"

Boone rolled his eyes and adjusted his hat with a smirk.

"Aspen and Boone, sitting in a tree, K-I-S-S-I—" Logan's off-tune singing was cut short by Boone's interjection.

"Alright, enough. What are we, twelve?" Boone smirked and swerved his horse close to Logan's to push him off course.

Logan laughed, too; his beaming, kiddish smile was always nice to see. His messy blonde hair curved slightly around the fitted part of his cowboy hat.

Taking in the group before me, I felt like I was the only ranch hand who didn't partake in the hat fashion choice. I understood why the guys did it, but I was more comfortable in a backward cap and less sweaty that way. Plus, there were so many styles of hats for the different seasons, and I couldn't get behind them all.

The banter kept the work light. By the time we finished getting the cattle settled for the vet, I was ready to head out. Apartment hunting with Theo was next on the agenda, and I was running late.

I barely had time to clean up, so I grabbed some cologne from the glove box and gave myself a quick spritz. In the rearview mirror, a streak of dirt stretched across my face, but I shrugged it off. I wasn't trying to impress anyone.

Pulling into Theo's driveway, I took in the sight of her small, dark brown bungalow. It looked even more cramped than I remembered—no shutters, no bright pops of color, and the neighbors practically on top of her. She needed more space, no question about it.

I raised my hand to knock, but before I could, the door swung open. Standing there was a woman who could've been Theo's twin–though her eyes were different. The woman's sharp blue gaze swept over me, head to toe, before a knowing smile tugged at her lips.

"You must be Rhodes," she said, holding a dish towel in one hand.

"Yes, ma'am," I replied, catching myself staring.

Her scrutiny softened. "Call me Sissy. 'Ma'am' makes me feel old. Theo's upstairs, come on in, but stay by the door. I don't need those boots tracking mud through my house."

"Yes, ma'am—uh, Sissy."

My mom raised me with strict manners. "No, sir" and

"Yes, ma'am" were ingrained in me, slipping out even when I didn't intend them to.

The house had a dated feel—wood paneling, tiled floors, and a cozy but cluttered vibe. The inside was cozy, the kind of authentic home you would picture in a small town. My eyes landed on a familiar box stacked in the dining room, the one I'd helped Theo move in months ago.

I spent the time alone looking at my surroundings, understanding what Theo meant when she said she had to find her own place before the baby was born.

"You ready?" Theo's voice broke through my thoughts.

She stood at the bottom of the staircase, dressed in white overalls and a fitted black long-sleeve top. Her hair was braided into pigtails, and there was just enough makeup to highlight her eyes. Smoky shadows made them pop, shimmering under the light.

"You look…" I trailed off, my brain scrambling to find the right words as I realized I'd been staring too long.

"Yes, I'm wearing makeup," she muttered, her voice tinged with self-consciousness. "You can stop staring."

I leaned in close, lowering my voice. "You look beautiful."

Her eyes widened, and for a moment, I thought I saw her swallow hard. Before either of us could say more, her mom's voice rang out from the kitchen.

"You two better get moving!"

"Thanks, Mom," Theo called back, sarcasm dripping from her tone as she turned away with a grunt.

I followed her out, jogging to catch up and as she stomped to the truck.

"Nuh huh, Honey. You're not opening that door for yourself."

She raised an eyebrow, but I beat her to it, opening the passenger door. As long as she was riding with me, she'd never open a door again.

15
Theo

I WAS a bit more dressed up than usual. After all, I had people to impress. Well, one person: the realtor showing me apartments today.

Our list wasn't long—just two options. That's all Faircloud seemed to offer. It wasn't a town geared toward single renters. Family homes dominated the market, and the apartments I'd scrolled through online were either out of my budget or unlivable. I'd saved enough to cover nearly a year of rent, but my budget was tight. Raising my limit would shrink my nest egg and force me back to work sooner, a thought I didn't want to entertain just yet.

"There you are!" A woman's bright voice interrupted my thoughts. She approached Rhodes and me on the sidewalk, binder tucked under her arm. Judging by her polished white pantsuit and straight blonde hair, it was Cassie, the realtor.

"I'm Cassie!" she chirped, shaking my hand and then Rhodes'.

She was stunning. Legs for days, a perfect smile, and

she smelled like lilacs and sunshine. Her bubbly demeanor was a stark contrast to my more reserved nature. As she turned her attention to Rhodes, my jaw tightened. Her gaze lingered a little too long, and the way she bit her bottom lip, I wasn't a violent person but…

Suddenly, I wished Rhodes had changed out of his work clothes. Dirt-smudged face and all, he still looked unfairly attractive. The way my thoughts drifted, thinking about how I should've climbed on his lap earlier, was almost embarrassing. His compliment hadn't helped either. Was I really that easy to fluster, or was Rhodes just impossible to resist?

"You must be Theo," Cassie said, breaking my internal spiral.

"Yup," I replied shortly, stuffing my hands into my overall pockets. Good guess, *Cassie*.

"And you are?" she asked, turning her full attention to Rhodes, eyes gleaming like he was some kind of dessert.

"Rhodes Dunn," he said with a polite wave. First and last name? Really? I fought the urge to roll my eyes. But, then again, when I'd put my last name in his phone, he had something to say.

Theo 1, Cassie 0.

"Let's get started," I interjected, ushering us toward the building before Cassie could keep ogling Rhodes.

The first apartment was a one-bedroom, and calling it small was generous. There wasn't even space for a crib in the living room. The outside was dismal—dead bushes, scattered trash, and a broken fence. The inside wasn't much better: an open floor plan with a kitchen overlooking the living room, one bathroom with a stand-up shower, and beige walls reminiscent of a Wendy's Frosty.

"This unit has one bathroom and a stand-up shower only. The beauty of this is the exposed brick wall." Cassie walked to the wall in question and slapped it like a used car salesman. A brick wall was the least of my concerns.

I glanced around for signs of in-unit laundry. No luck.

"Um, is there a washer and dryer?" I asked hesitantly.

Cassie shook her head. "But there's a brand-new laundromat just down the road! Top-of-the-line machines. If I had to use it, I wouldn't even mind!"

Right.

I needed in-house washing for all the clothes I would have to wash between spit-up and other fluids.

"Before you decide," Cassie added quickly, "there's an amazing walk-in closet! It's big enough for both of your clothes *and* the baby's things."

Both of our clothes?

Cassie's eyes ping-ponged between Rhodes and me, likely piecing together a scenario.

"You two are together, right?" she asked, gesturing vaguely to my bump.

Our simultaneous responses tangled into a jumbled mess.

"Oh, yes!" I blurted.

"No," Rhodes said at the same time, his tone firm.

The air between us grew heavy as we exchanged a quick glance. What had possessed me to say yes? Was it to make myself seem more stable to Cassie—or to stop her from making eyes at Rhodes? Either way, it was a mistake.

Rhodes, to his credit, recovered quickly. "Sorry," he

said smoothly, clearing his throat. "Yes, we're together. I didn't hear the question." Without missing a beat, he reached for my hand, lacing his fingers through mine like it was the most natural thing in the world.

The warmth of his touch sent a jolt through me, and my hand instinctively settled into his. It felt easy. Right. Like our hands were puzzle pieces meant to fit together. He gave a small, reassuring squeeze.

"You two are adorable together!" Cassie gushed.

I didn't want to let go. For a moment, the act felt real —too real.

"I'm sorry, Cassie," I said, forcing my focus back to the task at hand. "This place won't work. I really need in-unit laundry and a bathtub."

Cassie nodded, her bright demeanor unshaken, and pulled an iPad from her messenger bag. "Give me one second!" she said, tapping away on the screen with her long, manicured nails.

As the silence stretched, I became hyper-aware of Rhodes's hand in mine. I couldn't bring myself to pull away, even though this was just for show. On the outside, I played it cool, however, inside, I was buzzing with nervous energy.

"I found one!" Cassie announced, breaking the tension. "It's on the other side of town, but I think it will be perfect!"

Perfect? I wasn't so sure about her definition, but at this point, what did I have to lose?

We left the apartment and agreed to follow Cassie. I watched her stroll down the street and climb into a brand-new BMW, sleek and spotless. My chest tightened. She probably thought I was pathetic—a mom struggling to afford rent for even a half-decent place, dressed in donated clothes, and certainly not driving a luxury car.

Rhodes cleared his throat, standing with the passenger door open, waiting. I shook my head to snap myself out of my thoughts as he helped me climb in.

The drive was silent, not in a comfortable way. I had too much on my mind to make small talk. I couldn't bring myself to bring up what had happened earlier—us holding hands, me saying we were together. Just the potential of Rhodes questioning why I said yes made my stomach churn. My composure was already hanging by a thread.

What were we even doing? Spending time together was easy, sure, but there were no labels, and maybe that's why it worked.

By the time I stopped spiraling, we were pulling up to the second apartment.

This one looked promising. The bushes were alive, the area seemed well-kept, and there weren't too many steps. It felt like a good omen however small.

As Cassie unlocked the door, Rhodes placed his hand on the small of my back, urging me forward. The warmth of his touch steadied me as we followed her inside.

When the door swung open, I froze in awe. This place was everything I'd been searching for. The open floor plan was clean and modern, and it didn't feel cramped. Everything looked brand new.

A breakfast bar separated the kitchen from the living room, and large windows overlooked a well-kept parking lot. I wandered further in, taking in every detail. Rhodes trailed close behind as I stepped into the first bedroom. It had its own full bathroom attached, complete with a tub and a massive walk-in closet.

I spun around to face Rhodes, unable to stop the grin spreading across my face. He was smiling, too.

"What do you think?" he asked.

"It's perfect," I whispered, excitement bubbling under my breath as I tried not to let Cassie overhear.

I could already picture how I'd set it up—my bed in the corner, my baby girl's bassinet nearby. The second bedroom could be her nursery when she was old enough. This place wasn't just an apartment; it was a potential home, a space where we could start our lives.

Instinctively, my hand drifted to my bump. The realization hit me hard, bringing tears to my eyes. When I glanced up, I caught Rhodes staring at my belly, his expression softer than I'd ever seen. A small smile tugged at the corner of his lips as he stepped toward me. For a second, it felt like the rest of the world disappeared.

Then Cassie's voice cut through.

"So, this apartment is a little out of your budget."

Her words hit like a slap. My bubble popped so violently it almost left me dizzy.

Rhodes's smile vanished as fast as mine. He turned to face Cassie, voice tight. "How much?"

She hesitated, her eyes darting to her iPad. "A little less than double. But I *had* to show it to you!"

My temper flared instantly. "Why?" I snapped, stepping forward. "So I could get my hopes up just to have them crushed? To feel like life was finally about to begin, only to have it yanked out from under me?"

I was on a rampage now, anger burning away any

restraint. "You knew my budget before we started! How *dare* you bring me here knowing damn well I couldn't afford it."

Silence filled the space at my outburst.

Cassie shrank back as I stormed out the door. Before descending the steps, I spun around for one last jab. "Oh, and by the way? Your pantsuit is dumb, and your car is ugly."

The tantrum was cathartic, but the fallout hit me like a freight train. When I got to the sidewalk. I yanked on the handle of Rhodes's truck, only to find it locked. Of course, he'd locked it. The man was too rational for his own good.

Sniffling, I slumped against the tailgate, resting my head on the cool metal. Two apartments, and neither worked when the options were already limited. I was running out of time with just fourteen weeks left, and I still didn't have a place to bring my baby home to.

I took a deep breath and finally looked up to see *him*. His warm, reassuring smile made my chest tighten. Rhodes sat down on the bumper and shifted closer until our shoulders touched, a quiet but steady presence. Letting my head rest against his bicep, I felt a flicker of calm seep in, like I could finally start piecing myself back together.

"I know," I sighed in defeat. "I was really mean, wasn't I?"

"You should've seen Cassie's face when you insulted her car and pantsuit. Ruthless. But also kind of hilarious."

Despite myself, I laughed. Rhodes had this way of knowing when to lighten the mood. His hand found its way to my thigh, grounding me the same way it had that day at The Tequila Cowboy.

Rhodes made me feel safe, like my emotions, messy and raw, weren't too much for him. Like I could lay them bare without fear of judgment. It was a glimpse of the version of myself I could be if I didn't feel so heavy.

"I'm such an asshole," I mumbled.

"You're not an asshole," Rhodes said firmly. "But maybe send Cassie an apology card. And a candle. After we get food."

The corner of my mouth twitched. He wasn't wrong. However, at that moment, food and bed sounded like the only cure. Rhodes just knew what I needed, and I wasn't sure if that comforted me or scared me.

16 Rhodes

Rhodes2324 has won

TheoTheGreat09 Wants To Start A New Game With You

TheoTheGreat09 played CAZIQUES for 28 points

TheoTheGreat09: BOOM

Rhodes2324 played CHEATER for 12 points

**Rhodes2324: Theo Matthews, did you finally resort to using Google?

**TheoTheGreat09: The world may never know. Just accept the loss.

**Rhodes2324 played NEVER as a triple word for 24 points

AFTER STRIKING out at both apartments yesterday, Theo was noticeably deflated. She barely spoke during dinner and stayed completely silent during the drive home. The weight of her disappointment was tangible.

I knew how badly she wanted to find a place. Time was running out, and getting settled was her top priority. It made sense—she needed stability before the baby arrived. With her upcoming appointment weighing on her mind, housing should've been the least of her worries.

That's why, when she asked if I could help her look again today, I didn't hesitate. If it gave her even a sliver of hope or happiness, I'd do whatever it took. That's how I ended up spending my day off standing in a complete dump on the far side of town.

The neighborhood was isolated, with no stores nearby and her mom and friends a decent drive away. She was already hesitant to ask for help when her mom lived under the same roof. How could she possibly manage living this far out?

I practically begged her to let me turn around when we pulled up, but she's worked her Theo magic and convinced me to give it a chance.

The pictures online had been misleading to say the least. If I had to guess, they were taken a decade ago back when the place might've been *somewhat* livable.

This time, we weren't meeting Cassie. She'd officially parted ways with Theo after yesterday's fiasco. Instead, we were greeted by Phil—a five-foot-five bald man in a grease-stained button-down that probably fit him about as long ago as the photos were taken.

"I love this guy," Theo whispered to me, leaning closer.

"Of course you do," I teased. "He's not wearing a white pantsuit or driving a luxury car."

"Exactly."

It didn't take long for my instincts to be proven right. The first red flag came as Phil struggled to get the front door open. He had to throw his whole weight into it, and when he finally jiggled the handle loose, I half-expected the lock to crumble into pieces. Safety was clearly not a concern here.

Inside, it only got worse. The cabinets were broken, the floors were peeling, and the entire space felt like a hazard zone. I imagined Theo juggling groceries or, worse, the baby, only to trip on the warped flooring. The thought alone made my chest tighten.

Then came the final straw: a cockroach crawled across my boot and I jumped so high I might've cleared Phil's shiny bald head.

There was *no way* I was letting Theo move into this place.

"You see," Phil began, clearly trying to salvage the sale, "with a little paint and some area rugs, this place would look brand new."

Theo nodded enthusiastically, like he was onto something. "Ugh, you're so right!"

I stared at her, stunned. It was going to take a hell of a lot more than paint and rugs to fix this disaster.

"Would the landlord be willing to paint before I move in?" she asked.

Phil chuckled, scratching his head. "Oh, um, any non-essential upgrades like that would be up to you. You could just move in as is."

I didn't like this guy.

Watching Theo's hopeful expression flicker, I couldn't take it anymore. Disappointment after disappointment—it was too much. She didn't deserve this.

"Phil, buddy," I said, forcing politeness into my tone, "could you give us a minute?"

Theo's jaw dropped. She looked between us, clearly surprised and ready to protest, but no words came out. Phil shrugged and stepped out onto the metal platform outside—another problem. With winter coming, the slick surface was an accident waiting to happen.

Once Phil was gone, I turned to Theo, determined to address the disaster unfolding in front of us.

"What the hell was that about?" she snapped the moment we were alone.

"You can't live here," I said, cutting straight to the point.

"Excuse me?" Her eyes flared as she crossed her arms and cocked a hip. "Who are you to tell me where I can and can't live? It's within my budget, and it has everything I need."

She was fiery, but I wasn't backing down. "I'm telling you—you can't live here. The locks are a joke, the cabinets are one sneeze away from falling apart, and your unwanted roommate? He scurried across my boot a few minutes ago."

"Oh, yeah?" she shot back, sarcasm dripping from her tone. "Well, this is my last shot. I don't have a choice. I can't afford that second apartment we saw yesterday. I thought about it all night and don't even start on the first place. This one has a washer and dryer, a bathtub, and it's within my budget."

"There's a cockroach living here, Theo," I countered. "Where there's one, there are more. And you're miles from anyone who can help you if something goes wrong."

"Who gives a shit?" Her voice cracked as her frustration boiled over. "It's not like anyone would care anyway."

"I care," I said, softening my tone. "But bottom line? I can't let you and the baby live here."

"Oh, great," she scoffed, throwing her hands up. "What's your brilliant solution then? I've spent hours combing through listings, and this is it. This is all I've got."

She wasn't going to like my answer, but I said it anyway. "Move in with me."

Her eyes widened in shock. "Move in with you?" she repeated, disbelief coloring her voice. "Rhodes, how could you possibly think that's a good idea?"

"You'd have your own room. The baby would have her own space. My locks work, my cabinets aren't a death trap, and I can promise you, there's not a single cockroach in sight."

Theo stood rooted in place, her arms crossed tight, radiating tension. I stepped closer, gently placing my hands on her upper arms. I needed her to understand just how serious I was.

"You can't live here, Theo. I don't care if it's within your budget. Come live with me. Save your money. Find a place you and the baby truly deserve."

Her expression softened, the rigidity in her posture

melting as my words sank in. I could see the war waging in her mind, her pride clashing with practicality.

She deserved better than this. She deserved safety, comfort, and stability. Her mother's house wasn't an option—there wasn't enough room, and with her mom's hectic work schedule, it would be too much for everyone.

I could help. I *wanted* to help.

"Let me think about it," she finally mumbled, her voice quiet and uncertain. "That's a bold move, pun intended."

I let out a small laugh, relieved she hadn't immediately shut me down, and released her arms.

"Fair enough," I said, smiling. "Now, how about we get out of here? I feel like I need a shower just from standing in this place."

Slipping my arm around her shoulders, I guided her out of the sad excuse for an apartment.

"I kinda liked Stan, though," Theo replied, not pulling away from my embrace.

"Stan?" I asked, confused.

She smirked. "The cockroach. I named him Stan. Which means, yes, I saw him and still decided to look around."

"Desperate times, huh?" I muttered, shaking my head in disbelief as we stepped onto the metal platform.

Theo shrugged and nodded.

"I can't believe you named the cockroach."

This woman was something else.

17
Theo

YESTERDAY'S APARTMENT hunt was a disaster. The smell of mildew and dead bugs hit me the second I walked in. The place was musty, the paint faded, and I watched Stan dart out from under the fridge like his life depended on it. I tried to convince myself that some decorations and incense could make it livable, but who was I kidding?

Rhodes pulled me aside and confirmed every sinking feeling I had. I didn't want to be right. For once, I wanted to be wrong, so wrong. I wanted to hear that it wasn't that bad, that it was within my budget, so I should jump on the offer. Instead, he asked me to move in with him.

Asking Rhodes to come apartment hunting with me wasn't about pity or hoping he'd feel bad about what I could afford. That thought hadn't even crossed my mind, but now guilt had settled deep in my chest. I didn't want anyone to feel sorry for me—I'd had my fill of that in life.

If I moved in with him, we'd have to stop the flirty glances and fleeting touches I'd secretly started to crave.

My mind spiraled, replaying the feel of his hand in mine and the soft graze of his breath against my ear when he complimented me. Memories of the way I'd moaned his name in the shower, imagining it was his hands on me—it made my cheeks burn red hot.

"Ugh!" I flopped back onto the bed, groaning into the ceiling. What the hell was I supposed to do?

In moments like this, I wished I wasn't at odds with Penny and Aspen. They had no idea I was upset with them—it was my own internal conflict. I wanted to go back in time, shake some sense into myself, and fix everything. Nothing I was angry about even mattered. But now, the silence between us was too long, the embarrassment too heavy.

That was my problem lately: I felt too much and couldn't control it. The other day, when I snapped at Cassie, she was just trying to help.

I usually didn't care what others thought when making decisions, but right now, I needed guidance. This was too big to decide alone. Who better to ask than my mom?

Dragging myself out of bed, I trudged downstairs. Mom was at her craft table, working on a puzzle.

"Hi, Mom," I said, my voice soft.

"Hi, sweetie."

I pulled out a chair and sat down, reclining back to ease the ache in my lower back. Mom was piecing together a puzzle I'd brought her from Italy. She never traveled, but she always asked me to bring back puzzles from my trips. It was her way of exploring the world—a little adventure in the comfort of home.

"Can I ask your opinion on something?"

Mom slowly looked up, her eyebrows raised in surprise. "You never ask for my opinion."

I picked up a puzzle piece, fiddling with it between my fingers. "You know I've been looking at apartments."

"Yes, with that cute guy, Rhodes," she said with a knowing smile.

I glanced at her and rolled my eyes.

He was pretty cute, but that was besides the point.

"Well, none of them were...nice," I admitted, cringing at my lack of robust vocabulary.

"There's time," she reassured me. "You still have a couple of months before the baby's due."

She wasn't wrong, but I wanted to get settled before I was too pregnant to move comfortably. I turned the puzzle piece over in my hand, searching for where it fit. Placing it down, I grabbed another piece.

"The thing is, Rhodes asked me to move in with him."

I focused intently on the puzzle, avoiding her gaze. I slid another piece into place, only for her hand to stop me from picking up the next one.

"Look at me," she said softly.

I reluctantly met her eyes.

"So, what is it you want from me?" she asked.

"I don't know if I should," I admitted, though it wasn't entirely true. Deep down, I knew moving in with Rhodes was the best option. The thought of giving someone that much control over my life terrified me.

What if he got tired of me? What if he decided he didn't want the responsibility anymore? The idea of being vulnerable—of putting the baby and myself at his mercy—was paralyzing.

"I see your mind spinning." Mom's tone was gentle but firm. "I know I'm not great with emotions, so let's focus on logic first. What's your mind telling you?"

I exhaled slowly, organizing my thoughts. "It's the smart choice. Moving in with Rhodes would save me money. His house is close to you. The baby would have her own room, and the house has everything I've been looking for."

"But?" she prompted.

"But it also comes with that cute boy," I said, tears welling up. "And I'm scared it'll end badly."

"Which brings us to the emotions," Mom sighed and stood, pulling me into a hug. It was the same as when I was a kid—no words, just her arms around me, telling me without saying anything that she was there.

"I wish Dad were here," I whispered through the tears.

"Me too," she murmured, holding me tighter.

If Dad were here, he and Mom would sit me down, breaking everything apart from every angle. Dad would bring the emotional wisdom; Mom, the logical clarity. Together, they'd balance each other perfectly.

"I know I don't do emotions well," Mom said, pulling back to look at me. "But if I can give you one piece of advice? Follow your gut. I think you already know what you're going to do. You just needed someone to give you permission to trust yourself."

The moment Rhodes asked, I knew my answer. I just hadn't let myself admit it. Finding a stable, secure home was what I needed, for myself and the baby. I trusted

Rhodes because something about him felt steady and safe, kind of like my dad.

Maybe this was my dad's way of telling me to take this leap of faith, to trust the man who'd been through some shit himself and never turned away.

18 Rhodes

I SAT with my feet propped on the couch, my sweatshirt hood pulled snug around my face. Most nights, I was alone. It used to bother me, but now the quiet felt like an old companion. Loneliness had shifted into something softer, something I could live with. I wasn't truly isolated; I had people, if I wanted them. All I had to do was ask.

The TV was on, flickering in the background, but I wasn't paying attention. I couldn't tell you a single thing about what was playing.

The deep ache in my muscles had my full focus. Work today had been long and brutal, leaving me sore in ways I didn't think were possible.

The Cassidys were talking about expanding, eyeing the adjacent land for more pasture. Boone decided we should start clearing the woodline, prepping for a deal that wasn't even signed yet.

I didn't ask why we were putting in the work before anything was official. Boone was the boss, and questioning him wasn't my place. If I had to guess, he was trying to prove to his dad he was ready to take on more responsibility.

I'd be lying if I said I hadn't thought about what it might mean if Boone stepped into his father's role. A small part of me dared to hope that I'd be next in line to lead the crew. Mentally, I felt ready for it.

Stretching, I sat up and raised an arm above my head, only to have a sharp twinge shoot down to my fingertips. I winced. This soreness wasn't going anywhere anytime soon.

I needed to move, even though my body protested with every step. Pushing myself off the couch, my legs were stiff, and I couldn't hold back the groan that escaped. It turned into a laugh, though, as I thought about the fact that I'd be doing it all over again tomorrow.

Just as I straightened, my phone buzzed on the couch. Bending down despite my aching body's objections, I grabbed it.

Theo's name flashed across my screen.

It had been a day since I asked her to move in with me. As the hours passed, I spent my time waiting anxiously to hear her decision. I knew it wasn't easy, so I tried not to pressure her.

"Rhodes Dunn's office. How can I help you?" I answered, trying to sound more cheerful than I felt.

Theo let out a breathy laugh, the sound warming my chest. "Hey, do you have a minute to talk?"

I'd make the time if I had to.

I pinned the phone between my ear and shoulder,

heading toward my bedroom. "I'm not busy. Do you want me to come pick you up so we can talk in person?"

Theo sputtered, her words tangling into a mix of sounds. "What? Um, no, that's not necessary. I'm in my pajamas. I'll make it quick."

"Are you trying to let me down easy, Honey?" The nickname slipped out again, unbidden.

"Don't say it like that!" she exclaimed, her voice flustered.

"I'd rather look at you anyway. I'll be there in fifteen minutes."

I heard rustling on her end of the line, as if she were pacing or moving things around. "Rhodes, that really isn't needed. My answer—"

"How about ice cream? I'm in my pajamas too. Just throw on a sweatshirt and stop protesting."

Silence. I knew she wouldn't resist ice cream. It was one of her weaknesses, alongside Flamin' Hot Cheetos, pasta, and double chocolate cake.

"You evil, evil man," Theo muttered playfully. "You know I can't say no to ice cream."

"Time's ticking," I teased, making a tick-tock sound for effect.

"I'm going as fast as I can!" she giggled. "I'm hanging up now. I need to get ready."

Before I could respond, the line went dead. Shaking my head, I slipped on my sneakers, threw a hat on backward, and grabbed my keys from the entryway table.

As I drove through town, a smile tugged at my lips. I needed to hear her decision directly, to see her face when she told me. If it was a no, I wanted to be ready to counter her reasons with logic—or maybe just more ice cream.

Over the past few days, I'd started making subtle adjustments around the house, just in case she said yes. I lowered the plates to an easier reach and moved boxes out of the spare rooms to the basement. I wasn't ready to go through them yet—that was a job for future me.

Driving through town, I mentally ran through every argument I could make to defend my offer. Whatever her answer was, I was determined to show her this was the right choice.

"People move in with roommates they don't know all the time."

"You and the baby will both have your own space. I don't even use it."

"I don't sleep much these days anyway."

"You wouldn't be in the way. I'd actually enjoy coming home to you and the baby every day."

I sucked in a sharp breath through my teeth. Maybe I should keep that last one to myself. No matter how I phrased it, it sounded either desperate or creepy.

Just as I spiraled into anxiety over my internal confession, I pulled up to Theo's house. She must've been watching for me because I barely had the truck in park before she slipped through the front door and hurried toward the truck.

"Get back in!" she whispered, waving her hands as if shooing me away.

"Theo, you're never opening a door again as long as I'm here."

She groaned, tilting her head back dramatically. "Must you always be so noble?"

I chuckled, opening the passenger door for her. Once she slid into the seat, I leaned across to fasten her seatbelt.

My arm brushed against her lower belly, the other grazing her thigh. Theo inhaled sharply, a sound that I tried, and failed, not to notice. The faint scent of fresh linen from her clothes reached me. My head was so close to hers that her soft exhale sent a tickle down my neck.

Clearing my throat, I pulled back quickly, careful not to meet her eyes. If I did, I'd lose my resolve entirely.

As I turned to close my door, movement in the doorway caught my attention. Theo's mom stood leaning against the frame, arms crossed, watching us with a sly smile.

For a moment, I froze. There was no hiding the fact that she'd just witnessed me buckle her daughter's seatbelt like a damn knight in shining armor. With no better option, I forced a polite smile and gave her a quick wave before climbing into the driver's seat.

I buckled my seatbelt, deciding the best course of action was to pretend none of it had happened.

Theo, of course, had other plans.

"See what I mean?" she asked, smirking with an expression that said *I told you so*.

"Mom's love me," I replied with a grin, pulling away from the curb.

"Why am I not surprised?"

"I don't know, you tell me." I glanced at her out of the corner of my eye, finally taking in her outfit. She looked effortlessly attractive in a matching sweatsuit with her hair was braided into her signature pigtails, and the oversized fabric she wore flowed against her body–for some reason, it drove me a little crazy.

"I think it's that whole good-boy-next-door vibe you give off," she teased, waving a hand in my direction with her lips pushed out.

I scoffed, my filter vanishing as I replied without thinking. "I told you I liked being called a good boy."

"Ugh!" Theo gasped, laughing. "That's *exactly* what a good boy would say while ignoring the obvious innuendo." She shifted to face me, her bent leg pressed against the console.

"Who said I was ignoring it?" I quipped, my grin widening.

"The day Rhodes Dunn dirty-talks is the day hell freezes over." Theo was flirty. There was a look in her eyes that was beginning to make me feel like ice cream wasn't the only thing she'd devour.

"You're sassy today."

"Maybe I'm just a little anxious," Theo admitted, her tone softening.

"Acknowledging feelings, are we?" I teased, though my own nerves weren't far behind. I'd been bracing for her answer all day, running through every possible response she could give me.

"Rude!" she shot back.

"Maybe I'm a little anxious, too," I confessed, glancing at her briefly. She was biting her lip, her gaze locked on me. The look she gave me—half amused, half something deeper—threw my pulse into overdrive.

Before either of us could say more, I pulled into the ice cream shop parking lot. Her eyes lit up, and the look on her face went from wanting to eat *me* to being ready to demolish a chocolate cone with chocolate sprinkles.

Inside the shop, the cool air hit me, sending a shiver down my spine. Theo shivered, too, goosebumps forming on her neck.

She stepped up to the counter with a bright smile, greeting the girl working there. "Hi! I'll take chocolate ice cream, a large cone, with chocolate sprinkles, please."

Smirking to myself, I celebrated a silent victory.

"And for you?" The girl pointed her gloved hand at me as she started scooping Theo's order.

I stepped closer, pressing gently against Theo's back as I glanced up at the neon menu. My hand instinctively found its place on the small of her back.

"Cookies and cream with hot fudge, large," I said.

"Cone or cup?"

"Cup, please."

The girl nodded toward an older woman at the register. "You can pay down there."

Guiding Theo toward the register, I kept my hand on her back. She didn't flinch or brush me off, which felt... natural.

"Good evening! Just the large cup and cone?" the cashier asked.

"Yes, ma'am," I said, reaching into my pocket for my wallet.

"Oh, shit," Theo muttered, rummaging frantically through her purse. Her eyes snapped to mine, wide and apologetic. "I forgot my wallet. I'm so sorry!"

"It's okay, Honey. I've got it. It's my treat."

"I'll pay you back," Theo said firmly.

I smiled at the cashier and handed her a few bills. "Keep the change."

"Oh, why thank you, young man!" the cashier said brightly, her eyes lighting up as she dropped the change into the tip jar.

Stepping aside, I felt Theo close behind me, following me toward the pickup area.

"First of all, I *will* be paying you back. I don't like to take handouts. Second, do you realize you just tipped them like fifty percent?"

"First, it wasn't a handout. This was *my* idea. Second, you'd better get used to my niceness." I slipped my arm around her shoulder, pulling her closer. Her arms were tucked in tight, clearly still cold. "And third, I'm a big tipper."

"See? A good boy," Theo teased, leaning into my side. She was practically tucked under my arm now, like she belonged there. Hearing those words from her sent warmth rushing through me, banishing the cold.

"One cone, one cup!" called the girl from behind the counter, holding up our desserts.

Theo and I stepped forward in sync. I grabbed my cup, and she grabbed her cone. Without hesitation, Theo brought her ice cream to her lips, her tongue slowly tracing the side in a way that felt far too intentional.

Watching her was pure torture. Ice cream was a bad idea. I should've taken her somewhere less... enticing.

Her movements stirred thoughts I had no business having, and I had to shake my head to clear them.

Focus, Rhodes. Get your head out of the gutter.

"Can we sit on your truck bed?" Theo asked, snapping me out of my spiral. "I've always wanted to do that."

"You've never eaten ice cream in a truck bed? What kind of small-town girl are you?" I teased as we walked toward the door.

"The kind who avoided everyone except Aspen and Penny," she said, her voice softening at the mention of her friends, a shadow crossing her face. It was clear she hadn't spoken to them yet.

"Well, let's make your dreams come true," I said while holding the door open for her.

When we reached the truck, I dropped the tailgate but realized she was too short to climb up.

"Here, hold this and face me," I said, handing her my cup. She took it without question. I placed my hands under her arms and lifted her up to place her on the tailgate.

"You threw me up here like a rag doll," Theo said, laughing as she settled herself.

I flexed my bicep in response. Thank you to the years of hard, manual labor.

"Please don't do that again," Theo teased, nudging me with her shoulder.

"You don't like it when I flex?"

"Oh, it's not that. Cocky isn't a good look on you."

I smirked. *I could show her cocky.*

She dangled her legs over the edge, kicking them lightly. It brought me back to the night of Aspen's party, when she sat on the edge of the pool. Theo was magnetic, and the more time I spent with her, the harder it became to resist her pull.

"I think I should rip the Band-Aid off," Theo said suddenly. I looked up from my ice cream, meeting her eyes. "I've been thinking a lot about what the 'right' choice is," she continued. "And I don't think there's a definite answer."

Bullshit. There is a right answer–her moving in with me.

"I have to disagree," I interjected, scooping a bit of my ice cream and bringing it to my lips. "People move in together without knowing their roommate all the time. Plus, I don't get much sleep—"

"You didn't let me finish," she said, cutting me off.

I kept my eyes on my dessert, not wanting to look up and have to face her.

"But there's one answer I feel confident in. Logically, moving in with you is what's right. I trust you. It's weird—you feel familiar. So, if we're doing this, we need ground rules."

"Let's hear them."

"I *have* to pay you something. I can't not."

"No, you don't."

"Rhodes, please," Theo said, her voice firm. "I don't want your pity. I'm not a charity case, and I don't want you making this offer because you feel bad for me."

"That's not it at all," I said, finally looking up at her. "I want what's best for you and the baby. You deserve a clean, safe place to live. Can't you believe I want to do this because I'm kind? Because I'm your friend? Not because I have any other motive."

Her cheeks flushed pink, and her eyes locked on mine with an intensity that made me feel like she could see straight into my soul.

"Rhodes..."

"Plus, it gets lonely anyway. I'd like the company," I said, my voice softer.

There was a smudge of chocolate ice cream at the corner of her mouth. Without thinking, clearly lacking control, I reached out and wiped it away with my thumb before going back to my cup like it was nothing.

"What other rules do you have? Paying isn't an option," I said after swallowing the last bite.

"I don't know yet," she admitted, her voice softening. I wanted to crawl inside her mind and see what was going on up there.

"When do you want to move in?" I asked, hoping the question didn't sound as eager as I felt.

Theo cleared her throat, wiping at the same spot I'd touched moments earlier. "As soon as you'll have me. I think it's best to get settled before the baby comes."

"You're probably right," I agreed with a laugh.

"And I'll need to learn all your weird quirks to make sure you're good enough for the baby," Theo teased, her eyes twinkling with mischief. She stuck her tongue out playfully, making the moment even more ridiculous.

Shaking my head with a grin, I hopped off the tailgate, placing my empty cup in the truck bed. "Alright, that's enough sass for tonight," I said, holding out my hand to help her down.

"Wait!" Theo squealed, cramming the last of her ice cream cone into her mouth. Her cheeks puffed out like a chipmunk storing nuts for winter, pulling another laugh from me.

She took my hand and hopped down, steadying herself as her feet hit the ground. The mischievous glint in her eyes made me wary of what she might say next.

"You don't do anything creepy at night I should know about, do you?"

19
Theo

"UGH!" I groaned, flopping back onto Rhodes's couch. Or, I guess, *our* couch now. Was his furniture mine, too? If I had people over, would I say, *you can sit at my table*? Or would it be, *you can come to my room,* or just *the room*?

Too many questions for a brain running on fumes. Those were answers for another day. For now, all I needed was rest.

Rhodes and I spent the entire day moving my stuff in—not that there was much to begin with. My room at Mom's wasn't big, and after spending so much of my adult life on the go, I hadn't bothered collecting too many belongings.

The baby's stuff, though? *That* was a different story.

She had claimed the entire dining room at Mom's house with mostly gifts from the gender reveal and stuff accumulated over time. We loaded Rhodes' truck bed to capacity and filled the back seat to the brim. Luckily, we managed it all in one trip.

By "we," of course, I meant *Rhodes*. I was barely any

help. There wasn't much I could carry, and by my fourth trip inside, I was winded and in desperate need of a break.

While I caught my breath, Rhodes made three trips for every one of mine. When I got back to work, he still lapped me, and the whole time, he never complained or lost the determination.

Now, after getting the rooms semi-set up and my stuff into its designated spots, Rhodes still hadn't slowed down. Watching him do everything was unsettling. I wanted to pitch in more, lend a hand, but there was no denying how much I needed the help. Accepting help was becoming easier, but *feeling* helpless? Not so much.

I grabbed a throw pillow and pressed it over my face, muffling a loud groan. My feet were throbbing, and my ankles had swollen to three times their normal size. I hadn't even known that was possible.

"Ugh!" I yelled again, dragging it out this time.

The cushion under my legs dipped slightly. I didn't even bother moving to make room for Rhodes to sit down.

"Are you okay?" he asked, a small laugh escaping him.

"Does it *sound* like I'm okay?" I snapped, yanking the pillow off my face to glare at him.

Rhodes just smiled, unfazed by my snarky remark. He tapped my legs and pointed upward. "Lift them."

I shook my head.

"Theo, lift your legs. Let me try something that might help."

Help. There it was again.

As much as I hated feeling like the damsel in distress, the possibility of relief was too tempting. With a sigh, I gave in and lifted my legs.

"Wait," I said suddenly, pulling my legs back. "Do you have a foot fetish or something? Is this going into your spank bank later?"

"Haha," Rhodes replied dryly, his tone as unamused as his expression. He gestured with two fingers, beckoning my legs back. Somehow, like he'd cast a spell, they obeyed and settled across his lap.

He pushed my sweatpants up past my calves, and a wave of panic hit me. When was the last time I shaved? I debated pulling my legs back, but the ache in my feet won out. Rhodes wasn't the type to care about a little leg hair. Plus, shaving was getting harder every day.

Still, the reminder was a nudge: I needed to book an appointment with my wax lady. No way was I giving birth in a few months looking like an untamed jungle.

"I like your socks," Rhodes commented, pulling me from my thoughts.

I propped myself up on my elbows and looked down. The fuzzy cow faces stared back at me.

"I'm a sucker for a cow," I said with a small smile.

"Would you want to come by the ranch sometime? I could bring you to the barn and see the cattle I work with."

"I'd like that," I said. "I've been there so many times over the last few months, and I *still* haven't seen a single cow. I was starting to think the whole thing was a cover for something else. Drug ring? Money laundering, maybe? What does Boone Cassidy *really* want with Aspen?"

Rhodes scoffed and began applying pressure to the bottoms of my feet.

He wasn't denying it.

The pads of his thumbs worked deep into the tissue, massaging away the tension. It felt *really* good. And not just because of the relief—it was the way his hands moved. The veins shifting beneath his skin, the delicate precision of his fingers...Was it hot in here, or was that just me?

I stayed propped up on my elbows, watching as he worked. He moved to my ankles, then up one calf, kneading with just the right amount of pressure. A groan of relief slipped out before I could stop it.

"Where did you learn this?" I asked.

"The internet."

"What a weird search history you must have. *How to give epic foot massages*? I'm dying to know why."

Rhodes cleared his throat, set down my first leg, and moved on to the second. There was avoidance in his gaze, like he didn't want to answer the question fully.

"So, what are you thinking of wearing to the Halloween party?" he asked. My face crinkled into a curious expression at his shift in topics.

"What party?"

"Boone and Aspen's. The Halloween party they're having next weekend."

I frowned, caught off guard. A party? I hadn't heard anything about it. Maybe I missed a text? The thought stung, though I wasn't about to pull out my phone and check in front of Rhodes. Then again, it wasn't like I'd been putting in the effort lately. I'd been dodging Aspen and Penny for weeks, avoiding the confrontation I wasn't ready to face. Maybe after the baby was born. Maybe...never.

"I didn't know about it," I admitted finally, my voice quieter than I intended. "So I guess I'm wearing nothing. And no, I don't mean my birthday suit."

Rhodes chuckled, the sound warm and easy. "Why don't you come with me? I don't really want to go alone."

"Oh, Rhodes, I don't know." My gaze drifted back to his hands as they worked, steady and capable. "It'd be weird."

"Let me guess—you haven't talked to Penny or Aspen yet?" His voice softened, cutting through my carefully constructed walls.

"No," I sighed. "And I don't think a Halloween party is the best place to start."

"I have to disagree," he said, his tone light but insistent. "It's perfect. Everyone will be in costume—it'll lighten the mood. You'll all feel a little silly, and it'll make the conversation easier."

I bit my lip, considering. He had a point. Costumes and a crowd could act as a buffer, easing the tension I'd been dreading. And really, what was the worst that could happen? I'd already been avoiding them for so long; maybe facing them wasn't as terrifying as I'd made it out to be.

"Plus," Rhodes added, his voice dropping slightly, as if coaxing me, "Penny and Aspen aren't cruel people. They don't have a mean bone in their bodies. They care about you."

His words struck a chord I couldn't ignore, disarming me the way only Rhodes seemed able to. He was right. Penny and Aspen cared about me—even if I wasn't sure I deserved it right now. And maybe...just maybe...they missed me as much as I missed them.

I leaned back, letting the realization settle over me like a wave. Growing up, I'd never had strong friendships. I'd been teased, left out, labeled "poor" because I didn't have the newest clothes or gadgets. I'd carried that baggage with me all these years, dragging it into relationships that didn't deserve it. I'd built walls, assuming rejection where there wasn't any.

"Hey." Rhodes's voice cut through my thoughts. He paused the massage and tapped the bottom of my foot gently. "What's going on?"

"They've never done anything to make me feel unwanted," I admitted, my voice soft, almost hesitant. "I think...I think I've been projecting my own insecurities onto them."

It felt strange to say it out loud, but at the same time, it made so much sense. Hearing the words, giving them life, was like flipping a switch. A light bulb went off, illuminating things I'd tried to ignore.

"I wasn't the kind of kid who had strong friendships growing up," I confessed, staring down at my hands. "I was teased, bullied, and always left behind. Kids at school used to make fun of my clothes, but I won't bore you with the pity party. I guess I just assumed that's how everyone saw me."

Rhodes exhaled sharply, his voice rough with understanding. "Kids can be fucking cruel," he said. "But, Honey, you're not that kid anymore. And they're not those kids. I think you owe it to yourself and to them to have the conversation. Not that I'm telling you what to do," he added quickly, a small grin softening his tone.

I smiled faintly, nodding. "No, you're right. And the Halloween party...maybe it's the perfect place to start."

"Exactly." He smiled back, his expression full of encouragement.

I sat up, pulling my legs from his lap and scooting closer. Without hesitation, Rhodes lifted his arm, and like it was second nature, I nestled into his side. He pulled me closer, his warmth wrapping around me like a heavy blanket on a crisp autumn night.

"Thank you," I whispered, my words barely audible.

"Anytime, Honey."

I felt peace—no ache in my chest, no racing thoughts, just quiet comfort. With Rhodes's arm around me, I had a plan. I had a safe place. And for the first time, I believed everything might just be okay.

20
Rhodes

IT HAD BEEN a few days since Theo moved in, and honestly, not much had changed—except now I had someone to sit with at night and watch TV.

Slow, quiet living suited us both. I wasn't one for going out or having constant human interaction, and apparently, neither was my new roommate.

Theo had been introducing me to her favorite true crime documentaries, which was both endearing and mildly terrifying. She loved all things morbid. I was convinced that if she ever decided to kill me and bury my body, no one would ever find out.

Last night, during one of her chosen documentaries, she kept reminding me to pay attention to specific details because they'd "come back later." One thing I'd learned: it's never just a boating accident.

"Let's get moving, gentlemen!" I yelled, rallying the crew from the barn. It was the start of the day, and I was in charge. Boone was off with his dad, finalizing the land deal.

It wasn't unusual for me to play ringmaster of the circus we called Cassidy Ranch, especially lately. Something big was in the works, though I refrained from asking questions until I had reason to. I had a feeling that time was coming soon.

Four ranch hands, plus Logan, broke up their little powwow and ambled toward me, ready to get to work.

"We've got a few things on the agenda today," I started, glancing over the group. "Crowley, Jacobs—you're on fence duty. Check for any broken barbs or posts. If you find something, make note and report back." I nodded toward them, a silent dismissal. They didn't need to stick around for the rest of the assignments.

"Stanson," I continued, turning to the lanky ranch hand, "you're on stall duty."

Stanson groaned, crossing his arms over his chest like a sulking teenager.

Next to him, Ryker tried—and failed—to stifle a laugh.

"You think that's funny, Ryk?" I asked, raising a brow. When he didn't reply fast enough, I added with a smirk, "Fine. You're with him. Between the two of you, it should take half the time."

Ryker's grin faltered. "Yes, sir," he drawled sarcastically, giving me a lazy salute before turning on his heel. Without further complaint, the two headed off toward the cattle barn.

"Logan, you're with me," I said, already moving toward the day's project.

"Hell yeah," Logan replied, falling into step beside me.

"Rhodes! Wait up!"

I stopped and turned to see Boone striding toward me.

He wore his cowboy hat low, light-washed jeans, and a button-up with an Aztec print. A cleaned-up Boone was never a coincidence. Whatever he had to say, it wasn't small talk.

"Go on ahead to the stalls. I'll catch up," I told Logan.

He tipped his hat and sauntered off, as easy going as always.

Boone reached me, clapping a hand on my shoulder as we pivoted away from any lingering ears. When we were far enough from the others, he stopped and faced me, his expression serious.

"I need to talk to you about something," Boone said.

His tone set off a ripple of curiosity, maybe even concern. I crossed my arms, mirroring his stance. We definitely spent too much time together.

"What's up? Everything okay?"

"Oh yeah, more than okay." Boone's grin was so wide it threatened to split his face. His excitement radiated off him, impossible to miss. "We got the bid. Cassidy Ranch is expanding."

A matching grin spread across mine, and I reached out to pull him into a celebratory hug, slapping his back firmly. "That's incredible, man. You deserve this."

Boone stepped back, still grinning, but the shift in his tone pulled my full attention. "There's more." He shoved his hands into his pockets, a rare tell of nerves from my usually confident friend.

"My dad's stepping away, fully this time. He wants me to start learning the behind-the-scenes stuff."

I nodded, already knowing where this was headed. If anyone was ready to step into those boots, it was Boone.

"I've been thinking about this for a while," Boone continued, his eyes locked on mine. "You're the best damn ranch hand we've got, and I trust you. When I start focusing on the business side, I want you to take over."

The weight of his words hit me, and for a moment, all I could do was stare at him. A year ago, this offer wouldn't have been possible. Hell, I wouldn't have trusted myself with it. But now? Now it felt different.

"I'd be honored," I said, unable to keep the smile from my face.

"Good." Boone's grin was back in full force. "We've got a lot to discuss, but I know you'll kill it."

I nodded toward the barn, reluctant to keep Logan waiting too long. "Logan's expecting me."

Boone waved it off. "Just text him. Kid's probably standing around on his phone anyway."

He wasn't wrong.

Laughing, I fell into step with Boone as we made our way toward the main house. He was like the Oprah of job offers—spreading good news like candy, terrible at keeping surprises, and damn near impossible not to like.

Theo

I decided to make dinner tonight. Rhodes was running later than usual, and though it had only been a few days since I moved in, I was already picking up on his routines.

He woke up between 3:30 and 4:00 every morning, showered, and made coffee like clockwork. He probably thought I slept through it, but I was a light sleeper. The sound of his boots on the floorboards and the soft clink of his coffee mug had become familiar, almost comforting.

By the time he got home around five, he was usually tired, never grouchy. I didn't know much about what his days as a ranch hand entailed, I figured I'd learn soon enough.

Tonight, I wanted to surprise him with dinner. Cooking wasn't exactly my strong suit. Rhodes was the one with culinary skills but I could manage parmesan-crusted chicken. It was one of the few recipes I knew, something my mom used to make when I was growing up. Simple enough that even I couldn't mess it up.

I pulled the chicken from the fridge and set it on the counter, trying not to think too hard about how much I disliked working with raw meat. Thick cuts of chicken had become a food aversion lately—texture was an issue. Beans, too. Just thinking about them I had to hold back a gag.

After rummaging through the kitchen for a cutting board and meat mallet, I found what I needed and tried to commit their locations to memory. This wasn't my space yet, but I wanted it to feel like it could be.

Once I'd flattened the chicken, I needed a plate. Rhodes kept his plates on the higher shelves, well out of my reach, remembering from the first time I was here.

I grabbed a chair and dragged it to the cabinet, knowing this probably wasn't the smartest idea. Climbing up carefully, I opened the door, expecting to find plates on the third shelf. Instead, the space was empty. Leaning back slightly, I scanned the other shelves until I spotted them on a lower level.

Stepping down slowly, I pushed the chair aside and grabbed a plate.

For a moment, I paused. Why had he moved them? The thought tugged at me briefly, but I shook it off. Maybe he'd noticed me struggling to reach them before and adjusted without saying anything. That seemed like something Rhodes would do. He was a man of quiet, thoughtful gestures.

After a while, the rumble of a truck pulling into the driveway drew my attention. Through the picture window, his headlights cut through the twilight, announcing his arrival.

Perfect timing. My culinary masterpiece was nearly finished, and I had to admit it smelled incredible. If this didn't impress him, nothing would.

The front door creaked open, and Rhodes stepped inside. His presence filled the room, even from across the house. I leaned back slightly from the stove, just enough to catch a glimpse of him.

Dusty and tired and somehow still undeniably handsome, he paused in the entryway to remove his boots. As if sensing me watching, his gaze lifted, locking onto mine.

"Something smells good," he said, a warm smile spreading across his face.

I grinned back. "If you're lucky, it might even taste good too."

He wore a short-sleeved t-shirt, dark-washed jeans streaked with dirt, and his trusty cowboy boots. Easy on the eyes didn't even begin to describe this man. The way that shirt stretched just enough across his chest to show the outline of his muscular pecs, the snug sleeves hugging his biceps—*chef's kiss*. I wouldn't mind burning that image into my memory forever.

Rhodes tossed his hat onto the entry table and kicked off his boots. As I mindlessly stirred the pot of instant mashed potatoes, he ran a hand through his hair from root to tip.

The way I wanted to undress that man—piece by piece, layer by layer—was practically feral.

Dragging his feet slightly on the wooden floor, Rhodes made his way into the kitchen.

"You're making dinner?" he asked, opening the fridge to grab a water bottle. He cracked the lid and leaned against the counter, settling comfortably out of my way.

"Don't sound so shocked," I quipped, tearing my gaze from him and focusing back on the pot. If I kept staring, these mashed potatoes would turn into an inedible lump.

"I'm not," he replied, defensive but amused. "It's just nice that someone's taking the time to cook a homemade meal for me."

"When's the last time someone cooked for you?" I asked.

Rhodes took a sip of water, pondering. "How long ago was Easter?"

That was... sad. While I'd spent years traveling the world, meeting new people, and experiencing unique cultures, Rhodes had been here—alone. The thought hit me harder than I expected.

"What did you do today?" Rhodes asked, his sharp eyes clearly catching the shift in my mood.

"Well," I started, trying for nonchalance, "I tested out

your fancy washing machine. Did some laundry, I was running low on pajamas. I put more of my stuff in the room and started sorting through the baby's things."

"No documentaries?"

"Well, that too, but I figured that was a given."

Rhodes chuckled.

"By the way," I began, unable to hold back my curiosity any longer, "did the plates move? Or am I losing it?"

"I moved them lower," he admitted, casually leaning against the counter. "If I'm not here, you need to be able to grab one without climbing on something."

My lips pressed together in guilt as I looked away.

"You climbed something, didn't you?" he accused, his tone a mix of exasperation and amusement.

"In my defense," I said quickly, holding up a hand, "I didn't know you moved them. If I had, I wouldn't have!"

"Theo, that's not safe," he said softly, his voice laced with concern. There wasn't a hint of judgment, just genuine care, and it made my chest tighten. "What if you'd fallen and no one was here?"

Rhodes clicked his tongue and moved to grab utensils from the drawer.

"Nothing happened! I'm safe. See?" I gestured at myself and even spun in a slow circle to prove the point. "All in one piece."

Then, with a teasing grin, I shot back, "What about you, oh Holy One, who does no wrong? What did you do today?"

Rhodes laughed, the sound low and rich, shaking his head. "Oh, I'm no saint, Honey."

No kidding. This man could absolutely ruin me—split me in two, make me lose every shred of composure. I wouldn't be praying to God; I'd be on my knees for Rhodes Dunn.

I bit back the reckless urge to say something equally unladylike and tried to focus on steadying my thoughts.

"Boone's stepping away from the labor side of things and into his dad's role," Rhodes said, thankfully shifting the conversation.

"Wait—what?" I spun to face him as he settled at the small kitchen table.

"Boone's dad is retiring, handing over the ranch. Boone asked me to take over as lead rancher."

His grin was slow and steady, the kind of pride that shone brighter in his quiet confidence than in any words he could say.

"Rhodes!" I squealed, unable to contain my excitement. "That's amazing!"

He nodded, his stupidly cute smile still firmly in place, and I felt an overwhelming urge to hug him, to kiss his cheek—anything to touch him.

"Who else knows?" I asked, curious who he'd already told.

"Just you... and Boone's family, of course."

Just me. I was the first person he told. The realization created a rush of warmth that spread through my chest, bubbling up like champagne ready to overflow. My lips curled into a wide, uncontrollable smile, my cheeks aching from the force of it.

"Well, then this is officially a celebratory dinner!" I declared, turning back to the stove to pull the glass dish from the oven. Trying my best to hide the ache I felt. "I hope it tastes good. If not, pizza's on me."

I set the dish on the counter.

"Ooo!" I spun around excitedly. "I can even make cookies! Premade, of course, not from scratch. But hey, a cookie's a cookie."

My cheeks ached from how much I'd been smiling, but it didn't matter. Rhodes deserved every bit of joy tonight.

"I'm just happy I had someone to come home and share the news with," he said softly, his sincerity cutting straight to my heart.

And I realized, in that moment, I was just as happy to be the one he came home to.

21
Theo

"WHY IS HE CRYING?" Rhodes asked, pointing at the TV.

I barely spared him a glance, pausing the show for what felt like the millionth time. After dinner, I'd settled in to catch up on one of my favorite reality shows, and now Rhodes had decided to join me, clearly getting invested.

"Because the judges loved his collection."

"Okay, but... why is *he* mad?" He gestured toward another designer in a sequined blazer glaring daggers at the crying man.

"Because he thought the judges hated *his* collection more," I explained. "But instead, they called it 'a bold take on modern fashion,' and now he's pissed that the crying guy stole the spotlight."

Rhodes blinked at me, then back at the TV. "This is chaos."

"This is *art*," I corrected, tossing a popcorn kernel into my mouth.

I smirked to myself. Rhodes had started the night

scrolling on his phone, throwing casual glances at the screen, but every glance lasted a little longer until he was hooked. He'd never admit it, I could just tell.

I hit play and resumed the show, determined not to pause again even when he felt the urge to chime in because I knew he was bound to.

We sat in comfortable silence as the show carried on in the background. His phone was flat on his chest as he relaxed back, his hands behind his head.

After dinner, he'd helped with the dishes, we shared some casual small talk, and then he went off to shower. I thought maybe he'd head to his room and call it an early night since he had to go to the ranch in the morning, instead, he sat with me on the couch.

We shared parts of a blanket, which should have felt intimate, however it felt natural.

"So, let me get this straight," Rhodes said, leaning back. "They spend, what, a week making clothes?"

"Three days," I replied, holding up three fingers without looking away from the screen.

"Three days?" he scoffed. "To make outfits people either cry about or insult, and then some guy in a hat tells them, 'You're out'? That's the whole show?"

I gasped, clutching my chest in exaggerated horror. "Excuse me? *Some guy in a hat*? That's a *legend* you're talking about."

"A legend?" Rhodes raised an eyebrow. "For telling people their clothes suck?"

"For revolutionizing the industry," I said, rolling my eyes. "And it's not just about the clothes. It's about the drama, the artistry, the—"

"The drama," he cut in, smirking. "Got it."

I grabbed a pillow and threw it at him, but he caught it, laughing.

"You're such a guy."

"And you're way too into this."

"I am not," I said, crossing my arms. "It's just a fun way to relax."

"Uh-huh." Rhodes glanced back at the screen. "So... who's the guy in the fur vest? Is he supposed to look like that, or did he lose a bet?"

I groaned, his smirk was so damn cute. "That's Bruno. He's known for pushing boundaries."

"Boundaries between what? Fashion and bad decisions?"

"You wouldn't get it. Fashion isn't just about clothes—it's an art form." I nudged his leg with my foot.

Rhodes grabbed my foot and pulled it into his lap, his hands beginning to massage it in that infuriatingly wonderful way he had before. I tried to focus on the TV, but the man was a distraction.

He studied me for a moment, his teasing grin softening. "You really like this stuff, huh?"

My cheeks warmed and I nodded. "I do. It's kind of inspiring. Watching people pour their hearts into something they care about, even if it's ridiculous sometimes, you know?"

He tilted his head, a faint smile tugging at his lips. "I get that. I mean, it's not my thing, but... I get it."

Our eyes met, and something about the sincerity in his voice made my chest tighten. "Thanks. I think."

"Anytime," he said, leaning back. "Now, tell me—if I were a designer, what would I make?"

I laughed, my stomach shaking. "Oh, that's easy. A basic black T-shirt and jeans to show off your ass."

The words were out before I could stop them. My hand flew to my mouth as my cheeks flamed.

Rhodes grinned his smile on full display. "Theo, are you saying you like my ass?"

I groaned, burying my face in my hands. "Don't make me answer that."

He chuckled, pulling my hands away from my face. "It's okay. I like your honesty. And for the record, if I *were* a designer, I'd make clothes for people to relax in. No sequins, no fur vests, just comfort."

"Why am I not surprised," I teased.

We shared a laugh and I wasn't sure what I enjoyed more, the show or having him here with me.

By the time I was ready for bed, we'd made it through a couple of episodes. When I said we had catching up to do, I wasn't kidding. At one point, Rhodes got up to make popcorn after I dramatically complained about being hungry. I couldn't resist tossing a few pieces at him, which he effortlessly caught in his mouth with a cocky grin.

Then, we dug into a bowl of ice cream that now sat half-melted on the coffee table. Neither of us cared. We simply existed in the moment, enjoying the easy rhythm of our time together.

My eyes grew heavy, each blink lasting longer than the last. A yawn escaped as I nestled deeper into the soft pillow beneath me, the sound of the TV fading into the background. I was caught in that hazy space between awake and asleep, where the show still played, but my dreams started to take over.

"Theo, Honey," a soft voice called, nudging me back to the surface.

"No," I groaned, pulling the blanket higher over my face.

My body felt weightless, and I vaguely registered the warmth of the couch disappearing. I huffed, half-asleep, searching for it again. Instead of soft cushions, I found something solid, sturdy—something that smelled faintly of clean skin and coffee.

"I got you," that same gentle voice murmured.

Before I could piece together what was happening, I felt myself being carried. Then, I was placed onto a softer surface, the weight of blankets cocooning me like a cloud.

I rolled over, forcing my heavy eyelids open just enough to see a tall shadow looming over me. A soft smile tugged at my lips, my mind blurring the figure into a fragment of my dream. I felt a gentle brush against my cheek, soothing and tender, pulling me deeper into the lull of sleep and back into my dreamland.

The soft click of a door sounded faint, and I let it fade into the background as sleep fully consumed me. My last thoughts were of the faint familiar scent lingering in the air and the sturdy chest that had carried me so effortlessly away.

22 Theo

27 weeks pregnant
Baby is the size of a head of cabbage

Rhodes2324 Wants To Start A New Game With You

TheoTheGreat09 played DIVA for 9 points

TheoTheGreat09: diva is a female version of a hustler. FYI

Rhodes2324: Okay, Beyonce.

TheoTheGreat09: Rhodes... you know more than Zach Top and Toby Keith? SHOCKED

Rhodes2324: I can see you smiling right now. You're sitting right next to me if you forgot.

TheoTheGreat09: How could I when your phone volume is on max watching stupid videos?

I LOOKED UTTERLY RIDICULOUS—PUN totally intended. I agreed to go to the Halloween party with Rhodes. Well, not together, but at the same time, in the same car.

I'd been living with Rhodes a full week at this point, and I could only think of one complaint: he cared about nothing.

It was refreshing to be with someone as laid-back as I was. Our personalities meshed effortlessly, and we got along better than I could have hoped. He'd never admit it, but I knew he secretly enjoyed the shows we watched every night. Without fail, he'd come home, ask, "What are we watching?" and plop down on the couch after dinner. He'd stay there until I inevitably dozed off, nudging me awake just enough to guide me to bed.

Being six, almost seven months pregnant, and trying to fit into spandex was not a smart plan. After mindlessly scrolling, I saw this cute costume idea on Pinterest and thought I'd at least give it a shot.

Rhodes had been pestering me for days, practically begging to know what I planned to dress up as for Halloween. I wasn't about to tell him. The last thing I needed was for him to copy my epic idea or try to match me.

I wiggled into the black-and-white fabric, the stretchy material snapping lightly against my skin. When I turned to look in the mirror, I was no longer myself—I was a full-on pregnant cow.

The spandex bodysuit I found online was perfect, arriving just in time. I'd added my own flair: pink udders for my belly and a headband with floppy ears I'd hot-glued on. Using eyeliner, I drew a cute cow nose and a few other facial details to complete the look.

That was the beauty of Halloween—you could be whoever or whatever you wanted. It was the one time of year when looking completely ridiculous or insanely hot (or both) was socially acceptable.

The weather was warm, so my tattoos were on full display. The black ink that wrapped my arms in intricate florals and vines added an extra layer of personality to the costume. Honestly? I felt pretty damn good.

Spinning around to get the full view in the mirror, I smirked. My ass looked amazing, even in cow print. Feeling cute gave me the confidence boost I needed to tackle the night ahead.

The thought of seeing Aspen and Penny still made my stomach twist, but Rhodes had been right. I needed to do this—for myself and for my baby girl. My insecurities about past friendships didn't matter anymore. I couldn't let the ghosts of my childhood hold me back.

Running a hand over my belly, I smiled at the thought of her. What kind of mom would I be if I didn't show her how to stand her ground?

A quick glance at my phone told me time was ticking, so I gave myself one last once-over in the mirror. Satisfied, I strutted out of the bathroom with as much confidence as my swollen feet could muster.

At that exact moment, Rhodes's bedroom door flew open, and he stepped out, taking up the entire doorway with his broad frame.

"Absolutely not," I said immediately, shaking my head as I took him in. "Nope. This isn't happening."

He was dressed as a damn farmer—plaid button-up shirt, straight-leg Wranglers, and a cowboy hat perched on his stupidly perfect head.

Rhodes took one look at me and burst into laughter, doubling over with his hands on his knees. It was the kind of laugh that made his whole body shake. I couldn't tell if he was laughing at my costume or at the sheer irony of us unintentionally matching.

"What are the odds?" he wheezed, straightening up and wiping his eyes. "Looks like we planned this."

"One of us has to change," I said, glaring at him. "If we show up like this, people are going to get the wrong idea."

"I'm not changing," Rhodes said with a shrug. "This isn't even a costume. These are just my regular clothes."

"Do you know how long it took my pregnant ass to squeeze into spandex?" I shot back. "Way too long, Rhodes. Way too long."

He stepped closer, the scent of his cologne wrapping around me as his ruggedly handsome face hovered just inches away.

"Well, we're at an impasse, Honey."

I groaned, throwing my hands in the air as I stomped to the kitchen to grab my purse and slung it over my shoulder. He wasn't going to budge, and frankly, neither was I.

"Let's just go before I change my mind and decide not to go at all!" I called over my shoulder, walking toward the door.

Rhodes followed, a chuckle rumbling in his chest. Neither of us was going to win this battle, but at least we'd get the party started. Yee-fucking-haw.

I PURPOSEFULLY KEPT my distance from Rhodes, hoping that if we stayed far enough apart, no one would notice the unintended theme. A girl could dream, right?

But, of course, that dream shattered the moment we stepped into the barn. Mac noticed immediately.

"Y'all plan this?" he asked, pointing between Rhodes and me with a mischievous smirk.

"I was dressed first!" I blurted.

"False," Rhodes interjected smoothly. "I've been ready all day. I wore these jeans and boots to work."

"Yeah, well, squeezing into this spandex suit took longer, so I win."

"Did you win, D-I-V-A?" Rhodes teased, drawing out the letters in his deep voice.

"Okay, let's pause the very obvious flirting," Mac cut in with a laugh, throwing an arm around my shoulders. "Let me show you what we've got so I can get back to drinking."

Mac was dressed as the Joker, complete with slicked-back green hair and makeup that nailed the creepy smile. The tailored purple suit and a cigarette tucked behind his ear pulled the whole look together.

"Thanks, Mac," I said as he led me toward the tables stacked with food and drinks.

The barn was packed, far more crowded than I'd expected. I scanned the room, looking for familiar faces.

The main area was decked out with cobwebs and fuzzy spiders, bats hanging from the ceiling, and skeletons propped against the walls. Red lights cast eerie shadows over everything, setting the perfect Halloween mood.

This had Aspen's touch all over it.

"The rest of the gang is over in the far corner," Mac said, giving my shoulder a friendly pat before turning to Rhodes. "Catch you later, cowboy."

Mac disappeared into the crowd, and I timidly approached a pitcher labeled 'blood' on the drink table. It was hard to tell what was spiked and what wasn't, but I was craving something fruity.

"Want me to taste it and check for alcohol?" Rhodes's deep voice tickled my ear, sending a shiver down my spine. The speakers were loud enough to shake the walls, forcing him to lean in close so I could hear him.

"Please," I said, stepping aside as he grabbed a red solo cup. He filled it with just a splash, tipped it to his lips, and smirked.

"Straight juice. No alcohol," he confirmed, then filled the cup to the brim and handed it to me.

I took a sip and was immediately hit with nostalgia. It tasted like childhood—like trick-or-treating in neighborhoods with the best candy, hoarding juice barrels and king-sized Snickers bars like treasure.

Rhodes reached down, grabbed a beer from the cooler, and popped the top on the edge of the table with effortless ease.

Hot. My ovaries were practically doing backflips.

"You ready?" he asked, his voice low and close, his lips brushing against my ear again. Goosebumps spread down my arms as I nodded, my voice caught somewhere between a squeak and a hum.

"Mhm," I managed, taking a step in the direction Mac had pointed out earlier.

I needed to get this conversation over with before everyone else got too drunk—or before I backed out entirely.

As promised, the group was gathered in the corner, chatting and laughing. My stomach dropped, nerves twisting into a knot.

Boone and Aspen were the first I spotted. They were dressed as Bo Peep and her sheep—Aspen in a sweet pink dress with a scandalous neckline, and Boone covered in cotton balls, sheep ears perched on his head.

Penny caught my eye next, dressed as a slutty black cat in a faux-leather spandex suit even tighter than mine. Bless her soul—I had no idea how she planned to get out of that thing later. Judging by the way Mac was leaning against the wall, openly ogling her, I suspected he'd be the one helping her out of it.

Even Logan was here, which surprised me. He wore a simple lion's mane and a yellow T-shirt, whiskers and a pink nose painted on his face.

Taking a deep breath, I forced myself to move forward and join the circle.

"Theo! Rhodes!" Penny squealed, rushing over to hug me. Her warmth and excitement hit me like a tidal wave, and guilt twisted in my chest.

She had no idea what had been weighing on my mind, which pointed to how ridiculous my worries had been or how oblivious she was.

Penny's hug was tight and genuine, her vanilla-scented perfume wrapping around me like comfort.

"I'm so happy you're here," she whispered, pulling back slightly to beam at me.

"Me too," I said softly. I really had missed her.

Aspen quickly swooped in, nearly knocking Penny aside to hug me next. The love from my friends was overwhelming, and for the first time in weeks, I felt truly welcome.

"I'm glad you made it," Aspen said sweetly.

"Can I talk to you two for a second?" I asked, glancing between them.

They nodded immediately. I tapped Rhodes on the arm, handing him my drink.

He leaned down once more, his voice a low murmur against my ear. "I'll be right here."

I squeezed his arm in acknowledgment, then grabbed Aspen and Penny by the hands, leading them to a quiet corner by the hay bales.

"Is everything okay?" Aspen asked, sitting beside me on one of the bales.

"No," I admitted, my voice trembling slightly.

Penny's eyes widened, her face suddenly pale beneath her whiskers. "Is the baby okay?" she asked, her tone tinged with fear.

"The baby is okay," I reassured Penny quickly, seeing the panic flash across her face. "This isn't about that. It's me. I haven't been feeling great mentally. I should've brought it up sooner, but I didn't, and that's on me."

I paused, taking a deep breath when neither of them spoke. "I've felt excluded lately. It's like you guys didn't want to include me or plan things I could do, and it really hurt."

Aspen's eyes dropped, her face falling under the weight of guilt.

"I'm so sorry," she murmured. "That was never my intention. I thought keeping things normal would help. I didn't even think about it like that."

"Hell, I didn't even know about this party. Rhodes told me, and it was embarrassing to realize my two best friends didn't even think to invite me."

"I texted the group chat," Aspen said, her brows furrowing as her head tilted to the side.

Had she? My memory flickered. I'd opened their messages but hadn't replied in weeks. In my anger, I probably skimmed over everything without really reading it. And let's be honest—if Rhodes hadn't nudged me, I wouldn't have come even if I knew.

"I haven't checked the group chat in a while to be honest. I stopped answering, did none of that concern you either?" I asked, my temper beginning to flare.

The silence must have spoken volumes because Penny stepped closer, her expression softening. "You're always so independent. I thought you wanted space."

"That's the problem," I mumbled. "Just because I'm independent or like to do things on my own doesn't mean I don't want to feel loved or included."

Aspen recoiled slightly, inhaling sharply.

I wasn't trying to be harsh—I was being honest. I'd convinced myself that staying silent would protect my peace, in reality, I'd been protecting theirs. All the while,

I'd been at war with myself, harboring these feelings and letting them fester.

"Is that why you stopped answering us?" Penny asked gently.

I nodded. "I was throwing a tantrum. I felt like no one cared, like you all expected me to stay the same person I was months ago. But I'm not. I can't be."

"I'm so sorry," Penny said, her voice trembling as she reached for my hand, just like she had the day I told them about my pregnancy over tacos.

"I should've known better, should've said something," Aspen added. "I thought I was doing the right thing, but I see now I wasn't. I didn't know how to approach it and I'll own that. I'm sorry, too."

I wouldn't tell them it was okay—because it wasn't—but I accepted their apologies. If they could take responsibility, then I had to as well.

"I messed up too," I admitted. "I should've said something sooner. But it's hard. Really damn hard."

"Can I hug you?" Penny asked, arms already open.

I laughed softly and nodded. "Of course."

"Wait! I'm joining!" Aspen declared, diving in to make it a three-way hug.

Rhodes was right—talking to them dressed as Little Bo Peep and a cat made it all feel a lot easier. This was the conversation I'd needed for weeks.

"I'm sorry I shut down," I added, squeezing them tighter. "Feelings aren't my strong suit."

"Boo!" Penny said with a playful pout. "I should've pushed harder. I should've known something was off."

Aspen nodded. "I'm just glad we are talking about it

now. I knew something was wrong but I didn't know how to bring it up."

"I am too. Let's promise to speak up from now on," Penny said, holding out her pinky.

Aspen and I hooked ours with hers in unison. "Deal."

As we pulled apart, my eyes drifted across the barn to Rhodes. He stood with the guys, laughing and grinning in a way that made his whole face light up. His eyes crinkled at the corners, and his Adam's apple bobbed as he tilted his head back to laugh harder.

The flutter in my chest was warm, almost dizzying. I'd done this for me but it was because of *him*.

"I knew it!" Penny gasped, covering her mouth with one hand and pointing at me with the other.

"Knew what?" I asked, my voice pitching up as I quickly looked back at her.

"You and Rhodes," she accused, her tone dripping with glee.

"Oh, shit!" Aspen cackled. "I called it!"

"It's not like that," I stammered, waving my hands defensively. "We've gotten really close after he offered to let me live with him. It's just until I find my own place after the baby is born."

"YOU'RE LIVING WITH HIM?" Aspen and Penny shouted in unison from across the circle.

"Shh! Keep it down!" I hissed, glancing around the barn.

"For how long?" Penny asked. "And how do you keep your hands to yourself? I saw the way you just looked at him. I don't know if I could either." She wiggled her eyebrows up and down. "Oh my God! Does he walk around shirtless?"

"What is it with you and sexualizing everyone?" I laughed, shaking my head. Penny had always been like this—first about Boone, and now Rhodes.

"Ugh," she groaned, dramatically flopping her head forward. "I'm always horny, okay? I'm living vicariously through my friends until it's my turn."

"Um, hello? The Joker over there has been eyeing your boobs like they're his last meal," Aspen pointed out, nodding toward Mac.

Penny bit her lip, twirling a strand of hair. "He was, wasn't he?"

I grinned and shook my head. "We're not talking about Rhodes here. Not tonight."

"Fine," Penny sighed dramatically. "But you owe me answers."

Talking to them had lifted a weight off my shoulders. I'd stepped out of my comfort zone and spoken up about how I felt, and it felt good—empowering, even.

The past few weeks had taught me so much about myself and the people I cared about. Without Rhodes's gentle push, I might've let my insecurities destroy friendships with two women who'd changed my life.

They'd saved me when I first arrived in Faircloud, and I knew they'd keep saving me for years to come.

And as for Rhodes... I couldn't quite push him away, no matter how hard I tried. Maybe I never wanted to.

23
Rhodes

I FELT HER WATCHING ME. It took everything in my power not to glance in her direction. I wanted to give her privacy and space to handle this moment. As much as I was dying to know how things were going, I'd wait as patiently as I could.

Pride swelled in my chest for Theo. This clearly wasn't easy for her, yet she cared enough about the relationship to be uncomfortable and vulnerable. I admired that more than I could say.

Besides trying not to be nosey, keeping my eyes to myself was a special kind of torture because she was testing me in that spandex suit. It hugged her perfectly, and my legs felt weak at the sight.

I counted my lucky stars when she left me alone in the hallway at home. She'd come out of the bathroom dressed like that, and I was a goner. Then she opened her mouth. I didn't know feisty women were my thing. Maybe just when it came from Theo.

"Aspen wants everyone to go to the fall festival for a

mini 'Friendsgiving' the weekend before Thanksgiving. Would you be in?" Boone asked.

I barely registered the words. I was focusing so hard on not looking at Theo that my brain wasn't computing anything else.

"Yeah, sure, that sounds—"

"I need him for a minute!" Theo yelled, grabbing my biceps and yanking me away before I could finish. I still had her drink in my hand; the red liquid sloshed dangerously at the force of her pull.

"Whoa there," I laughed.

"No time!"

She dragged me far from the group, out the barn doors and into the cool Texas night. The sky was inky black, and the sound of crickets filled the air. Her small legs moved in quick bursts as I followed behind her.

"It went so good!" Theo huffed, coming to a stop. She spun around, her smile so radiant you could see it from space. The apples of her cheeks were prominent, smooth, and round. "I'm really proud of myself. I can't believe I did it." She laughed and threw her hands in the air. "It shouldn't be groundbreaking—an adult talking about her feelings—but for me, it was. Oh my God!"

She rambled, and it was adorable.

Without warning, she threw herself at me, wrapping her arms around me in a tight embrace.

At first, I hesitated. Did I hug her back? Did I go for a friendly half-hug or a full one?

Fuck it.

I wrapped my arms around her and rested my chin on top of her head.

If I got the chance to hold Theo Matthews, I sure as hell was going to take it.

She burrowed deeper into my chest, and I couldn't stop myself from smiling.

I didn't want to let go. Theo's body fit perfectly against mine, like she was made to be here, in my arms, for eternity.

She leaned back slightly, her arms still looped around my body as she looked up at me. Even dressed as a farm animal, she was breathtaking.

My gaze flicked between her eyes. The playful smiles we'd been wearing faded, replaced by something heavier, deeper.

Electricity crackled where our bodies touched, and the urge to close the space between our faces became almost unbearable. I wanted to kiss her—to feel those plump, sassy lips against mine and lose myself in her.

Like she could read my thoughts, Theo rose onto her tiptoes and pressed her lips lightly to mine. The warmth of her touch unraveled me. My eyes drifted shut as I melted into the kiss, her soft breath mingling with mine. Her lips, gentle yet insistent, sent a rush of heat spiraling through my chest.

She must've felt it, too–the pull between us was undeniable. It wasn't just me.

My hand wove into her hair, pressing us closer. The taste of her on my lips was heavenly and utterly intoxicating.

Kissing Theo was better than I'd ever imagined. I wanted to be stuck with her forever, stuck in this moment under the stars.

With a final lingering press of our lips, Theo pulled away, though I could sense we were both reluctant to break the connection.

"Thank you," Theo whispered, her voice barely audible as her gaze dropped to my mouth, then back to my eyes. Her lips were wet and swollen, and I knew mine must have been the same.

"I don't know why you care so much," she added, her voice tinged with vulnerability.

Smirking, I lifted a hand and gently tucked a stray strand of hair behind her ear. Her pigtails were cute, but seeing her hair wild and loose? It did something to me—something I couldn't put into words.

"I just do," I said softly, letting the weight of my words hang between us. Little did she know, I wasn't going anywhere.

She leaned into my touch, her eyes fluttering closed briefly before opening again with a small, raw smile. This moment—it felt real.

"You can tell me all about the conversation on the way home," I said reluctantly, knowing we couldn't stay wrapped up in this bubble forever. "We better get back to the rest of the crew before someone comes looking." Not that I cared because after tasting those lips, I was hooked. I'd let the world know how infatuated I was with Theo Matthews.

She sighed. "You're right," Theo said, stepping back with hesitation. "I'll grab more 'blood' and meet the girls by the fire."

I nodded, letting my hand linger against hers for just a

moment longer. "Let me know when you're ready to go, okay?"

Theo nodded, clutching her drink with both hands as she turned and walked away. I couldn't help but watch her, my gaze following every step.

When she rejoined the girls, I made my way back to Boone. Across the yard, Mac and Logan were deep in conversation. By the look on Mac's face, it was serious, and he seemed completely out of his element.

"What the hell was that about?" Boone asked, raising an eyebrow as he sipped his beer.

"What was what?" I replied, feigning innocence.

"Theo pulling you away. The hug? Did I see you kiss?"

I glanced toward the fire. Theo was laughing, her smile brighter than the flames rising from fire.

"She had a good talk with Aspen and Penny. I helped her work through some stuff, that's all," I said casually, though Boone's skeptical look told me he wasn't buying it.

"Oh yeah? A little bird, also known as Aspen, told me you two are living together."

"Since when are you a gossip?" I shot back, taking a long sip of my beer.

Boone grinned, unbothered. "The girls are right; it is kinda fun."

Sighing, I adjusted the cowboy hat Boone had loaned me for the night. I wasn't going to admit it out loud, but I was starting to like the damn thing.

"She needed a place to stay, and I had the room. That's it. Things could've been different, now it's..." My voice trailed off.

I owed Boone the truth. A few months ago, I'd given him endless grief over Aspen. I couldn't be the pot calling the kettle black.

"I saw the way you looked at her," Boone said, his voice quieter now. "That wasn't very roommate-like."

"Do I like her? Yeah, absolutely. She's the first woman to make me feel something since Jess. But things are complicated," I admitted, the words tasting heavier than I expected.

"Because she's pregnant?" Boone crossed his arms, his tone sharp, like he'd fight me if that were my problem.

"Jesus, no. Because she's my roommate."

Boone smirked. "I don't see the issue."

"Of course you don't. You got with your neighbor *and* your employee," I retorted, rolling my eyes.

"Coworker," Boone corrected, holding up a finger like he was giving a lecture.

"Whatever. The point is, it's not that simple."

Boone's grin softened into something more sincere. "Look, if you feel something, you should explore it. Your shot at love wasn't like the rest of ours, but that doesn't mean you don't deserve to be happy. I'm not gonna judge you for seeing where it goes."

His words settled the storm in my chest, even if just a little. Truth was, I did like spending time with Theo. I looked forward to coming home to her. I couldn't help but wonder—what would it be like to come home to her and the baby?

"I wouldn't even know where to begin," I confessed.

"Win her over. Do cute shit. They love cute shit," Boone said, chuckling.

I laughed, shaking my head. Though, he wasn't wrong —Theo *would* like cute shit. I'd just need to figure out what would make her smile.

"Take it slow," Boone added, clapping me on the shoulder. "See what happens. But don't put your happiness on hold just because you're living together. Do what feels right."

It was worth a shot. If things didn't work out, we could be adults about it... right?

By the fire pit, only Aspen and Logan remained. Theo was lounging in her chair, her eyes half-closed. After living with her, I'd learned the signs that meant she was ready for bed: droopy eyes, slackened mouth, and uncontrollable yawns. Watching her now, I saw the trifecta.

"I think we're gonna head out," I told Boone, nodding toward the fire pit. He gave me an understanding look and motioned for me to go.

When I reached Theo, her sleepy smile tugged at something deep inside me.

Leaning down, I whispered softly, "Come on, Honey. It's time to go."

She groaned, her eyes fluttering open just enough to see me. She stumbled slightly as she stood, but I steadied her with a hand on her elbow.

Murmuring her goodbyes, she hugged everyone left in the circle before we made our way to the truck. Once we were out of sight, I scooped her up, carrying her the rest of the way. She didn't protest, just nestled into my chest, warm and trusting.

After buckling her into the passenger seat, she

snuggled up against the window, her eyes closing almost instantly.

The entire drive home, my mind wandered. I thought about how much I cared for her, how much she consumed me. When we pulled up to the house, I realized I'd have to help her get ready for bed which started a whole slew of feelings.

"Come on," I murmured, coaxing her awake as gently as I could.

Theo grumbled incoherently, but let me guide her inside. She barely stirred as I helped her wash her face, her makeup melting away under the warm washcloth.

When we got to the last step—her spandex costume—I hesitated.

"We have one more step," I said, sitting her on the edge of the bed.

Her room was a mix of her personality and her past: photos of her and her friends, a black comforter she'd brought with her, and trinkets scattered on the nightstand. Little by little, she was making this place her home. I liked that.

Reaching behind her, I unzipped the fabric, loosening it enough for her to tug the sleeves down. She struggled, sleepy and incoherent, until I stepped in to help.

Just as I turned my head to give her privacy, I caught sight of a strap on her shoulder.

Thank God.

I helped her out of the costume, leaving her in what looked like a swimsuit or some kind of undergarment. Whatever it was, it offered just enough coverage to keep things from being awkward.

I rummaged through her dresser, eventually pulling out a set of matching pajamas. The fabric was soft and the pattern was simple. When I turned back, Theo was already curled up on her side, her breathing slow and even, teetering on the edge of sleep.

Did I even bother?

Groaning softly, I ran a hand down my face. Forget the pajamas. Tossing them onto the dresser, I made a quick decision: I wasn't going to undress her completely. That was a line I wouldn't cross, especially not without her consent.

Instead, I stood by her bed, unsure whether I was being helpful or just plain intrusive. She looked so peaceful, her features softened and serene, like every worry she carried was momentarily set aside.

My gaze drifted lower, landing on the gentle swell of her belly. It was impossible to ignore now, a quiet reminder of the life growing inside her. Something stirred deep in my chest—something I hadn't felt in a while. A strange, unfamiliar longing.

For a fleeting moment, I let myself imagine this was *my* life. That I belonged here. That this was the family I'd always dreamed of.

The thought hit hard, and I blinked rapidly, forcing away the sting of tears gathering in the corners of my eyes.

Maybe the tears weren't for Theo or the baby, but for myself. For the life I thought I'd be living by now. I'd always wanted a family and a house full of laughter and love, the kind of happiness you see in picture frames at the store.

But that wasn't my reality. Not yet.

I reached down and brushed her cheek with my thumb, the faintest of touches, just enough to feel the warmth of her skin.

One day, I told myself. One day, it would be my turn.

For now, I stepped back, letting her rest. As I watched her breathe softly, her hands cradling her belly even in sleep, I couldn't shake the feeling that maybe, just maybe, this was where I was supposed to be after all.

24
Theo

"YES," I managed between needy pants. My back arched, and my legs began to quake, shaking uncontrollably at the sensation of his tongue against my delicate center. This felt so fucking good.

"Please," I begged. My mouth opened to scream, but no sound came out.

Reaching my hand down, I intertwined my fingers into locks of dark hair, gripping and pulling him closer. I needed more. More what? I didn't know, but I was desperate to chase this arousal.

Shoving my pussy into his face, I let out a frustrated groan because I knew he wasn't giving me everything he could, he was holding back. This man was teasing me on purpose, my body aching for more. A vibration sent tingles up my spine as he chucked against me, burying his face deeper. His facial hair rubbed against me in just the right way, a sound I'd never made before slipped past my lips

"You're so needy for me, Honey," Rhodes muttered, using his tongue to form circles around my clit. He swirled one, two, three more times and ran his tongue down my slit, taking his time to clean my dripping center.

"Do you hear that?" Rhodes mumbled into me.

He delicately licked my entrance. The soft, lingering edging nearly as arousing as the fast and devouring pace. A mixture of fast and slow movements riled me up just to bring me back down, creating a steady hum at the base of my spine.

So close to release, the feeling was building up stroke by stroke of his tongue. Before I could make my move to wrap my legs around his head to demand more, Rhodes stopped, and a cool breeze filled the space where he was.

Angry, I huffed and sat on my elbows, my eyebrows pushed together.

"Did I say stop?" I asked, tilting my head to the side.

Rhodes stared at me, a sexy smirk on his wet lips. It was me on his lips, me who he was devouring like it was his last meal. His hair was tousled, sticking up like he'd just gone round for round in the ring.

"You think you're in charge?" Rhodes quipped, kneeling between my legs and looking down at me desperate beneath him. He was shirtless, every one of his muscles defined. Pecs, abs, biceps; they each deserved my undivided attention. I wished I could lick them all, take my time exploring every dip and curve.

"I may let you have your way outside the bedroom, but in here, you are mine," Rhodes growled. "Turn around and bend over."

I shot up, gasping for air, my hand clutching my chest in an attempt to steady the wild rhythm of my heartbeat.

Was I sweating? I wiped the back of my hand across my forehead. *Yep, definitely sweating.*

Horny and desperate, I sat there for a moment, trying to pull myself together. My dreams had been... vivid. Dirty. Completely consumed by Rhodes.

This wasn't the first time I'd used my imagination to

dull this restless, aching need, but it was becoming a problem. A *serious* problem.

I couldn't deny it anymore. I was painfully attracted to my roommate. And with every fleeting glance, every accidental brush of his hand, my resolve was crumbling. How much longer could I pretend I wasn't losing control?

Frustrated, I threw the blanket off my body, the cool air washing over my overheated, sticky skin.

That's when I noticed it.

The tight spandex I'd worn last night was gone.

Wait... what?

Memories of the night before came rushing back. I'd been exhausted—barely able to stay awake, much less get myself ready for bed.

Which meant...

My pulse spiked again.

Rhodes.

He must've helped me undress.

The thought sent a jolt through me, reigniting every ember of sexual frustration I'd tried to snuff out.

This is getting out of hand.

And the worst part? Deep down, I wished he hadn't stopped.

Fuck.

I stood up and paced back and forth. There was no way I was going to get rid of the arousal. This was no longer an itch.

I *wanted* him badly. I *needed* him biblically.

Then, I thought about our kiss. That damn kiss that I initiated. I was pulled into the moment and on emotional overdrive. Adrenaline was pumping through my system, excitement lighting me on fire.

His lips were soft; he tasted like warmth and good decisions.

I needed a cold shower. That would do the trick. I needed to douse this fire I felt inside me.

Did I really *want* to?

Maybe this was my chance to make a move and put the desire to rest.

My nipples ached; they were hard against the tight clothing.

Fuck it.

A feral part of me took over; I was blinded by my libido. Rummaging through my drawers, I found a tank top and shorts that were barely a scrap of fabric.

I stepped out of my clothes from last night and into this, something suggestive enough to give Rhodes a tease. Running my hands through my messy hair, I left it wild and untamed as it cascaded around my face.

My mind was made up. The no-shit, get what she wants woman wasn't at rest, she was ready to play. I'd pull out the big guns to reel Rhodes in. I was tousled, horny, and ready to shake shit up.

I stepped out of my room, my bare feet padding down the cool hardwood hallway. Each slow, deliberate step was a performance, a reminder of the confident persona I always wore. When I reached the kitchen, my practiced calm faltered.

Rhodes was already there, one step ahead of me.

He stood at the counter, his back to me, wearing nothing but a pair of low-slung pajama pants that clung to his hips. His broad, muscled back was a masterpiece, every ridge and dip tempting my fingers to trace the lines. When he turned, the expanse of his chest and abs—defined, utterly devastating—came into view.

My mouth went dry.

I'd walked out with every intention of making him squirm, but now I felt like the one out of her depth, striding into a gun fight with only a knife.

Forcing a breath, I pushed down the looming nerves and wore a sultry smile. "Good morning," I said, casually raking a hand through my hair in an attempt to feel loose and free.

Rhodes turned his head, his green eyes meeting mine with an intensity that made my pulse kick up five notches. The mug in his hand paused mid-lift as his gaze flicked down, taking in my tank top and bare legs.

"Morning," he said, his voice a low rumble that sent a shiver down my spine.

I sauntered to the cabinets, letting my hips sway just enough to catch his attention. As I reached for a glass, I deliberately overextended, the hem of my shirt riding up to reveal a hint of skin.

"Could you help me?" I asked, glancing back at him with wide, innocent eyes.

His jaw tightened, and for a moment, he didn't move, his gaze lingering just long enough to make the air between us crackle. Then he cleared his throat. "Sure."

Rhodes stepped closer, his presence as commanding as ever. He reached over me, his chest brushing lightly against my back. The scent of him—clean, woodsy, with a hint of soap—wrapped around me, making my knees weak.

I stayed frozen, every nerve ending alive as his arm hovered above me. I could feel the heat radiating from his skin, the tension tangible. He grabbed the glass and handed it to me, stepping back before I could react.

"Thanks," I murmured, my voice slightly unsteady. I turned and poured juice into the glass, taking a seat at the island to ground myself. "How'd you sleep?"

Rhodes leaned against the counter, mug in hand, his biceps flexing just enough to draw my attention.

"Pretty good. You?"

"Like a baby," I replied, swirling the juice in my glass before looking up at him. "Though I did have an... interesting dream." *Tease*. I'd use the dream to play with him, have him at my mercy. What man could deny hearing more about a dirty dream, especially if it involved him?

Rhodes' brow arched slightly, the corner of his mouth curving in a way that was maddeningly attractive. "Oh yeah? What about?"

He stepped closer, resting his elbows on the counter across from me, his stupidly attentive eyes locking onto mine. The heat between us was almost unbearable.

I hesitated just long enough to let the tension build, then lowered my gaze to the rim of my glass, running a finger along its edge.

"Well," I said softly, lifting my eyes to meet his. "You and me."

"Hmmm." He hummed, leaning in closer. Not an ounce of shock appeared on his face. "And?"

I lifted a hand to my neck, trying to soothe the tension there.

"It's... a bit embarrassing," I admitted, leaning back in my chair and placing my hands on the cool marble countertop.

Rhodes' eyes fell to my breasts that were barely contained by the thin-strapped tank I wore, no bra. He could easily see the peaks of my nipples forming beneath the fabric. I changed my posture, pushing them out to seem irresistible.

Licking his lips, he stood up straight and walked towards me.

"Tell me," he purred, affected by the atmosphere in the kitchen just as much as I was.

"We were in my room."

"Yeah?"

Rhodes came closer, rounding the island.

"And you were with me, in my bed."

"Mhm."

Another step.

"I was on my back."

"And?"

One more.

"You were between my legs."

Rhodes stood close to me, and I spun the kitchen chair making sure I was facing his direction. He peered down as I looked up, my mouth slightly parted.

"What was I doing?" Rhodes cocked his head to the side, arms crossing over his broad, bare chest. His muscles bulged and the veins became more prominent.

I gulped, blinking slowly at him and bit my bottom lip.

"Tell me, Theo. What was I doing?"

With an intentional pause, I let the room fall silent, anticipation gnawing at me before I responded in a hushed whisper.

"Devouring me."

Rhodes smiled, leaning his tall frame down so he was inches away from my face. My skin was prickling, and my core throbbed. His change of demeanor turned me on; I barely recognized the man before me.

Rhodes was soft and gentle but seeing him ravenous and hungry made my skin crawl. I'd love to see him come undone beneath me.

His pupils dilated, and his gaze touched my lips.

"Did you like it?" he asked, his tone not wavering as he pushed forward, playing my game.

Shame-filled pleasure took over, making me defiant to his approach.

"Yes."

We were nose to nose, stuck in a whirlpool of tension neither of us wanted out of. I needed him now more than ever. There was no way I'd be able to turn back from this. No showerhead or hot dream would take away this ache.

Making the first move, I reached out and ran my fingers against his abs, feeling every dip under my touch.

"You were such a good boy," I whispered in a sultry tone, angling my face millimeters away from his lips. Our breaths tangled, a heady mixture of heat and longing.

That was all it took to shatter Rhodes's control. His lips crashed into mine with a passion that left me breathless.

I leaned into him, my hands curling around the back of

his neck, pulling him closer, desperate to close the distance between us. Our mouths moved together, a wild, unrelenting rhythm. I couldn't tell where I ended and he began.

Rhodes cupped my face with both hands, drawing me to my feet. My teeth caught his lower lip, tugging lightly before letting go. The sharp snap as it sprang back made him growl, his eyes darkening as they fluttered shut.

With a swift motion, he spun me, backing me toward the living room. We moved as one, never breaking apart, our kisses frantic and fevered. Hands roamed, lips clashed, it was chaos, raw and electric, a frenzy that neither of us could control.

This was the first time I was going to have sex while pregnant; there was a lot I was unsure of. What would be comfortable? How would my body react? I couldn't let the anxiety impact the moment. I trusted Rhodes.

Rhodes took control, and I was willing to let him, every ounce of defiance stripped away with a single intimate touch. Sitting down on the couch, he pulled me to straddle him. One leg lay on either side of his waist while I leaned down to let my tongue explore his.

"I'm gonna enjoy this," Rhodes muttered against my lips before diving back in. "I've been thinking about you, needy and naked for me, for way too long." I knew he meant it because I could feel how hard his cock was as it twitched between my legs. I rocked my hips to rub along his length, giving me the friction I needed to pleasure myself.

Rhodes' hands dipped into my shorts, cupping my ass and squeezing. The feeling of his calloused palms against my sensitive skin set me ablaze. My hands grabbing his cheeks and my body moving in rolling motions against his. The tank top felt too tight, rubbing against the sensitive skin of my nipples adding to the friction.

I was feral.

Rhodes pulled away, pausing the kiss as he panted.

"Are we doing this?" he asked, leaning his head against the back of the couch.

"I think so," I replied, my thumbs gently rubbing his cheeks as I stared into his eyes, lost in a pool of dilated pupils.

"What do you want?" His hands still roamed my body, exploring the curve of my hips under my clothes.

That was a good question. Was an intense make-out enough? Did I want to go further?

The slickness between my legs told me my answer.

I leaned, pressing my breasts against his bare chest. "You."

"If we do this, there's no going back." He was caring and cautious, leaving it up to me. Even in a lust filled moment, he was considerate. I could *feel* how badly he wanted me. Wanted this. Yet, he considered me and my feelings above the raging ache of his cock.

"I know."

Without any more questions or hesitation, Rhodes leaned farther back and removed his hands from my body. Like a king, he draped his arms on the back of the couch and nodded past me.

"Then stand up and strip for me, Theo."

Scrambling, I climbed off of his lap and stood. My

heart was in my ears, beating loud enough to drown out any sound.

I was molten as I hooked both thumbs into the waistband of my shorts and shimmed out, standing bare to make a show out of my strip tease. Rhodes was staring at me like I was a work of art, a sparkle in his eyes I'd never witnessed before. That gave me the courage to keep going.

Slowly, I removed the tank top and let it hang from my fingertips, twirling it back and forth before dropping it to the ground with a smirk.

I was standing completely naked in front of Rhodes Dunn. My friend. My roommate. My deepest desire. The man I shouldn't be getting involved with but fuck if I could hold back any longer.

He was the first person to witness me naked while pregnant. I'd been hiding myself and my body from the world–he was the first one to truly *see* me.

"You are *beautiful*. A masterpiece." Rhodes said, his gaze raking over me from head to toe.

Usually, I hated the extra attention, but right now, I soaked in every bit I could. I craved it, craved him.

"Look at you," Rhodes scoffed in almost disbelief. He reached his hand towards me, his palm up. I placed my hand in his, and he guided me to him to resume my position.

Rhodes leaned up, placing both hands on either side of my belly. Coming closer, he left a soft kiss on the swell. There were those damn butterflies again, the gentle touch of their wings tickling my insides. My core throbbed in anticipation and my heart kicked with longing. There was a crack, like ice was melting away.

"I think it's your turn," I spoke softly, dropping my intense stare down to the hard cock in his pants.

"Not so fast, Honey. I want you to tell me exactly what I did to you in that dream."

My cheeks blushed at the thought of *real* Rhodes between my legs, pleasuring me with his tongue. Not many men have done that before. It was far too intimate for casual hookups.

Instinctively, I wanted to protest. I stood before him for a moment, wondering what I could do to pivot the situation.

"I can see you overthinking," Rhodes said, standing to tower over me.

Maybe if I sank to my knees, he would forget about the dream. I could blow his mind and give him the best head he probably ever experienced, and we'd move to the main event.

"Forget the dream," I replied, moving to put my hands in his waistband to pull down his pants and let him spring free.

Rhodes was built, long and thick which I could see clearly through his pajamas. He could rip me in two, making walking quite difficult. He had the power to destroy me and not just with his cock.

"Theo, Honey, sit. You're not going to distract me that easily. My mind is made up and I'm a man who knows what he wants." Rhodes laid his hands over mine, removing them from his defined hips. He even had that V that made all the girls stupid.

Rhodes spun me, pushing me lightly to sit down.

Now, *I* was in the vulnerable position. He was in complete control, and it didn't worry me that I was at someone else's mercy.

With a shaky exhale, I closed my eyes and let my head fall back.

Rhodes pushed the coffee table away to fit between me and the couch, dropping between my legs. I was on display, wide and ready for him to play.

The slickness between my legs was all for him, the wetness more than I'd felt before. It seemed nothing turned me on like the thought of Rhodes on his knees for me.

"What did I do first?" Rhodes asked, peppering kisses on the inside of my upper thigh. That single move made me putty; my skin was hot, and I let out a desperate whimper.

"You used your tongue," I somehow managed to say, watching intently.

Rhodes followed my instructions, starting at my entrance and he licked up, painfully slow, savoring my taste. The sensation of his hot, wet tongue against my core was almost too much.

"Mhm, like that." I sighed with pleasure.

"Now what?"

"Suck on my clit." I was throbbing. I'm surprised he didn't feel it against his lips as he latched onto me and sucked, pulling away and coming back again. "*Fuck*, like that," I growled. He repeated over and over, intentionally slow to torture me.

"Rhodes," I moaned.

"Did I use my fingers?" He asked, running his pointer finger down from my clit to my entrance. He stuck in the tip just enough to make me want more. I pushed my hips down, trying to take it for myself.

"Do you *want* my fingers, Theo?"

"Yes."

"Yes, what?"

"Yes, please," I begged, spreading my legs as wide as they could go. The colder air hit me, adding to the satisfaction.

Rhodes shoved one finger in, toying with me as he pumped in and out. His free hand reached down and grabbed his length, jerking inside his pants.

"That's it," he growled. "You're so wet. Is this all for me?"

I nodded, moving my hips to create friction against him.

"Can you take one more?"

"Yes," I groaned in response.

Rhodes laughed and pushed in another finger, returning his mouth and using his tongue to play with me. Between the penetration and his tongue, I was a panting mess. My hips bucked and my clit rubbed against his lips. The stubble on his face scratched the sensitive skin, just as it had in my dream.

He picked up his speed, devouring me with no mercy. Sucking, licking, sopping his way up and down my slit as I moaned his name. I screamed at the top of my lungs riding out my orgasm.

"Fuck!"

Rhodes hummed in agreement, burying his face deeper as I came against his lips.

He pulled back, a wicked, deadly smirk tugging at his lips. The sight sent a shiver down my spine, equal parts thrill and torment.

As Rhodes straightened, he wiped his glistening mouth with the back of his hand, his eyes dark with unspoken intent.

Straight from a raunchy porn film, he put the two fingers that were inside me into his mouth and sucked so hard his cheeks hollowed.

Lord…

"You taste so good. I bet you feel even better," Rhodes whispered, leaning down to kiss me. I tasted myself on his lips. The mixture of me and him on his tongue was erotic.

"Lay on your back," he demanded and I listened. I was never the submissive type, but the commanding tone of Rhodes' voice altered my brain chemistry.

Laying down was easier than getting up in my current state. My body was exhausted from the orgasm, like I'd run a marathon at record speed.

Finally, fucking *finally*, he pulled down his pajama pants. From my back, I watched the fabric disappear, revealing rock-hard length. I wasn't disappointed by what I saw. Just as I expected, Rhodes Dunn outdid every cock I'd seen.

This man was built to fuck.

I wanted to taste him, feel the velvety skin slam into the back of my throat. The drool was pooling in my mouth, salivating like a damn dog.

Doing the hottest thing a man could do, he ran a hand

down his length and wiped a bead of come from the tip. I bit down on my bottom lip and secretly wished it had been *me* cleaning him up.

Rhodes left one foot on the ground and placed his bent knee on the couch for support. Both of his hands came down on either side of my face as he hovered inches above me.

I reached up and entwined my fingers into the locks of black hair. It was smooth and clean, like silk beneath my fingertips.

I pulled him down, placing a long, hard kiss on his lips. He returned the gesture, and we both allowed a moment to lean into the kiss, my tongue and his finding a rhythm.

"Theo, I'm going to fuck you. I need to know you agree." Rhodes spoke, hurried against my lips.

"I want your bare cock buried inside me. Fuck me, please."

Rhodes groaned and tilted his head up to the ceiling, saying a silent prayer. My fingers in his hair pulled the ends and yanked his attention back.

"Honey, you have no clue what hearing you say that does to me."

I could guess because I felt his thickness twitch in agreement.

"We don't need a condom for obvious reasons. Plus, I'm clean; I haven't had sex since, well." I looked down at my belly.

"I haven't been with anyone in… awhile." Rhodes looked ashamed to admit that, but to me, it made it mean that much more.

Without another word, he lined up his cock to my entrance. I shifted in frustration, my body needing him inside me, now.

His face tensed as he pushed past my walls. With every inch he gave, he paused for a moment for me to adjust. As badly as I wanted to close my eyes to focus on the way he stretched me, I kept my attention strictly on Rhodes, taking in how devastatingly handsome he truly was.

"I can take it," I whispered, urging him to fill me all the way.

He took his time despite my encouragement. I moaned his slow pace, sending my head spinning. The head of his cock was so deep inside me. I wasn't used to feeling this full.

Pleasure felt different while pregnant, everything was heightened.

Rhodes's eyes closed as he picked up speed but I continued to watch him shove into me less controlled. The concentration he needed to keep himself together was clear by the pinched brows. Sounds of satisfied grunts filled the air mixed with my own high pitched moans.

He angled himself up, rubbing against the exact spot I needed. This time, I couldn't help it when my eyes closed. The control I once had was nonexistent.

"Rhodes!" I screamed, my voice breaking at the end of his name. This is what I needed. This is exactly what I'd been craving since that night in the shower.

Rhodes took my leg and hoisted it onto his shoulder, driving in my heat deeper. He felt *so* good.

"Come for me, Honey," Rhodes begged. "Come on my cock."

My vision blurred, and time slowed as I did exactly what Rhodes asked. I came, my climax taking charge.

My walls squeezed his cock as the pleasure consumed me.

"I'm not done with you yet. If I stay like this any longer, I'm going to bust sooner than I'd like," he purred, hovering over me. "Ride me, Honey. Have your moment in control." That turned me on more than the sight of his glistening cock as he pulled out of me. I smiled wickedly, ready to make him regret ever giving me the chance.

Placing my hand on his chest, I pushed him off me. He sat down and obeyed, spreading his legs slightly like a king on his throne.

He looked divine, his hard length slick and ready to welcome me as I took a seat on *my* throne.

I angled my entrance right above him. He held his cock steady for me as I sank down, filling myself from tip to base again, but this time, it was smoother because I was used to his size.

The new angle felt euphoric. My movements were limited, but I was able to rock, causing his tip to hit the perfect spot which was enough to cause that stinging feeling to build at the base of my spine.

Rhodes' hands grabbed my hip and he lifted me up, thrusting his hips, pounding into my slick core.

"I thought I was in control?" I quipped, flipping my hair to one side and latching onto his exposed neck to stifle a moan. I sucked and nibbled my way to his ear, dragging my tongue to taste his now slick skin.

"You are; I thought I'd lend a hand. I know how much you love the help," he panted, dripping with sarcasm.

Placing both hands on his shoulders, I used him as support to show him just how much I didn't need his help. I was done fucking around, I'd make this man crumble.

Frantically, I rode him to oblivion. I screamed, and he groaned. I huffed, he sighed. Our bodies slammed together, creating a symphony of erotic noises.

"Keep doing that," Rhodes begged. He wasn't going to last much longer and that fueled my ego.

Fucking the best I could, I threw my head back and didn't let up.

"You fill me so well, Rhodes." I rocked harder, the friction on my clit spiking my blood pressure. "I'm so fucking full of your cock."

His hand came to my throat, holding with enough pressure to make my head spin. I'd never been choked before but the way it added to the pleasure, I'd be exploring that more later.

"Eyes on me," he groaned, the hand from my neck grabbing my chin as he forced it down. "I want you to watch as I fill you."

I looked down at where our bodies were joined, my hips fluid as I moved against him.

On an exhale Rhodes grunted one last time before he came, closing his eyes to enjoy the moment. I didn't stop right away, dragging out the last bit of pleasure I could.

It felt dirty knowing he was raw inside me, that he would be dripping down my leg. It was a good kind of dirty, that kind that made me want to do it again and again.

"Was I a good boy?" Rhodes teased, a devilish glint shimmering in his eyes.

"On your best behavior," I replied, placing a long gentle kiss on his mouth, my tongue darting out to run along his bottom lip. "Give me a breather, and I'll be ready for round two." Rhodes laughed against me, which pinched my heart.

"Woah," He replied, placing his hands under my ass and standing to lift me off his cock. "I'm going to need a full cup of coffee and a meal before we do that again."

He carried me to the kitchen while I placed soft kisses on his neck. I'm glad I didn't have to walk because my legs were as wobbly as a newborn calf.

Rhodes placed me down on the island and stood between my legs, caging me in his arms. He looked down at my pussy. His fingers dipped down and shoved the come dripping out back inside of me.

"What do you say about me cooking us breakfast? My requirement is that you sit your pretty ass right here, naked, so I can enjoy the view?"

I bit my lip and nodded. How could I object to that?

Rhodes kissed my cheek and turned away. Now, I was the one with a view. His *pretty ass* was all I needed.

"Can we have french toast?"

"Is that what you and baby girl want?"

I nodded in agreement with a soft smile on my face, one he couldn't see.

I liked hearing him say, *baby girl*. Warmth bubbled and radiated from within. My heart was a little more open every moment I spent with Rhodes. As foreign as being vulnerable felt, I could get used to this as long as I knew he was the cause.

25
Rhodes

I'D OFFICIALLY FOUND my new kink, being called "good boy". Before, I meant it as a joke, but hearing her use that nickname while begging me to fuck her was *erotic*. My dick was hard again thinking about it.

I was in trouble. Deep, deep trouble. I had a taste of Theo and I knew there was no going back.

This morning, I completely lost my composure. After the kiss last night, Theo had consumed every single one of my thoughts. I'd gone to bed thinking about the way her lips felt against mine, how she tasted, and the way she'd run to me, adrenaline-fueled and eager to share every emotion.

Then, this morning happened. Seeing her in that poor excuse for a tank top and those even skimpier shorts sent my thoughts careening off the tracks like a runaway freight train. I'd told myself I could handle these urges—that I could keep my feelings in check. Hell, up until that moment, I'd done a decent job. The combination of her looking downright devastating and making such a bold move shattered my restraint.

It'd been a long time since I'd been with anyone. My hand had been my only release.

Being with Theo felt different—like a blessing I didn't realize I needed. Knowing how deeply I felt drawn to her and seeing how badly she wanted me too made giving in feel not just right, but inevitable. In that moment, there were no doubts, no hesitations. I let myself fall, fully and completely, and I didn't regret a single second of it.

Now, we lay tangled together on the couch, naked and blissfully spent after devouring an insane amount of French toast. The energy we'd burned earlier had left us ravenous, and the meal had only added to the contented haze.

My arm rested around her as she lay on her side, one leg draped over me. The blanket was wrapped snugly around us, keeping us cocooned in warmth. It was pure, unfiltered heaven.

The sun filtered through the curtains, casting a soft golden glow over her face, highlighting every delicate feature. The freckles scattered across her nose, the curve of her cheek, and those beautiful, plump lips I'd kissed not so long ago.

I couldn't help but stare, memorizing the details of her face like they were the answer to every question I ever had. Her taste still lingered; the scent of her arousal was consuming.

I rested my hand on her belly, gently tracing the curve of its swell. A peaceful silence filled the room, wrapping us in a moment that felt untouched by the outside world. It was just me and Theo.

"I've been thinking," Theo murmured, her fingers trailing lazily across my chest in a soft figure-eight. "I want to decorate a nursery for the baby. Would that be okay?"

"Of course," I replied, looking down at her as she snuggled against me. "What were you thinking?"

"I thought maybe we could paint the walls? But I understand if you don't want to, it is your house, after all."

"Theo, this is your home too," I said firmly, brushing a stray strand of hair from her face.

She hesitated, her gaze flicking away. "I'm only staying here. I'm a guest."

"Cut that out," I replied gently but still firm. "You're not a guest. You're here as much as I am. If anything, you've made this place feel like a home."

Since moving in, Theo has filled the void of what I didn't realize was missing. She made me laugh, cared to listen about my day, and often made dinner so when I came home tired, I didn't have to be hungry. With her here my life was infinitely better, and the idea that she thought of herself as temporary stung.

"Rhodes, it's true. You were kind enough to open your house to—"

Before she could finish, a firm thump beneath my hand startled me. My eyes shot to hers. "Did she just…?"

Theo's face lit up, her head lifting to meet mine. "Yes, she did," she giggled. "She must like you."

A strange, unexpected pressure gripped my chest. My hand stilled, but I didn't move away.

"Keep your hand there," she urged, her voice soft and coaxing. "She'll do it again. Say something."

"I don't even know what to say," I admitted, the words catching in my throat.

The baby kicked again, this time with more force. It was incredible, this little life making itself known so distinctly.

Theo laughed, her joy bubbling over. "Looks like that was enough."

"Can she... hear me? Does she know who I am?" I asked, the question almost whispered.

"Maybe. Babies can start picking up on familiar voices even now. That's why some people play music for them or talk to them, they recognize it when they're born."

The idea that she might already know me, even in the smallest way, made my heart twist. I wanted to keep my hand there forever, to feel her move again.

I leaned down and kissed the top of Theo's head, letting my lips linger as I searched for the right words. She moved her hand from my chest to rest it over mine, silently telling me she wanted me to stay.

"Will she move like that a lot?" I asked after a beat.

"Yeah, but she usually gets more active when she hears something she recognizes."

"Hmm."

"Does it... weird you out?" she asked tentatively, her voice laced with uncertainty.

"What? That she moves and you can feel it?"

"That, and... me being pregnant. And us—" she hesitated, the words faltering. "You know, being together like this. I know the situation isn't exactly ideal."

"God, no. Not at all. It's beautiful," I said, my voice resolute.

Her cheeks flushed a soft pink, and the smile that followed was breathtaking, like a bright star lighting up the night sky. I wanted to remember it forever, to hold onto it for the times when life felt dark.

"Do you have a name picked out?" I asked, eager to learn more about the little one growing inside her.

"I do," she said with a mischievous glint, "it's a secret. Not even my mom knows."

I respected that, even if the curiosity burned in the back of my mind. I felt weird referring to her as, "the baby," because she was more than that but in time, that would change.

"Why don't we plan to work on the nursery next weekend?" I suggested, brushing a strand of hair from her face. "After your appointment this week, maybe I can come with you, and we can pick up what you need?"

Her expression shifted, the light dimming as she cleared her throat. "Oh, no. I can go by myself. Don't worry about the appointment. I'll grab a few things tomorrow."

Her words stung more than I wanted to admit. I'd overstepped, pushed too far. Embarrassment tightened my throat and I forced a smile. "Okay," I said softly.

Before the moment could settle into awkwardness, I tilted her chin gently with my fingers, drawing her attention back to me. Her hazel eyes met mine, and for a second, everything else faded away.

"Wait, stay like that!" she exclaimed, sitting up and scrambling to climb over me, her excitement infectious.

She waddled down the hallway as fast as she could while still naked. I laughed to myself and shook my head; she was something else.

Theo disappeared for a few moments before returning with a camera around her neck. Grinning at me, she approached with her face in the viewfinder.

"You looked handsome. I need to capture the moment."

"Oh no, I look crazy." My hair was a mess, *and* I was naked.

"It's for my eyes only! Please," she begged, dragging out the last word.

Saying no to her was impossible.

"Your eyes *only*," I repeated and pointed a finger at her.

"Cross my heart."

I placed one arm above my head, making sure to flex my bicep a little, and held my smile. The blanket was lying right below my pecs, revealing a sliver of my abs.

Theo came closer, pulling the blanket down to lay barely above the base of my cock.

"Seriously?" I laughed and shook my head.

"Oh, please. You know you look good. Remember, my eyes only, " she said in a suggestive tone, which made me wonder what she would be doing with these.

I posed a few more times, going with the flow as she snapped away, cheering me on.

"Yes, that's perfect!"

I moved again.

"The lighting is amazing."

Click of the camera.

"Give me a smolder."

I obeyed the best I could because what the hell was a *smolder*?

Theo smirked, a devilish grin, as she came close and straddled my hips. Her free hand rested on my stomach, dancing incredibly close to the edge of the blanket that was barely covering my manhood.

She held the camera in the air, hovering over our bodies as she snapped another picture. Looking at the screen, she laughed.

"Now, that's hot."

She spun it for me to see, and she was right; hot didn't do it justice. In the photo, you could see Theo's bare legs around my waist, revealing just enough to be suggestive. My abs were defined, and her hand was clearly reaching for *something*.

I reached out, taking the camera from her.

"My turn."

"No way!" She protested, putting up her arms to block her face. I took the picture anyway; her breasts were on full display.

"This one is for *my* eyes only." I grinned. "Now, smile."

Theo rolled her eyes and obeyed, cheesy as ever. Her hand covered her breasts, making the photo less revealing. I was going to frame every picture I took, maybe make my own special photo album.

I angled the camera down, snapping a photo of her covered breasts and her pregnant belly. Twisting the camera back to her, she leaned in and smiled.

"That's a good one."

"They're all good ones."

26

Theo

28 weeks pregnant
Baby is the size of lettuce

GETTING in and out of this damn car was harder by the day. It was so low to the ground that I practically had to plop into the seat, sacrificing grace and dignity in the process.

I timed my errands carefully. Rhodes usually got home at a predictable hour, give or take some ranch-related delays, so I could count on him to help me out if needed. Waiting a few extra minutes for him was better than attempting another traumatic solo exit from the car.

Today's plan was simple: run to the store, grab paint and supplies for the baby's nursery, and get back for Rhodes. Ideally, we'd pull into the driveway at the same time, and he'd swoop in to help me out.

Time was ticking. Each passing day brought me closer to my due date—early January—and it was already November. With the holidays approaching, time always seemed to speed up, even if I didn't have much family to celebrate with.

I'd envisioned the perfect nursery, my Pinterest board finally coming to life. Neutrals, darker tones, and a vibe that screamed "kick-ass" rather than "cutesy." Longhorns, cow print, and tasteful patterns were all part of the plan. Still, I had to temper my enthusiasm—this was temporary. I'd save the grand ideas for when I had a place of my own. For now, a little paint and maybe a rug would do.

POP!

The sound jolted me, and I clenched the wheel, my eyes squeezing shut in reflex. Was I hit? Did I hit something?

The car sputtered, its speedometer slowly ticking downward as it lost power.

"Shit, shit, shit!" I cursed, yanking the wheel to steer toward safety. The car coasted to a stop, its tires landing half on the shoulder and half on someone's front lawn. Oops.

With a final gasp, the engine died. The dashboard went dark, and the wheels refused to budge.

What do I do now?

My first thought was Gus—he was the only one I trusted with Betsy. Digging through my purse, I found my phone and dialed his shop. The line rang endlessly before a voicemail finally picked up.

"Thanks for calling *The Rolling Wrench*. We'll be closed for vacation and return next week. Please leave your name and number, and we'll get back to you shortly. Keep rolling."

Gus's monotone delivery didn't do justice to the

upbeat tagline, which was clearly the work of his teenage daughter, Indie.

Groaning, I leaned back against the headrest, weighing my options. The list was short. Too short. I only had one other person I could call.

Swallowing my pride, I dialed the number. As the phone rang, unease crept in. What if the car was beyond repair? This wasn't any car—it had been my dad's. Losing it would mean losing one of the last pieces I had of him.

"Hello?" Rhodes's chipper voice broke through my spiraling thoughts.

"I'm stuck," I groaned.

"Stuck like you can't get off the couch? Or stuck on the floor because you dropped the remote and thought you could grab it yourself?"

"No, smartass. Stuck on the side of the road because my car broke down."

"Oh, shit." His tone shifted. "Where are you?"

"Just outside town. I tried Gus, he's on vacation. I can't sit here until next week—I'll die."

Rhodes chuckled. "So dramatic."

"You like it, though. Otherwise, you wouldn't be so nice to me."

"True," he admitted. "I'll come to your rescue, but I'll need to bring a friend."

"I can't believe this is happening."

"It's okay, Honey. We'll take care of it."

I sighed, a mix of relief and anxiety washing over me. I knew he'd help, but the thought of losing the car still weighed heavily.

"Let me grab Boone, and I'll head your way. Text me your location."

While I waited, I rested my forehead against the steering wheel, letting my thoughts wander—probably not my best idea. I thought about Rhodes, the sex, the car, and the future. Everything felt interconnected, tangled together by a fragile thread.

We hadn't addressed the sex since it happened, which, in hindsight, was either very mature or incredibly childish. We'd carried on as if nothing had changed, but I knew deep down that it had.

Being with Rhodes wasn't only physical. It felt deeper, more meaningful. When he looked at me, I felt seen. When he listened, I felt heard. And now, as he rushed to help me, I felt cared for.

That scared me. I was good at compartmentalizing sex and intimacy. To me, they were two entirely separate things. But being cared for? That set my heart on fire and left me teetering on the edge of an emotional cliff.

The rumble of a truck pulling up snapped me out of my thoughts. A flatbed trailer attached, it backed carefully toward the front of my car. Boone hopped out of the driver's seat, and Rhodes emerged from the passenger side.

I swung my legs out of the car and waited as Rhodes approached. Boone had already popped the hood and was inspecting the engine, smoke curling out in thin wisps.

"How are you holding up?" Rhodes asked, hands on his hips, head tilted.

"I'm fine."

He raised an eyebrow, clearly not buying it. Maybe the tear stains on my cheeks gave me away.

Huffing, I rolled my eyes. "I'm afraid the car can't be fixed. I don't think I can handle that."

He nodded, a sad smile tugging at his lips as he extended his hand. I placed my fingers in his palm, and he squeezed gently, pulling me out of the metaphorical hole I was stuck in.

When I stood, he wrapped his arms around me, pressing my face against his chest.

"We'll get it fixed," he promised.

I hoped he understood the weight of that vow. This wasn't only about a car—it was about the memories tied to it.

"We'll have to tow it back to your house," Boone said, walking over to us and wiping his greasy hands on his jeans.

"Thanks for coming to help, Boone." I offered him a small smile, which he returned with a nod.

"You got it—whatever you need," he said, pulling me into a quick side hug. "We'll get her up and running."

Boone and Rhodes had dropped everything to come to my rescue. They didn't treat it like an inconvenience or burden; instead, they brought comfort and calm, assuring me it would all be okay.

The people I'd grown close to here in Faircloud weren't part of the insecure, disconnected past I'd left behind. These friendships were genuine, transformative. I'd found family here—a support system beyond my mom.

If I thought too much about how incredible they were, I'd start crying again.

"Maybe we should take it to Gus's shop?" I suggested, hesitant.

"He's out of town," Rhodes reminded me. "The car would sit outside until he got back—and who knows when he'd have time to fix it?"

"Gus has always worked on this car. I trust him."

"I get that," Boone said, stepping in. "But I really think it's better off at Rhodes' place for now. When the shop opens, I'll bring the trailer back, and we can take it there if we need to."

I glanced between the two of them. I wanted to trust their judgment, but my stomach twisted in knots.

"We're going to load her up, okay? Do you trust me?" Rhodes asked, his voice soft and reassuring.

I nodded reluctantly.

"Let's get you into the truck," he said. "Do you want the front or the back seat?"

"The back," I mumbled.

Rhodes guided me to Boone's truck and opened the door, helping me climb in. I sat with a heavy weight in my chest. Guilt gnawed at me—had I neglected something with the car? Had I forgotten to check the oil? That wasn't like me. I prided myself on being responsible, but now I felt the sting of doubt.

Outside, Boone and Rhodes worked efficiently, loading Betsy onto the trailer and securing her in place. It probably only took twenty minutes, but my anxious thoughts made it feel like an eternity.

The drive back home was silent. I stayed in the back seat, lost in my spiraling emotions. Once we arrived, Boone helped me down from the truck.

Without a word, I walked inside and plopped onto the couch.

There was more to how I was feeling, a deeper ache.

I missed my dad.

Since finding out I was pregnant, I hadn't let myself dwell on his absence. But now, it hit me like a ton of bricks. The grief was overwhelming, an ache so deep it felt like I'd run straight into a wall.

My body sank into the couch as the tears came.

There was no stopping them. The dam broke, and the flood poured out in relentless waves.

I missed him so much.

He should be here. He was supposed to be here—to see me through this, to share in the joy and challenges.

Grief is a complex thing. It's an emptiness, a void that refuses to be filled. It's heavy, persistent, always lingering in the background no matter how hard you try to move forward. And in moments like these, when life changes in monumental ways, it becomes unbearable.

The sound of the front door opening barely registered through my sobs. Boots thudded softly on the floor until they stopped beside me.

"Theo, Honey," Rhodes said gently, sitting down next to me.

He wrapped an arm around my shoulders, tucking me into his side. In that moment, his presence was grounding, a refuge in the chaos of my emotions.

"I miss him," I choked out.

"I know," Rhodes said, his hand moving in slow, comforting circles on my back.

"He should be here. I needed him. I still need him."

"Let it out," he murmured.

And I did. Gasping, sobbing, the words spilling out between broken breaths. The world blurred into the background, but Rhodes stayed steady, his warmth and care surrounding me.

"He would've loved being a grandfather," I managed through the tears. "That's what hurts the most. I keep picturing what his face would look like when he'd see her for the first time—the light in his eyes. She'd probably have a dozen Oklahoma State onesies and ridiculous Pistol Pete hats."

Rhodes chuckled softly, the sound vibrating through his chest.

"Tell me more about him," he encouraged, his voice low and steady. "What was his name?"

I smiled faintly, even through the tears. "Frank. He always hated his name." I chucked at the thought. "He was the best dad a girl could ask for."

I closed my eyes and let the memories flow—riding bikes in the neighborhood at night, late grocery runs for ice cream, the way he made everything feel okay. He was my first protector, the first man to show me my worth.

"What was your favorite thing about him?" Rhodes asked, his hand brushing gently over my hair.

"When I was ten, I would've said his version of the chicken dance," I said with a watery laugh.

The memory played in my mind, his arms flailing wildly in the most ridiculous, endearing way.

"But now? It's how he made me feel. He was home. Nothing else has ever compared to that."

Rhodes didn't say much, letting the silence settle

around us. He was a quiet anchor in the storm, grounding me without judgment.

"Why don't you head to bed? I'll bring you something to eat," he offered, placing a soft kiss on my head.

"I'd like that," I said, untangling myself from his embrace.

"And maybe later, you can tell me more about him. Show me pictures too, if you're up to it."

I nodded. It had been too long since I'd let myself look at the photos, the memories too painful to face. However, I was ready to stop avoiding them.

It was time to honor my feelings, to allow myself grace. That was a promise I intended to keep.

27
Theo

AGE 9

I HATE SCHOOL. *I hate school. I HATE school.*

I wasn't going back, no matter what Mom or Dad said. They could send me to work instead—like, real work. I could babysit Mrs. Schwartz's dog, bag groceries at the store, or maybe even help out at the diner. Anything would be better than stepping foot in that place ever again.

This morning, I was excited. I wore my new sneakers—pink and teal, the coolest shoes I'd ever had. They matched my backpack perfectly! I even spent some of my birthday money on them because I thought they were that amazing.

The girls at school didn't think so. They made fun of them, whispering behind their hands and giggling like they always do. Usually, I ignore it, but today? Today, it got to me. The mean words, the whispers, the looks.

I yelled back at them, saying the same kinds of mean things they'd been saying about me. But, of course, the teacher didn't see them being mean. She only saw me yelling, so I got in trouble. I had to sit inside for the rest of recess while they stayed out and played jump rope like nothing happened.

Now, I was sitting on the bus, holding back tears the whole ride home. My backpack sat on my lap, and I stared out the window, biting my lip so hard it hurt. When we got close to my stop, I couldn't hold it in anymore. The tears spilled out, drop after drop, and all I wanted was to be home.

The brakes squealed, and the bus stopped. I didn't even wait. I jumped up, wiped my nose with my sleeve, and ran off. My new sneakers hit the sidewalk, but I didn't care anymore if they got dirty.

When I got to the house, I threw my backpack on the floor, bolted upstairs, and slammed my bedroom door behind me. I collapsed onto my bed, curling up into a ball as the tears kept coming.

Why couldn't I just be normal? Why couldn't they like me? I just wanted to fit in, to have friends, to not feel like this all the time.

There was a soft knock on my door.

"Theodora? It's me."

It was Dad. His voice was quiet, almost like he didn't want to scare me. "Everything okay?"

"I'm fine!" I shouted, even though I wasn't. I didn't want to talk about it. "I'm just doing homework. I have a lot!"

The doorknob turned, and he came in anyway. He stood there for a second, looking at me as I played with the little string hanging off my bedspread.

"There's no way that string is that interesting," he said, trying to make me laugh.

I didn't laugh. I didn't even look at him.

He sat down on the edge of my bed, close but not too close.

"Princess," he said softly.

That did it. The second he called me that, I lost it. I started sobbing, my shoulders shaking so hard I couldn't even sit up straight.

Dad pulled me into his arms, holding me tight. I buried my face in his shirt, and even though it smelled like work—sweat and sawdust—I didn't care. It was comforting.

"Why are they so mean to me, Daddy?" I hiccuped through my tears.

"I don't know, Princess," he said, stroking my hair.

"They said my shoes were ugly. And my clothes were old. And then I yelled, and I got in trouble, and they didn't!"

"Let it out," he whispered. "If you keep it all inside, it'll just make you stinky."

That made me giggle, even though I was crying. He always said that, how bottled-up feelings make you rotten. No one likes someone rotten, he'd say.

"It's okay to feel mad and sad," Dad said. "You're allowed to feel hurt when someone is mean to you. And it's okay to be angry when things feel unfair. You're not wrong for feeling that way."

I nodded, sniffling against his shirt. The tears were slowing down now, but I didn't let go of him.

He didn't let go of me, either. He just held me, letting me cry until I couldn't anymore.

When the tears were gone, we sat there on my bed. He started telling me about his day, about some silly thing that happened at work. I listened, my head resting on his chest, his voice soothing me like it always did.

I don't know what I'd do without him.

28
Theo

SLEEP HIT me like a bat cracking against a hundred-mile-an-hour fastball. When I say I was down for the count, I mean there was no waking me.

Rhodes, ever the gentleman, brought me grilled cheese and tomato soup in bed. I devoured the meal, then spent the rest of the night alone—my request. He had offered to stay and keep me company, but I politely declined. As much as I was opening up to sharing, my need for alone time ran deep. I was a loner at heart, recharging best in solitude.

I loved my friends, but my true peace often came in the quiet company of myself.

Rhodes understood and left me to indulge in an unhealthy amount of reality TV without so much as a raised eyebrow. Before heading to bed, he popped his head in to check on me, catching me mid-battle with a fistful of Oreos. No judgment, just a simple smile and a soft goodnight.

However, this morning, the house was eerily quiet.

I woke up to find Rhodes nowhere in sight. It was strange. He had the day off, and I half-expected to see him in his usual spot in the kitchen, leaning against the counter with a cup of coffee in hand.

Stretching my arms above my head, I rolled my neck and shuffled toward the front door. I grabbed my flannel jacket, deciding to check outside.

The November air was crisp, biting against my skin as I stepped out. My slippers scraped against the concrete as I waddled toward the driveway, where the boys had left my car after towing it home yesterday.

In the meantime, I'd left a voicemail at Gus's shop, detailing the problem and asking him to call me back. I was anxious to get Betsy in for a tune-up sooner rather than later.

As I approached the car, something caught my attention—the hood was still up.

Did they leave it open all night?

I took a few more steps, and that's when my heart stopped.

Rhodes was bent over in the driver's seat, tinkering with something.

My vision blurred, and my feet rooted themselves to the ground.

Panic surged through me, sharp and overwhelming.

"What... what are you doing?" I blurted, my voice shaky, not directed at anyone in particular.

Rhodes stood up, wiping his hands on a towel before flinging it over his shoulder. He chuckled. "Good morning to you, too."

I repeated myself, this time more firmly. "What are you doing?"

He hesitated, sensing my unease. "I thought I'd take a look under the hood, see if it was something I could fix."

Rhodes stood in front of me, wearing his flannel jacket, backward hat, and jeans tucked into boots. There was a smudge of dirt on his cheek, as if he'd rubbed his face in frustration.

"Why?" I asked, tilting my head, my voice sharp.

"I was researching last night and thought—"

"No one touches this car but Gus," I interrupted, my voice rising. "I wanted to bring it to his shop. I asked you to tow it there, but you insisted on bringing it here."

"Theo, it's okay," Rhodes said, stepping toward me cautiously.

"It isn't okay!" I snapped. "What if you didn't fix it? What if you made it worse? I need this car, Rhodes!"

His expression softened and I still couldn't meet his eyes anymore. My gaze darted to the car, and the panic settled deeper into my bones.

"You know how much this car means to me. Yet you went against my wishes."

This car wasn't just metal and bolts. It was my dad's legacy, our project, something meant to be *ours* until the end. Trusting one other person to work on it had been hard enough.

Rhodes placed his hands gently on my arms. The moment his touch reached me, my eyes closed, and I drew in a shaky breath.

"First," he said softly, "I need you to take a deep breath and count to five."

I obeyed, inhaling deeply, holding the breath, and exhaling slowly on his count.

"Second," he continued, his voice calm and steady, "Gus isn't going to be back in time for your appointment. He's out until next week. I wanted to see if I could fix it so you wouldn't have to wait."

When he put it like that...

"I think I know what the problem is," Rhodes added, "but it's not safe to drive right now. I'll take you wherever you need to go, and I'll make sure she's running by the end of the week."

His tone was gentle yet firm, leaving no room for doubt.

The tension in my shoulders eased, and I could finally see past my panic.

"Okay," I whispered, the word a mantra to ground myself. "Okay."

"We'll go to your appointment today. Whatever happens, we'll deal with it, and then we can swing by the store to pick up a few things for the nursery. How does that sound?"

Rhodes's hands lingered on my arms, steady and reassuring, waiting to make sure I was okay before letting go.

"That sounds good," I replied, nodding more than necessary, my throat tight as I swallowed hard.

He gently turned me toward the house, his hand guiding me from the small of my back.

"We've got time to eat before we leave. What can I make?"

I took a deep breath, counted to five, and exhaled—just as Rhodes had coached me earlier. It helped, though I was still wound tighter than a spring.

"I can't eat until after my appointment," I said, my stomach growling in protest. I had to fast beforehand, but his mention of food made the hunger kick in full force.

"Well, then you've got all day to decide what you want."

Rhodes pulled me closer, tucking me under his arm as we climbed the porch steps.

I felt a pang of guilt for how I'd reacted. Seeing Rhodes working on the car had sent me spiraling into fight-or-flight mode, and I chose to fight. The loss of control, the panic—it was unlike me, but it had overwhelmed me in the moment.

It wasn't until I was buckled into the passenger seat of Rhodes' truck that I realized we were heading to my baby's appointment *together*. Strangely, the thought didn't unsettle me as much as I'd expected.

My leg bounced uncontrollably as we sat in the waiting room. The same faded wallpaper and faint antiseptic smell filled the space, triggering memories. This was the first time I'd come to an appointment with someone, and it left me feeling a bit off-kilter.

I'd choked down the sugary drink they made you take nearly an hour ago, and I was ready to be done with this. I was proud of myself for getting my blood drawn earlier all alone, but my nerves ramped up the longer we waited, more of an opportunity for people to see us here.

I'd made Rhodes stay behind when I checked in. The

last thing I needed was the receptionist getting the wrong idea and turning future visits into awkward encounters.

"I feel like I'm having déjà vu," Rhodes whispered in my ear. "Pretty sure this place looked exactly the same when I was a kid."

"The wallpaper hasn't changed?" I asked, arching a brow.

"Nope. Neither has that weird clown picture over there." He nodded toward a particularly unsettling photo on the wall.

A laugh escaped me, easing the tension in my chest.

An older woman seated in front of us turned, her gaze piercing. When I finally met her eyes, she smiled warmly and closed her magazine.

"Aren't you two just adorable?" she gushed. "I wish my daughter had someone to go with her. I've had to be there every step of the way."

Ouch.

"Thank you," Rhodes replied smoothly, placing a hand on my thigh. "We're just so excited to welcome our little girl into the world."

Play along, Theo. It's all pretend.

"Oh, yes!" I chimed in, probably too enthusiastically. "We can't wait." My hand rested instinctively on my belly, and a pang of longing surged through me.

"When are you due?" the woman asked.

"January 18th," I said with a soft smile.

"I hope you two make beautiful memories together. I'll keep your baby girl in my prayers."

Outward affection from strangers made me uncomfortable, so I nodded politely and redirected my attention to the TV in the corner. Judge Judy blared, and I feigned intense interest.

Rhodes chuckled beside me, his hand remaining on my thigh long after the interaction ended.

"Theo Matthews," a nurse called from the doorway. I stood, and Rhodes's hand slipped away.

"I'll be right here," he assured me with a soft smile, his eyes crinkling slightly at the corners. His fingers brushed mine briefly, sending a jolt through me.

"Would you... want to come?" I asked quietly, leaning closer to keep the older woman from overhearing.

Rhodes studied my expression, his brow furrowing slightly. After a moment, he nodded and stood, falling into step beside me.

Why I'd asked him to come back was beyond me. Maybe I just didn't want to be alone for once.

I reached for his hand, and after a brief hesitation, he intertwined his fingers with mine. Together, we walked down the hallway to the exam room.

Once inside, I perched on the examination table, my feet dangling nervously over the edge.

The nurse returned to take more blood. My stomach churned at the thought. They'd already done this once, and the idea of repeating it multiple times made my skin crawl.

"Here we go, Ms. Matthews," the nurse said kindly. She looked young, fresh out of school, with a sweetness in her tone that eased some of my dread.

I extended my arm but turned my head away, focusing on Rhodes. He held out his hand, and I reached for it gratefully.

His thumb traced soothing circles over my knuckles, grounding me as I braced for the needle.

That small, tender gesture released a breath I hadn't realized I was holding. For the first time in a long while, I felt like I wasn't facing this alone.

29
Rhodes

AFTER THE AMOUNT of blood Theo had drawn, you'd think she'd be wiped out for the day. But when it came to shopping, she somehow found a second wind.

This morning, I'd seen her at her most vulnerable—upset, angry, and detached. The heartbreak in her eyes was palpable, and all I wanted was to put a smile back on her face.

Taking a look at her car had made sense to me. Why wait for Gus to come back, only to have him sit on it for who knows how long? I had enough knowledge from tinkering with ranch vehicles alongside Boone to make an educated guess. Once I had the part, I could fix it today without Gus' help.

Theo didn't realize it yet, but she'd have to accept my help, whether she liked it or not.

Now, I followed her through aisle after aisle as she navigated the store. We'd come for paint, but the cart was steadily filling with other items.

Theo stood in front of the wall of paint swatches, her hand resting on her belly. The array of colors before her looked like a rainbow, each hue blending into the next.

Earlier, while we waited in the exam room at the doctor's office, she'd shown me her Pinterest board for the nursery. She wanted neutrals, a dark accent wall, and Western-inspired decor. She'd mentioned she didn't want to go overboard since living with me wasn't "permanent."

I wasn't thinking of temporary solutions. My goal was to give her exactly what she envisioned because who knew what the future might hold?

"What about this one?" I asked, stepping away from the cart to tap on a light brown swatch that reminded me of milky hot chocolate. It was moody yet beautiful—just like her.

Theo grabbed the swatch, adding it to the growing pile in her hand. She looked like she was hoarding rare Pokémon cards, ready to trade at any moment. The colorful cards fanned out in her palm, each one carefully selected.

"That pairs really well with the accent color," she said, pointing to a soft emerald green.

Sure. What did I know?

She reached into the cart and pulled out a blanket she'd found on a random shelf. Holding it up to compare the two colors, she nodded to herself, her bottom lip caught between her teeth in thought.

That small, familiar motion set my blood humming. My mind betrayed me, flashing back to the morning when she'd bitten her lip just like that—naked and aching beneath me. Heat surged through my body, and I shifted uncomfortably, desperate to redirect my thoughts.

Theo had become the best part of my life. She fit so effortlessly into my home and my routine that I hardly remembered what it was like before she was here. Free time was now spent with her, whether watching TV, playing Scrabble, or just talking.

Thursday nights used to be solo grocery runs after work. Now, I swung by the house to pick her up first. Dinner had gone from frozen pizza to shared meals, more work but worth every second.

Theo wasn't just a part of my life—she completed it in ways I hadn't even realized were missing. She accepted me for who I was, never asking me to change.

I loved that about her.

Loved.

"What do you think?" Theo's voice broke through my thoughts. Her hazel eyes were locked on mine, and she laughed softly, shaking her head.

"I think the baby, who shall remain unnamed, will love it," I teased, trying to recover from my wandering thoughts.

"Oh, come on," she groaned, turning to face me.

We were close now, nearly chest to chest—if it weren't for the bump—in the middle of the aisle. Her eyes widened slightly, and her smile faded as the air between us shifted.

I couldn't look away. The apples of her cheeks, the freckles scattered across the bridge of her nose, and the warm intensity of her gaze had me rooted in place.

Something came over me—maybe it was all the baby stuff, or the way she'd slowly let her walls down for me. Maybe it was the memory of her coming undone in my arms or the quiet intimacy we'd built over time.

I lifted my hand, cupping the side of her face, my fingers brushing behind her ear. Without hesitation, Theo tilted her head up, her lips just inches from mine.

"Whatever you want, Honey. I'm happy with it," I murmured.

Was this a mistake? The last time we'd been this close, it was her choice—driven by desire. This time, it was mine—driven by something much deeper.

"Can I kiss you?" I asked, my voice barely above a whisper.

Theo hesitated for a moment, then licked her lips and nodded.

I leaned in, pressing my lips to hers in a gentle kiss. Theo kissed me back, and we both closed our eyes, savoring the moment. Her soft, pouty lips moved against mine in a controlled rhythm—not frantic or needy like the other day, but slow and tender.

Here I was, standing in the middle of a store, kissing Theo. The world around us faded away. All it had taken was one look, and every hesitation disappeared, replaced by the simple need to follow through on what I'd been craving since that first taste.

Theo's hands slid lazily around my waist, pulling me closer. I could've stayed like that forever, her warmth grounding me, her lips sending sparks through my veins. Time seemed to stand still, and I clung to the pure bliss of the moment.

As much as I wanted to keep going, I knew I couldn't. If I did, I might not be able to stop.

Reluctantly, I pulled back, letting my hand linger on her cheek, my thumb brushing her skin in a soft, reassuring gesture.

"What was that for?" Theo asked, tilting her head, her hazel eyes searching mine.

"I don't know," I admitted honestly. The moment had taken over, and I'd simply acted.

Theo smiled, rising onto her tiptoes to plant another quick, lazy kiss on my lips. It was sweet and fleeting, but it left me wanting more.

"What was *that* one for?" I teased, a grin tugging at my mouth.

"I don't know," she replied, her smile widening as she took a small step back.

I could get used to this, get used to Theo kissing me simply because she wanted to.

After leaving the first store, we stopped at another, this one filled with decorative items. Trinkets and random nonsense covered the shelves, but Theo seemed completely in her element. She picked up objects, studied them briefly, then set them back down. I followed quietly as she searched for the pieces to bring her vision to life.

"Okay, which one?" Theo asked, spinning around with a teddy bear in each hand.

In her right hand was a dark brown bear with a cute red bowtie. In her left was a lighter brown bear, less fuzzy, with bright blue eyes and a soft pink bowtie.

I studied both, genuinely trying to picture them in the nursery.

"That one," I said, pointing to the light brown bear.

"That was my favorite!" Theo said, tossing it toward the cart. She must've put a little too much enthusiasm behind the throw because the bear came flying straight for my face.

Quickly, I reached out and caught it just before it hit me, laughing as I dropped it into the cart. "Careful, you've got quite an arm."

Theo lifted her arm and flexed dramatically. "I know you want a ticket." She kissed her bicep with a playful smirk.

Laughing, I shook my head. "Only if it's front row."

"Front row and VIP, baby," she shot back, winking before turning to continue down the aisle.

"What else is on your list?" I asked, leaning on the cart's handle as I pushed it.

"I want some floating shelves for her books, but I don't know where they are."

We wandered through the aisles, Theo adding far more to the cart than just shelves. Clothes, blankets, pillows—even a rug somehow found their way in. By the time we grabbed the shelves, the cart was so full it was becoming a chore to push.

Theo finally stopped and stretched, hands on her hips, arching her back like she'd just finished a marathon.

"I'm beat!" she declared, doubling over dramatically.

"Oh, wait—I forgot to grab—"

"No way!" Theo cut me off, raising a finger to silence me. "You forgot nothing. My ankles can't take another step. You might actually have to carry me to the car."

I'd do it, too.

I laughed, raising an eyebrow.

Her lips twitched in amusement, but she shook her head, scoffing as she realized I was joking. "Bastard."

A ding caught my attention, and I noticed a red six flashing on a register.

The items in the cart were on the surface, scanned in, and placed into our bags. When the man behind the counter said our total, I pulled out my wallet and inserted my credit card before Theo could protest.

"Rhodes," her voice was low and testing as she turned to glare at me.

"Theo," I replied, feigning nonchalance while typing in my pin.

The cashier stayed oblivious to the silent war raging between us. Theo's narrowed eyes burned into me, but I kept my expression calm and casual.

When the receipt was handed over, I grabbed the bags and headed for the truck, still ignoring the daggers she was throwing my way.

We walked in silence. I loaded the bags into the back and helped her into the passenger seat without saying a word.

Once we were on the road, she finally let loose.

"I don't need your money."

"I know."

"I don't need your pity."

"I know."

"I can do it on my own."

"I know."

Theo let out an exasperated groan, throwing her head back against the seat.

"Then why do you insist on helping me? Doing things for me without asking?"

I glanced at her, my voice steady. "Is it really that hard to see, Honey?"

30
Theo

I WAS FALLING for Rhodes Dunn, and there wasn't a damn thing I could do about it. I was gone—long, *long* gone—for those green eyes and that big, unyielding heart.

The kiss in the store had been playing on a loop in my mind. It had caught me completely off guard; when I turned around and found him so close, I'd been stunned. But I didn't mind. Truthfully, I'd been waiting for that moment. Every night when he came home from work, telling me about his day, I fought the urge to wrap my arms around him and melt into his warmth.

I was starting to love the little world we'd built together. It wasn't flashy or complicated—just Rhodes and me, existing in an easy kind of bliss. He'd come home, I'd have dinner ready, and we'd spend the evening enjoying each other's company. I had to admit, my cooking skills had come a long way. On his days off, I'd watch him work magic in the kitchen, always eager to learn his tricks.

There was no external noise, no chaos. Just us, savoring the quiet joy of our own little bubble.

If I was being honest, the intensity of it all scared me sometimes. I'd never imagined this kind of life for myself. I was supposed to be a free bird, untethered, flying wherever the wind took me. Settling down was never part of the plan. Yet here I was—happy. Happier than I'd been in years. And falling hard for Rhodes.

I avoided thinking about the future, about the inevitable end to this arrangement. Moving out after the baby was born wasn't something I wanted to dwell on. Rhodes never brought it up, and I wasn't going to either. For weeks now, I'd felt myself falling for him, and honestly, how could anyone not?

I thought about Jess sometimes—about how she'd left him. It gutted me to know how deeply it had hurt him, that the kind, steady man I knew now had once been so broken. Every now and then, a nagging doubt crept in, making me wonder if there was something I didn't know about him, some piece of the puzzle I was missing. I trusted my instincts. I trusted who Rhodes was.

Was it foolish, getting this attached when I was about to bring a baby into the picture? Maybe. However, the way Rhodes cared for me told me everything I needed to know. He would care for my daughter the same way—with unwavering devotion.

I needed to talk this out, to sort through my feelings with someone who'd listen, maybe two someones.

Since Halloween, Aspen and Penny had been checking in more often, which I was grateful for. Today, they'd suggested a spa day—pedicures, mimosas for them, and sparkling grape juice for me.

It felt good to get out of the house, to clear my head

and process what I was feeling. Processing wasn't something I was used to doing, it was becoming part of this new chapter in my life. Not only was I learning to embrace someone else's presence without running, but I was also allowing myself to feel. And, more importantly, to accept those feelings.

The emotions came in waves. Sometimes anger, sometimes sadness, but also moments of pure happiness. And through it all, Rhodes was there. He always seemed to know exactly what I needed.

If I cried, he'd wrap me in a hug and press a kiss to the top of my head. If I was angry, he'd listen patiently while I vented—whether I was railing about a real problem or something trivial, like pumpkin spice only being available once a year. When that anger dissolved into sadness, he'd be right there, holding me again.

After receiving the results from my doctor's appointment and finding out the glucose test came back normal, I'd thrown myself into his arms. He handled the happiness, too.

"The warm water is heavenly," Penny sighed, leaning back in her chair.

"I second that," Aspen agreed, lazily swishing her feet in the basin.

I smiled, clicking the buttons on my chair to activate the back massager. These chairs were the best part of pedicures, hands down.

"I couldn't tell you the last time I had a pedicure," I said, turning my head to look at the girls. "Probably Italy. Or maybe France?"

"Ugh, I bet that was amazing," Penny sighed wistfully.

"I'd *love* to go to France someday. It's on my 'must-travel-before-I-die' bucket list."

"We could go sometime," I suggested, smiling at them. "A girl's trip—I could show you two around."

"Yes!" Aspen gasped, clapping her hands in excitement.

"I'm going to start planning. This will be my entire personality for the foreseeable future," Penny declared. She was a planner to her core, always down to the smallest detail. Thank God for her because I was the opposite.

"Well, it'll have to wait until after the baby comes," I said, running a hand along my bump.

"She's going to be here so soon!" Penny cheered, sipping her mimosa.

"I know! I can't believe it."

Time was ticking. Thanksgiving was just over a week away, which meant I was closing in on thirty weeks of pregnancy. Thinking back on everything that had happened since I returned to Faircloud—it was overwhelming.

Thirty weeks. Seven months. Two hundred and ten days.

"How's it going, living with Rhodes?" Aspen asked, leaning forward slightly.

Luckily, the women doing our nails were occupied with manicures, leaving us free to chat without prying ears.

"Really good," I admitted honestly, feeling the perfect segue to confide in my friends. "We get along well."

I looked down at my nails, absently picking at my cuticles.

Aspen cleared her throat, drawing my attention back. She could always tell when I had more to say.

"You slept with him, didn't you?" she asked, her voice laced with curiosity.

I nodded, unable to hold back the laugh that bubbled up. I had *proof*, too. Reaching into my purse, I pulled out my phone and opened my photo gallery. These pictures were supposed to be for my eyes only, but Aspen and Penny didn't count.

I handed my phone to Penny, the first photo pulled up. "Here's your proof."

Penny grabbed the phone, and Aspen leaned so far over I thought she might fall out of her chair. Penny zoomed in immediately—I'd bet good money it was on Rhodes' abs.

"Oh, *hell* yeah," she laughed, nodding appreciatively. "This is hot."

"Keep swiping," I encouraged.

"Was he good? I bet he's so good," Penny said, practically drooling. "I'd swallow him whole and make sure he knows I don't have a gag reflex."

"It was amazing," I admitted with a grin. "I'd absolutely go back for seconds."

The pictures had become my guilty pleasure. It was embarrassing how often I'd opened them just to stare.

"I want these framed, please and thank you," Penny said, her eyes still glued to the screen.

"The smile on your face says it all," Aspen added, her attention on me.

"I think I might be falling for him. Hard," I confessed, cringing slightly. "I wasn't expecting it."

Saying it out loud felt strange. The truth was, Rhodes had become my person. He was the one I wanted to talk to after a tough day, the one I hoped would be there for my next doctor's appointment. He was the constant in every scenario I pictured for my future.

"Oh, babes," Penny said, handing my phone back and touching my arm gently. "Falling in love is scary, and you never see it coming."

Aspen nodded. "That's how I felt with Boone. Taking the job on the ranch wasn't supposed to lead to a relationship, but now? I couldn't be happier."

"It's weird for me," I admitted. "I always thought I'd live my life on the go. But with Rhodes, he makes me *want* to stay. I want to settle down—have a family."

"Have you told him?" Penny asked.

I laughed, though it sounded more like a dying animal. "Oh, God, no. I wouldn't even know what to say."

Did I want to tell Rhodes? Yesterday's kiss made me believe he felt *something*, too. Would putting it into words make things... weird?

"How did you do it, Aspen?" I asked, searching for some guidance. Whatever she did clearly worked.

She laughed, shaking her head with a sly grin. "I was naked in his bed, wearing nothing but his cowboy hat."

"I love that for you," Penny giggled, reaching over to high-five her. "You know what you need to do."

I raised a skeptical eyebrow. Penny's ideas always came with a side of caution.

"It's a good idea!" she insisted.

I sipped my sparkling juice, glancing at Aspen, who

was clearly gearing up for whatever wild plan Penny was about to pitch.

"You should print the photo of you on top of him and put it in his wallet. Maybe print a few. Then put one in his truck."

I nearly choked, the juice threatening to shoot out of my nose. The sound I made drew every eye in the salon, which only made the choking worse. My cheeks burned, tears prickling at the corners of my eyes.

"Wait!" Aspen exclaimed. "That *is* a good idea."

"See?" Penny said, grinning triumphantly.

The woman doing my pedicure arrived just then, settling into the low chair in front of me and getting to work.

"What if someone else sees it?" I whispered.

"That's the fun," Penny replied with a wink.

I had to admit, it *would* be funny. It could break the ice, and if I didn't make a move, who's to say things would change?

"I've always been direct about what I want," I mused, almost to myself. "Why stop now?"

"Exactly," Penny said. "After this, let's go get them printed. I want one for myself anyway."

She winked again, and I couldn't help but laugh.

31
Theo

AFTER RHODES HAD FIXED my car, he made an appointment with Gus to have it checked out. Not that I didn't trust him or his amateur mechanic skills, but he thought it might ease my mind to have a "professional I trusted" take a look.

Instead of Rhodes taking me, my mom offered. He'd been around so much over the past few weeks that I felt guilty leaning on him again. When I mentioned it to my mom, she said it would be a good opportunity for us to spend some time together. I couldn't argue with that. Now that I wasn't living with her anymore, I saw her even less, and it had been weighing on me.

Rhodes dropped my car off early this morning before heading to work. He didn't want me driving it until he was sure it was in perfect condition. He even arranged for Boone to pick him up and take him to the ranch.

This man and his thoughtfulness—he really was chipping away at the walls around my heart, walls that had only just started to thaw.

My mom picked me up, and we were on our way to the shop. The trees flashed by in a blur, the silence only broken by her not-so-subtle prying questions.

"So... care to fill me in about Rhodes?" she asked, hands perfectly positioned at ten and two on the steering wheel, eyes focused ahead. I rolled my eyes and leaned my head against the headrest.

"Do I have to?"

"I mean, no, you're a grown woman. But I'd like you to."

When she put it like that...

"Fine," I sighed, feeling the weight of the moment settle in. "Things are good. He's been really sweet, and I think I'm starting to really like him."

My mom nodded, her lips curving in a knowing smile. "Do you still feel good about moving in with him? Any regrets?"

I shook my head. No regrets. Sure, the emotions he stirred in me were a little unsettling, but I didn't feel the urge to run like I used to.

Rhodes was like comfort, and I was drawn to it in a way I hadn't been before.

"I'm happy."

"That's all I ever wanted for you," she said softly. "Your dad would've wanted it, too."

Dammit. Hearing her mention my dad stirred up a flood of emotions. I'd been working through so much already—figuring out how I felt about Rhodes had brought up a lot of reflection. Now this? How much could one woman handle?

The tires crunched on the gravel as we pulled into Gus'

shop. My car was parked safely in the garage, the bay door up. Gus knew better than to leave it out in the open—I would've given him hell if he had.

I slid out of the passenger seat, my feet dragging as I walked toward the shop door. My mom trailed behind, adjusting her blouse and smoothing her hair. It was cute that she was trying to look put together for the grumpy mechanic inside.

"Gussy!" I called out, using the nickname I'd given him in hopes of getting his attention.

The inside of the *Rolling Wrench* was an homage to hold time shops. There were decorations most popular in the 50's—reds and cream colors decorated the space. The floors were a black and white checkered pattern that held years of scuffs.

I heard a grunt followed by the rolling of an office chair, and then some muttered words, probably Gus grumbling under his breath before he finally emerged.

"Why are you so loud?" Gus appeared, his red beard braided into a single thick plait, his wild mop of red hair tied back into a messy bun. His towering frame filled the space behind the desk, tattoos visible as his shirt sleeves were rolled up to his elbows.

"Why are you so *grumpy*?" I shot back, leaning my forearms casually on the reception desk.

"I was fine until you walked in here," Gus replied, still rummaging through papers without looking up. I knew he hadn't looked at me yet because the moment he saw my mom standing there, he'd forget all about being grumpy and turn into the big teddy bear I knew him to be around her.

"Can you believe he talks to me like this, Mom?" I emphasized the last word, just to rile him up. Gus' head snapped up, his eyes landing on my mom, and he immediately cleared his throat, his cheeks turning a faint shade of pink. I couldn't hold back the laugh at his sudden shift in demeanor.

My mom giggled, pushing a few stray hairs behind her ear. "Oh, Sweetie, he's just kidding."

What a traitor! I rolled my eyes and stepped aside to let my mom take my place.

Within seconds, she was deep in conversation with Gus, their usual flirty banter flowing effortlessly. I decided to let her have her moment. Pulling out my phone, I started texting Rhodes.

> Me: My mom is flirting with Gus 🤢

> Rhodes: Lol, come on, it's sweet.

> Me: Sweet? Gus is anything but sweet.

> Rhodes: From what I hear, he's sweet to your mom. (;

> Me: Stop.

> Rhodes: Stop what? I mean, yeah, he is. Didn't he come by to check on her while you were gone?

> Me: That is not what you meant by 'sweet.'

> Rhodes: Dirty, dirty mind, Honey...

I scoffed, locking my phone. Tapping my fingers on the

desk, I waited for them to get it out of their system before I butted in.

"Listen, my ankles are killing me, and I have to pee again. Is the car safe to drive or not?"

Gus stopped what he was doing, turning his gaze to me slowly, his expression filled with anger as he growled, "Whoever did the work did a pretty decent job. I guess that means you won't need me anymore."

I stepped closer, placing my hand on his, which was resting on the desk.

"Aw, I'll always need you, Gussy."

"Thank God," he muttered, tossing the keys at me across the desk.

Technically, I didn't need to stay here. I could just leave and let my mom have her moment. They needed to go out already—it'd been years of lingering gazes and playful words.

"Hey, Gus!" I called from the garage bay, leaning out with my car door open.

"What now?" Gus grumbled, his voice tinged with irritation.

"Instead of me paying you, how about you take my mom out on a date? She's free tonight." I gave him a playful salute before sliding into the driver's seat.

From where I sat, I could see my mom's expression. Her jaw dropped, eyes wide with shock. I couldn't help but laugh as I fired up the engine. The car roared to life with its familiar purr, and my heart fluttered with relief.

Rhodes had done it—he'd fixed it. Was there anything that man couldn't do?

I pulled out my phone and sent him a quick text before pulling out of the shop and heading home.

> Me: You really are good at everything, aren't you?

> Rhodes: the cars good?

> Me: Yup, she's purring perfectly

> Me: Idk how I'll ever thank you

> Rhodes: no thanks needed :)

32
Rhodes

TheoTheGreat09 Wants To Start A New Game With You

TheoTheGreat09 played BORED for 8 points

TheoTheGreat09: PLAY ME BACK!

TheoTheGreat09: What if I said please?

TheoTheGreat09: On your way home, can you grab a milkshake? Chocolate please? The baby wants it.

Rhodes2324: Of course

Rhodes2324 played NEEDY for 9 points

LOGAN and I were on repair duty for the day. There was a hole in the back of the chicken coop that needed fixing to keep predators from sneaking in and slaughtering the brood.

Lately, Logan had been my shadow. Everything I did,

he mirrored. With the transition approaching, it was time for Logan to get more hands-on experience alongside me, broadening his skills to solidify his role as my second-in-command. He'd soon take on the same role I had with Boone once I stepped into full leadership.

Life was good. I was happy. I found myself smiling more when I looked in the mirror, finally recognizing the man staring back. My work was improving, nights were less daunting, and I knew part of that was because of Theo.

What we had—still undefined—was working. Together, we fit seamlessly. Touches lingered, kisses were stolen, and our time together felt unmatched. We'd built a life entirely our own.

At work, I thought about Theo. At home, I wanted Theo. At night, I dreamed of Theo.

Little by little, I noticed a spark returning to her eyes. She wasn't hiding anymore but showing herself—to me and the world. Just the other day, she went out for a girls' day with her friends. Whatever this was between us, it seemed to be good for both of us. The thought of it ever ending churned my gut with dread.

I wanted to tell her she was a part of my happiness.

I wanted her to know she never had to look for a new place.

I wanted to show her how much I craved her, as long as I lived in a world where she existed.

"Do you still have the business card for that guy who fixes boots?" Logan asked, chipping away at the rotted wood around the coop's hole. "These boots are falling apart, but I can't bring myself to get rid of them."

He stood to his full height, a few inches shorter than me. I'd been supervising, half-watching while lost in my thoughts.

"Yeah," I said, clearing my throat and uncrossing my arms. I reached into my wallet, searching through the cards and scraps of paper I kept there.

Something new caught my attention. Without thinking twice, I pulled it out.

"Oh... wow," Logan choked, coughing into his fist. "I don't think I was meant to see that."

Quickly, I held the photo to my chest. It was a picture of Theo from the other morning after we'd had sex—the one she took. Her hands were on my abs, my cock just out of frame.

"Oh my God," Logan groaned, covering his eyes with one hand and pointing to the ground with the other. "There's another one."

I bent to pick up the second photo, this one taken by me.

Theo. *Fucking* Theo. She'd printed these photos and slipped them into my wallet, fully aware I'd find them. I probably should've been irritated that Logan had seen her like that, but instead, I felt a sense of pride. She was mine in those moments—intimately, entirely.

Shaking my head, I stared at the photos a little longer, remembering the way her body felt against mine. My skin prickled with a lingering desire, yearning for her all over again.

I shoved the photos back into my wallet for now, knowing I'd look at them later. I handed Logan the card.

"The coast is clear. You can open your eyes now."

He peeked through his fingers, grabbing the card skeptically.

"Why is it always me?" he muttered as he took it from my hand.

"What do you mean?" I asked with a laugh.

Logan shivered, like he was recounting war stories with an old buddy. "I walked in on Boone and Aspen at the Farm Stand while Boone was, uh, under her skirt."

I barked out a loud laugh, my head tilting back. Poor Logan.

"Sorry for adding to the trauma."

"So... you and Theo?" Logan asked cautiously, like he wasn't sure he should.

What could I say?

We're roommates? Friends? Hooking up?

That I had feelings for her? That I couldn't imagine my life without her?

All of it was true.

Honesty felt easier. Lies snowball, and eventually, the truth gets lost.

"I don't know," I admitted. "I like her, a lot. But we haven't talked about it. We're just... going with the flow."

Going with the motions felt right for us. We were adults, and allowing fate to control things took the pressure off.

Logan nodded like he understood. "Do you have a plan?"

I didn't know what to do. I didn't want to interrupt the good thing we had going, but I knew it was a conversation we'd have to eventually. Avoidance couldn't be the answer forever.

"Again, I don't know," I confessed. "She's dealing with a lot right now. I don't want to complicate things for her."

Would bottling it up make me a hypocrite?

Logan bit the inside of his cheek, pondering what I'd said. "Look, I don't know much about this kind of thing, but if it were me, it's better to say something now than regret it in the future. Besides, what's the worst that could happen? At least you'd have your answer."

That's what scared me. I was living in my own world where Theo was mine and there was no uncomfortability. If I were to ask her the question, I feared it would drive her away, that she would leave. I don't know what I'd do if she left me, too.

WHEN I GOT HOME, I called out for Theo as I walked through the door. My boots were kicked off by the entryway, my keys tossed onto the table, and my hat thrown over the back of the couch. A chocolate milkshake was in my hand as I made my way to the kitchen.

"One milkshake, ready to be devoured," I announced.

Theo appeared from the hallway, and damn, she looked adorable. She was dressed in a matching pajama set—hot pink with pinup cowgirls—and her hair was piled messily on top of her head, little strands framing her face. My fingers itched to brush them back.

She held out her arms, squeezing her hands in a playful "gimme" motion, which I happily obliged.

"Thank you," she cooed, placing her head against my chest. My arms wrapped around her instinctively, and without thinking, I kissed the top of her head.

"Dinner's in the fridge," she said, pulling away to sit at the island. "I made soup earlier, so you'll have to heat it up."

I'd made my way to the fridge and dished out my serving of food, popping in the microwave. When I turned around, I stared pointedly at Theo until I was able to pull her attention away from her dessert with a smirk on my face.

"What?" she asked, chocolate dribbling from the corner of her mouth. I ripped a paper towel and handed it to her across the island.

"You nearly gave Logan a heart attack today."

She tilted her head, with a pinched and puzzled expression, like she was digging deep into her mental filing cabinet to figure out what I was talking about.

"I'll give you one hint: photo."

There was a beat before the color drained from her face, quickly replaced by a flush of pink.

"I said your eyes only!" she protested.

"Coming from you." I shook my head with a laugh. "You're telling me it's just a coincidence that you pulled a bold move like that after you spent the day with *Penny*?"

Theo's silence spoke volumes as she returned her attention to the milkshake, like I was no longer in the room.

"Hmm?" I prompted again, leaning back against the counter, arms crossed.

"Okay, fine!" she relented, throwing up her hands. "It was Penny's idea, but I wasn't expecting Logan to see!"

"And what did Penny say exactly?"

Theo mumbled something too low for me to hear.

"A little louder, Honey."

"She said she'd swallow you whole," Theo said in a rush, her voice barely above a whisper. "And that she doesn't have a gag reflex."

"Jesus," I muttered, running a hand over my face.

Theo giggled, avoiding my eyes. "She also said she bets you're good in bed."

Now it was my turn to flush. I wanted to ask what her answer to that question was but my voice got caught in my throat.

"Did you at least... like it?" she asked timidly, her hazel eyes flicking up to meet mine for a brief second before going back to her shake.

"Yes," I admitted, letting out a sigh as I approached the counter. I placed my hands on the cool marble, leaning in. "Theo, look at me."

She stubbornly kept her eyes on the milkshake, stirring it as if I wasn't standing right there.

"Your soup is ready," she finally said, pointing toward the dinging microwave.

I grabbed my food and set it down, minimizing distractions.

"Honey," I said softly.

That did it. She looked up at me, her expression softening. "Yes?"

"What are we doing here?"

I had thought about this the whole way home. I

needed to know where she stood. Pretending everything was fine while we danced around our feelings wasn't sustainable. Deep down, I knew she felt the same pull I did, but I needed to hear her say it.

"I'm eating my milkshake," she said playfully, "and you're eating the soup I made after scrolling Pinterest for hours."

"That's not what I meant," I replied, raising an eyebrow.

Theo groaned, tilting her head back. "Couldn't you let me avoid it a little longer? Feelings are hard."

I shook my head.

She sighed, her voice softening. "I like you, Rhodes, but I'm afraid putting a label on us will ruin the ease of what we have." She gave me her full attention. "I'm content with where we are."

I felt the same, and it was good to know we were on the same page.

"I'm happy, Theo," I said. "I like this, but I'd be lying if I said I wasn't teetering on the edge of wanting something more."

Her eyebrows shot up in surprise.

"I don't want to scare you away," I added.

She straightened her posture. "I'm not some shy thing, Rhodes. I can have fears. That doesn't mean I'll run."

"I didn't mean it that way," I said quickly. "I just didn't want to put my feelings on you and make things harder. I also can't ignore that I see something between us."

She let out a deep breath, relaxing in her chair. "I'm not going anywhere."

That small reassurance eased the knot in my chest.

"I really enjoy my time with you," I said. "What we have is effortless, and I appreciate that. Stepping into something like this isn't easy for me after... well, you know."

A flicker of understanding crossed her face.

"I know," she replied. "It's not easy for me either. The way I feel is foreign yet, it's also comforting. I don't know what to do with that. However, with you, it's been easy to step into a life and feel settled."

"I don't want to add more pressure to you, or the baby, things have changed a lot for me."

Theo nodded, her shoulders relaxing as she settled back into her chair. "Me too. Me too. I like our bubble though. I'm not saying I don't ever want to step into something more, but right now I'm content with what we have. I hope you understand that."

I did. I understood where she was coming from. However, I wasn't going to wait forever to put a label or make what we had deeper. For now, I'd go at her pace. I chose not to tell her I was falling in love with her, directly. I knew I was. When I looked at her, I saw hope, strength, and the life I'd always wanted.

One day, I'd tell her everything. For now, I kept it to myself and let the vague confession linger a little longer.

33
Rhodes

Theo is 29 weeks pregnant
Baby is the size of a butternut squash

IT WAS NURSERY DAY.

Theo was dressed in worn overalls and a snug T-shirt, her bare feet tapping softly against the hardwood floor as she surveyed the room. She looked ready, eager to get started. I was dressed in my backward cap and an old pair of mesh shorts that I didn't care about getting dirty.

The first thing we needed to do was paint, which was the most exciting part for me.

I poured the milk-brown paint we'd picked out into two flat trays, watching the creamy color swirl before it settled. Placing a roller in each tray, I turned to Theo with a grin.

We'd woken up early, shared a quiet breakfast, and I savored a strong cup of coffee before we dove into the project

Since our conversation the other day, nothing had

really changed—but somehow, everything had. The glances we exchanged lingered, the touches felt more intentional, and the unspoken energy between us shifted into something that felt undeniably deeper. The words I'd neglected to say out right were clearly understood.

"Alright, Honey, grab that roller and get to work," I instructed, grabbing a small brush to start on the trim. Theo wasn't tall or agile enough to cover more than what was directly in front of her.

Instead of insisting she sit this out, I wanted her to feel helpful. She could paint the middle of the walls, and I'd take care of the rest.

"Sir, yes, sir." She gave a mock salute. As Theo picked up her roller, flashing me an excited smile, it hit me that this was more than just a room we were painting. It was the beginning of something beautifully new.

"One pass at a time. We don't want it to look spotty," I reminded her. Theo nodded, her pigtails swaying with the movement.

BEFORE I COULD FINISH TRIMMING a whole wall, Theo was done. When I tell you she probably covered a three-foot radius, I was being generous. Each wall had a stripe right across the middle.

"Okay, now what?" she asked, swaying her body back and forth. I was lying on the ground, paintbrush in hand, trying not to get paint where it didn't belong. My attention couldn't be swayed because I refused to tape before I started the project. Call it masculine stubbornness.

When I didn't answer her right away, she took a step closer to me, and I could feel her looming above, staring. That made my hand start to shake.

"I said, now what," she repeated herself.

Letting out a laugh, I rolled on my back and stared at her. "I've got to keep trimming the walls before we can use the extended roller and paint the rest."

"What can I do?"

"Let me finish this wall, and then you can paint more."

Theo stepped away, the paint roller dangling from her hand. I resumed my job, focusing completely on the wall, needing it to be perfect.

The sound of crinkling plastic broke my concentration. Theo was pacing back and forth across the drop cloth, her bare feet shifting it noisily with each step. She looked restless, clearly bored out of her mind.

A cold hand touched my cheek, causing me to jolt the brush against the wall. Glancing over, I saw Theo, brown-handed, smirking at me.

"Did you just put a handprint of paint on my face?" I asked, my tone laced with disbelief.

Theo nodded, biting her bottom lip to stifle a grin.

"Are you really *that* bored?"

"I don't like sitting here doing nothing, so I let the intrusive thought win," she quipped, shrugging innocently.

"Clearly," I replied dryly.

Theo stepped closer, her other hand tucked suspiciously behind her back.

"What are you doing?" I asked, raising my hands defensively, already bracing for whatever mischief she had planned.

"Having some fun," she said, inching toward me with a grin that screamed trouble.

"Theo," I warned, slowly standing and gripping my paintbrush like it was some kind of weapon. Not that it would stop her.

Her grin only widened as she crept closer, her eyes glinting.

Glancing to my right, I quickly bent down and put my hand in the paint, too. I gave her a testing glance, and she didn't back away. I approached her, my pace matching hers as we danced like two fighters in the ring.

"Watch your step!" Theo squealed and pointed at the ground. Like the fool I was, I looked away from her and immediately regretted my choice because she pounced. Her paint-covered hand found its mark, landing on my T-shirt.

I laughed and spun around, placing my painted hand on her back as she tried to escape. Theo spun with a gasp, her jaw unhinged.

"What? Didn't think I'd give it back?"

Theo moved quickly. As I wrapped her in my arms, her back pressed against my front. She wiggled, trying to move from my grasp, but was unsuccessful. Her ass rubbed against my cock, jolting it awake. With the paintbrush still in my hand, I dragged it across her belly and then up her arm in a swift motion.

Out of pure luck, Theo was able to break free enough to spin and face me, both hands coming up to cup my cheeks.

Our breaths were labored, panting inches away from each other. Her paint-smeared palms left two marks on my face. I reached mine to hers, cupping one cheek. We were a mess—paint-splattered and chaotic, our light brown smudges matching the walls we'd been working on.

My eyes darted between hers, a frantic pinball trapped in its machine. The need to close the gap, to kiss her, to mix my paint with hers, overwhelmed me.

So, I gave in.

My lips crashed against her, firm and unrelenting. My hand stayed on her face, grounding us in the chaos as she melted into the kiss, pulling me closer, eliminating any trace of space between us.

I walked us backward, her back hitting the wall with a deep thud. Our lips didn't stop, neither of us coming up for air as my tongue explored her mouth frantically.

Theo's hands left my face and trailed down my body, streaks left in her wake. The cool sensation was felt under my shirt as she reached my stomach.

I pulled away from the kiss, her slender fingers dipping into the waistband of my shorts.

"Was this your plan all along?" I asked.

"Maybe," she replied, bringing her bottom lip between her teeth.

"All you had to do was ask, Honey."

She kissed me again, using one hand to pull me closer by the collar of my shirt. Fumbling for the claps of her overalls, I refused to break away. I'd feel my way around because there was no chance I'd stop the kiss.

Finally, the front of her overalls fell down, revealing the tight shirt that spread across her breasts. Theo pushed me, rolling us over against the wall, so now she was on top. With the thud of my back against the wall she broke and stared at me with a wicked grin.

"It's my turn to taste you," she muttered against my lips, giving me one last kiss before sinking to her knees.

"Theo," I protested.

"Be a good boy and take it." She pulled down my pants, boxers and all, allowing my cock to spring free. It was hard and aching, knowing Theo was on her knees before me. "I hope I can fit all of you in my mouth."

"Fuck," I groaned, my head falling back, making contact with the wall.

Theo took me, slowly teasing the tip with her tongue. I needed to watch her, see her with a mouth full of *my* cock. When I looked down, her eyes were already on me and she hummed in approval like she'd been waiting.

Through hooded eyes, she took me all the way until my tip hit the back of her throat, not once taking her eyes off me. Tears began to prick, and she gagged slightly but didn't stop.

Seeing her gag on my cock sent a tingle up my spine, release already knocking.

I had to look away; I couldn't bust yet.

Theo dove in, placing both hands on the backs of my legs and moving her mouth along my shaft. Her tongue popped out, swirling around the base as I buried deep in her mouth.

One hand that was on the back of my thigh moved inside, a finger dragging up and along my balls. The feeling was indescribable. My skin pricked as she held me in her palm.

"Theo, fuck!" I groaned, my head snapping down to watch again. She was grinning. She knew she had me.

My cock sprang from her mouth as she pulled away. Without warning, she lifted my dick and her tongue ran from base to tip. It tickled but in the best way possible.

The warmth from her mouth left my shaft and latched onto my balls, using her tongue to create circles on the sensitive skin.

The arousal was almost too much. I closed my eyes, and little white stars burst behind my eyelids. It was euphoric in a way I'd never experienced. Theo broke me, snapping a thread I'd been keeping taught.

"Stand up. Now," I growled, wanting to pick her up by those slutty pigtails.

"So soon?" she cooed, sitting back on her heels and batting her eyes at me.

"Theo. Up." The words came out short and to the point; elaboration was unnecessary.

I was ready to fuck.

If this was her goal, to make me lose my shit, she won.

Theo stood on command like a good girl, arms crossed behind her. I took my cock in my hand, stroking it as I stared at her swollen mouth, saliva dripping on her chin.

I used my finger to beckon her closer, and she stepped towards me without hesitation. My hand reached out and wiped the dribble with my thumb.

"Dirty, girl," I purred. "Get undressed."

Theo obeyed. In seconds, she was naked in front of me for the second time, and it was a sight I'd never get used to.

I pulled the shirt over my head and bent down, dipping my hand in paint. Slow and full of anticipation, I stalked to her, but she didn't budge. I took her breast in my palm and pinched her hard peak, the paint leaving a handprint over her breast

"This is mine," I said.

Doing the same to the next breast.

"And this."

I circled her, like a hawk with its prey. Bringing my hand back, I slapped it against her ass. There was a loud crack, and Theo winced. Another hand print left behind. With every touch, I was marking her, marking my territory so she'd hopefully get the hint that this was all mine. Every inch of woman that stood in front of me.

I stepped up behind her, my breath tickling her ear.

"Hands on the wall, Honey. Now."

My voice was commanding, not going to take no for an answer. Luckily for me, there was little protest. Theo walked towards the wall and placed both hands in the wet paint.

"Like this?" She asked, giving me a glance over her shoulder.

"Just like that," I praised. Moving closer with deliberate steps, I kicked each of her feet wider so I could see her dripping pussy on display. "When it dries, I'll be able to see those hands whenever I step foot in this room and remember exactly what I'm about to do to you."

Spreading her, I bent down and spit between her legs.

Not that she needed it; this woman was soaked for me. Theo whimpered when my warm saliva hit her exposed skin.

I slapped her ass again, this time the other cheek and watched it recoil. Holy, *fuck*.

Taking a moment, I admired her beauty. The curve of her ass, those pigtails draped down her back, and the paint I'd place on her skin.

"I want you to keep these legs spread for me, okay?" I asked, stepping up closer behind her, lining my cock at her entrance. Theo wiggled her ass, begging for me.

With my cock in my hand, I rubbed it along her entrance, teasing her. I was ready to plunge into her heat, feel her clench against my shaft as she let loose.

I'd thought about this endlessly over the past few weeks. My body ached for her since the first taste, but the gentleman in me had kept those desires in check—barely. Now, knowing she'd let me cherish her again, I was never going to hold back.

I was completely lost in Theo—the curve of her smile, the depths of her hazel eyes, the irresistible pull that seemed to draw me closer with every breath. She didn't know it yet, but she was stuck with me. Forever.

I pushed into her with no warming up this time. She'd take all of me like I knew she could.

Slamming into her tight heat, I pumped over and over as our bodies connected. She was slick with need, my cock sliding effortlessly in and out as she moaned my name.

"You're mine, Theo." I bent to whisper into her ear, not letting up on my thrusts. "You have me."

"Rhodes," Theo moaned, her head falling forward as her forehead hit the wall. "You fuck me so good."

My hands that were on her hips, pulling for leverage, released. The moment I saw those pigtails months ago, I wanted to know what they'd feel like wrapped around my fist. Now was my chance.

Reaching up, I grabbed the hair in my hands and yanked her head back towards me. She gasped, looking at me from the side of her eye. My hips stopped, my cock still inside her.

"I'm going to do something. If you don't like it, tell me," I whispered in her ear, placing kisses on her exposed neck.

I took my hand, reaching around, a knuckle applying pressure to her behind. Theo moaned, and her jaw went slack.

"Fuck, yes," She cried, bending more, but my hands in her hair kept her head in place.

"Do you like it when I put pressure there, Honey?" I asked, adding more.

Theo nodded, panting at the sensation. I took her positive response as an indication to keep going.

I fucked her hard as I slammed my hips into her, my knuckle giving her just enough pressure from behind. The room was filled with a symphony of grunts and moans. My legs were burning from how I was angled to pump inside her. Between the slight pain and the slickness around my cock, I wasn't able to hold back any longer. With a loud exhale, I released inside her, pumping until I knew I was empty and she was filled with *me*.

"Oh, fuck Rhodes," Theo panted, as she rode her

climax, coming undone around my shaft. "You're so good."

I laughed, pulling from her and standing to stretch my legs. Sex with Theo was better than I could've ever imagined. She was so responsive. I liked the praise.

Theo spun around, holding her palms up covered in paint from the wall. We both took a look at where she'd been standing, and two hand prints stared back at us.

"I'm not painting over those," I said, coming up to wrap her in an embrace. Our naked bodies pressed together, and I soaked in the warmth of her bare skin on mine.

"What will we tell people when they come in here?" She asked into my chest. "Two random handprints on the wall?"

"I don't care," I replied, kissing the top of her head. Theo giggled and pulled away, looking up at me.

I couldn't stop the smile spreading across my face. I was grinning like an idiot—a happy, ridiculous idiot—looking at the woman who had reignited something in me I thought I'd lost forever.

One look at her, with those messy pigtails and worn overalls, and I felt something stir in me for the first time in ages. It was her acceptance, her quiet attention, that made me feel cared for again. It was her moving into my house that finally made it feel like a home.

34
Theo

30 weeks pregnant
Baby is the size of a head of broccoli

"THEO, Honey, we are going to be late," Rhodes shouted from the living room as I worked tirelessly to pick an outfit that *actually* fit.

Finding cute or even remotely presentable clothes to wear in public at thirty weeks pregnant was a challenge. Tonight, Rhodes and I were meeting our friends at Faircloud's Annual Fall Fest. I hadn't been to the festival in years—probably not since high school. Other than the summer block party, this would be the first time I'd be surrounded by most of the town. With that came an unavoidable pressure to look halfway decent, a pressure that normally wouldn't faze me.

After what happened between Rhodes and me in the nursery—the whole "hands on the wall, now" moment—we'd slipped into this unspoken rhythm. The more we saw each other, naked and vulnerable, the more we just... meshed. Things were flowing.

Subconsciously, I wondered if I was obsessing over how I looked because I wanted to prove to the town that I deserved Rhodes' attention.

Finally satisfied that I looked presentable, I shut off the bathroom light and headed to the living room. I'd settled on a pair of maternity jeans, my favorite boots, and a flowy sweater—perfect for when the evening chill set in. Instead of my usual pigtails, I'd gone for a half-up, messy bun perched on the crown of my head.

"You look pretty," Rhodes said, his voice warm. He stood there looking effortlessly gorgeous in his jeans and backward hat, like he hadn't even tried.

Ever since *that* moment in the nursery, my desire for him had been relentless. It was like a switch had flipped inside me, and my once-manageable libido was now in overdrive. His hands. That smile. It all drove me to the brink of distraction.

I bit my lip, letting my gaze travel from his boots to his hat, my imagination running wild with ideas of how we could spend the evening without ever leaving the house.

"Down, girl." He chuckled, stepping closer and wrapping his large, rugged hands around my biceps. His touch sent a shiver through me. "I can practically see what you're thinking." He leaned down and brushed a soft, teasing kiss across my lips. "As tempting as that is, we promised them we'd be there."

When he pulled away, I groaned dramatically and stomped my foot like a tantruming toddler.

"Why do you always have to be so responsible?" I

grumbled, grabbing my purse and turning away from his grip.

"One of us has to be," he said with a knowing wink. "Besides, by me being responsible, you get to keep having all those dirty thoughts. Isn't that more fun?"

A laugh escaped me. He wasn't wrong. As we headed out the front door, my mind filled with images of Rhodes doing all kinds of deliciously inappropriate things to me.

"Oh, it's fun, all right," I teased, sighing dramatically. "The things you're doing to me in my head right now…"

Rhodes let out a deep laugh. "You think this is funny? I'm soaking—"

"Please don't finish that sentence," he interrupted, shooting me a pointed look as he opened the passenger door of his truck.

I climbed in, but before he could shut the door, I grabbed his shirt collar, pulling him in for a slow, lingering kiss. When we finally broke apart, his eyes darkened with restraint.

"Theo," he said, his tone half-scolding.

I grinned, unapologetically asking, "What?" in a timid tone.

"You're trouble."

Rhodes shut the truck door and rounded the front as I pulled my camera from my purse. Lately, I'd been trying to take more pictures, capturing moments I never wanted to forget.

Flipping through the camera's gallery, I got lost in the memories. There were so many photos of Rhodes. Despite the distraction the other day, we'd finally finished the baby's room. I let Rhodes do most of the work—

truthfully, I wasn't much help and mostly got in the way. Instead, I stayed off to the side, documenting the day in snapshots. One shot showed him standing with his back to me, paintbrush in hand, shoulders tense with focus. Another was from when I'd called his name, catching him off guard. He'd turned to me with a smirk, his expression soft, raw, and so completely unposed. Seeing him look at me like that—with joy—tugged at something deep inside me.

The more I saw him smile, the more he gave me pieces of his heart, the harder I fell for him.

I thought back to the other night, when he'd been buried inside me, cherishing my body. He told me, more like *demanded* that I was his. Even though I didn't say anything out loud, in my head I agreed.

Old Theo would've ran. She'd have packed her bags and fled to another city or even another country. This version of me didn't want to bolt. Instead, I wanted to dig my roots deeper into Faircloud. Because of him.

Lost in my thoughts, I didn't even notice Rhodes had climbed into the driver's seat. When I came back to myself, we were already on the road.

"Where'd you go?" he asked, his voice laced with curiosity.

He always knew when I checked out, could sense when my mind wandered. I wasn't ready to share my thoughts, not yet. I knew he felt something too. For now, I wanted to hold onto this quiet peace a little longer. Who knew what would happen when the simplicity of *us* was replaced by rules and titles?

"I was just looking at some photos I took," I said

casually, clicking through a few more. One flashed on the screen—a shot of my bare belly, framed by a bra and low-hanging pajama pants. I'd been taking progress photos, wanting to document my pregnancy so one day I could show my daughter what it was like when she was in Mommy's belly.

"Can I see?" Rhodes asked, slowing to a stop at an intersection.

I nodded and turned the camera toward him. He leaned in closer, one hand resting on the steering wheel and the other draped over the center console.

"I can't wait to meet her," he murmured, a small, tender smile forming on his lips.

I couldn't wait either. The thought filled me with an ache so sweet, I almost blurted it out. But I held back—I wasn't ready to say it aloud yet. Instead, I shifted the conversation.

"So, how are we going to act around everyone tonight?" I asked, my tone light but my question loaded.

"What do you mean?" Rhodes responded, his brows knitting together slightly as he kept his eyes on the road.

"Oh, come on. You know what I mean. We've clearly fallen into... whatever this is. We can't be kissing or hugging or touching like we do at home."

Rhodes nodded slowly, processing. "I guess you're right. I hadn't really thought about it like that. Everything's just felt so..." He trailed off, searching for the right word.

"Natural," I supplied softly, because I felt it, too.

"Exactly." He hummed in agreement, the sound low and warm. Then he sighed, glancing at me briefly. Our eyes met, and for a second, the truck felt smaller, the air heavier. "Theo, I think we should talk—"

"Please, not right now," I cut him off, my voice dipping into a quiet plea as I leaned my head back against the seat. "Not here. Not before we spend the night with our friends."

He nodded again, his jaw tightening as he swallowed hard, the tension in his throat betraying how much he wanted to say.

I knew we needed to talk about whatever was happening between us—about what we were becoming—but I couldn't handle it right now. Not here. It had to happen at home, where I'd have the space to cry, to feel, to try to untangle the overwhelming knot of emotions Rhodes had tied around my heart.

I felt so much for him that I didn't even know where to begin.

We pulled up to the parking lot; Boone, Aspen, Penny, Mac, and Logan all gathered around the bed of Boone's truck, clearly waiting for us. We weren't *that* late. I took a deep breath, closed my eyes, and grounded myself, counting back from five like Rhodes has often told me. I had to center myself, get these emotions out of my head, and enjoy the time with my friends. Things have been going well; I wanted to keep them that way.

Smiling, I opened the passenger door and swung my feet over the seat.

"Don't you dare," Rhodes whispered, catching my attention before I could hop down. I knew what he meant. I hadn't opened a door as long as I was with him, but it was too late. I'd wait and at least let him help me down.

Rhodes came around and helped me out before we made our way over to where our friends stood.

"It's about time," Mac joked, half his lips turning into a smirk. "We've been waiting for ages." Penny reached out, smacking Mac on the chest. He gasped and rubbed his skin like he was in real pain.

"Don't listen to him," Boone said, rolling his eyes. "He got here probably a minute ago. His truck's still warm."

"Now that we are all here," Aspen said. "Where did we want to start?"

Faircloud came alive whenever there was some kind of festival or activity. The streets were lined with string lights, attaching at each lamppost wrapped in red and orange leafed garlands. Laughter echoed through the streets as children darted between booths, their faces painted, high on candied apples. The sound of chatter blended with the soft strumming of a local band playing under the gazebo in the middle of Faircloud Park. An acoustic guitar, a violin, and a mandolin weaving a familiar tune of old-time folk and country.

I let out a breath, a sense of pride rushing through me. Seeing the scene before me thrilled me to raise my daughter in a town like this.

"What if we got some apple cider first?" I suggested, hanging the camera around my neck.

The crowd agreed, and we wandered across the street, walking under the arched entrance surrounded by pumpkins and cornstalks. We were greeted by rows of booths and local vendors popping up to sell their creations. Knowing Aspen, she probably took out a small loan to come here. If there was a small business she could support, she was there, no questions asked.

"What about this one?" Logan asked, pointing to a booth called *The Cider Press*. He was the first to approach the booth, and we all filed in line behind.

Rhodes stood behind me, and we were at the back of the line. I could feel him step closer, the heat from his body radiating off and seeping into me. The urge to step into him, lay my head back, and soak in his comfort was so strong, but I kept forward. I decided to bring the camera to my face, snapping a few pictures of all my friends in line, the shop's name in the background.

To break the spell of Rhodes' closeness, I called out, "Okay! Everyone, look here and smile!"

Our friends turned around in unison, their faces lighting up for the camera. Penny threw up double peace signs while Mac stuck his tongue out like a fool. Boone, the romantic, kissed Aspen's temple, making her smile stretch wide enough to reach ear to ear.

I pulled the camera back to check the shots. The image was perfect—the twinkling lights framed them beautifully, and the blurred trees in the background added just the right touch of atmosphere.

"Alright, now it's your turn," Rhodes whispered in my ear, his breath warm against my skin.

"Me?" I scoffed, lowering the camera. "No way. I'm the photographer."

He gave me a knowing look. "I know my way around a camera. Remember?"

Of course, I remembered. I'd printed the photos he'd

taken and placed them on my nightstand—a little secret I didn't plan to share.

"Go on," he urged, holding his hand out for the camera.

With a dramatic eye roll, I handed it over and stepped into the frame next to Mac. He wrapped one arm around me and the other around Penny.

"Don't blink," Mac teased, his smile mischievous.

"Thanks, genius. Now I'm definitely going to blink," Penny quipped, nudging him with her hip.

Laughing, I grinned fully at the camera, a real smile I hadn't felt in what seemed like ages. Rhodes snapped several photos, adjusting the angles as he went. Finally, he lowered the camera and gave an approving nod.

"How'd I do?" he asked, tilting the screen toward me.

I leaned in, my heart warming at the sight. The photo was perfect—natural, happy, and genuine. It felt like seeing a piece of myself I hadn't recognized in a while.

"Want one of just you two?" Mac offered, holding his hand out for the camera.

I looked at Rhodes, who met my gaze with a shrug. With a small nod, I handed the camera to Mac.

"Alright, lovebirds, arms around each other," Mac said with a grin.

I stepped closer to Rhodes, wrapping my arms around his middle. He pulled me under his arm, his embrace solid and warm. As Mac snapped the picture, a single word whispered through my mind: *home*.

THE EVENING DRIFTED on as we wandered from booth to booth, soaking in the festive atmosphere. Events peppered the night—a wood-cutting contest, sack races, and, my favorite, bobbing for apples. While I'd usually dominate an apple-bobbing contest anywhere else, there was no way I was risking my dignity in front of half the town.

Boone, on the other hand, couldn't resist. "Let's do it!" he called, pointing at the lineup of bins. "I bet I'll win."

"Doubt it," Mac shot back, rolling up his sleeves. "You've got about as much chance of winning as wrestling a hog in the mud."

My face scrunched, and I looked at Penny and Aspen, who looked back at me with the same confused expression. Mac spoke in his own language most of the time; no one understood it but him.

"Game on!" Boone declared, tossing his cowboy hat onto Aspen's head. "You two in?" He nodded toward Logan and Rhodes.

"Hell yeah," Logan said, pulling off his hat and hesitating, unsure where to put it. I held out my hand, and he grinned, handing it over.

I looked up at Rhodes, who seemed hesitant to join in. Leaning closer, I nudged him with my elbow. "Do it. I want to see you win, it'll be hot."

That did the trick. "Say less," he replied, pulling off his

baseball cap. "I'd put this on your head, but it doesn't have the same meaning."

Laughing, I took the hat and teased, "Go show them who the real man is."

Rhodes chuckled and followed the guys to the lineup. Each of them knelt in front of a bin filled with water and apples, ready to compete. Aspen, Penny, and I stood together, watching from the sidelines. I couldn't help smiling like a fool as Rhodes leaned forward, the light catching on his profile.

Watching him like this, so effortlessly confident and playful, I knew one thing for sure: I was absolutely *gone* for this man.

At the older man's call, everyone dove in, heads plunging into the water as they scrambled to grab apples with their teeth. The challenge was simple: the first to clear their bucket won.

I couldn't take my eyes off Rhodes. His head dipped into the water, and he quickly came up with an apple clenched between his teeth. Water streamed down his face, his soaked hair falling messily across his forehead. He shook his head to fling off the droplets, sending a small spray around him.

"Keep going!" I cheered, a little too enthusiastically. A few people glanced my way, and I cleared my throat, reining in my excitement as I shifted to quieter clapping.

Penny was next to yell. "Let's go!" she called, her voice carrying over the crowd.

Aspen joined in, jumping up and down as she cheered for Boone. "Come on, Boone! You've got this!"

The three of us laughed as we watched the guys on

their knees, water splashing everywhere as they struggled to snag the apples. The ridiculousness of it all made it even more entertaining.

I brought my camera up and started snapping away, taking photos of everyone around us as well as the contest.

Finally, Logan shot to his feet, arms raised in triumph, an apple still dangling from his mouth. "Victory!" he declared, his muffled voice earning a round of cheers from the crowd.

I waved his hat in the air and cheered with the rest of the spectators. Around us, the guys were coming up for air, shaking water from their faces and grinning through their defeat. The whole scene was pure chaos and hilarity, and I loved every second of it.

The judge handed Logan something; it looked like little pieces of paper. It occurred to me none of the guys knew what they were trying to win except for bragging rights to stoke their pride.

Logan jogged up to Rhodes, conversing about something I couldn't quite interpret. I turned my attention away, trying not to seem like I was prying or listening in.

"How was that?" Rhodes asked when he joined me, using the hem of his shirt to dry his face. The move exposed a sliver of his stomach, and I couldn't help but notice how the water clung to his skin.

"Pretty hot," I replied, giving him a playful nudge with my shoulder.

The rest of the evening was spent indulging in deep-fried apple slices drizzled with caramel—sweet, sticky, and utterly delicious. As the festival began winding down, the crowd started thinning, and it felt like the perfect time to call it a night.

After saying our goodbyes to everyone, Rhodes helped me climb into his truck. We headed home, the quiet hum of the drive soothing after the noise of the festival.

But curiosity was gnawing at me. I couldn't shake the memory of Logan and Rhodes talking earlier.

"So, what was Logan saying to you after the contest?" I asked, glancing at him.

Rhodes cleared his throat, keeping his eyes on the road. "He gave me the tickets he won," he said casually, as if it wasn't a big deal.

I frowned. "Why would he do that?"

"He didn't think he'd use them," Rhodes replied, his tone maddeningly vague.

I laughed lightly, though it wasn't because I found it funny. "You're being cryptic."

Exhaling, Rhodes glanced at me briefly before focusing back on the road. "They're tickets for a weekend getaway," he admitted. "Logan doesn't have anyone to go with, so he gave them to me."

My breath caught. My cheeks flushed with heat. "But... you do?"

Rhodes's hand tightened slightly on the steering wheel. "I took them because I thought you might like them," he said quietly. "After the baby's born. As a gift. I figured it might be a chance for you to take a break—if you wanted to."

His confession hit me hard, like a wave crashing over me, leaving me unsteady and breathless. My heart swelled, and my mind raced to process what he'd just said. I stared ahead, blinking rapidly, as I tried to string together a response that didn't sound as shaken as I felt.

If I ever took a weekend getaway, the only person I'd want there with me would be him. But instead of saying that, I nodded and quietly murmured my thanks.

Rhodes and I were treading into dangerous territory. I didn't know how much longer I could go without addressing the big, fat elephant in the room. I'd never felt love like this before, and the urge to scream it, to shout it from the rooftops, was all-consuming.

No wonder all the movies always have an epic love confession because I was bursting at the seams. I was moments away from standing outside of his window with a radio, blasting old-time country love songs.

35
Rhodes

MY HEART POUNDED in my chest, each beat quick and uneven. Anxiety clawed its way in now that we were on the road. I couldn't quite pinpoint why I was so nervous about Theo meeting my mom. She was kind, and so was Rob. It wasn't about them—it was me. My own mental struggles had taken hold, making this moment feel too big. Because it was. Whatever this thing between us was, it felt real now. And I wanted that. God, I wanted it so badly.

The slow nights, the stolen laughs, the time we spent learning each other. The way I'd sneak glances while she'd brush her hand against mine like it was an accident. Truly, it never was. I was unraveling the mystery of this woman piece by piece, discovering the secrets she hid from the world.

Like how much she loved physical touch and words of affirmation, even though she'd never admit it. If I told her she looked good or pulled her into a hug, she'd melt, the icy front she had softening into nothing.

In the mornings, she loved waking up to the smell of coffee, though she never drank it.

She hated the "big light," always preferring the living room to be wrapped in a soft, amber glow. It was these little quirks, these tender glimpses, that made her feel like home.

I wanted to tell her, take a leap into us and turn the unspoken words into reality. Maybe today. Maybe I needed to have my mom see her, meet the woman I've fallen into a beautiful life with. But before I could, I had something I had to do first.

What day was better than Thanksgiving?

Fuck. Now I was *really* panicking. My mom was meeting Theo on a holiday which meant, we were spending a holiday together.

Theo's mom was working the night shift, and there was no way I could leave her home alone. The thought of her by herself would gnaw at me all night. I'd wonder if she was okay, if she'd eaten, if she felt *lonely*. The idea of her sitting in that quiet house made my chest tighten.

So, I asked if she wanted to come with me. And to my surprise, she agreed without a single protest.

"How ironic," she said from the passenger seat of my truck, breaking the comfortable silence.

"Hmm?" I kept my eyes on the road, glancing briefly in her direction.

"Somehow, we still managed to go to the grocery store on a Thursday. You really are a man of routine."

I let out a fake laugh, which earned a genuine giggle from her. My mom had forgotten the mashed potatoes for dinner, leaving it to us to pick up a box of instant on the way in.

"You know what else would be ironic?" Theo asked, teasing me now. She was poking at me with that familiar glint in her eye, her bottom lip caught between her teeth as if she was trying to hide a smile.

"Let's hear it," I said, side-eyeing her for a second before returning my focus to the road.

"If Indie was there. Your precious routine would still be intact."

"That precious routine," I repeated, mock-serious, "is what keeps me sane."

Routine was one of the few things in my life I had complete control over, and I clung to it for the comfort and stability.

"It's admirable," Theo said softly, her gaze shifting out the windshield.

"You think so?" I asked, genuinely curious.

"Yeah. You've clearly worked hard to overcome some serious stuff. I didn't mean to minimize it." Her voice carried a note of regret, and I realized my joking must have come off as defensive, though it hadn't been.

"Honey," I said gently, "I was kidding. I know you weren't making fun of it. Let's be real—I think you kind of like my routine."

She laughed and leaned her head back, the loose strands of her hair falling from her pigtails, framing her face in a way that made my chest tighten.

"Honestly? Yeah, I kind of do," she admitted. "I used to thrive on spontaneity, but now I'm starting to appreciate settling down and finding structure."

I nodded, understanding what she meant. Even I felt I wasn't the same man when we first met.

When the truck came to a stop in front of the store, I turned to her. "Want to come in or wait here?"

"I'll come in," she said, but then her expression shifted to one of confusion. "You've got something on your face."

I reached for the visor mirror to check, but as I pulled it down, a small photo slipped out and landed in my lap.

"What's that?" Theo asked, already reaching for it. She picked it up, her fingers delicate as she held it. Her face softened, her cheeks flushing a light pink as her eyes focused on the picture.

"You kept it?" she asked, her voice barely above a whisper. She stared at me, her eyes glassy and wide with disbelief.

"Yeah," I admitted, my gaze steady on her. "I like it. I'd put it on the dashboard, but we said our eyes only, remember?"

She smiled then, running her fingertips lightly over the colors on the photo like she could touch the memory itself. I'd chosen the one where she was smiling—not that I didn't appreciate the other photos, especially the one where she was practically naked. However, it was that smile, so unguarded and full of life, that made my heart stop every time I saw it.

"I'd be okay if you did..." She paused, clearing her throat before handing me the photo back. "Put it there."

Those words felt like a silent nudge that she was okay with people seeing her in my life, seeing that maybe she was something a little more. I didn't press but nodded, taking that picture and placing it front and center along the plastic of my dash.

My Theo.

WE WERE in and out of the store faster than I expected. Apparently, last-minute grocery shopping on Thanksgiving wasn't much of a thing in Faircloud. Just as Theo had predicted, Indie was working the register.

She lit up the moment she saw Theo—bright smiles, cheerful energy, the whole package. It was the same every time we came in together. When I came alone? Flat smiles. Minimal enthusiasm. Like she was counting the minutes until her shift ended.

Was it me?

Theo was still laughing as we made our way back to the truck, clearly enjoying the little show Indie put on for her. I couldn't help but laugh too, the stark contrast between how Indie treated us hitting me as ridiculous.

"Is it something I say?" I asked as I opened the truck door for Theo to climb in.

"I think it's what you *don't* say," she replied, settling into her seat. "It wouldn't kill you to smile and ask how her day's going. People feed off energy, you know."

I nodded, humming in acknowledgment. I hadn't really thought about it like that before.

"So... you're telling me it's my face?" I asked, smirking as I leaned against the open door.

Theo tilted her head from side to side, lips pursed in mock deliberation. "You *do* have a bit of an RBF."

My eyebrows shot up. "An RBF?" I echoed.

"Resting bitch face," she said matter-of-factly. "For someone who feels a lot, you don't show it well. I've come to the conclusion that you have a very boring face—boring but, luckily, quite handsome."

I laughed, shaking my head. "That's it. I'm shutting the door now. Hands and feet in."

Theo grinned and quickly adjusted herself, making sure nothing was in danger of being caught as I closed the door.

Climbing into the driver's seat, I started the truck and headed toward my mom's house. It wasn't far, just a couple of minutes away, but Theo managed to fill every second with a detailed rundown of how I could improve my facial expressions. Coming from her, of all people, it was rich.

"For someone who only started feeling her emotions a few months ago," I said, cutting her off with a teasing glance, "you sure talk a big game."

Theo gasped, mouth dropping open in mock outrage. "Rude!" she squealed, slapping my shoulder.

I just laughed, my chest warming at the easy banter between us. She always knew how to pull me out of my head, and right now, I couldn't be more grateful for it.

The anxiety that was there eased as the jokes flew between us, and when I finally pulled up to the house, I let out a breath of air.

Theo carried the grocery bag in one hand, and I guided her to the front door. Step by step, we climbed the short set of stairs leading to my mom's bright yellow door.

I skipped knocking, pushing the door open and stepping inside like I had a thousand times before. The warm aroma of my mom's cooking greeted us immediately. She was an incredible cook—probably where I'd inherited my own skills, though I'd never claim to be half as good as she was.

"Ma!" I called, shutting the door behind us and pulling off my boots. Theo, in her platform slippers, slipped them off with ease and left them neatly by the door.

The familiar creak of the hardwood floor welcomed us as we made our way toward the kitchen. There, my mom twirled around with grace, an apron tied neatly around her waist, stirring something on the stove. Rob was perched on a stool at the kitchen island, his focus on a crossword puzzle spread out before him.

"Hi, sweetie!" my mom beamed, looking up from her pot with a radiant smile.

"Mom, Rob, this is Theo," I said, motioning to the woman beside me. She stood tall, her smile warm and genuine, the crinkle at the corners of her eyes and the way her cheeks lifted making it clear she wasn't holding anything back.

"It's so nice to meet you both," Theo said, waving politely.

Rob was the first to move, hopping off the stool with the energy of someone half his age and wrapping Theo in a dad-like hug. Rob embodied comfort with his rounded glasses, perpetual soft smile, and blond hair streaked with just a touch of gray.

"It's my pleasure," he said, stepping back and extending a hand. "Can I take your coat?"

Theo quickly handed me her purse and slipped off her light flannel, revealing her overalls and a fitted T-shirt underneath. "Thank you," she said softly, her voice full of sincerity.

"Did you get the potatoes?" my mom asked as she came over to hug me. I nodded to Theo after pulling away. She turned and pulled her into an embrace, too.

"It's so nice to finally meet you," my mom said, holding Theo by the shoulders and giving her an affectionate squeeze.

"You too," Theo replied with an easy smile. "Rhodes has said nothing but amazing things about both of you. Thank you for having me."

"Oh, it's our pleasure," my mom said, taking the grocery bag from Theo's hand. "I always make way too much food and end up sending most of it home with Rhodes."

"It's true," I added with a grin. "I'll be eating turkey and cranberry sandwiches for a week."

Theo reached for her purse back, but I shook my head, gesturing to the empty seat next to Rob. "Go on," I whispered. "Take a seat."

She smiled and nodded, settling into the chair.

"So, Theo," my mom began as she started prepping the potatoes. "Tell us a little bit about yourself."

"Oh, wow," Theo said with a light laugh. "That's always a tough question." I moved to stand behind her, resting my arm on the back of her chair. She leaned into me instinctively. "Well, I love photography and nature. Oh! And I love to travel."

"Me too," Rob chimed in, setting his pencil down. "What's been your favorite place so far?"

"Egypt," Theo said without hesitation, her eyes lighting up. "I did a magazine spread there. The pyramids were stunning, and I even got to ride a camel."

She was breathtaking, her face glowing with excitement as she talked about her work.

My mom gasped, spinning around from the stove. "You're kidding! That sounds incredible. I'd love to hear all about it."

I stepped back, letting Theo get swept into the conversation with my mom and Rob. Their voices blended into a lively hum as I stood there, taking it all in. Watching her mesh so seamlessly with my family tugged at something deep inside me.

It wasn't just about today—it was the future I could see unfolding before me. Theo coming around more often. Laughter at the dinner table. The baby cradled in my mom's arms. Theo smiling just as she was now, fully at ease, sharing more and more of herself with the people who mattered most to me.

I glanced down at her, my heart swelling at how effortlessly she fit into my life, like she'd always belonged there. My gaze lingered on her belly, and for a moment, I drifted, picturing the little girl she'd soon bring into this world.

No matter where I stood in Theo's life, one thing was certain—I would make sure that little girl never carried the weight of feeling unwanted, never believed for a second that her existence was a burden.

I would make sure she always knew she was loved.

Theo's laugh pulled me back to the moment. I smiled, leaning against the counter, and let myself revel in the sound of it—of her—knowing I was exactly where I wanted to be.

Dinner had been devoured, bellies were full, and everyone wore the satisfied smile that only my moms home-cooked meal could bring. Theo and Rob were deep in conversation at the kitchen table, her laugh mingling with his low chuckle. I felt my mom's gentle tug on my arm, pulling my attention away from Theo. Reluctantly, I followed her out to the front porch.

The air was crisp, carrying the faint scent of fall leaves and the distant hum of crickets. The sun dipped low behind the trees, painting the sky with warm streaks of orange and pink. We settled into the rocking chairs, the old wood creaking beneath us. For a while, we rocked in companionable silence, the rhythm soothing. I waited for her to break it first.

"She's a sweet girl," my mom said at last, her voice soft and thoughtful.

I nodded, a small smile tugging at my lips. "She is."

"How are things going?" she asked, her tone casual but her eyes sharp. "With her living with you, the baby...everything?"

I knew this was coming. My mom had been cautiously supportive when I'd first told her Theo was moving in. She raised me to care deeply for others, to give without expecting much in return. She was also a mother, protective and perceptive, always looking out for me in her own way. I'd brushed off her curiosity, skimming the surface of my feelings for Theo. But now, it felt impossible to avoid the truth she already seemed to know.

"It's going really well," I admitted. "Things have definitely...shifted since she moved in."

She hummed in response, her chair creaking as she rocked back and forth. "I can tell. I see the way you look at her. I don't know if I ever saw you look at Jess like that."

Her words hit me like a jolt. I turned to face her, my brow furrowed. "I loved Jess more than I'd ever loved anyone."

She gave me a knowing smile, the kind only a mother could. "Sweetie, she was your first love. Of course, you thought that. But you had nothing to compare it to." She paused, letting the words sink in before continuing. "You were just a kid. That love was real, but it barely scratched the surface. Love as an adult...that's different. There's more at stake when you've got responsibilities, when you've lived through heartbreak and learned how to grow."

Her words lingered, pulling me into my own thoughts. If Jess and I had been in this position, would I have handled things the same way? I thought back to the emotional moments I'd shared with Theo over the past few months. The truth was, I wouldn't have been capable back then. Jess had been my first love, but I'd been emotionally immature, unsure of how to speak my truth or even understand my own feelings.

"You've come so far," my mom continued, her voice warm with pride. "I see the man you've become because of everything the boy went through. And as hard as it was, I think it's made you better."

I nodded, letting her words settle. She was right. Being with Theo didn't just feel different—it felt right. When I was with her, Jess wasn't even a shadow in my mind. I was so immersed in Theo, in our life together, that my past felt like a distant echo.

"I can see the wheels turning," my mom said, cutting through my thoughts. "What's going on up there?"

"For the first time in a long time, I'm not thinking about Jess," I admitted. "I'm not stuck in the past or replaying what went wrong. I'm thinking about the future. About what could be."

Her lips curved into a soft smile. "And that's because of Theo?"

"Yeah," I said, the answer coming easily. "It's because of her."

"Have you told her that?" she asked.

I laughed, shaking my head. "No, not yet."

"What's stopping you?" she pressed.

I exhaled, running a hand through my hair. "I need to close the chapter with Jess first. I can't start something new with Theo knowing there's still...unfinished business."

There were boxes in my basement—memories of Jess. Old photos, letters, pieces of a life I'd once thought would be forever. It didn't feel right to dive headfirst into a new beginning while those pieces of my past loomed below. Theo deserved me with a fresh start, and so honestly, so did I.

"You lost a love that felt like everything back then," my

mom said gently. "You needed time to grieve it, to heal. You've got this incredible opportunity in front of you. The life you've always dreamed of, with someone who truly fits. I know you thought that life would be with Jess, but life has a funny way of giving you exactly what you need. That girl in there, talking to Rob about Egyptian history? That says a lot."

A laugh rumbled in my chest. "It does take a special kind of person to be interested in Rob's endless trivia."

"Oh, trust me, I know," my mom teased. "I've been listening to it for nearly two decades."

I didn't need to say it aloud for my mom to know. I was in love with Theo—not falling, not inching closer. I'd already fallen, head over heels, and hit the ground hard.

The next step was clear. Close the chapter on my past and give Theo the love she deserved, the love I was finally ready to give.

36 Rhodes

Theo is 32 weeks pregnant
Baby is the size of a cantaloupe

"ALRIGHT, what am I making for dinner?" I called to Theo, who was sprawled on the couch, feet propped up, scrolling aimlessly on her phone.

I'd come home from work not long ago to find her fast asleep, drool pooling on my throw pillow while some old true-crime show droned on about a missing murder weapon from twenty years ago. Now she was awake, but something felt... off. Theo wasn't one to zone out on her phone.

Her responses were minimal, and there was a pained expression etched onto her face that she couldn't quite hide.

The rain outside began to hit the window, we were supposed to be getting a pretty nasty storm tonight.

From the living room, a faint groan answered my

question, followed by the soft rustle of fabric as she shifted.

"Hey, is everything okay?" I asked, walking around the couch, the kitchen towel slung over my shoulder.

"Yeah," she sighed, her forearm draped lazily over her eyes, the other hand resting protectively on her belly. "I'm just... not very hungry."

Her tone told me something else was going on. "Can I do anything?" I asked, gently taking her arm and nudging it away from her face. She cracked one eye open, gave me a tired look, and then closed it again.

"Maybe... chocolate milk?" she finally murmured, holding out her hands.

I helped her up, feeling the weight of her leaning into me as she stood. She waddled toward the kitchen, one hand on her lower back. She barely made it to the island before collapsing onto one of the stools with a groan.

"Chocolate milk it is," I said, heading to the fridge.

"Wait, what about strawberry instead?"

I smirked, grabbing both the chocolate and strawberry powders from the cabinet. Setting them on the counter, I turned to face her, crossing my arms. "Your call, but you seem conflicted."

Theo stared at the options, her brow furrowing. "No... chocolate," she decided, then hesitated, her lips twitching in indecision.

I waited.

"Ugh!" She groaned, throwing her head back dramatically. "I don't know what I want!"

Laughing, I grabbed both containers and walked toward her. Kneeling in front, I gently turned her stool to face me. Placing my ear against her belly, I held up the chocolate powder.

"What are you doing?" Theo asked, laughing despite her mood as her fingers found their way into my hair.

"Letting the baby decide," I said matter-of-factly. "Alright, little girl, which one is it?"

I switched to holding up the strawberry powder, and right on cue, the baby gave a solid kick.

"That doesn't actually work!" Theo giggled, shaking her head, though the smile on her face was worth every second of my theatrics.

"Apparently, it does," I teased, standing up with mock triumph. "She wants strawberry, but you want chocolate. How about I make both?"

Theo bit her lip, nodding. "That works."

As I grabbed two glasses, my phone buzzed in my back pocket. I set the glasses on the counter and answered, tucking it between my ear and shoulder.

"Hello?"

"Hey, man," Boone's voice came through, rushed and urgent. "Hate to do this to you, but I need you back at the ranch. It's bad—a calf's tangled in the barbed wire. She's panicked, and the vet won't make it in time. She's already torn part of the fence down, and the other cattle are starting to wander. I'm afraid they'll break loose."

"Shit," I muttered, pouring milk into each glass while keeping an eye on Theo. "I'll be there as soon as I can."

"Thanks. Sorry to pull you back like this."

"No worries. I'm on my way."

I hung up, stirring the drinks quickly and setting them in front of her. She watched me with a mix of curiosity and concern, an expression that was shadowed by something deeper.

"That was Boone," I explained. "There's an emergency at the ranch. I've gotta go. I'm not sure how long I'll be."

"Oh shit," she murmured, worry flickering in her eyes. "I hope everything's okay."

"Theo," I said gently, placing a hand on her arm. "Are you sure you're alright?"

Her lips pressed into a thin line, and for a moment, I thought she might tell me. Instead, she nodded. "I'm fine. Go. Boone needs you."

I hesitated, my gut telling me not to leave her like this. Theo gave me a small, encouraging smile, her hand resting on my forearm.

I leaned down, pressing a kiss to her forehead. "I'll be back as soon as I can."

As I turned to leave, I couldn't shake the feeling that something wasn't right.

BOONE WASN'T WRONG—THIS was bad. The poor calf was tangled so tightly in the barbed wire that for a moment, I stood there unsure how I could even begin to help. The storm didn't make it any easier. Rain poured in unrelenting sheets, drenching everything and turning the dirt beneath my boots into a slick, treacherous mess. Thunder rumbled low and ominous, a promise that the worst was yet to come.

Right now, the priority wasn't the calf—it was the fence. I couldn't risk the rest of the herd spooking and bolting. Slamming the shovel into the wet ground, I dug a new hole for the replacement post, mud splattering my jeans and boots with every movement. Boone had managed to get the calf to drier ground, working to untangle the barbs while coordinating with the vet over the phone. With the storm rolling in, the vet's arrival would be been delayed.

"Rhodes!" A voice cut through the storm, faint and unfamiliar at first.

I froze, my hands gripping the shovel tightly as I squinted into the downpour. The rain blurred everything, but I could make out a figure running toward me, their movements frantic.

"Rhodes!" they called again, louder this time, and my heart stuttered. It wasn't Boone. This voice was feminine, urgent.

Dropping the shovel, I shielded my eyes with one hand, trying to make sense of the scene through the chaos of rain and wind. The figure grew clearer, a bright pink raincoat, hood pulled tight against the storm.

"Aspen?" I called, disbelief lacing my voice. What the hell was she doing out here in this weather?

By the time she reached me, she was out of breath, her face partially hidden beneath the hood. "What are you doing here?" I demanded, grabbing her arm and dragging her under the shelter of a massive weeping willow. The thick branches offered little relief from the downpour, but it was better than nothing.

"Have you checked your phone?" she asked, her voice trembling.

"No. Why?"

She yanked her hood down, revealing a pale, frightened face. Water streamed down her cheeks, though whether it was from the rain or something else, I couldn't tell.

"It's Theo," she said.

Time stopped. The rain, the wind, the thunder, all of it faded into a hollow, numbing silence. My heartbeat pounded in my ears, drowning out everything else.

"She's been trying to call you," Aspen continued, her voice trembling.

Fumbling, I pulled my phone from my back pocket, swiping at the screen to clear the water. Twenty missed calls stared back at me, Theo's name flashing in all of them.

"Wha-whats going on?" I muttered, my voice cracking as I looked back at Aspen.

"She called me to get you," Aspen said, her words hurried and frantic. "She didn't want to scare you, but she said she wasn't feeling right. Something's wrong. I don't know what, but—"

She didn't get to finish because I was already running.

My boots slipped in the mud, my legs burning as they pushed forward through the slick field. My truck was still parked near the fence line, and I barreled toward it.

"Rhodes!" Boone's voice shouted after me, I didn't stop. I couldn't.

I reached the truck and yanked on the handle, only to realize I hadn't unlocked it. "Damn it!" My hands fumbled for the keys, my fingers shaking as I tried to focus.

"What's going on?" Boone had caught up to me, his breathing heavy as he stood just behind me.

I turned to face him, my chest heaving, rainwater dripping from my hair and chin. "It's Theo," I said, my voice breaking under the weight of her name.

The look in his eyes shifted instantly—concern morphing into alarm.

I didn't wait for him to respond. I flung the truck door open and climbed in, slamming it shut behind me. My hands gripped the steering wheel tightly as I started the engine, my mind racing with every worst-case scenario imaginable.

I broke every Goddamn speed limit back to the house.

"Theo!" I yelled, barreling into the house. Dirty boots be damned, I didn't give a fuck.

"I'm in here!" She called from down the hall in her bedroom. I strode in, my boots slamming against the floor. Coming to a halt when I saw her sitting, bent and holding her belly, I had to catch my breath.

She looked up, her eyes sad and turned down.

"There's something wrong. I'm having these weird contractions and I'm scared." She panted.

"It's okay," I said, stepping closer to her. "It's okay."

"I'm sorry, I didn't know who else to call," she said between labored breaths, trying to push through the pain.

"Don't you dare be sorry. I'm here," I reassured, crouching down to be at her eye level. Her hazel orbs stared at me, a red tinge to the whites of her eyes like she had been crying. "What do you need from me? Do you want to go to the urgent care in town? The city? Theo, tell me what you need and I'll make it happen."

She thought for a moment, taking steady, practiced breaths like the ones learned from all those childbirth books.

Watching her now made me realize how out of touch I was for her to give birth. I silently hoped this wasn't the moment because I desperately needed to know more. To know how to be able to help her through it.

Finally, she nodded and tried to stand.

"Urgent care," she breathed and I swooped her up in my arms, carrying her out of the house and to my truck.

I DIDN'T WASTE a second as I pushed through the emergency doors, Theo cradled tightly in my arms. My heart was hammering, adrenaline coursing through me like a wildfire. Calm wasn't an option.

Theo let out a quiet whimper against my chest, and guilt twisted inside me like a blade. I'd known something wasn't right earlier, and still, I left her.

Never again.

Out of the corner of my eye, I spotted a wheelchair against the wall. I didn't care whose it was or what rules I might've been breaking. Nobody was going to stop me. Carefully, I lowered Theo into it and wheeled her toward the reception desk, my pulse a steady roar in my ears.

"Sir, you can't just—"

"She needs a doctor, *now*," I growled, my voice sharp and edged with panic. I leaned across the desk, fists planted, daring anyone to argue. "She's thirty-two weeks pregnant and in pain. Get someone here. *Now*."

"Rhodes," Theo's soft voice cut through the fog in my head. She reached out, her fingers brushing against my forearm. "I'm okay," she whispered, her eyes meeting mine.

Her touch, her voice snapped me back to reality. I blinked, realizing how I must've looked: wild-eyed, frantic, out of control. This wasn't helping her. It wasn't helping the baby.

I took a shaky breath and closed my eyes, forcing myself to count backward from five. When I opened them again, I straightened and offered the terrified receptionist a tight, apologetic smile.

"I'm sorry," I said, my voice calmer but still laced with urgency. "*Please*, can you get her a doctor?"

Theo nudged her way forward in the wheelchair, her calm composure a stark contrast to my barely contained panic. She started speaking to the woman behind the desk, her tone soothing, her strength humbling me.

I stepped back, raking a hand through my hair as I tried to pull myself together. Fear was clawing at my insides, raw and relentless. The thought of anything happening to her or the baby was too much. My actions had been out of line, and I knew it. But damn it, I was scared. I was more scared than I'd ever been in my life.

"Sir, we're going to take her back now," the receptionist called to me after a moment, her tone much gentler.

I moved quickly, closing the distance between us in a few long strides. Theo was sitting quietly, her hands gripping the wheelchair's arms, her breathing slow and measured.

"Can I go with her?" I asked, my voice low, almost pleading.

Theo reached for me, her pinky hooking around mine. That small touch unraveled me. She looked up, her face pale and steady, as she managed a soft, reassuring smile. "I'll be okay," she murmured.

I squeezed her hand, reluctant to let her go but knowing I had to. As a nurse approached to take her back, she gave me one last look—a look that told me she was holding it together.

And then she was gone, leaving me standing there, helpless and a bit hollow.

I spent the rest of the night in a stiff waiting room chair, my legs bouncing restlessly, my mind spinning in endless loops. Hours seemed to stretch into days. At some point, I must've drifted off because the next thing I knew, a doctor was standing in front of me.

He was tall and thin, with kind eyes behind wire-rimmed glasses, the sort of face you instinctively trusted. I shot to my feet, every muscle in my body tense as I waited for him to speak.

"She's okay," he said, his voice steady and reassuring. "The baby is okay too. It was a case of Braxton Hicks, false contractions that can feel very real and understandably scary."

A breath I hadn't realized I was holding rushed out of me, leaving me lightheaded with relief.

"We've put her on bed rest," the doctor continued. "Very limited activity until the baby comes. We don't want to risk inducing labor, so we'll monitor her closely. She can go home in the morning."

I nodded, the weight of his words sinking in.

She was okay.

The baby was okay.

That was all that mattered.

37
Theo

THE COUCH HAD BECOME my best friend. Since that night in the hospital a couple days ago, I'd barely moved from this spot.

When Rhodes was here, I never wanted for anything. He catered to my every wish, my every need without hesitation.

I was hungry? He was in the kitchen, whipping up something to eat.

Had to use the bathroom? He was there, helping me get there.

Cold? He'd drape an extra blanket over me without a word.

Normally, I'd feel overwhelmed by someone hovering over me like that. Suffocated, even. But Rhodes had this way of making it feel natural, seamless like caring for me wasn't a burden but something he *wanted* to do.

The morning we came home from the clinic, I was so exhausted from the poking and prodding that I passed out on the couch almost immediately. While I slept, he found my phone and called my mom, letting her know what had happened and that everything was okay. The next day, she came over, and we spent time together.

Today was the first day I was completely alone since the scare. It was also the first day I started to feel like myself again. The doctors had made it clear we were playing a waiting game now—keeping the baby comfortable for as long as possible until it was time.

Any day now, I thought. The idea filled me with equal parts excitement and anxiety.

I kept things simple and easy: watching TV, preparing light meals, and napping when my body demanded it. With the quiet came thoughts I couldn't escape.

Over the last few days, I'd been stuck on how Rhodes had reacted at the hospital, the memory of his face etched into my mind.

I'd never seen him like that before—pure, unfiltered fear in his eyes. Every word he spoke was laced heavy with concern. The way he moved, the way he carried me, it was like the world around him didn't exist. In that moment, I knew there was nothing he wouldn't do to keep me safe and to protect the baby.

And that's what I think I needed to know. Before this, there had been doubt, small but persistent, about letting someone into my baby's life.

Would they truly have her best interests at heart? Would they leave when things got hard? Would they love her as much as she deserved to be loved?

After all, she wasn't even his. Rhodes had no obligation, no expectation to stay or to care for her, yet he had already attached himself. The way he cared for me, the way his hands would instinctively cradle my belly like he was holding something precious. I knew, without a shadow of a doubt, that Rhodes not only cared deeply for me but for her, too.

I stretched out, my body sore from too much stillness. My muscles needed movement, a reminder they still served a purpose. For the first time today, hunger pricked at me. Lately, I'd felt off. I had no energy, no motivation to eat properly, let alone consume a balanced meal. Not ideal, but my body wasn't interested in cooperating.

Before I could rise, the front door creaked open, the hinges groaning like they were in desperate need of some TLC. My head snapped toward the noise just as the unmistakable beat of *My Humps* blasted through the house.

"What the—?" I scanned the room, heart racing. No one was in sight as the door stood wide open with the absurd song echoed loudly.

"Hello?" I called, sitting up straighter, equal parts curious and alarmed.

Then I saw Boone. He shimmied into the room, perfectly in sync with the song's beat, his body moving in hilariously awkward rolls and exaggerated hip sways. My jaw dropped, and laughter bubbled out of me as I clapped in delight. Boone's grin stretched wide as he danced his way toward me, stopping in front of the couch to drop low and shake his ass.

"Are you serious right now?" I managed between fits of laughter, wiping at the tears pricking my eyes.

Without breaking rhythm, Boone handed me a hot chocolate from the farmstand, complete with a festive bow. Before I could ask what on earth was happening, movement at the door caught my attention again.

This time, it was Mac, and *he* was dancing to *My Humps*, a sight I *never* thought I'd see.

If Boone's moves were endearingly awkward, Mac's were like a poorly rehearsed male stripper audition. He spun, pumped his arms, and threw in a chest pop that looked like it belonged on *Jersey Shore*. I lost it, laughter overtaking me until my sides hurt.

"What the hell are you guys doing?" I yelled over the obnoxiously loud bass, my cheeks aching from smiling so much.

Mac sauntered toward me with exaggerated seduction, placing a finger over my lips to silence me. Then, still in character, he handed me a takeout box and winked before retreating to stand beside Boone.

I stared at them in disbelief, my expression a mix of amusement and shock. It was like the Chippendales dancers had invaded the living room.

Just when I thought the ridiculousness had peaked, the door thudded shut behind me.

Enter Rhodes.

As the final verse of the song blared, Rhodes rolled his hips, his hand resting behind his back like a cowboy in a dance-off. Unlike the others, his moves had an irresistible swagger, his brawny frame teasing me with every sway and roll. My mouth went dry as my eyes trailed down his body, lingering on the way his jeans clung to his hips. I bit my lip, thoroughly entranced.

Suddenly, my appetite roared back to life.

Rhodes approached, his movements deliberate and

confident, until he stood directly in front of me. He dipped low, rolling his hips in a slow circle that had me gripping the couch cushion for stability. Then, with a flourish, he produced a bouquet of flowers from behind his back and offered them to me.

I gasped, my bottom lip trembling as I took the familiar bouquet—the same flowers he'd brought on our first dinner together. The laughter faded, replaced by an ache in my chest as I blinked back the happy tears threatening to spill.

Rhodes stepped back, blowing me a kiss before all three men lined up in front of me. As if they'd rehearsed this minutes before, they launched into a coordinated routine. Body rolls, waves, and spins—they moved in perfect sync until Mac fumbled the body wave, earning a round of groans and laughter. Boone ended the routine with an overly dramatic move, dropping to the floor to hump the air like his life depended on it.

The music cut off, leaving the guys panting and a bit sweaty from their impromptu performance.

"Well," I said, shaking my head, "that's one hell of a way to deliver food."

"Did we seriously miss it?" A familiar female voice called from the front door. I turned to see Aspen and Penny stepping inside.

Penny let out a dramatic groan, stomping her foot. "We told you doofuses to *wait*! Ugh!"

Boone shrugged, utterly unapologetic. "We couldn't help it. Mac was nervous and wanted to 'get it over with.'"

"I wasn't nervous, you asshole," Mac shot back, dropping onto the couch by my feet with a huff. "I just wanted to get it over with, because unlike some people, I'm not much of a dancer."

"I could tell," I teased, giving him a soft smile. "But hey, you gave it your all."

I sat up, pulling my feet beneath me. Whatever just happened here would live rent-free in my brain forever. There was no way I'd forget the way Rhodes could move those hips.

Bow wow.

"Not that I don't love seeing you all," I said, looking around at my unexpected audience, "but why are you here?"

"Rhodes had this idea to brighten your spirits," Aspen explained, settling cross-legged on the floor. She placed a box, muffins, if my guess was right, on the coffee table.

"We thought we'd bring the fun to you this time," Penny added, sliding onto the couch beside me. She leaned her head on my shoulder, her familiar warmth an unspoken comfort.

I glanced up and caught Rhodes leaning against the doorframe to the kitchen, his arms crossed casually over his chest. Our eyes locked, and my heart gave a little kick, as if it had just noticed what my brain had been processing for a while now. His smirk deepened, the corners of his eyes crinkling in that way that made me feel like I was the only person in the room.

Warmth and joy spreading through me like the first sip of hot chocolate on a cold day.

These were my people, my messy, wonderful, mismatched family. They listened when I spoke, cared when I needed it most, and showed up in ways I hadn't realized I needed.

Even with the room full of laughter and love, my focus stayed on the man leaning in the doorway. The one who made all of this happen, who orchestrated this ridiculous, perfect moment, because he knew exactly what I needed, even when I didn't.

BY THE TIME the sun had dipped below the trees, casting the world in darkness, my friends finally decided it was time to leave. My body felt heavy with exhaustion, but my heart was full, brimming with joy and the warmth of their company. After lingering goodbyes and promises to see each other soon, the house grew quiet, leaving just Rhodes and me to recount the day.

"Thank you," I murmured, snuggling into his side. His arm wrapped around me, pulling me closer, his body radiating warmth. Rhodes' thumb traced soft circles on my side, a soothing rhythm that matched the peaceful quiet settling over us.

"I'm glad it turned out well," he replied with a chuckle. "Trying to teach Mac to dance, though, that might go down as one of the hardest things I've ever done."

I laughed, the memory of their hilarious attempts to dance flashing in my mind.

"I can't believe you pulled it off. What did you bribe them with?" I teased, glancing up at him.

"Nothing," Rhodes said simply, his voice steady and sincere. "I just asked if they wanted to do something to make you feel better, and they were all in."

His confession struck me silent. My throat tightened as a wave of emotion washed over me.

"I—we love you, ya know," Rhodes added, his hand moving to my hair, his fingers combing through it with gentle affection. That single slip-up hung in the air, heavy and meaningful.

"I know," I whispered, my voice thick with the effort to hold back everything I wanted to say but couldn't yet bring myself to admit.

He shifted, his tone soft yet firm. "I've been thinking. I think you should sleep in my room. After the other night, I'd feel better keeping a closer eye on you, at least until the baby comes."

His confidence left no room for argument. It wasn't a suggestion; it was his way of protecting me, of easing his own worries.

I tilted my head to look up at him, our eyes locking. "I'm just down the hall, Rhodes. You know that."

"I haven't slept through the night since," he admitted quietly, his voice raw with vulnerability. His words settled over me, making my skin prickle.

I swallowed hard, the intensity of the moment wrapping around us like a cocoon. His gaze didn't waver, and neither did mine.

"Consider it you doing me a favor," he added, his voice a low rumble that sent a shiver through me. "I need to know you and the baby are okay." He reached up, his hand cupping my jaw as his thumb brushed against my bottom lip. The tender touch undid me.

"Okay," I breathed, my voice barely above a whisper as I gave in quickly. My heart was overwhelmed by the depth of his outward concern.

He leaned down, his lips capturing mine in a kiss that was soft and unhurried. I melted into him, letting his touch and his warmth drown out everything else. His kiss was all-consuming, a quiet promise that I could stay wrapped in this feeling forever.

Time stretched as we sat there, lips moving together in a dance that felt both endless and fleeting. When we finally parted, my lips tingled. The moment left me breathless, my thoughts spinning in a haze of him.

Eventually, we decided it was time to head to bed. For the first night of many, I fell asleep wrapped in Rhodes's sheets, surrounded by the rich, clean scent of him.

Safe, warm, and utterly content, I drifted into a peaceful sleep, cradled by the man who made me feel cherished in a way I never thought possible.

38 Theo

> Penny: Theo, can you please describe in DEEP DETAIL how each of the guys looked dancing to my humps? 😌
>
> Aspen: I can't believe we missed it!!!
>
> Penny: I've had RAUNCHY dreams about it

> Theo: a girl doesn't kiss and tell...
>
> Theo: just know, it was HOT 😓

> Penny: GASP!! ID TELL YOU 😲
>
> Aspen: SECRETS ARENT FUN THEO

PENNY CHANGED THE GROUP CHAT TO 'GIRL CODE VIOLATION'

"I REALLY DON'T WANT a baby shower," I groaned, folding a blue-printed onesie and adding it to the pile.

Sprawled out on my bed, I worked through the stack of baby clothes I'd collected so far. With the baby going to be here within the month, there was still so much to prepare.

The mountain of stuff I already had felt overwhelming. I'd been chipping away at it since the beginning, trying to stay ahead of the chaos, but Penny's latest suggestion was not helping.

"Come on, Theo, pleeease!" Penny begged, dragging out the last syllable as she clasped her hands dramatically.

"I've been planning this for ages!" Aspen chimed in from our three-way FaceTime call.

"Seriously?" I deadpanned into the camera. I hated being the center of attention, and outside of my two best friends, I didn't have anyone I wanted to invite. Socializing with a bunch of near-strangers wasn't exactly my idea of fun.

"Well, okay, maybe a couple of weeks," Aspen admitted, glancing away. She was clearly at work—her background was unmistakably the Farmstand shelves.

I finished folding the clothes the baby wouldn't fit into for a while and placed them in a labeled bin, sorting everything by size and season.

My plan was simple: store it all in the basement and retrieve each tote as needed. Rhodes was down there now, spending his day off reorganizing to make space for them. What kind of man cleans his basement on his day off? A good one. *My* good one.

"I really don't want anything big and elaborate. The gender reveal was plenty, and while I loved it, it completely wiped me out."

Penny leaned back in her chair, nodding. "Fine, fine, I get it. Nothing big, but I still—" she paused, her eyes going wide as someone walked into her office. She waved them off with a sharp nod toward the door.

"Who was that?" Aspen asked.

"No one," Penny dismissed the question with a shrug. "Anyway, I still want to do something for you. You deserve it."

For a moment, I wavered. Letting my friends have their fun was tempting, though the thought of hosting and entertaining made me feel instantly drained. I decided to stick to what felt right for me.

"I appreciate it, but really, I'm okay." I smiled softly, setting a folded onesie aside for good measure. "Maybe we could just have a small get-together? No gifts, just the three of us and maybe the guys hanging out."

Aspen's face lit up. "I could bake some goodies!"

"I'll bring the fun," Penny added, grinning.

"Rhodes might be up for cooking something," I said, making a mental note to ask him later.

"Speaking of Rhodes," Aspen said with a sly smile, "how are things going?"

"Ooh, ooh, did he like the pictures?" Penny wiggled her eyebrows suggestively.

I burst out laughing. "Yes, he did. He keeps it in his truck, actually. So... I guess you could say things are going great." My cheeks warmed, and despite myself, a grin spread across my face. Just thinking about him made me feel giddy and warm all over.

"Hot!" Penny sighed dramatically, leaning back in her chair until she nearly disappeared from the screen. "That is every girl's dream."

When she sat back up, her attention was caught again by something off camera.

"You're happy," Aspen said softly, resting both hands on the counter as she peered at me.

I couldn't deny it, I wasn't going to deny it.

"I am," I admitted, the words coming easily. "Rhodes has been so supportive, so kind. Being with him is... easy. I've always liked being alone, but being with him is better. He makes me feel understood, heard. He gives me a kind of comfort I haven't felt in a long time."

Penny and Aspen stayed quiet, their expressions tender as I confessed. My mind drifted back to the last few months, the time since Rhodes had walked into my life and quietly, steadily, changed everything. Who I was before, who I'd become, and who I wanted to be—these were different versions of myself I could barely reconcile.

Before Rhodes, before the baby, I was a lone wolf. No ties, no plans to settle. My life had always been about chasing the next adventure, the next country, the next thrill. I thrived on independence, visiting home only when the ache of missing my mom and my friends grew too sharp. Faircloud, Texas, had been nothing more than a pitstop, a place to refuel before I figured out my next destination.

I had sworn I would never get attached to anyone. Never again. Loss had taught me that. It had come too early, too fiercely, and it had left scars no one could see but me. It turned me cold, quiet, and detached, not cruel but guarded. I could take care of myself. I *would* take care of myself. No one would have to sacrifice for me, not ever again. Because sacrifice led to hurt, and I had carried enough of that for a lifetime.

When I met Rhodes, I was reluctant. Yet, something

deep inside me whispered that I could trust him. I wasn't a religious person, but the parallels between Rhodes and my dad were impossible to ignore. From the moment we sat outside the bathroom at The Tequila Cowboy, I felt it, felt like I'd known him my whole life. He was sent, put into my life for whatever cosmic reason.

Rhodes was gentle yet firm, steady and kind. Being with him was like stepping into a time capsule. It brought me back to the girl I used to be, the girl who once believed in love and connection and safety. I felt cherished, not just tolerated.

Somehow, without me realizing it, he became my center. He took a piece of my heart, and it didn't stop there. That piece grew with every glance, every smirk, every quiet act of kindness. Until he didn't just have a part of me. He owned it all.

"I have to go," I mumbled, standing abruptly.

Before Penny or Aspen could respond, I ended the call and left my phone on the bed.

Their words and my internal reflection had sparked something in me.

I was done waiting. Done sidestepping labels and dodging the inevitable. I knew, deep down, that saying the words out loud wouldn't change the life we had built. I also knew I needed to say them—not for him, but for me.

Because I was happy, and I wanted him to know.

My legs carried me down the hall and into the kitchen, my only thought was to find him. The basement door creaked as I opened it, and I descended the stairs slowly, one step at a time. The lights were on, but the silence was deafening.

"Rhodes?" I called softly, my voice trembling as I reached the bottom of the stairs.

I turned the corner and found him sitting on the floor with his back to me. His legs were crossed, a tote in front of him, its lid discarded to the side.

Quietly, I moved closer. That's when I saw the tears streaming down his face. He held a picture frame in his hands, the dark wood encasing an old photo of him and Jess. The box before him was filled with remnants of their time together, a sweatshirt, a jar stuffed with folded notes, and other mementos of a love that had ended.

My chest tightened. I wanted to cry with him, to share his pain. Instead, I lowered myself down beside him, the swell of my belly making the motion slow and awkward. I rested my hand lightly on his arm.

"I'm so sorry," I whispered, my voice barely audible. He didn't deserve this—didn't deserve what had happened to him. Rhodes was one of the best men I knew: kind, gentle, and a soul so pure it shone. He deserved love, real love, the kind that cherished him as fiercely as he cherished others.

"This box has been sitting down here since she walked away," he said after a moment, his voice rough and broken. He scoffed, tossing the picture back into the box like it burned him. "I came down here ready to throw it all away. I didn't even plan to open the stupid thing, my curiosity got the best of me. I thought I could look at it and be okay."

I leaned into him, resting my head on his bicep. My fingers trailed down his arm until they found his, threading together, our warmth mingling in the stillness.

"I don't regret the time I spent with her but I don't miss her at all," he admitted, his voice cracking. "When things were good, they were some of the best moments of my life. But seeing all this again?" He gestured to the box with his free hand, his head bowing in defeat. "It hurts. It brings back every thought, every doubt about myself I worked so hard to bury."

"People come into our lives for a reason," I said gently, my thumb stroking his hand in quiet reassurance. "They're part of our journey, part of what shapes us into who we're meant to be. Jess is a part of that for you—of why you're the man you are today. The man who's so kind and caring, who loves so deeply."

He was quiet for a long moment, his chest rising and falling as he absorbed my words. Then, in a voice barely above a whisper, he said, "I loved her. I loved her with everything I had. And it wasn't enough. *I* wasn't enough."

My heart clenched. "Rhodes," I said, shifting to kneel in front of him. I placed my hands gently on either side of his face, turning him away from the box filled with the weight of his past. "She made a choice, and she will regret that for the rest of her life. She'll look back one day, angry at herself for giving up someone like you, for leaving you behind. That's her burden to carry, not yours."

I held his gaze, my thumbs brushing softly over his cheekbones. His eyes, red and raw from tears, searched mine, as if looking for some truth in what I was saying.

"You are *more* than enough," I whispered, my voice steady. "And anyone who doesn't see that? They're the ones who don't deserve you."

The room was quiet except for the sound of our

breathing, and I watched as some of the tension eased from his shoulders. In that moment, I hoped he could see himself the way I saw him: a man worth every bit of love he had to give and so much more.

"This box is the past," I said softly, my voice steady but gentle. "It's proof of how far you've come. She doesn't deserve your tears."

I reached up, brushing away the tear that slipped down his cheek with the pad of my thumb. His eyes closed at the touch, and he drew in a deep inhale, holding it for a moment before releasing it, a long exhale that seemed to carry the weight he'd been carrying. I stayed quiet, patient, as he repeated the motion, each breath lighter than the last.

Quietly, I began to count backward from five, my voice calm and deliberate, letting him know I was here, that he was safe. His eyes shot open on the last count, locking onto mine. The intensity in his gaze rooted me to the spot, the stillness between us thick and consuming.

"Why did you come down here, Theo?" Rhodes asked, his voice low and curious. His head tilted slightly, and his hands moved to rest on the tops of my thighs.

He knew me too well. He could tell there was more to my presence than comfort. There was no avoiding or denying it, he needed to hear everything I'd been holding back.

"I—" I paused, searching for the right words, my throat tightening with the weight of what I wanted to say. "I've been thinking a lot lately. About who I'm becoming. About where the last few months have taken me and where I want to be in the months ahead."

I shifted slightly closer, my knees pressing into him.

"I've experienced something I didn't realize I was missing, a kind of love and support I didn't know I craved until I finally felt it. For so long, I relied only on myself, out of fear. Fear of letting people in. Fear that they'd leave."

Recognition flickered across Rhodes's face, and I swallowed hard.

"You saw that. You felt it," I continued, my voice trembling but resolute. "And instead of letting me drown in it, you taught me to swim. You didn't just jump in and fix all my problems. You showed me the way, set an example, and gave me the space to figure it out for myself."

Every word brought me closer to the truth I'd been skirting around, the confession that made my heart pound like thunder in my chest. It wasn't easy. I wasn't used to this kind of vulnerability, but I knew if I didn't take the chance, nothing would change.

I shifted closer, leaning in until our faces were so close I could feel the warmth of his breath.

"Seeing this box, these memories..." My voice softened, heavy with emotion. "I know it might make you feel like you're not enough, like you're unworthy of love. But that's not true. She didn't leave because *you* were lacking. She left because she was a fool."

Rhodes' expression broke, his guarded vulnerability melting into something open and raw.

I leaned closer still, our lips separated by just a whisper of space. My heart raced as I finally let the words fall, the three words that had been building inside me, aching to be said.

"I love you."

I pressed a soft, lingering kiss to his lips, and he melted into the touch. His arms came around me, pulling me closer, grounding me in the moment.

And in that quiet, intimate space, the weight of my confessions filled the air, weaving us together in a way that felt unshakable.

"I want you in every part of my life," I said, my voice trembling with the weight of the confession. "You've broken down my walls and wiggled your way into my heart. I can't imagine a time or place where you aren't the center of my attention."

Rhodes's gaze softened, his eyes searching mine. "I came down here to get rid of this box," he began, his voice low, the perfect balance of husky and tender. "It's the last tie I had to her, and I needed to let it go. To throw it away and make space, make space for what's right in front of me."

He exhaled deeply, his shoulders relaxing as his words spilled out like a confession. "You're that space, Theo. You're the opportunity I didn't know I was waiting for. You're the one who showed me it was okay to leave that part of my history behind. Being with you, cherishing you, and receiving your care and love... it erased all the awful things I believed about myself. You've made me see I'm worthy of love."

My heart clenched at his words, the sheer vulnerability of his declaration sinking into me. I smiled, the warmth of his love wrapping around me like a comforting embrace.

"I love you, too, if that wasn't already clear," Rhodes said, a teasing laugh escaping him. He leaned in, capturing my lips with his. The kiss wasn't rushed or frantic—it was unhurried, deliberate, the kind that made me feel every ounce of his affection and devotion.

"Crystal," I murmured against his lips, my smile pressing into his.

Rhodes pulled back just enough to look into my eyes, his smirk lingering. "Thank you," he said, his voice brimming with sincerity. "Thank you for trusting me enough to let those walls down. I promise I'll take care of your heart and be the man your father would expect me to be."

His words shattered me in the best way, the floodgates opening as tears spilled down my cheeks. My breath hitched, and Rhodes leaned in, kissing the wet trails with a tenderness that made my chest ache.

"You and that little girl in there," he said, his hand sliding to rest on my growing belly, warm and steady, "will always be my number one priority."

My stomach fluttered in perfect timing, and as if on cue, the baby shifted, brushing against Rhodes's hand.

He stilled, his face lighting up with awe. "She loves you, too," I whispered, my voice thick with emotion.

"I have to tell you something," I said, leaning closer to him. My lips brushed his ear as I whispered the secret I hadn't told a soul.

Rhodes's eyes widened for a split second before softening with understanding. His expression was gentle, a quiet acceptance radiating from him. He nodded, his lips finding mine again—once, twice, and then a third time, each kiss more certain than the last.

Then he stood, pulling me up with him in one smooth, effortless movement.

"This box," he said, gesturing to the forgotten remnants of his past, "can wait. There's something much more important I need to do first."

His hand found mine, the warmth of his grip grounding me even as a spark of anticipation lit in my chest. He led me up the stairs, his steps purposeful, down the hallway to somewhere that only heightened the anticipation thrumming through me.

The promise in his touch sent a shiver down my spine, and as we walked, a rush of arousal bloomed, pooling low in my belly. Whatever awaited us, I knew it would be nothing short of unforgettable.

"I'm going to cherish you. Take my time devouring that sweet pussy while you cry out just how much you love me," he purred against my lips before slamming the door to his bedroom shut.

39
Rhodes

AS I LAID her gently on my bed, I leaned down and captured her lips in a slow, lingering kiss. The faint scent of Theo, mingling with the familiar smell of my sheets, was intoxicating. The ache in my jeans only grew stronger. I didn't think I'd ever get used to this—to her being here, in my bed, in my house, and most of all, in my heart.

I stepped back, needing a moment to take her in, a vision of beauty that stole the air from my lungs. Theo wasn't just gorgeous, she was breathtaking in a way that was all her own. Unique, radiant, and utterly mine.

"What?" Theo asked with a soft laugh, lifting her hands above her head, letting them drape over the pillow.

"I can't get over how stunning you are," I said, settling into the space beside her. "And the fact that you *love me*."

Her laugh deepened, warm and full of affection. She reached up, cupping the side of my face, her touch tender.

"I do love you," she said, her voice steady, filled with conviction. She kissed me again, her lips lingering as her gaze locked onto mine. Her hand slid from my cheek to my neck, her fingers brushing the sensitive skin as she tilted my head back, exposing the base of my throat.

The movement sent a sharp jolt straight to my cock, my body alive with anticipation. When her tongue flicked against my skin, a shiver rolled down my spine, heat spreading through me in waves. My breath hitched, my body responding instantly to her touch.

A low growl escaped me as I pulled back, flipping the dynamic—it was my turn to explore her. I started with her neck, teasing the delicate skin with my lips and teeth, each bite leaving faint marks of possession. She was mine, and I savored every inch of her, tasting the undeniable truth of it.

I trailed warm kisses down her chest, the soft skin peeking out from her v-neck T-shirt inviting my lips. Theo felt like velvet beneath my touch, and I took my time, savoring the way her body responded. A quiet moan escaped her, her fingers threading through my hair as she tugged lightly at the ends, sending a thrilling shiver down my spine.

My hand slid to her stomach, and I gently lifted her shirt, exposing more of her. My lips followed, pressing kisses to her skin. I paused to look at her through hooded eyes, catching the way her head tilted back as she lost herself in the moment. Her soft movements and the way she rocked her head, savoring my touch, only made me want her more.

"The way I feel about you," I murmured against her skin, pressing a kiss just above her navel, "it's like nothing I've ever felt before."

I moved lower, leaving a trail of warmth with every

kiss, my voice low and full of meaning as I whispered, "You complete me, Theo Matthews."

In one motion, I pulled down her pants. She lifted her hips to help me the best she could, her center coming close to my face. I bent down, placing a kiss there, too, and she hissed from the unexpected touch.

Instead of diving in with my mouth, I used my finger to tease her already dripping wet slit. Responsive to my touch, she was every man's dream. I ran my finger up and down, stopping a moment to play with her clit before plunging inside of her.

"Oh, fuck," she moaned. "Again, Rhodes. That's so good."

I followed her request, curving slightly as I pulled in and out in a swift motion. One dip was all I was willing to give before I paused, needing the reassurance again.

"You're mine, Honey," I growled, warmth rushing through my body at her praise. "I need to hear you say it, *you're mine*."

"I'm yours," she moaned as I fingered her again, her walls clenched around me in pleasure. Knowing she could take it, I used another finger to spread her. I wanted desperately to taste her, devour her.

I lowered my head, keeping a slow, steady pace with my fingers as I licked her clit, the nub swollen from her arousal. I flicked it once, twice, and then sucked. She squirmed beneath me, the pleasure shooting through her. My cock was so fucking hard seeing her respond to me, so I did it again until I got the same reaction.

My free hand shot down to my shaft, rubbing it through my jeans, the friction sending a cascade of anticipation through every nerve. I was needy, desperate for relief, so I sat up and pulled my fingers from her to undo my jeans and let my length spring free.

Theo sat up in disbelief, but before she could groan in protest, her face shifted. A devilish grin took place when she saw me reach down and palm my shaft.

"Does me playing with my cock turn you on?" I asked, kneeling on the bed, my pants down to my knees as I pleasure myself. Each stroke slow and deliberate. My hand pumped, my thumb swiping along the head as a drip of precum took form.

Theo nodded feverishly, her eyes not moving from my length.

"Then touch yourself, Honey. Show me how wet you are," I growled, jerking my shaft. My eyes were fixated on her pussy, her legs wide open, giving me the best damn show in town.

Like a good girl, she followed instructions. Theo hand moved to her center, playing with her swollen clit. Arousal consumed me, making my vision blurry as I worked my shaft. Watching her play with her pussy before me was a delight.

Biting my lip, I rubbed my tip and brought my hand down the shaft using the liquid that seeped to guide me along.

"Faster," Theo panted, her eyes not leaving my shaft.

I did as she asked, jerking myself faster. She followed my pace, matching my energy as she ran a finger down and dipped inside her core. She touched herself as she watched me, and knowing she was getting off like this was euphoric.

"Good boy," she purred and laid her head back. Theo's body tensed up, her leg beginning to quake as she dove in and pulled out to play with her clit in small circles. "I'm so close," she moaned.

"That's it, Honey. Let go," I encouraged her, cock still firm in my hand.

Theo let out a groan and the flush in her cheeks grew stronger as she came, the sight sending me over the edge. Watching her come undone with her own touch was enough for me to feel the tingle at the base of my spine.

"Theo," I groaned. "I'm gonna come. Open your mouth. I want you to taste what you do to me." I shifted closer and her jaw fell open, ready and willing.

My balls tightened and a rush of warmth spread through my shaft before I came. Some landed in her mouth but the rest was on her chin and cheeks.

She opened her eyes and brought the hand she'd been using to play with herself to her cheek. Like the dirty girl I'd come to learn she was, Theo wiped me from her skin and sucked her fingers.

I ran my hand along my length a few more times before I let go and made a move to get off the bed.

"You stay there," I said, leaning down to give her a gentle kiss. I brushed a strand of hair from her forehead and looked into her eyes with a smile. "We gotta get you cleaned up."

I left my room, Theo dirty and spent in my sheets. When I returned, I ran the warm washcloth along her and proceeded to take my time cleaning her up.

This woman was mine and I'd spend the rest of my life proving that to her.

40
Rhodes

Theo is 37 weeks pregnant
Baby is the size of canary melon

LIFE HAS BEEN A WHIRLWIND. Days and nights blur together, tangled up in hot, breathless moments of passion or wrapped in quiet comfort on the couch.

The holidays came and went in a flash, a joyful blur of laughter, stolen kisses, and the kind of peace I didn't know I'd been missing. For once, I wasn't just surviving the season with my mom and Rob—I was *living* it, showering Theo and the baby with gifts and soaking up every second of having her close.

Now, January settled in and the baby countdown was shorter every day. It's been weighing on Theo; I saw it in her tired eyes and in the way her shoulders tensed under the pressure. She needed a break, even if I *had* to push her to call Penny and Aspen for a girls' night.

So here I am, parked at The Tequila Cowboy with the

guys, a beer in my hand and my thoughts still wrapped up in her.

Mac was tending the bar while Boone, Logan, and I took up a few barstools. Conversation flowed, discussing the newest development in the return of Boone's sister, Ellie. She'd been gone for months, missing out on a lot of news that had happened over the last eight or so months since she left Faircloud.

"I'm kinda surprised she didn't come home for the holidays," Logan said, taking a sip of his beer. "I mean, she's never missed a holiday."

"She FaceTimed us on Christmas. It was nice to see her face," Boone said, a small smile playing at his lips. "She looks good—healthy and happy."

It'd been hard for him when she left, especially with how long she'd gone without keeping in touch. Everyone worried about her.

"Any update on when she's coming home?" I asked.

"Apparently, she's ready. Plans to come back for good in a few weeks."

Logan's head snapped up, his attention suddenly glued to the conversation.

I couldn't help feeling there was more to Logan's interest than just hoping she'd return home safe. That kid had followed her around like a puppy dog most of their childhood. With Logan's parents hardly ever around, he spent more time with the Cassidys than his own family. And since he and Ellie were close in age, they were practically inseparable back then. It wasn't until Logan hit working age that he started tagging along with us guys instead. Let's just say, if he'd ever confessed his love for her, I wouldn't be the least bit surprised.

"Good. I'm glad she's not letting that dickhead keep her away forever," Mac said with a grin, leaning his hands on the bar top. "Still stands, if she wants, I'll egg his house."

"Me too," Boone muttered, exhaling a deep sigh as he leaned back on his stool. His attention dropped to his beer bottle.

"What does that mean for Aspen and the farmstand?" Mac asked, following up.

Boone shook his head. "Ellie made it pretty clear she doesn't want to go back to all that. She wants to, what was it?— 'move on and find something for herself.'"

We all nodded, letting the words settle. I hoped, for her sanity, she found something worth settling down for.

Conversation flowed easily between us, and it felt good to catch up with my friends. My fingers itched to text Theo, to check in on how her night was going. Aspen and Penny were coming over to watch a new reality show, something about finding love, while doing face masks and other "girl things."

I pulled my phone out, staring at the screen after Boone had rushed off to the bathroom, leaving me alone on a stool. A space separated me from Logan, who was deep in conversation with a local. My finger stopped over Theo's contact, trying to convince myself that I didn't need to hover. I'd done enough of that. Still, the urge was there—I couldn't help it.

"Hey, Rhodes. Long time, no see." A familiar voice cut through the noise, sending a shockwave of tension through my body. My heart raced, a spark of recognition short-circuiting my thoughts. There was no way I was hearing this right.

I turned slowly, praying I was wrong, but my face immediately stung with the realization. The one person I didn't want to see again, the one person who'd done so much damage, was sitting next to me.

Jess.

I swallowed hard, forcing my attention forward as I brought my beer to my lips, taking a long swig to calm the knot in my stomach.

"Hi, Jess," I muttered, not meeting her eyes.

My ex-girlfriend—the one I'd cried over, drunk myself stupid over, nearly lost myself over—was there, casual as ever. Anger boiled inside me, simmering at first, then growing with each passing second. My body was tense, radiating fury, and I knew she could feel it. There was no way she couldn't.

"Not to sound rude, but why are you sitting here?" I asked, my voice colder than I intended. The bar was practically empty—plenty of seats, yet she chose to sit here, knowing full well how much that simple action would hurt.

Jess scoffed, arms crossing over her chest as she leaned back. She looked bothered, as if my question had offended her.

"I didn't want to sneak around and avoid you. This is my town, too."

I let out a bitter laugh, shaking my head. "Your town? Rich," I replied, taking another long pull of my beer, staring straight ahead.

I caught Mac standing on the opposite side of the bar, filling a pitcher. His eyes flicked toward me, trying to remain casual. I could see the worry in his gaze. He wouldn't intervene—he would watch from a distance, keeping himself far from the tension brewing at this end of the bar.

"Come on, Rhodes. Are you still not over it?"

Her words hit me like a slap, though this time, I didn't hesitate. I turned to face her, leaning forward on the bar with my elbow, my voice a low growl.

"Over *it*?" I spat, the words dripping with venom. "You have no idea what you did or how much it destroyed me, do you? I kept my mouth shut, let you go because I thought you needed space. But me? I went through hell, hit rock bottom after you left, and your first comment to me is asking if I'm '*over it?*'"

Her face was unreadable now, lips pressed tight as I finally let out everything I had kept inside for so long. I'd never said these words to her before—hadn't given her the satisfaction of knowing how much she'd broken me.

And in that moment, something shifted. I realized I wasn't affected by her anymore. The anger, the hurt—they were real, but they weren't for her. They were for the guy I used to be, the one who had lost himself because of her.

"To answer your question," I said, my voice steady with a sharp edge, "I am over it. But that doesn't mean I have to be okay with you sitting next to me and acting like you deserve forgiveness."

Jess's jaw tightened and she didn't flinch. "I did what I had to do, Rhodes. You weren't going to leave with me, so I made a choice."

"Just like I made a choice to give up a full-ride football scholarship for you," I shot back, the words cutting through the air like glass. "Every decision I made, every single one, was for *you*, Jess. And what did you do? You threw me away. Years together, gone. For what?"

We had never hashed this out, not like this. We'd never sat face to face and said all the things that burned inside us. Maybe now was the time. Maybe now was the *only* time.

"It was high school, Rhodes," she said, her tone dismissive as she shifted in her seat to face me head-on. "It wasn't that deep. Did you really think we'd stay in Faircloud forever once we graduated?"

"Yeah, I did. After I gave up my dream for you, I thought that would be enough to show you how serious I was about us."

She didn't answer. For once, Jess had no snappy comeback, no sharp retort. She just stared at me, her mouth slightly parted, utterly speechless.

"You destroyed me," I said, my voice quieter now, but no less firm. "It's taken me all this time to love myself again, to find myself again. You know what? Things happen for a reason. I'm healing with people who actually care about me. I hope you're happy, Jess, because while I don't feel for you, I respect what we had."

I brought the beer to my lips, taking a long pull as the words settled between us like smoke in the air.

Jess leaned back, her expression unreadable, though a flicker of something—curiosity, maybe amusement—sparked in her eyes. "Hmm," she murmured, tilting her head. "So, is the talk around town about you and Theo Matthews true?"

I froze, the bottle still pressed against my lips. When I finally lowered it, my voice came out low, sharp as steel. "That's none of your damn business."

Jess stood, a slow, knowing smirk curling at the corner of her mouth. "I'll take that as a yes."

"And what does it matter to you if it is?"

She shrugged, feigning indifference. "I thought we could have a civil conversation, but clearly, you're not ready."

I let out a dry laugh, sharp and humorless. "Oh, cut the gaslighting bullshit. I'm not gonna sit here and play nice. I haven't said a single thing that isn't true. If it stings, that's on you." I waved a dismissive hand, already done with her games.

I was letting her get under my skin, giving her exactly what she wanted—a reaction. Exhaling slowly, I closed my eyes and counted backward from five, forcing myself to let it go.

"Look, I truly hope you're happy with whatever life you've built for yourself," I said, my voice calmer now. "But leave me the hell out of it."

Jess's expression twisted, her eyes flashing with something almost cruel. "Good luck with your mundane, monotonous life stuck in this town," she bit out. "You and your friends have no clue what real life even is."

"Alrighty," Mac cut in, his voice firm as he planted both hands on the bar top. "Time for you to take your tantrum somewhere else. My bar is off-limits to people like you."

Jess shot me one last scathing look, her gaze sweeping over me from head to toe like she was trying to find something—some weakness, some crack in my armor. Finding none, she huffed and spun on her heel, storming out of the bar.

The second the door swung shut behind her, Boone reappeared like he'd been waiting for the coast to clear. He slid onto his seat, eyebrows nearly touching his hairline. "Well, damn."

"Do you want to share?" he asked, his voice full of concern.

I shook my head, taking another sip of my beer. Seeing Jess in person and watching her walk away again gave me something I hadn't expected: closure. I thought trashing her things, our memories, was enough but this was what final felt like. As angry as I was, it wasn't about her anymore. It was about the guy I'd been—the one who'd stayed stuck in his own head for too long.

"There's really nothing to say. She came in, sat down, we exchanged a few words, and she left."

"I heard," Boone replied with a raised brow. "She hit a nerve with Theo."

Mac stood and waited as Logan leaned in, both of them waiting, their eyes focused on me.

Rolling my neck, I let out a slow breath. "Fine," I said. I told them everything. I told them about the moment Theo and I shared in the basement, how I'd confessed my feelings to her. I talked about how I couldn't imagine my life without her, how she and the baby were becoming part of my world. I spoke about how lost I had been after Jess, and how, for the first time in a long time, I was finally feeling like myself again. It was as if the universe had conspired to bring Theo into my life, and I into hers.

The guys listened quietly, nodding, their faces lighting up as they celebrated my happiness. Mac bought a round of shots, and we all toasted to the journey ahead.

By the time the night had stretched on longer than expected, I left and headed home, eager to find Theo waiting for me. I expected everyone to be gone, and Theo wrapped up in my bed, naked, but when I walked in, I found three women asleep on the couch, the TV blaring.

A smile tugged at my lips as I took in the scene. This was us now. We'd grown together, through the mess and the chaos, into something real.

I leaned down, pressing a soft kiss to Theo's forehead before turning off the TV and heading to bed.

She'd hear about Jess tomorrow. I know she would laugh, maybe even roll her eyes and come up with something witty about the ridiculousness. I did want to tell her, because she deserved to know, but that chapter finally closed. For now, I just wanted to bask in the peace of knowing I'd finally found my way home.

41

Theo

I WASN'T sure if this was my brightest idea, but I refused to tell Rhodes I'd been experiencing contractions since early this morning. The moment I confessed, he'd scoop me up and drag me to the hospital without a second thought.

From all the baby books I'd read, I knew labor could take hours, sometimes even days, after contractions started. I'd been carefully counting the time between each one, and so far, they were five minutes apart, lasting roughly a minute...

Oh, shit.

I glanced over at Rhodes. He was fast asleep, sprawled on his stomach, his back rising and falling with each peaceful breath. He looked so calm, so undisturbed. Maybe I should let him sleep a little longer.

I was stalling.

The truth was, I was terrified. I'd been begging for her to come out for weeks, cursing my aching back, the shortness of breath, and the belly that made even rolling over in bed feel like an Olympic event. But now that the moment was here? I was frozen with fear.

My pulse thundered in my ears, muting everything else around me. My nerves screamed, paralyzing me as I thought about what was coming. The next time I stepped foot in this house, it would be with my baby. Life as I knew it was about to change forever.

I sat up, leaning against the headboard, clutching my belly as a contraction tore through me. I took a deep, shaky breath.

"Rhodes," I whispered through clenched teeth.

Nothing.

"Rhodes," I called again, louder this time. Still nothing. Out cold like he'd flipped a switch.

When the pain eased for a brief moment, I reached over and shook him violently, thinking that would've done the trick. Rhodes stirred, groaning as he rolled onto his back, his eyes barely cracking open.

"For the love of God!" I shouted as the next contraction hit, sharp and unrelenting.

That woke him up.

Rhodes shot upright, leaping out of bed like he was ready to fend off an intruder. "Theo, what the hell?" he demanded, his voice groggy as he adjusted his pajama pants.

It didn't take long for him to notice the pain etched across my face. His expression shifted instantly, panic flashing in his wide green eyes. "Oh, shit," he breathed.

"Mhm," I groaned, clutching my belly as another contraction rocked me.

These were the real deal, none of those fake Braxton Hicks teasers from weeks ago. This was *it*.

Swinging my legs over the side of the bed, I let them dangle as Rhodes bolted from the room. I could hear him sprinting down the hall, his footsteps pounding against the hardwood. He'd been preparing for this moment for weeks. The baby-go bag was stationed in the kitchen, packed and ready, just waiting for its moment to shine.

Moments later, Rhodes came skidding back into the room, the bag slung over his shoulder as he tossed in the last-minute essentials.

Meanwhile, my body refused to cooperate. Part of me thought, *Maybe I'll just have the baby right here.*

Rhodes must have noticed the panic in my face because he crouched down in front of me, his eyes softening as he cupped my cheek. His touch was grounding, pulling me out of the chaos in my head.

"It's going to be okay," he said gently, his voice steady. "You're a champ."

I nodded, tears pricking my eyes as the weight of the moment crashed over me.

"Please, don't leave me," I murmured, my voice trembling.

Rhodes's green eyes locked onto mine, steady and unflinching. His thumb traced soothing circles on my cheek. "I'm not going anywhere, ever," he said firmly. "You have me, all of me, forever."

I swallowed hard, nodding as he helped me to my feet.

From there, we moved like the well-rehearsed team we were, running through the steps we'd practiced a thousand times: my clothes, the final packing, and to the door in record time. We'd even used a stopwatch during practice runs to shave seconds off our time.

Just as we reached the front door, I froze.

"Wait!" I shouted, my hand on the doorknob.

Rhodes paused mid-step, his arms overloaded with my purse, the go bag, a blanket, and a pillow.

"Did we get my camera?"

He groaned, rolling his eyes with a smirk, but nodded. "Yes, Honey. That was item number one."

Sure, it sounded ridiculous but it was a necessity.

With that, we were out the door, barreling toward the adventure of a lifetime.

CONTROLLED breathing was the one thing I clung to. Not the nonstop beeping of monitors echoing down the hall, not the parade of nurses bustling in and out of my room to check my vitals. Just in and out, over and over. If I stayed inside my head, maybe I could make it through this.

We made it to the emergency room in record time, thanks to Rhodes. Even with me unraveling in the passenger seat, he'd remained a steady anchor, his calm presence grounding me in a way I didn't think possible. He hadn't flinched, hadn't let my panic disrupt his focus. He was solid, everything I desperately wanted to be in that moment.

Now, I needed space. The constant coming and going,

the poking and prodding—it was too much. Overwhelming. I'd sent everyone away: my mom, my friends, even Rhodes. Peace and quiet were all I could ask for right now.

Being alone was my comfort zone. It had always been. Solitude sharpened my thoughts, let me navigate the chaos of life on my own terms. I was a lone wolf by nature, fiercely independent. Somewhere along the way, that had started to change.

Meeting Rhodes had shifted something in me. For years, I'd kept everyone at arm's length: my mom, my closest friends, anyone who tried to peer too deeply into the walls I'd built. However, with him, it had been different. I let him in without hesitation, drawn to something in him that felt achingly familiar, like a forgotten song I'd always known. He felt like home.

Lying here in this hospital bed, ready to bring this child into the world, the realization struck me hard: Rhodes reminded me of my father. His gentle strength, his unwavering patience—it all stirred memories I hadn't dared to confront in years. He didn't shy away from me, even when I was at my most vulnerable. He stayed persistent and steady, pulling me back to a time when I felt safe, when I wasn't so afraid of loss.

I think I fell in love with him the day he sat beside me on his couch, wrapped me in his arms, and asked me about my dad. He saw the broken pieces of me, the ones I tried so hard to hide, and instead of turning away, he wanted to understand. He wanted *me*.

For most of my adult life, I'd run—traveled as far as I could from this town, from the pain of attachment because the closer you got, the greater the risk of losing. And I couldn't bear that again. Losing my dad had carved out a part of me that I thought would never heal. It left me convinced that wanting anything, love or connection, only brought heartbreak. I thought I'd buried that fear, grown past it, but it had lingered, festering beneath the surface all along.

And then there was Rhodes. He taught me something I hadn't dared believe in: that love could survive the wreckage. After everything he'd been through, his own feelings of abandonment, of being unwanted, he still found the courage to open his heart. He didn't let the scars define him. That night in his basement, when he let me see him stripped bare, vulnerable in a way that mirrored my own fears, he gave me hope.

Hope that maybe, just maybe, love could be worth the risk.

42
Rhodes

I PACED BACK AND FORTH, convinced I was wearing a path into the hospital floor. Theo had asked me to step out of her room, she needed a moment to collect herself. I hadn't even thought to argue. She was about to face something monumental, something terrifying, and if space was what she needed, I'd give it to her. Even if every part of me ached to be by her side, holding her hand, whispering that she wasn't alone in this.

The waiting room felt impossibly small, even with all our friends and her mom there. Aspen, Boone, Penny, Logan, and even Mac were scattered across the stiff chairs, their quiet conversations blending into the background noise. Meanwhile, my thoughts were spinning out of control.

It reminded me of the last time we were here, the fear that had gripped me so tightly I could barely breathe. This time, fear had no place. This was supposed to be a moment of joy, of hope—a new life beginning. A baby girl. She wasn't mine by blood, but that didn't matter. No one could tell me she wasn't mine in every way that counted. I'd watched her grow, watched her mom fight for her, for them both, with a strength that left me in awe. She was my family, and so was the woman in that hospital bed.

Since that day in the basement, I'd made a promise to Theo—a vow. I would take care of her, no matter what. She was my priority, my heart, and nothing in this world could change that.

I ran my hands over the back of my head, the tension in my shoulders refusing to ease. My boots echoed against the worn linoleum, a sharp rhythm that matched the restless thrum in my chest. The fluorescent lights buzzed overhead, glaringly bright.

"Rhodes."

The soft voice behind me startled me, pulling me from my frantic thoughts. I turned on my heels, heart racing as if it already knew who it was.

Theo's mom stood in the hallway, hugging herself tightly. She'd arrived not long after us, promising to stay as long as we needed her.

"Hi, ma'am," I greeted her, trying to steady my voice. Then I caught myself. "I mean, Sissy."

A small smile curved her lips as she stepped closer, placing a warm hand on my arm. Gently, she guided me to the side of the hallway, away from the bustle of passing nurses and beeping monitors.

"If you don't cut it out, you're gonna drive yourself insane," she said, her tone firm but kind.

She wasn't wrong. Normally, I could rein in my racing thoughts, find some sense of control over my emotions.

Not now. Not with Theo in there, and the weight of everything pressing down on me.

"I know," I admitted, sighing as I dropped my head. My voice came out quieter than I intended. "I'm just impatient. I need everything to go smoothly. I need everyone to be okay."

Sissy nodded thoughtfully, her eyes softening. "You know," she began, "you remind me a lot of my husband."

I blinked, tilting my head. The unexpected comparison triggered my curiosity. She must have noticed my confusion because she continued without missing a beat.

"He was so in tune with his emotions. Frank never let Theo face anything alone—he was always there, her rock. Where I... well, I was the rational one. The logical side of things. I've always struggled to share how I feel, to express my emotions openly. That's where Theo gets it from."

Her voice faltered for a moment, but she pushed through.

"When Frank died, Theo changed. She wasn't my little girl anymore, and honestly, I didn't know how to handle it. I did the only thing I could think of: I packed us up and moved. A new town, hours away from Oklahoma. A fresh start. I thought it might help, but she wasn't the same, and neither was I. I was broken, and I didn't have the tools to fix either of us. All I could do was try to be the best mom I could."

Her words hung in the air, heavy with unspoken grief. She sighed, her shoulders slumping ever so slightly.

"You did a hell of a job," I said, meaning every word.

Sissy scoffed softly, nodding as her gaze drifted to the

hospital room door where Theo was resting. Her expression shifted, pride flickered in her eyes, mixed with something deeper.

"I know," she said, a quiet smile tugging at her lips. Then she turned back to me. "The reason I told you all of this is because I think you're good for Theo. I think you bring something to her life she's been missing for a long time." Her voice grew warmer, and her hand gave my arm a reassuring squeeze. "You're an amazing man, Rhodes. To see her trust you the way she does, enough to move in with you so quickly, of all things…"

We both chuckled at that, the brief moment broke the tension in my chest.

"I know you must be special," she finished, her smile deepening.

Her words settled over me, steadying me. For the first time since we got here, I felt a little less restless. A little more certain. We were going to be okay.

"I love your daughter," I said, my voice steady, my gaze locked with Sissy's. "She's the special one."

Her lips curved into a soft smile as she reached out to squeeze my hand. "You treat her right, and that baby, too."

"I will," I promised without hesitation.

She gave me a knowing look, her eyes twinkling with pride. "Good. Now, go take a seat. You're gonna need all the energy you can get." She added a wink, and I couldn't help but grin as I nodded.

The moment between us eased, and I followed her suggestion, settling into a chair with the rest of our friends. Talking to Sissy had felt like a lifeline, a moment of validation that I hadn't known I needed.

I loved Theo Matthews more deeply than I'd ever thought possible. This love wasn't just a feeling; it was a force, a tether that bound us. Her happiness was mine, her fears were mine, and with every beat of our hearts, I could feel us syncing, becoming one.

Aspen returned from grabbing coffee for everyone, and of course, Penny followed. Those two had packed bags and prepared for an overnight stay, ready to take shifts so Theo was never alone. Not that it would come to that—not while I was here. Nothing short of Boone physically dragging me out would make me leave Theo's side. And knowing Boone, that scenario wasn't out of the question, which was probably why the girls had made plans.

I glanced around the waiting room, my chest swelling with an unexpected warmth. Seeing everyone here, friends who had become family, filled me with a deep sense of gratitude. Faircloud wasn't just a place anymore; it was home. And now, that home was growing, its arms expanding to embrace a new chapter, a new life. I sat there, surrounded by the people who loved her, I knew there was nowhere else I'd rather be.

"Rhodes?"

An unfamiliar voice called out, pulling me from my thoughts. I turned to see a nurse peeking into the waiting room. I was on my feet before I realized it, crossing the room in a hurry.

"That's me," I said, my voice steady.

"Theo is asking for you. It's time."

My stomach flipped, the weight of her words sinking in. I glanced back at the group. They were all watching me, their faces soft with encouragement. I found it in me to count down from five, closing my eyes to focus on the deep breath.

Following the nurse into the room, my heart pounded as I saw Theo. She was breathing heavily, her face scrunched in pain as she gripped the sides of the bed. The sight of her like that hit me like a freight train, but I pushed through it, rushing to her side.

"I'm scared." With panic laced in each word, she reached out her hand for mine.

I didn't hesitate. I slid my hand into hers, wrapping my fingers around hers as tightly as she needed. The warmth of my touch was a promise. I was here, and I wasn't going anywhere.

"I got you, Honey," I murmured, my voice as steady as I could make it.

I stood right by her side as the doctor entered the room, the door clicking shut behind her. The staff moved swiftly, setting everything up, but my focus never wavered from Theo. She shifted into position, and I stayed there, whispering encouragement, grounding her through the storm.

The room filled with the sounds of her pain—yells that cut through me like a knife. Still, I kept my voice steady, guiding her through every push, every moment, until finally, the tension broke. A sigh of relief was followed by the most beautiful sound I'd ever heard, the cry of a newborn.

Tears pricked at my eyes, and I didn't fight them. I watched as they lifted the baby, so small, so perfect, and brought her into the world. She let out another cry before they laid her on Theo's chest, her tiny body rising and falling with each precious breath.

Theo was crying, too. Silent tears streamed down her face as she held her baby close, skin to skin. I stood, my legs unsteady beneath me, overwhelmed by the moment.

They were perfect—both of them. My heart felt like it could burst knowing with absolute certainty that they were my whole world now.

I turned, digging through the bag we'd brought with us. Theo had insisted I pack one thing in particular, and my hands found it easily. I lifted the viewfinder to my eye, framing the scene in front of me: Theo holding the baby, a radiant smile lighting up her tear-streaked face. I clicked the button, capturing the moment forever.

"Hi, baby," Theo cooed, her voice soft and full of wonder as she placed a gentle hand on the baby's back.

I set the camera down and stepped closer, reaching out a tentative hand. My finger brushed against the baby's tiny, delicate hand, her skin impossibly soft.

"Hi, Frankie," I whispered, my voice cracking under the weight of the love flooding my chest.

43
Theo

SHE WAS FINALLY HERE.

Frankie lay peacefully in her bassinet next to my hospital bed, and all I wanted to do was hold her. I wanted to press her perfectly round face to mine, kiss the tip of her button nose, and promise her I'd never let her go.

This was the fresh start I'd been searching for. Looking at her, I knew it was all worth it. Every sleepless night trying to find comfort, every tough decision—everything had led to this moment. And then there was him. The man who had stood by my side from the moment I returned to Faircloud. Helping me, supporting me, loving me. Rhodes had taught me that slowing down and settling into life was worth it. All that running, running from this town, running from myself, was nothing but preparation to bring me here.

Did I regret the choices I'd made? No. I understood that every twist and turn had guided me back to Faircloud, to my mom, to my best friends, and to Rhodes. This was where I belonged. I belonged *home*.

The door creaked open, and Rhodes stepped in, his hands full, a huge grin lighting up his face.

"I've got crackers, a cookie, and some sour gummies," he said, depositing his haul onto the table tray before collapsing into the chair he hadn't left much since I'd given birth.

"Gummies, please," I whispered, careful not to wake the baby as I reached out my hand.

My mind wandered as I chewed, slipping into memories and moments of quiet reflection. The past few days had given me plenty of time to think. Breastfeeding in silence—though I hated it because getting Frankie to latch was an exercise in frustration. Quiet moments while she slept and the nurses insisted I rest proved to be the time for the deep thoughts to come rolling in, like when I stared blankly at the wall, waiting for Rhodes to return.

The weight of unspoken words pressed on me, climbing up my throat and begging to be released, to bridge the space between us.

"Rhodes?" I asked, my voice soft as I popped another gummy into my mouth and chewed slowly.

"Hmm?" He glanced at me, brushing crumbs from his jeans.

I hesitated. Talking about things like this didn't come naturally to me. Confronting my emotions and voicing them out loud still made me squirm, it was all still new, but I was working on it. I squared my shoulders and decided to say it anyway.

"When I lost my dad, I became a shell of myself." Rhodes sat up straighter, giving me his undivided attention. "Moving here was the best decision my mom ever made. It gave us a second chance, a place to start over with a new identity. I wasn't just the girl whose dad had died anymore. The teachers didn't give me special attention out of pity, and the whispers in the hallways stopped. I finally had the opportunity to be *Theo*. When I looked inside, she wasn't there. Instead, I found someone new, someone I didn't recognize."

A tear slipped down my cheek, warm against my skin. I wiped it away with a quick sniffle, trying to steady myself.

There was so much I wanted to say, a whirlwind of thoughts and feelings pressing to get out. But this mattered—telling Rhodes mattered.

"I retreated. I stopped showing attachment or letting myself care because deep down, I blamed myself. This voice inside me screamed that it was all my fault—that if I hadn't begged my dad to come to my stupid soccer game, he'd still be here." I laughed bitterly, the sound hollow and humorless. "God, it sounds ridiculous, doesn't it? Ten-year-old Theo believed it. She carried that weight around for a while. It changed her, changed me into a person who detached from most things. If I had the chance to talk to her, she never would've imagined we'd make it through—that we'd be okay, that we'd have real friends. Friends, I almost pushed away because my mental health was dragging me down again."

I turned to Rhodes, finally meeting his gaze after all this time. His green eyes held steady, unwavering. Mine brimmed with tears until they spilled over, and when they did, I broke. My sobs were uncontrollable, raw and unfiltered, as if all the pain, all the emotions I'd buried for years were finally clawing their way out.

"Honey," Rhodes said softly, his voice a soothing contrast to my chaos. He reached for my hand and shifted me gently, making room in the hospital bed so he could climb in beside me. He pulled me into his arms, holding me the way only he could, with quiet strength and unspoken understanding.

I took a shaky breath, resting my head against his chest. His presence steadied me, gave me the courage to keep going.

"Through all of this, I found you," I whispered. "It sounds crazy, maybe even stupid. From the moment we really met on that street, I felt it, a pull. Like I'd known you my whole life. It was as if the breath I'd been holding for fifteen years finally released."

Rhodes tilted my chin up, his thumb gentle beneath it, guiding my eyes to meet his.

"I know I've told you I love you—and I know you feel the same. But Rhodes, I am so madly, deeply in love with you that it hurts. The thought of a life without you leaves an ache in my chest, I can't imagine ever filling. When I'm with you, I'm happy. I feel alive again, like that warm, tingly feeling I'd forgotten existed is finally back."

Rhodes gave me a smile so soft, so full of love, that it stole my breath. It was the kind of smile I wanted to capture in a picture forever, to hold onto for those moments when I doubted whether I truly deserved the love he was so willing to give.

"And that baby over there," I said, my voice low and reverent, "she's yours. I'm yours."

His lips found mine, tender and passionate, grounding me in the warmth of his embrace as we lay entwined in the hospital bed. Frankie's soft coos drifted from her bassinet beside us, a sweet reminder of a future we'd create together.

When I broke the kiss, his hand remained on my cheek, his thumb brushing over my skin in a way that soothed every worry, every doubt.

"And I'm yours, Theo," he whispered, his voice thick with emotion. "I wouldn't want to be anywhere else."

A smile tugged at my lips as I leaned up to kiss him again, this time lingering just a little longer, savoring the taste of him, the feel of his lips on mine.

"You gave me a second chance," Rhodes murmured against my mouth. The words were so quiet, so intimate, that I pulled back to meet his gaze, captivated by the vulnerability in his eyes.

"You showed me I'm capable of being loved again," he continued, his voice steady yet brimming with emotion. "That even with the nagging feelings of not being good enough, of not deserving this, I can still find love, real love. Whether you realize it or not, you were the one person who made me feel again, made me believe again. I was yours before you ever even knew it, Honey."

His confession left me breathless, my heart swelling with an intensity I could barely contain. In that moment, I knew there was nothing more powerful, more grounding, than the love we shared and I was putting my heart in the hands of the guy my dad would've approved of.

"You're never going to believe what the cafeteria had!" Aspen announced, bursting into the room with her mouth half-full. The entire crew followed her, filling every inch of free space as they piled in.

"Shhh!" Penny scolded from behind, craning her neck to peek over Aspen's shoulder. "There's probably a sleeping baby!"

Rhodes and I glanced at each other, then at our boisterous visitors. I couldn't help but smile.

"Oh my God," Penny squealed softly, tiptoeing toward the bassinet to get a closer look at Frankie. She acted like it was her first time seeing her, though she'd been in and out of this room plenty over the past few hours.

"Look at you two," Mac teased, leaning casually against the wall with his arms crossed. "Were we interrupting something? I mean, the hospital might not be my first choice for... well, you know. But hey, to each their own."

I shook my head, laughing as Rhodes let out a scoff, shifting slightly to face the crowd.

"How's Mama feeling?" Boone asked, coming up to the bed and tapping my foot playfully.

I shrugged, tilting my head to rest it against Rhodes' shoulder. "Tired. Drained. Used." I giggled, and the sound set off a ripple of laughter among our friends.

"Well, at least the glow hasn't gone anywhere," Aspen chimed in, perching on the edge of the bed. Boone slid his arm around her shoulders, pulling her close.

"I think that glow's courtesy of someone else," Mac muttered under his breath, earning a few snickers from the group.

I took in the scene before me, my heart swelling with gratitude. All my friends, gathered here, showing their love and support—it was almost overwhelming. I was so damn lucky to have them.

For the first time in a long while, I didn't question where I belonged. It was here, with these people, with Rhodes and Frankie. This was home.

The End

Epilogue

Rhodes

FRANKIE COOED in the back seat, her little face lighting up as Theo made the funniest, most adorable faces at her. I couldn't help but smile, watching them through the rearview mirror. There, in that moment, I saw Theo in her element—shining as a mom, a role that suited her so perfectly.

Adjusting to life with an infant was definitely as challenging as everyone had warned me, but it didn't make it any less beautiful. I loved the quiet mornings, just me and Frankie, while Theo got a few extra hours of sleep. The early sunlight would spill into the room, and it was just us on the couch, the silence wrapping around us like a comforting hug.

This little girl, she had me in a constant tug-of-war with my heart. Every time I looked at her, I felt this overwhelming rush of love—a love so pure, so fierce, that it almost took my breath away. It wasn't like the romantic love you feel when you find your soulmate. No, this was something else—stronger, important, and it tingled in every fiber of my being. Theo called it "cute aggression," and honestly, she wasn't wrong.

Today was special. Theo, Frankie, and I were headed to Cassidy Ranch to see the cows. I'd promised Theo I'd take her there someday, and considering I worked here, it probably should have happened sooner. Life with a newborn had a way of making time slip through your fingers. It had only been four months since Frankie was born, and Theo and I had been dating from the very beginning. These past few months had been filled with so much joy, laughter, passion, and tenderness.

I parked the truck in front of the barn and jumped out, opening the backdoor to help Theo out. I moved to the other side to grab our baby girl.

"Alright, show me the cows!" Theo demanded, planting her hands on her hips. "I can't wait any longer."

I chuckled, finishing up buckling Frankie into the carrier strapped to my chest.

"Patience, Honey," I teased, leaning in to press a soft kiss to the top of Theo's head. Before we arrived, I'd asked Boone to bring some of the cattle over to the smaller grazing area beside the barn, so we wouldn't have to go inside and spoil the surprise I had planned.

The gift waiting in the barn was something I'd been planning for months. From the moment I first laid eyes on that little girl, I knew I'd do anything in my power to keep her safe, to give her the world.

I reached for Theo's hand, threading my fingers through hers, and we walked together toward the animals. There was a new calf on the ranch, just a couple of days old, its wobbly legs and unsteady steps enough to melt anyone's heart—especially Theo's.

Over the past few months, there had been another big change. Boone's dad had officially retired, which meant I was stepping into the role of head rancher. Taking on two huge responsibilities at once had been overwhelming at times, though having Theo by my side made everything seem lighter. She made everything easier, and every moment with her felt like a gift.

I was happy. So damn happy. My life was shaping up in ways I hadn't dared to dream of. I had love in every corner of my world. People who cared for me, who wanted the best for me. But Theo—Theo was the best thing that had ever happened to me. The best chance I'd ever taken.

"Shut up!" Theo squealed, her hand flying to her mouth. "Look at the baby!" She pouted her lip and, without hesitation, let go of my hand to run towards the fence. I couldn't help but laugh at her excitement.

"Your mom is crazy, do you know that?" I asked Frankie softly, pressing a kiss to her delicate baby hair.

When I caught up with Theo, she was crouching down by the calf, trying to coax it closer with the same sound you'd use to call a cat. It wasn't working, she didn't care. She was having fun, and I wasn't about to stop her.

"Look, Frankie. That's a cow," Theo said, turning towards our daughter. She gently took Frankie's hand in hers and made a mooing sound, mimicking a cow. "Cow goes moo."

This woman. My heart swelled with love.

Frankie's little legs kicked in excitement at the sound of Theo's voice, a smile lighting up her face as she babbled something in response.

"They are cute!" Theo said, her smile stretching so wide it could've rivaled the sun. I could see the joy in her eyes as she interacted with our daughter, our little family.

Theo had made it clear from the start that Frankie was

mine, too. That this journey into motherhood wouldn't have been the same without me. At first, I'd brushed it off —uncomfortable with the thought of claiming Frankie would be mine. She wouldn't let me shy away. She bought me a hat that said "DAD" in big, bold letters, and I wore it every day since, a constant reminder of just how much I was a part of this beautiful, chaotic life we were building together.

"I have another surprise," I murmured, gently turning Theo away from the pen. She tilted her head, a puzzled look crossing her face. In my back pocket, I had a bandana. I pulled it out and handed it to her. "Put this on."

"Oh, Rhodes. Are you trying to get kinky?" she teased, raising an eyebrow.

I laughed, almost snorting. "As much as I'd love to, it would be a little tricky with the baby strapped to me and, well, pretty inappropriate."

I placed both my hands on her shoulders, guiding her into the barn. "Stay right here," I said, my voice soft but firm, before stepping away to flick on the bright overhead lights. I took a position next to the surprise, leaning on the bumper, anticipation building.

"Okay, you can look."

Theo slowly pulled off the bandana, her face scrunching in confusion. "The surprise... is an old truck?" she asked, taking a cautious step closer. She ran her fingers over the dented hood, tracing the chipped and faded paint, evidence of years of wear. It wasn't much to look at, but it meant everything to me.

"I guess I should explain," I said, stepping closer.

"Please," she urged, her voice softening.

"This is my 'new to me' truck."

"You have a truck already," she said, her brow furrowing. "Why would you trade that thing for this? No offense." She cringed as she circled the beat-up vehicle.

"I want to give you my other truck," I said, my heart pounding. "I'd take this one."

Theo froze, her eyes wide in shock. "Your very expensive, very new truck?" She tilted her head, her hands perched on her hips, clearly taken aback.

"Yes. I want you to have it, so when you have Frankie, I know you'll be safe."

Her face softened, and we stood there for a moment, just looking at each other. I watched her eyes glisten, her gaze flicking between the old truck, Frankie, and me.

"Rhodes, that's a lot," she whispered, her voice thick with emotion.

I shook my head, stepping toward her. "No, it's not. I told you before, when I bought that truck it was with the idea of having a family. I want the people I love most to always be safe. You are my family, Theo. You and Frankie deserve it."

Theo's hands reached up, gently cupping my face, her touch sending a shiver down my spine. She leaned in and pressed a soft kiss to my lips.

"I don't know what to say," she murmured against me.

"Just tell me you love me, and we can call it even," I said, my voice low, playful.

She smiled, kissing me again, a sweetness in her lips that left my heart racing. "I love you, Rhodes Dunn."

I pulled away, tucking her under my arm, the sense of her warmth and affection grounding me in that moment.

"Plus," I added, my voice teasing, "I thought when Frankie gets older, she could help me work on it."

Theo stopped mid-stride, spinning me to face her. She grabbed my hand, shaking her head in disbelief. "You are the most incredible man to walk this earth," she whispered, her eyes shining.

I smiled, my heart full as I looked down at her. I'd vow to give Frankie and Theo the life I never had. I would make sure they never had to worry about anything, that they always felt like my top priority. Theo Matthews would one day carry more of my children, and she would take my last name. And I couldn't wait for that day to come.

Acknowledgments

First, I want to thank my fiance, Nate. If you're looking for someone to thank, he's your guy! Without his support and push, Faircloud, Texas, would never have been created. Thank you for being my real-life PERFECT man. You make all the romances I'll ever write seem small compared to the love you give to me. Rhodes (as great as he is) doesn't compare to you.

Keona, my amazing partner in crime, my right hand. Without you, I think I'd be lost. You keep me on course. You are my compass. I love us and all the texts, facetime, and voice memos we share talking about life, books, and everything in between. I'm so lucky to have found someone to invest their time and energy into me and my journey.

Vanesa, my hype girl. You have made writing Rhodes so dang fun. From your commentary through book one, to the comments you send me now. Thank you for taking the time and being a part of my author journey. You get a standing ovation from ME!

Kayla, Danie, Arthi, and Brittany. Thank you for beta reading for me (most of you for the second time, hehe). The fact y'all loved TSWW so much you came back for more? I'm honored. The amount of joy I had reading your comments, DMing you all through your reading, is indescribable. You all make being an author so much fun!

And, to the readers. The amount of love and support I received from TSWW was insane! As someone who thought about 10 people would read her story, my heart was SWELLING with pride. I can't wait to keep writing more books, more swoon-worthy men for YOU ALL!

About the author

M. Hartley is a hopeless romantic with a passion for crafting heartfelt stories about small-town charm and rugged fictional cowboys (with big hearts and big…) When she's not writing and drinking a glass of sweet red wine, she can be found doting on her beloved dog, Hank, or indulging in her absurd Swedish Fish addiction. Dedicated to making readers fall head over heels for romance, M. Hartley believes there's nothing better than a love story that lingers long after the last page is turned.

If you missed her first book, The Story We Wrote, it is available now on Kindle Unlimited and paperback.

M. Hartley is most active on Instagram so make sure to follow her to stay up tp date on all things Faircloud (and more!)

Made in United States
Orlando, FL
27 March 2025